GEORGANA'S SECRET

PROPER ROMANCE

Georgana's Secret

Arlem Hawks

THORNDIKE PRESS
A part of Gale, a Cengage Company

LIBRARY OF CONGRESS CIP DATA ON FILE.
CATALOGUING IN PUBLICATION FOR THIS BOOK
IS AVAILABLE FROM THE LIBRARY OF CONGRESS.

ISBN-13: 978-1-4328-8966-1 (hardcover alk. paper).

Published in 2021 by arrangement with Shadow Mountain

Printed in Mexico
Print Number: 01   Print Year: 2021

To Jeff, who is both the
wind in my sails and my anchor.

And to Elizabeth Bowler, Rebecca
Johnston, and many others — the real
cabin "boys" who served in the
Georgian Royal Navy.

PROLOGUE

Lushill House
Bromley, England
June 1799

Footsteps, firm and steady, sounded on the stairs. Each one tore at Georgana Woodall's young heart as she waited in the hall outside the nursery because they brought Papa's goodbye closer and closer. She brushed her tears away quickly, in case Grandmother was following Papa. Grandmother had no tolerance for tears — from girls of seven or their mothers.

Papa's handsome face appeared above the steps, then his blue uniform with the gold trim, then his smart black boots. He stopped at the top of the stairs. She held his gaze for a moment, then dropped her eyes back to their comfortable spot on the floor.

Her father went down on one knee. She didn't look at him until he cupped her chin in his hand. "What are these tears, George?"

Against her will, the corner of Georgana's mouth ticked upward. "Grandmother does not like it when you call me that."

"Then it shall be our secret." He put a finger to his lips, which forced a full grin from her. Papa rarely went against his mother's commands, and then only by order of the Admiralty.

"Mama doesn't like it, either." Georgana didn't especially like it herself, but she wouldn't tell him that.

His face softened. "Well, if Mama wishes me not to call you George, I will try to remember." His hand fell to his side, and he rose to his feet.

Georgana's throat tightened. It was time for goodbye.

"Come, Georgana," he said. She waited for him to tell her to be brave. Sometimes he added that to his practiced farewell.

Instead, he caught her up and lifted her to his shoulder.

Georgana let out a squeal, then a giggle through her tears.

"We have time for one last sail before I leave." His eyes twinkled, the way they sometimes did when Grandmother wasn't around.

He glanced about to be sure they were alone, then walked quickly to the servants'

8

stairs. She held on tight, one hand on his epaulet and the other around his head. They emerged from the servants' quarters into a sun-bathed and silent garden.

"Ready, Captain?" he asked.

Georgana extended her arms out to the sides like yardarms on a mast. Papa stalked forward, slowly rocking back and forth to imitate a ship. She drew in a breath still shaky from her tears. There wasn't much wind, but she imagined a stiff breeze off the ocean pulling at her dark curls and billowing her dress like a sail.

Someday Papa would take her to sea. Until then, she had to pretend.

A white lace cap appeared above the bushes, cutting a swift path toward them through the rose garden. Georgana's heart leaped into her throat.

"Storm off the larboard bow." Her voice came out in a squeak.

Papa halted when he saw Grandmother's cap. "Hard to starboard," he said softly.

They were escaping? "Hard to starboard," Georgana echoed.

Papa wheeled around and dashed for the edge of the house. She bounced against his shoulder, turning her head to see if Grandmother had spotted them. The old woman's drab gray dress came into view just as Papa

9

rounded the corner.

"Alfred? Georgana?" The shrill sound grated on Georgana's nerves.

Papa didn't stop but slowed his pace as they reached the kitchen garden. He started to sway again, exaggerating the motion. "Captain, the wind is too much!"

Georgana giggled as she was tossed from side to side. "Hold steady!"

"I can't. The gale's caught us!" He tilted harder, his actions more and more wild until Georgana slipped from his shoulder and into his arms. Her laughter shook loose the tightness in her stomach that had grown in anticipation of the looming goodbye.

Cradling her to his chest, he sat on a nearby bench. "You have a wonderful laugh. Like sunshine on a winter day."

She liked his laugh, too. She liked the way it made Mama smile. Her smile didn't come out very often when Papa was gone. Grandmother chased it away.

"Don't ever lose that laugh, little one."

Georgana pressed her face into his waistcoat so the words wouldn't come spewing out. She did lose her laugh. Like Mama's smile, her laugh stayed locked away when they were left to Grandmother's charge. Mama said Georgana should never tell Papa about what happened when he was at sea.

10

Mama didn't want him to worry.

Papa kissed her forehead, his eyes wet. "I love you, George. Someday I will not have to go."

Someday. It seemed an impossible promise.

He squeezed her tightly and rocked her, gentle as a ship in a quiet harbor. He chewed the corner of his lip. Georgana followed suit until she drew a sad smile to his face with her imitation.

She closed her eyes. For a moment, she forgot his departure, forgot Lushill House, forgot the cruel words waiting on Grandmother's tongue. She focused on the feel of Papa's strong, safe arms around her.

All too soon, she was standing on the front steps, holding Mama's trembling hand, as Papa grasped the carriage door. He paused, then looked back. He tipped his bicorn hat, and Mama choked down a sob.

Then Papa vanished into the coach, and the horses lurched forward, dragging the carriage and Georgana's father toward Portsmouth and the ocean.

She gritted her teeth against her tears. Perhaps if Grandmother saw her efforts to remain composed, she wouldn't shout.

The carriage hadn't cleared the yard before it began.

"Inside." There was no kindness in Grandmother's tone. "Back to your studies, Georgana. I will not have the stupidest girl in England for a granddaughter." Her hard eyes flitted to Mama. "Compose yourself, Susan. Ridiculous outbursts have no place in this house."

Someday . . .

A flash of gray sleeve preceded Grandmother's slap. Georgana stumbled back. Mama's grip on her hand kept her from falling. The stinging flesh of her cheek brought new tears to her eyes.

"Please," Mama whimpered, "let her alone. She is only —"

"I said to go inside!" Grandmother shrieked.

Georgana looked back to the road as Mama pulled her obediently into the manor. She shuddered as she tried not to cry. If only her father had seen. Maybe they wouldn't have to live like this.

But Papa's carriage had turned a corner and was lost in the trees. And all happiness with it.

CHAPTER 1

Eleven years later
Portsmouth, England
July 1810

Lieutenant Dominic Peyton tried to feel sorrow over his departure, but his efforts were in vain. The ocean's siren song called him to the window of his study, where he strained for a glimpse of the waters he knew he couldn't see from this distance, though he thought he could pick out the tips of HMS *Deborah*'s masts above the rooftops.

Not long now, he told his impatient soul.

The anticipation of boarding a ship again stirred up an excitement he'd striven to quell the last few weeks, in order to not pain Mother.

He regretted leaving his mother, of course. She had no one else but him. Only his concern for her kept him returning to land.

Dominic tucked his bicorn under his arm and took one last look around the study

13

with its neglected books and rows of sea-shells, rocks, and driftwood lining the shelves. One token for each time his ship had docked since his second year in the navy. Fourteen years of this silly tradition, but his mother still loved it, placing each gift with care.

He strode down the hall to find his mother in the drawing room, mending one of his stockings. She stared over the rim of her spectacles, holding the stocking so close it nearly touched her nose. With hair still more brown than gray, she seemed too young to have difficulties with her sight. An ache sliced through his heart as he watched her work. Misfortune was her lot, though she hardly deserved it.

After a few more stitches, she cut the string and sat back. "Ah, my boy. Are you ready?"

He nodded. The servant had already taken his trunk to the hired coach.

"And here I am dawdling." She folded the stocking neatly and stood. "I thought I had finished these, but I found one hiding in my basket."

Dominic took it from her and shoved it in his pocket, wishing he could force down his restlessness as easily. "Thank you."

She reached up to touch his cheek. "Anything for you, Son."

Mother didn't cry anymore when he left. She'd always been brave — braver than he was, to be certain. What any captain wouldn't give for a ship full of men with a will as strong as his mother's. It would make for the most formidable crew in His Majesty's navy.

Her arms encircled him, and she rested her head against his shoulder. "Do you know why I named you Dominic?"

He grinned. When he was small, she had often sneaked into his room after the nurse put her boys to bed. She would whisper songs and stories as she rubbed his back, and she always ended with that question. Now she asked it whenever he left.

"No, Mother." That was his usual answer. And then she would tell him stories about the Irish grandfather she'd named him for.

She frowned at him, then fussed with his brown hair. He should have had the barber cut it shorter. It would be unmanageable before long.

"Your father made me a bargain."

Dominic blinked. He hadn't heard this version of the tale before.

"If I didn't complain about the name he gave his heir, I could name the next child. And then he named your older brother

15

John, so he could fit in with all the other little English heirs of the same name." She huffed dramatically, and Dominic laughed.

She stepped away to survey her work with his hair. "I so wanted you to be a girl."

"You've kept that back for twenty-six years, and now you see fit to tell me?"

His mother swatted his arm. "Once they put you in my arms, I wished for nothing else but you. I wouldn't trade you for a dozen girls."

"Would you trade John, then?"

She shook her head in exasperation, and the sparkle left her eyes. She loved John, shameless dastard that he was. "You mustn't tease, Dominic. Surely you are above that."

He ducked his head, trying to rid himself of the simmering in his gut at the thought of his brother. It was the same sensation that rose at any mention of his father. Years had dimmed his indignation but hadn't removed it.

She smoothed his sleeve. "I named you Dominic because I saw the strength of your grandfather in you, even as a tiny infant. I knew you would distinguish yourself just as he had."

Dominic couldn't resist. "And you knew Father would hate an Irish name."

Her eyebrows raised, but she kept her

16

mouth shut. So loyal, though the man hardly deserved it.

The clock on the mantel struck nine. His orders were to report to the *Deborah* at ten.

"You'd best be on your way," his mother said before he could.

"Is there nothing I can do for you?"

She clasped her hands before her. "Not now, but soon."

He touched her arm. "What is it?" His mother never asked for anything.

She looped her arm through his and marched him from the drawing room. The hallway barely fit the two of them walking side by side. "Someday we will have time to go to London for the Season."

London? What on earth would she want to do in Town? And during the Season, when the city was overcrowded with people?

"I thought you hated London." He stopped before the door. The lone footman of the house pulled it open, then flattened himself against the wall to allow them to pass by.

"We must go somewhere to find you a wife, since none of the Portsmouth girls have caught your eye."

A wife? Dominic's stomach lurched like a landsman's the first week at sea. Marriage was the least of his worries. And with the war's end nowhere in sight, and tension rising in the Americas, he didn't anticipate a rest from service soon. Unless, of course . . .

"When do you think they will promote you to captain?" his mother asked as they exited the house. "I thought for certain you would have earned it after your last voyage."

An unexpected, intense pang pulsed through Dominic's core. These last few weeks he had tried to forget all about the promotion. "It should come soon, I think." He pasted on a smile. "All in good time."

"After the promotion, perhaps we can go to London as you wait for your command. A post-captain would be quite the conquest in the marriage mart."

He kissed her cheek. "Goodbye, Mother. I'll send word of when you can expect me as soon as I know our orders." The crew received orders only after they boarded, a naval practice his mother despised.

"Be careful, Son."

Dominic hurried into the coach and set his hat on the seat beside him. He let his head fall back, wondering if his face was burning like the secret he kept.

Before the door closed, Mother poked her head in.

Dominic straightened, hoping she hadn't

18

seen his relief. "What is it?"

"I nearly forgot. There is something you can do for me. I wish you to make inquiries while on board."

Interest piqued, he leaned closer. Thank heavens she hadn't renewed talk of promotion and Town. "What sort of inquiries?"

"I knew Captain Woodall's wife when she was a girl," his mother said, lowering her voice. "Her family lived very near mine before I married. She died a few years ago, leaving behind a daughter. I have thought of that little girl often, but none of my London acquaintances have heard of her in quite some time. They say she vanished soon after her mother's death, and no one has seen her since, though she should be in Society by now."

How odd. Families usually pushed their daughters into Society's brazen lights, not hid them. "Did the captain send her to a school?" That was a reasonable explanation. "Or to kin, perhaps?"

His mother shook her head. "Her only relation is the captain's mother, who still lives at his house near London."

Dominic's eyes narrowed. Very strange, indeed.

"I thought, while under his command, you might ask about the girl." She wrung her hands. "Not in a forward manner, of course. I wouldn't want to jeopardize your relationship with the captain. But surely someone on that ship knows something."

He covered her hands with his. "I will ask, and I will write as soon as I can." Would she consider inviting the Woodall girl to stay? It would be nice for his mother to have a companion while he was away, and he didn't think it would take much convincing, seeing as the girl had little family to speak of.

As the carriage pulled away, he pressed his forehead against the window, watching as his mother vigorously waved a handkerchief from the steps of her little house. His little house, legally, but he never thought of it that way. She had originally let the house on her meager annuity from his father's will, and Dominic had bought it a few years ago with prize money accrued from conquests at sea. He wished he could give her more than a few bedrooms and a cramped living area, but even saving so much of his earnings, he couldn't afford better. That was why, when the promotion had come, he'd turned it down.

Dominic kneaded his temples, trying to push down his lingering doubts about his refusal. He had made the right decision. A working lieutenant's salary was better than the half pay a post-captain received while waiting for a ship. And with so many new captains hoping for a command, he did not know when he'd be back at sea. Better to stay a lieutenant and keep his mother in that tiny home than deplete his funds.

Dominic breathed deeply, anxious to leave behind the stale air of the carriage in favor of the sharp brine of an ocean breeze. Just the thought stirred his heart, but his joy was doused by that ever-present tinge of regret.

He insisted to himself that he had turned down the promotion for his mother, which was true. Yet a small part of him whispered that wasn't the whole truth.

Dominic scooted to the opposite side of the coach to look out the other window. The docks grew closer, and beyond them, the vast ocean. Tiny specks of birds circled the stately masts that rose above the city. He could almost hear the gulls calling as they wove through the maze of ropes. Bound-up sails clung to the yards, begging for the captain's cry to unfurl so they could catch the wind.

This was why he could never marry. His heart belonged to the sea. He both feared and hoped it always would. Waiting for a position as captain would keep him aground for months. Better to serve another man and keep the freedom of the sea than be his own master in the prison they called land.

Georgana brushed at her father's hat once more, then set it and the brush on the desk. It was time for Papa to leave his quarters, but he stood motionless at one of the windows. He'd started doing this in the mornings when they docked a few weeks ago. She didn't know how to pull him out of his meditation. Her hand found the back of her neck, and her fingers twisted into the cropped ends of dark hair. Three years, and the missing tresses still unnerved her.

"Are you ready, sir?" she asked. He didn't move.

Georgana lifted the sapphire coat from the back of a chair and crossed the cabin. She held it out, waiting for him to put his arms into the sleeves.

"Sir?"

He whirled around, and the raw pain in his eyes made her step back. What had she said? His usual stoicism was gone.

"Why are you here, George?"

"I . . ." She ducked her head. He had heard her come in with breakfast, hadn't he? The tray sat untouched on the table except for the roll she had eaten.

"You should be in London," he whispered, his red-rimmed eyes never leaving her face. "Making your debut in Society, receiving gentlemen callers, dancing and laughing to your heart's content. Not waiting on a sorry old captain aboard a dank ship."

Georgana glanced behind her at the door. The marine usually on duty while at sea was not at his post now that they were in port. Still, her heart pounded at the thought of someone overhearing.

She mouthed the word, *Papa.* No sound came out. The word hadn't crossed her lips since they boarded HMS *Deborah.* "You brought me here to protect me." She spoke quietly. She moved closer, unsure if he could hear what she said. Her arms came up to offer him the coat again, and he finally shrugged into it. "I want to be with you."

"If only I had . . ." He shook his head. Since taking command of the *Deborah,* streaks of silver had tinted his light brown hair at the temples. She wondered if it was life at sea or their secret that had taken more of a toll on him. Gone were the days of playing ship in the kitchen garden. She hadn't seen the playful, carefree side of her father since before Mama's illness. "George, will you fetch me some tea? I need a moment to compose myself."

The image of Grandmother screeching those words at Mama's crumpling face filled Georgana's mind. *Compose yourself, Susan! Ridiculous outbursts have no place in this house.* Georgana wiped sweaty palms on her breeches and pulled her knitted Monmouth cap onto her head.

"And if you see the new lieutenant, instruct him to meet me in my quarters."

She nodded. "I assume Lieutenant Jarvis will be showing him around?"

"Yes, though Lieutenant Peyton will be his superior as first lieutenant. I need to speak with Peyton before Jarvis gets his hands on him."

Georgana paused at the door. "You didn't promote Jarvis to second-in-command?"

"I wouldn't make that man first lieutenant if he were the last man on this ship," her father muttered, turning back to the windows.

"Does Jarvis know?"

"I informed him yesterday evening."

She shuffled silently from the room, her stomach sinking. Jarvis had already taken to strutting about the upper deck as though he were the first lieutenant. He would not receive this seeming demotion calmly. Indeed, she was shocked there hadn't already been an outburst. His anger must be boiling beneath the surface, waiting to break free.

That did not bode well for anyone on this voyage.

A ruddy-faced lieutenant was waiting for Dominic when he stepped onto the quarter-deck of the *Deborah.* The man's narrow eyes took him in from hat to boots before offering his hand. They shook, and the strength of the lieutenant's grip surprised Dominic.

"I am Jarvis," the young man said. Dominic guessed him to be a few years younger than himself, perhaps three or four and twenty.

"Peyton. I am pleased to meet you," he returned.

"It's a sorry ship you've come to."

Dominic glanced around. It didn't seem in bad condition. The decks were clean, the rigging sound. "I just came from another *Leda*-class frigate. I did not mind it so much." The *Deborah* was older than his last assignment, to be sure, but most ships in the class hadn't seen more than ten years of service.

Jarvis laughed. "She's terrible in a storm. We lose half the crew to seasickness."

"Ah, I see." Dominic couldn't remember the last time he'd been seasick, even in a gale. "But the Leda class flies like the wind." Which was really all one needed in a ship.

"I suppose that is a benefit," Jarvis said, though he didn't look convinced. He glanced toward the hatchway. "Have you met Captain Woodall?"

"I have not, though I hear nothing but praise." That might have been a stretch. Captain Woodall had the reputation of being a good but safe captain, which was unusual for the commander of a frigate. As was his age. The Admiralty liked appointing young and daring men to captain their frigates.

Jarvis grunted as a boy scurried up the ladder and onto the deck.

The boy raised a hand to the brim of his tan cap and bowed his head. "What is it, George?" Jarvis asked brusquely.

"The captain wishes to see Lieutenant Peyton in his quarters immediately." The boy kept his eyes on the deck at their feet. His jacket overlapped his thin form. Though clean, his clothes showed signs of wear. A ship's boy, and not one destined for commission.

"Thank you, tell him I will be down directly," Dominic said.

The boy saluted again and fled down the stairs without another word.

"That is George Taylor." Jarvis folded his arms across his chest. "A third-class boy. Or so the muster book says."

Something in his sour tone made Dominic pause. "What do you mean by that?"

"He tends to the captain, helps the steward, carries on the duties of a personal servant. But he rooms with the captain and eats food from his table. And he never takes watches."

"That is strange." Third-class boys weren't supposed to be coddled. It didn't prepare them for life as seamen. "Is he a relation to the captain?"

"A distant relation. The boy's father was master and commander of the sloop *Caroline* that went down in the Mediterranean a few years ago. The previous first lieutenant," Jarvis swallowed, blinking rapidly, "said the boy joined soon after, since he didn't have any other family to speak of." The man cleared his throat and looked up toward the yards.

Dominic pretended not to see the show of emotion at the mention of Lieutenant Hargood, the officer he replaced.

"I had best find the captain. Thank you, Jarvis." Dominic left the man staring aloft and followed the boy — George — down the ladder to the gun deck. Dominic didn't

27

know where the second lieutenant's aura of bitterness came from, but he sensed something stewing behind the lowered brows and hard-set jaw.

CHAPTER 2

Georgana balanced a tray with tea things in her arms and waited for the steward to ready her father's dinner tray. She could almost hear Grandmother's shrill disapproval at the now-tepid water in the teapot. Preparing and serving tea had been the subject of many lessons with Grandmother, instructions that still echoed in Georgana's head after three years apart. But Grandmother never had to navigate the gun deck of a swaying ship in the middle of a watch change without upending the tea tray.

Georgana stood at the galley until the steward passed with the captain's dinner. Hanging lanterns swung gently about the deck, sending shadows running behind the cannons. The steward cut through the group of men milling about the deck. She followed on his heels, head down. If the crew didn't see her, they wouldn't talk to her. And while the men didn't notice her much, the boys . . .

"Hoy, George!" A hand grasped the back of her coat, forcing her to a halt. In the noise of the group, the steward didn't realize she'd stopped.

Georgana tried to breathe. She knew who held her coat. Most of the other boys tripped her or shoved her, then went back to their tasks, but Walter Fitz never let her go quickly.

She turned and tried to pull the coat free, but his grip held. The teapot sloshed water over the tray, and the other boys snickered. Georgana cringed as warm water splashed her dry, cracked hands.

"You going to walk right by without greeting your betters?"

She did not point out he was far from her superior. Though he might be stronger than she, they were both third-class boys. "I must bring the captain his tea." She used the gruff voice she'd tried so hard to master, but even her deepest tone sounded pitifully small.

"You're bringing the captain his tea?" Fitz smiled darkly. "You do that a little too well for a man."

Georgana's hands shook, rattling the tea things. Fitz had joined up in Portsmouth with his father, the new coxswain. He

30

couldn't have guessed her secret in so short a time. "Let go of me." She pulled again, but he didn't release her.

Instead, he whipped her to the side, and she crashed into one of the eighteen-pounder guns that lined the deck. The silver teapot clattered over, knocking the lid off. Water surged over the tray. Then he jerked her back toward his messmates.

"Stop, please!" she cried, still clinging to the tray.

"What was that, Prince George? Couldn't hear you." He sent her swinging the other way again.

A stitch in her jacket popped and reverberated up the seam. She fought to keep anything else from tipping to the floor. Eyes from around the deck fell on her, but no one stepped in to help. Not even the marines, tasked with keeping the peace on board.

"Too good to eat with us, are you? Having your dinner with the captain again?"

Georgana tried to wrench herself away and tripped, her knee pounding into the floor. The tray fell from her grasp, its contents clanging across the deck. She gasped at the pain that shot up her leg. Fitz tried to yank her back to her feet.

"That is enough." No one could mistake

the authority in the voice.

Her knee hit the deck again as her coat went slack. She almost fell flat but was stopped by a hand on her shoulder. Her head stayed lowered as the hand grasped her under the arm and helped her up. Heat rose to her face at the silence filling the gun deck. Men who had been climbing the ladder froze. All within view saluted the newcomer.

"Your name?" Lieutenant Peyton asked.

Georgana chanced a peek. The taller boy stood at attention, widened eyes his only sign of fear.

"Walt Fitz, sir."

"You will respect your shipmates, Mr. Fitz. Do not let me see this happen again."

Fitz nodded eagerly. No one was sure how to act around the new officer yet.

"Go fetch more water, George," the lieutenant said in a kinder tone. He picked up the fallen silver and set the tea things on her tray.

Georgana hurried back to the galley. How humiliating! As though being under the protection of the captain didn't give her enough unwanted attention. She didn't need Lieutenant Peyton making her more of a target.

The cook grumbled when she asked for

more water but refilled the pot from his kettle nonetheless. To her dismay, the first lieutenant was waiting at the ladder. The men had finished changing watch, leaving the gun deck mostly clear.

"Are you all right, George?"

She touched the brim of her cap and mumbled a yes. He was supposed to be on deck with his men.

"Don't let them treat you that way." The lanterns painted his face a dull yellow. But even in the poor light, she could tell he was handsome. The crew might have called him a "pretty boy" if he weren't ranked so high above them. She would know — that was what they called her, though in a jeering manner. The juvenile softness of her face didn't compare to his high cheekbones and angular jaw.

"Stand up to them," he said. "Don't let them toss you around. They will not give you respect otherwise."

Defend herself? That would not go well. Though in age she had them all beat by three years at least, Fitz could down her in a matter of moments, she was sure. He was skinny as a bowsprit but neared the lieutenant's height at only fifteen years old. She turned to go without responding to the lieutenant's suggestion.

"I could teach you, if you like."

Georgana paused. No one had offered to help her with anything since she stepped onto the ship. She lifted her eyes to meet his, but the earnestness of his gaze made her look quickly back to the floor.

"No, sir." She bowed her head. "But thank you all the same."

The lieutenant nodded, then bounded up the ladder like he'd been called to dinner instead of to stand on a damp deck late into the night. Georgana watched him go, then walked into the glow of the captain's quarters, lit with several tallow candles in glass-paned lanterns. Her father scribbled notes at his table, several maps lying before him. He didn't look up when she entered and shut the door.

Georgana could do with a few more people like Lieutenant Peyton on the crew. Perhaps this latest addition to the wardroom was worth angering the second lieutenant after all.

Jarvis slammed his empty glass on the table. "Escorting a convoy. Ridiculous! This is a job for a brig, not a frigate."

Sitting at the head of the wardroom table, Dominic glanced around at the men. None of the other officers paid the drunk lieuten-

34

ant any mind. Not even Moyle, whose cheerful and easy demeanor made him a natural listener — a good trait in a third lieutenant. Most of the senior officers had sailed with this crew before. They must have learned to ignore Jarvis when he tried to empty his stash of liquor in one evening.

"It's the captain's fault," Jarvis grumbled. "I'd wager he asks for the cowardly assignments."

Dominic returned his attention to his plate. Once full of pork and potatoes, it now sat empty. All too soon their fresh stores would be gone — eaten or rotten. He had to remember to enjoy the fresh food while he could. But even after they resorted to lackluster rations, there was always Antigua to look forward to. Not that Dominic enjoyed English Harbour, the Royal Navy's home in Antigua. He disliked the rank port city. But outside the harbor he could find many an oasis.

Dominic closed his eyes, trying to remember the fruits brought into Antigua's markets from all over the Caribbean islands. He hadn't sailed to that part of the world in years. The promise of exotic fruit sweetened the mundane task of escorting a fleet of merchantmen to the island.

Jarvis tilted his glass toward Dominic. "We

won't have a single prize this mission. Just you wait and see. Captain doesn't care for taking ships and earning money for his crew."

Dominic drew in a breath. As first lieutenant it was his duty to defend the captain. "And here I thought we sailed for glory of God and country."

"Why sail on a frigate, if not for prizes?" The slur of Jarvis's voice made him nearly impossible to understand.

A middle-aged man with dark, curly hair entered the wardroom with his wooden plate of food. He nodded a greeting to Dominic but didn't acknowledge the rest of the officers as he passed them and entered his cabin.

The French surgeon did not take his meals with the rest of the officers. Dominic couldn't tell if this was his choice or the rest of the wardroom's. The crew didn't seem to know much about Gilles Étienne, except his French heritage and experience as a surgeon. Dominic couldn't imagine being pressed into serving the enemy of his country, but Étienne seemed to endure it without protest.

Moyle leaned back in his chair with a contented sigh. His plate sat empty before him. "Captain Woodall was not always like this. I was a midshipman under his command. Always cautious, mind you, but he had a keen mind. He knew his strengths and never entered an engagement he couldn't win." Moyle tended to stay quiet as the others talked, but a full belly must have loosened his tongue. "He had a spotless record and boasted plenty of prizes."

"And then his wife had to go and die," Jarvis mumbled into the empty glass he still tried to drink from. "Ruined a good captain."

The callousness of Jarvis's grumblings struck something within Dominic. "You can hardly fault a man for that." He fought to keep the steam out of his voice.

"Three years, Peyton. How long does a man need?"

Out of the corner of his eye, Dominic caught a movement through the bars of the flimsy wood partition between the officers' quarters and the rest of the messdeck. George dipped through the doorway and froze in a silent salute.

"What is it, George?" He gave the boy what he hoped came across as an encouraging smile. The lad didn't acknowledge it, keeping his eyes on the ground.

"The captain wishes to speak to Mr. Jordan, sir."

The sailing master rose from his seat. "Perfect timing." He set his napkin over his chair before following the boy's hurried retreat.

Dominic watched them go. Poor boy. George didn't seem cut out for naval life. An apprenticeship on land would suit him better. Dominic would bring up the idea the next time he spoke with the captain. He had few connections on land, but surely the captain had acquaintances who could secure the boy an apprenticeship as a clerk or shopkeeper. Better yet, a place at school.

His mother's parting request nudged Dominic's mind once more. The captain's daughter. He had put off his inquiries as he settled into his position on the new crew, but several shared meals with this group had brought enough familiarity. They clearly weren't afraid of talking about the captain on his own ship.

"Does the captain have any family?" he asked. An innocent enough question.

"A daughter," Moyle said. He was slight compared to Jarvis's stocky form. Dominic had a few inches on both of them, and deep down he itched to discover if that would give him an advantage in a scuffle against the second lieutenant.

Jarvis continued to stare at his glass as

though confused why it was empty. "A pity."

Dominic pushed his plate away and threaded his fingers together on the table. "Does she live with relatives?"

"Why? Are you looking for a wife, Peyton?" Jarvis gave up on his glass and slumped back.

Dominic snorted. "Hardly."

"I thought I heard him say she was at a school in York." Moyle shrugged. "She should be in Society by now."

The purser spoke up from Dominic's left. "They can't have much of a relationship, I should think. I've never seen a letter arrive from York."

The captain was a man alone in the world. If not for his mother, Dominic would be in the same situation.

The conversation lulled after the purser's comment. Jarvis dozed off, and Moyle went back to the upper deck for his watch. Dominic declined a game of cards with the other officers and sought the limited privacy of his cabin. Seeing the timid George and discussing the lonely situation of the captain had put him in a strange mood that he wanted to sleep off before he was needed on deck.

Georgana sat at one of the windows, letting

the light of the full moon flood the paper in her lap. The ship's creaking seemed louder in the stillness of night, interrupting her father's quiet snores. He'd drawn the curtains around his hanging cot to block out the soft light. It was a rare moment of solitude.

She skimmed her pencil across the blank page, outlining the crest of a wave.

Grandmother had never let her draw the sea. Or people. She said it kept them wallowing in their past. Now Georgana drew only the sea. Wave after wave washed over pages in her sketchbook. Something about the sea compelled her to draw it night after night. Was it the delicate foam that adorned a gentle crest, or the strength of a surge as it crashed against the hull? The sea could be whatever it wanted. It never had to ask permission.

She sketched so many pictures, she'd started discarding them out the window when her father wasn't looking. The drawings weren't particularly beautiful, so it wasn't a loss to watch them melt into the sea. Grandmother had never let her forget what a poor artist she was, and Georgana still heard the woman's critiques hissing in her ear as she drew.

Georgana set down her pencil and placed

her hand against a cool windowpane. Moonlight skipped across the ocean's black surface. Lanterns, tiny dots poking through the darkness, twinkled to mark the position of the merchant ships.

A laugh drifted down from the quarterdeck, disrupting the quiet. Georgana grasped the handle on the window and cracked it open. The laugh sounded too jovial for Jarvis and too deep to be Moyle. Must be Lieutenant Peyton.

She listened as she continued her drawing. She couldn't make out words, but the cheerful hum of conversation soothed her.

The lieutenant hadn't stopped giving her attention, something Fitz and the other ship's boys added to their list of grievances against her. Though they kept quiet in his presence, they harassed her more frequently now. She rubbed her knee, still sore from the confrontation a week ago. Lieutenant Peyton was harming more than helping, but he didn't see that. Just like her father hadn't.

Georgana squeezed her eyes shut and tugged at the back of her hair. Father had done what he thought was best, stealing her away to be a cabin boy. On board, Grandmother couldn't reach her. She couldn't even find her.

Flashes of memory shot through

Georgana's mind. Blood on her hands. Tears rushing from her swollen eyes. Grandmother standing over her with the poker.

The scar running across her palm had faded, but a little ridge that ran from wrist to fingertip still pressed against her pencil as she drew. Her grandmother's anger over Georgana's mourning for her mother had come to a blazing head that night. Perhaps Georgana's display of emotions had run her patience too thin. The beating that ensued had been the worst of Georgana's life.

And Papa, nearly mad with grief, stole her away that very night. They told Grandmother she'd gone to a school in York. A lie. In the heat of her pain and his outrage, the deception had seemed the best plan. With Georgana on board, Papa would know she was safe.

But sailing the seas with her father had not been what she'd imagined. Though she insisted he not fret his decision, after three years, she worried as much as he did of the damage to her reputation should she be discovered. Grandmother might have let her out in Society by now. She could be married and settled far away from the woman. Many girls were by eighteen.

Lieutenant Peyton laughed again, and Georgana leaned in toward the window. Her ear rested against the crack, reaching for the carefree joy of the sound. For all the trouble he was causing, she wasn't sorry he'd joined the crew, if only because of the sound of his laughter and his easy smile.

Her eyelids grew heavy, and her head sank against the windowsill. She dozed, ears filled with the gentle lapping of waves and the new lieutenant's pleasant voice.

CHAPTER 3

Dominic never tired of the sea breeze. The sails snapped in each gust that carried them closer to Antigua. With two weeks behind them, they still had at least a month to go. And that was if good weather held. The merchant ships moved much slower than a frigate would on its own.

Jarvis paced behind him on the forecastle, every so often scanning the horizon. Dominic hid a smirk. Their slow pace had begun to wear on Jarvis.

Dominic stood beside the boatswain, Mr. Byam, who arranged lengths of new line to replace a damaged halyard. The portly man worked nimbly while giving instructions to his son, Charlie. The young man nodded, then hurried to the shroud to climb the mast.

Dominic watched Charlie ascend to the yardarm. He was quiet like George but with more confidence. "He's a good lad."

The boatswain beamed. "It's our first voyage with him as my mate." The smile slackened. "Would have brought his mother along as well but for the captain. He forbids women from being on board, in line with the Admiralty's order." The man shielded his eyes from the sun as he watched his boy aloft.

Dominic had noticed the absence of women on the *Deborah*. Despite the Admiralty's orders, many captains allowed carpenters' and boatswains' wives aboard to help with the work. But Captain Woodall was notorious in navy circles for keeping the rules.

"That would have been something, a whole family sailing together," Dominic said.

The boatswain sighed. "That it would have."

And something to consider. If Dominic were captain, he could certainly bring his mother with him. And wife, even. He played with the buttons on his coat sleeve as he pondered. It was a tempting idea.

But how would a woman fare in the harsh conditions of a warship? Or in battle? She surely wouldn't enjoy the cramped quarters and lack of privacy. Though he'd heard of several women who had braved battle and discomfort to be with their husbands, he could not see any lady of high society appreciating life on a frigate as he did.

Dominic turned his face to the wind and closed his eyes. Even if their finances were enough to make it through the waiting period to receive a command, he didn't see his advancement improving his mother's situation. Dominic removed his bicorn and brushed at an invisible spot on its surface. Besides, if he married, he'd have two people to leave. More, if children ever came. All those people to worry about while he was at sea living the life he was destined for.

He shook his head, clearing his mind. Too much deep thinking for one afternoon.

The bell erupted in eight clear rings, signaling the end of his watch. Dominic nodded farewell to the boatswain and headed for the main hatch. Moyle enjoyed backgammon, didn't he? Dominic needed something to take his mind off the future.

The boys from Dominic's division circled the entrance but didn't go down. A few yards away from them, he couldn't hear what they said, but he saw Walter Fitz's lips moving. A head appeared through the hatch, and Dominic groaned.

George.

Before Dominic could shout, Walter

kicked George, who lost his grip and vanished down the hatch. Dominic's stomach leaped. Every seaman slipped down the hatch at least once during his career, but he could only imagine what the force of a kick would add to such a fall.

The boys' roaring laughter dissolved under the click of Dominic's shoes. The group cowered back, except for Walter. Dominic wanted to slap the defiant look from the boy's face. He settled for grabbing a fistful of shirt and pulling the boy to him.

"Are you all right, George?" he called down the hatch, holding Walter tight as he strained to free himself.

"Yes, sir." He could hardly hear the shaking voice over the crash of waves.

The coxswain, Walter's father, hurried over from his place at the helm. "Something the matter, Lieutenant?"

Inside, Dominic seethed, but he tried to keep his voice even. "There is, Mr. Fitz. Your son will not respect his shipmates and has earned himself another watch because of it."

The boy squirmed. "I just finished my watch."

Dominic shouted to Jarvis over his shoulder. "See this lad gets a hearty share of duties this watch."

The second lieutenant shrugged and motioned for the boy to join him on the forecastle deck. Dominic let go, and Walter slunk away.

"They're only boys, sir," the coxswain said. "They didn't mean to hurt anything." Hurt anything? It wasn't *things* Dominic worried about.

"Get control of your son, Mr. Fitz, or I will. Actions such as that can endanger more than just the boys he torments." He scowled at the other boys, who backed up even farther. Then he hurried down the ladder to the gun deck.

George held on to the capstan, balancing his weight on one foot. The cylindrical capstan, waist-high to most men and riddled with notches to insert handles for hoisting and hauling, came nearly to his chest.

"Are you all right?" Dominic asked.

The boy nodded, scooting toward Captain Woodall's quarters. He lowered his other foot but groaned the moment he put pressure on it.

Dominic took hold of his arm before he could try another step. Most likely he twisted the ankle when he landed from the fall. "Let us get you to the surgeon."

The boy shook his head sharply. "I need to get back to the captain." He squinted at

Dominic, little droplets wetting the corners of his eyes.

"You won't be much use to the captain if that foot doesn't heal properly. Come, I'll help you."

Georgana winced as the surgeon removed her shoe, then stocking, pulling at the tender flesh beneath. Lieutenant Peyton put a hand on her shoulder. She couldn't meet his eyes. His kindness was just one more reason for the boys to tease her.

"Now, what have you done to your foot, Mr. Taylor?" the surgeon asked. He spoke English with ease but could not hide his thick French accent. She didn't like the amused look in his dark, glittering eyes.

The lieutenant spoke up. "The boys —"

"I tripped going up the ladder," Georgana said quickly.

Étienne glanced at Lieutenant Peyton but said nothing. Her insides writhed as the man took her foot in his hands. She'd stayed away from Étienne and the previous surgeon for fear they would see through her disguise. He prodded the purpling skin with his fingers, pain lancing up her leg.

She twisted her head away, teeth clenched. Her face met the soft scratch of wool, and she tried to focus on the sensation. It took all her strength to not let the tears escape as he felt along her ankle. Finally Étienne released her foot.

A hand tousled her cap, and only then did she realize she was leaning into Lieutenant Peyton's arm. She sat up quickly, grateful for the dim lighting of the surgeon's room to hide her flushed face. Leaning into him like a young lady swooning in a ballroom would do nothing to convince him she didn't need his help.

"It is not broken, *Dieu merci.*" Étienne went to a chest and retrieved a bottle of amber liquid. He pulled the stopper off the bottle, and an acrid smell permeated the room. "I will apply a compress of *vinaigre* for the swelling. It should not hurt so much in a few days."

Georgana's shoulders fell. A few days? She wasn't going to be able to keep this from her father.

Étienne soaked strips of cloth in a vinegar paste and wound the strips snuggly around her injured foot. She fought to keep her face stoic. The lieutenant pitied her enough. No need to make it worse.

"Eh voilà," the surgeon said. He moved away to return his supplies to their places. "I will need to replace the compress when it dries."

"Thank you, sir." She wobbled as she stood, and Lieutenant Peyton grasped her upper arm to steady her. The throbbing in her foot stopped her from shaking off his hand. If she were dressed as befitted her gender, he would not have dared take her arm in such a manner.

But she wasn't. She was a pathetic ship's boy who couldn't stay out of trouble despite her greatest efforts to remain unseen.

A strange homesickness for England soured her stomach. She'd never been homesick for that place before. England had always meant Grandmother. But she couldn't decide which bully she would rather face — Grandmother or Fitz and his gang.

The lieutenant thanked Étienne, who raised his hand to his forehead in a lazy salute. Lieutenant Peyton slowly led her out of the room and into the darkness of the orlop deck, the belly of the ship she only went to during battle.

They worked their way up to the messdeck, where Fitz's comrades gave them wary looks over their game of cards, then onto the gun deck. After the dank air of the orlop deck, the fresh air coming through the hatchway felt wonderful against her warm face. Her arms shook from the strain of pulling herself up the ladder without the use of her injured foot.

"Will you lie to the captain?" Lieutenant Peyton asked, his voice low. He took her arm again. "I think he ought to know what happened."

Georgana's head snapped up. He was going to say something. She could only imagine what new regulations Papa would create, further alienating her from the other boys and raising more suspicions. And they'd never leave her alone if Fitz were disciplined.

The lieutenant watched her, brows knit. Late afternoon light filtering through the hatchway caught the vibrant brown and green that swirled in his eyes.

"You can't tell him," she blurted.

Lieutenant Peyton sighed. "I will not say anything for now. But if this keeps happening, I will go to the captain."

Georgana saluted. She needed to stay clear of Fitz and his gang, for everyone's sake. "Thank you for your help, sir." She removed his strong fingers from her arm, and he didn't protest. Then she hobbled into the captain's quarters, one shoe and one empty stocking dangling from her fingers.

CHAPTER 4

Dominic didn't expect to see Captain Woodall on the quarterdeck. He usually didn't show himself above deck prior to the forenoon watch. Dominic seized the opportunity, walking quickly aft. George's plight had not left his mind since the incident with the other boys more than a week ago. He would keep his promise of not telling the captain everything, but something had to be done.

The captain stood at the very back of the ship, watching the horizon turn from deep blue to pink. Dominic joined him just as the bell rang four times from the other end of the ship. Six o'clock.

"Good morning, Captain."

Captain Woodall did not respond but rested his elbows on the bulwark.

"How is young George?"

"Nearly recovered from last week's fall." The captain removed his bicorn and ran a hand through his graying hair. "The ladders get so slippery some days. Can't be helped, unfortunately."

Dominic leaned into the rail. So the lad had kept to his story.

"Sir, pardon my boldness, but he does not appear suited to life at sea. Does he have connections that could find him an apprenticeship as a clerk or something less brutal than a career in the navy?"

Captain Woodall pressed his lips together. "The lad's father wished him to be at sea."

Dominic tapped his thumbs against the bulwark. He didn't know why he felt so foolish making this inquiry. He never had trouble speaking his mind. "He has been at sea three years, has he not? Perhaps it is time to advance him past third-class boy."

"He is fine where he is." It came out as a growl, as close to losing his temper as Dominic had seen from the captain in the three weeks since they set sail from Portsmouth.

"But what of his future?" Dominic persisted. "He cannot stay a ship's boy all his life. If his father was master and commander, surely he deserves a higher rank." Second class, at least. And if his father were a gentleman, first class. A higher rank could solve George's problem with Walter Fitz.

Punishment for harming a superior was severe.

The captain didn't respond.

"Why not prepare him for midshipman? I could train him in the things he doesn't know. He is fourteen? Fifteen? In a year or so he could be ready for advancement."

"Will you still be here?"

Dominic rested his gaze on the glowing horizon. Would he?

"I heard the stories of your last battle on HMS *Morning Star.*" Captain Woodall laced his gloved fingers together. "Captain Daniels was wounded early, and you commanded the ship nearly the entire engagement. Sank one French corvette, disabled another, only ten dead."

"Twelve." Twelve unmoving forms in canvas laid out on the deck, waiting to slide into a watery grave.

"A lieutenant who can take that sort of command . . . ," the captain said, watching him. "He should have his own command."

Dominic swallowed. The captain had slyly changed the subject.

"I would like to assist George in any way I can as long as I can."

Captain Woodall straightened, letting his hands fall to his sides. "Lieutenant, have you ever thought you made a correct decision but then later doubted that decision?"

An odd switch of the conversation. The captain clearly had no desire to discuss George.

Dominic's declined promotion weighed heavily on his mind. Yes, he did have doubts like that. He thought he had made the best choice for his mother, refusing the glory of his own command. The sea's cheerful splashing at the stern mocked his sincerity.

"I will let you continue your rounds," Captain Woodall said. "Join me for dinner tonight. And bring Jarvis and Moyle."

Dominic touched his fingers to the brim of his hat. They had never been invited to dine with the captain thus far in the journey. Perhaps this was a step toward better camaraderie between the wardroom and the captain. A smile touched his lips. The captain hadn't said yes or no to his request to train George, but he would count it as progress.

Georgana was used to standing while others ate. It was a punishment Grandmother had sometimes inflicted when she did poorly in her lessons. Her father rarely ate with the officers on purpose so she would not have to wait on them like this. She wouldn't have minded had the soreness in her ankle gone away, but she did not admit its continued weakness to her father.

Tonight all the senior officers sat at the captain's table. Lieutenant Peyton and the sailing master, Mr. Jordan, sat closest to her, with Jarvis and Moyle on the other side of the table. Jarvis's narrowed eyes flitted to her every so often. She focused on the white and black floor tiles to keep from reddening.

Her father raised his glass, more water than anything else. The risk of intoxication and letting slip their secret terrified him. With a dull voice he toasted the king, as naval officers always did at dinner. The lieutenants and sailing master followed suit, Lieutenant Peyton with more vigor than the rest.

The first lieutenant turned and held his glass out to Georgana, eyebrow lifted. She stared at the drink. Did he want more? There was plenty inside, and the steward took charge of refilling.

Then it dawned. He was offering her a drink. Georgana quickly shook her head.

Lieutenant Peyton shrugged and turned back to the table. No one except her father seemed to notice. He eyed the lieutenant as Moyle raised the next toast.

"To sweethearts and wives," the third

lieutenant said.

"And may they never meet." Jarvis grinned wickedly, as if the joke were new and not muttered on every ship in the Royal Navy. Fortunately for him, she couldn't imagine him having a wife, so he likely would never encounter that particular problem.

Lieutenant Peyton set down his glass before the others had finished. "How is your daughter in York, sir?"

Georgana's breath stopped. It wasn't a secret among the crew the captain had a daughter, but no one ever mentioned Miss Woodall. Georgana's skin went cold.

The captain cleared his throat, stabbing at his meat with unwarranted interest. "She is well. Thank you."

"Does she enjoy York?"

Georgana wanted to flee. If only she had somewhere to go.

Irritation flashed across her father's face but didn't stay long. Had the lieutenant seen it? "She enjoys her school well enough, I suppose."

The lieutenant cocked his head. His brown hair had an unruly look to it, as though he'd spent his entire watch at the prow of the ship. "Have you ever considered bringing her aboard?"

Georgana went rigid. Her eyes darted to

58

Jarvis, who was too absorbed with his glass to notice her. If he looked up, she knew he would see her fear.

First Fitz, and now Lieutenant Peyton was having suspicions. Her stomach tied itself into knots.

"My daughter is where she should be." Her father twirled the stem of his glass between his fingers. "So many questions today, Mr. Peyton."

Jarvis snorted. "Didn't you know? Peyton is looking for a wife."

Lieutenant Peyton laughed. "I have a few years before I wish to concern myself with that responsibility."

The lieutenant was single? She found that hard to believe.

Moyle leaned forward. "I doubt Miss Woodall would find life at sea to her liking. The navy is too rough a world for a young lady used to genteel society."

"Are you saying we are not genteel society?" Jarvis motioned for the steward to refill his glass. The man drank much more than he used to when Lieutenant Hargood was on board. Only six months had passed since Hargood's death, but those months had hardened Jarvis. The two lieutenants had been the best of friends.

"Yes, that is exactly what he is saying."

59

Her father placed his hands firmly on the table. "I know very few women of Society strong enough to endure life in the navy."

"Certainly such women are a force to be reckoned with," Lieutenant Peyton said.

She waited for the lieutenant to glance back at her, but he never did. Her breathing started again when talk turned to their course for Antigua. She stretched her injured ankle, trying to do so without drawing notice, and wondered how much longer until they returned to their duties.

Lieutenant Peyton's questions had hit too close for comfort, and she wanted to be alone to calm her racing heart.

CHAPTER 5

Dominic scanned the open sea before him. Ten. Eleven . . . Ah, there was the twelfth. All merchant ships accounted for.

Men lined the decks of the *Deborah,* pulling ropes to reposition the sails. They'd ventured too far from the merchantmen, but the stiff westward wind would get them back in place in no time. They were nearing a month at sea, and so far they'd avoided bad weather or altercations with other ships. If their good luck held, they could easily reach Antigua in another three weeks.

Midshipmen shouted to their divisions, following the sailing master's orders. Captain Woodall paced the starboard side, George trailing behind him. The boy looked so slight compared to the other men, even to the boys his age.

Timothy Locke, one of the boys who wandered about with Walter, stuck out his foot as George passed, sending the lad sprawling. George scrambled to his feet before the captain could see.

Dominic sighed and ran a hand down the side of his face. Those boys wouldn't listen. George had to take action. Nothing Dominic did seemed to dissuade the teasing.

At the end of the watch, Dominic hurried to the gun deck to catch George while the captain was busy with the sailing master. Dominic watched the boy slip into the captain's quarters and followed. Captain Woodall's clothes that George had cleaned that morning hung about. A few smaller shirts and pairs of breeches hung in the corner alongside a long strip of linen. Used to wrap George's ankle, Dominic guessed.

"George."

The lad startled and whirled. He must not have heard Dominic enter behind him. His face paled.

"Are you occupied? I have some things to teach you in the wardroom."

George's feet remained glued to the floor.

"Come, it will be good for you," Dominic prodded.

The boy touched the brim of his cap. "I-I'll be down directly, sir."

"Very good." Dominic smiled, hoping to dispel the fear in George's face. The boy didn't move until Dominic left the room.

He glanced over his shoulder in time to see George snatch the piece of linen and shove it into a trunk before pulling the other clothes down. The poor boy was too timid. But Dominic would cure some of that.

When Dominic reached the officers' quarters, only Moyle was there, as evidenced by the snores coming from his cabin. The young man could sleep through most anything. Dominic usually had to wake him for the first and middle watches. Dominic nudged the wardroom table to one side. That should be enough room.

Whistling drifted through the wooden bars of the partition between the wardroom and the rest of the messdeck. The hatch's ladder blocked Dominic's view, but it didn't take him long to guess who the whistlers were.

The tune belonged to a rather vulgar song called "The Handsome Cabin Boy," about a ship's boy who turned out to not be a boy at all, but the captain's mistress. The whistling could only be coming from the third-class boys, heralding George's presence on the messdeck.

Dominic set his jaw. As much as he wanted to knock the boys' heads together to teach them a lesson, he refrained. He couldn't fight George's battles for him anymore.

He met George at the wardroom door.

The whistling boys sat just around the corner at a table covered with tin cups and a deck of cards. One raised eyebrow silenced them. Then he pulled George in and shut the door.

"The time has come to face your foes, Mr. Taylor."

George nodded obediently. "Yes, sir." He kept close to the door, eying Dominic warily.

"Do you have older brothers?" Best to see what he'd already been taught.

"I have no siblings at all, sir."

So they would start with a clean slate. No matter. Dominic positioned himself a pace away from George. He removed his jacket and flung it over a chair, then loosened his black cravat. Next he rolled his sleeves up to his elbows.

When he looked up, George's eyes were bulging. "What are we doing, sir?"

"I'm teaching you how to hold your own against those boys." He spoke softly, though he didn't think the boys in the mess would be able to hear. "This might be easier without your coat."

George shook his head emphatically and pulled the edges of his coat more tightly around him.

Dominic shrugged. "Whatever you wish. Now, first we will work on balance. You know how to balance with the rocking of a ship. Balancing against a blow isn't so very different. Throw your weight into the force."

He pushed the boy's arm, and George stumbled away, nearly falling into the door of one of the cabins.

"Stand firm. Come, try again. Push back into my hand."

"I don't think this is a good idea." George cowered back toward the door as if to run.

Dominic stepped forward to stop George's retreat but then halted. The forceful teaching of Dominic's superiors had worked well on him when he was young, but George did not seem the same type of boy. "They will not quit until you have proven you are not an easy target."

"They still won't like me." Surprisingly, it did not sound like George minded.

"But they will respect you. That is all we are trying to achieve. If you are to advance in the navy, you must gain their respect." Dominic moved George back to the middle of the wardroom.

"As a third-class boy, I do not plan to advance far in the navy."

Dominic pushed him again. George struggled to keep his balance. "Your father was commander of the *Caroline*. You shouldn't even be third class. Now, plant your feet, like they are nailed to the floor." Dominic tried again, and George pushed back feebly. "A little wider stance, to give yourself a good base. And don't forget to lean in."

The boy sighed, shoulders sagging. Something about the way his head tilted gave him a slightly feminine look. Dominic felt for the lad. Someday, as George grew older, he would become stronger and the childlike softness would fade. Perhaps then he would come to own the legacy his father had left him.

It was the sort of legacy Dominic wished his own father had left. He shook away the pitiful longing. Those days were gone. No need to wallow in what could not be changed.

"I do not wish to advance in the navy," George said.

"What *do* you wish to do, then?"

The boy looked up. His bright eyes looked puzzled, as if no one had asked him such a question before. "I . . . I don't know."

"Well, then, you have until we return to England to decide. I will help you find whatever position or apprenticeship you would like, and I will help you convince the captain to let you go."

George had never held his gaze for so long before. Dominic couldn't tell if he was considering his decision or determining if a lieutenant he hardly knew was trustworthy.

"Until we return, we should work on your self-defense," Dominic said, breaking the silence. "It will be a long journey if that harassment keeps up. And it doesn't seem they will tire of it soon."

After a pause, George nodded once and readied himself. He only faltered back half a step this time. "Good, good!" Dominic tried harder to push him over, and George leaned into the force with more strength. The boy's face pulled into a concentrated scowl as they practiced again and again.

Finally, Dominic pushed as hard as he thought Walter had on the gun deck. With a growl, George pushed back. Not enough to bowl Dominic over — the boy didn't have the weight for that — but enough to make him stumble back. Dominic chuckled, a grin splitting his face. George breathed heavily.

"Well done, George. We'll make a fighter of you yet." Dominic rested against the table. "Shall we learn more tomorrow after morning watch?"

The boy did not answer for a time. He simply stood, pulling his jacket firmly over his chest. "Yes, sir," came the quiet answer. His eyes dropped to the floor again, and he rushed out of the wardroom.

Dominic stroked his chin. They had not technically made much progress. He adjusted his cravat and retrieved his jacket from the chair. But something in George's countenance had shifted. Such a small change, and yet somehow he knew it was an immense shift for the frightened orphan.

Georgana lay in her hammock, enjoying the gentle sway of the *Deborah*'s midnight course. She didn't understand how getting pushed over dozens of times could make her legs and back this sore. But she preferred it to the bumps and bruises of getting knocked around by Fitz.

She'd given up on drawing early tonight. Her mind wandered back to the wardroom too often to focus on sketching. In the three years she'd been at sea, no one had ever tried to befriend her. The crew envied or scorned her relatively sheltered life, and the officers distrusted her closeness to the captain. But Lieutenant Peyton showed none of that.

She shifted, and the rafters her hammock hung on creaked. Did the lieutenant really think standing up to Fitz and his friends would stop the heckling? She didn't think she could become a convincing enough fighter to scare them off.

But he did. He had stood in the wardroom in his cream waistcoat and breeches, arms uncovered and shirt open around the neck. She recalled the playful curve of his lip when she'd started to grasp what he was teaching.

Georgana pulled the blanket over her blushing face. He had simply taken pity on what he thought was a poor boy, and now she could not chase him from her mind. Her lips trembled, and her eyes filled with tears. She could not remember another person, besides her parents, who had shown her compassion. The few friends she had in Portsmouth as a young child had faded into the shadows of her memory.

Grandmother's image pounded on the doors of her mind, just as she had pounded on the doors to Mama's chamber. Mama would often lock herself and Georgana in her room to escape Grandmother. Those days her shouting intensified beyond her normal cruelty.

Georgana rolled to her side and brought her knees to her chest. She would never be rid of that woman. Three years free from her grasp, and the woman's screams still sent shivers up Georgana's spine.

You stupid, stupid girl.

I can only praise the heavens I was blessed with sons and never cursed with mistakes like you.

Stop mumbling, girl! God gave you a tongue to use it.

How dare you speak to me in such a tone! Do you see what a horrible girl you have brought up, Susan? But one can only expect it from such a mother.

Mistake! Mistake!

Georgana flinched as each phrase echoed through her head. She swallowed a sob. What if Grandmother was right? What if she was nothing but a stupid mistake?

Lieutenant Peyton's encouraging smile peeked through Grandmother's storm. He didn't see her as a tongue-tied dolt, or if he did, he didn't show it. Two tears streaked down her face. She clutched her hands together around her knees, fingers scratching against the cracked, ugly skin.

Lieutenant Peyton had grasped these hands to put them in a defensive position. She winced in horror at their roughness. They weren't the fingers of a lady. Of course the lieutenant must have expected such hands from a boy at sea. Still, embarrassment washed over her. Her fingers hadn't

70

always been this coarse.

Georgana sat up, and the hammock swayed. Papa breathed loudly from his hanging cot in the opposite corner. She wiped her eyes on her sleeve, something else that would have earned Grandmother's scorn. She stole from her hammock and crept to her father's writing desk.

Starlight caught on the glass panes of a lantern perched atop the desk. She twisted the latch and eased the lantern's little door open. The tallow candle inside stood nearly half the height of the lantern, with a few cooled drips down its pale side.

Georgana pulled the candle from its place. She dug her thumbnail into the bottom of the candle and dragged it upward. The tallow curled up before her thumb in a long ribbon, which she caught in the palm of her hand. She did this twice more to smooth out the indentation in the candle before returning it to its place and securing the lantern's latch.

She cupped the curls of fat in her hands and rubbed them together as she returned to her hammock. The hard tallow softened under her fingers, until she could smear it over the fronts and backs of her hands. A few days of this treatment, and she needn't be so embarrassed.

What a foolish thing to care about, given her situation. Georgana tucked herself back into the hammock. Almost daily since boarding the *Deborah*, the pendulum in her heart swung to and fro. Some days she mourned the loss of stability she had at Lushill House and the loss of her reputation should she be found out. Other days she felt that she and her father had been right to steal away in the dead of night. She did not know how long she would have to endure this, but she did not want the alternative.

This prison of a ship was better than Grandmother.

Perhaps Lieutenant Peyton's friendship was only the beginning of a better life at sea. As second in command, his respect could influence the rest of the crew. He was well liked among the men, more so than her father.

Her hands stilled. She arranged them on top of the old blankets so as not to stain her shirt, then slowly lay back and closed her eyes. The lieutenant's face filled her mind, and she let the images remain there, bringing a warmth she'd never felt before.

CHAPTER 6

"Good, George. Good!" Dominic motioned for the lad to pause his punching. Half a dozen days of practicing had not turned George into a fighter, but he was learning quickly. The wardroom was warm and stuffy that morning, and already Dominic had lost his cravat and coat. Now he unbuttoned his waistcoat and added it to the pile. He pulled at his loose shirt, letting cooler air dry the sweat.

He didn't know how George kept going with his jacket securely buttoned.

"Now, I don't want you to think about hitting my hand this time." Dominic raised his hand again. A thin layer of grease coated his palm from the lad's fist. He'd never known a boy to worry over dry skin unless it started to crack, but young Mr. Taylor was an odd one.

The boy cocked his head.

"When you swing, I want you to try to

73

punch the wall." He motioned behind him with his head.

George obediently walked toward the back of the wardroom, glancing at Dominic out of the corners of his eyes. Dominic laughed, grabbing his arm to stop him. "No, stay where you are."

"But I can't reach the wall."

Dominic repositioned the boy. Maybe a different explanation would work better. "Hit my hand, but instead of aiming for the surface of my hand, imagine going through it. A cannonball doesn't stop at the hull, it pounds straight through."

"Unless it misses." Was that a grin on George's face? Dominic blinked, and it was gone.

"Those are French guns." The fleeting spark in the boy's eyes gave him hope. "Don't be a French cannon. Be a sound English cannon."

George chewed the corner of his bottom lip and stared at Dominic's hand. His fist shot forward. Dominic's hand smarted when the boy made contact. The punch was harder than any of his previous ones.

"Much better. Again."

A stocky form stomped through the door, and George snapped into a salute. "More practice, Peyton?" Jarvis asked. His watch clearly hadn't cured the foul mood he woke up in. The second lieutenant didn't wait for an answer before entering his room and slamming the door.

They wouldn't see him for several hours, Dominic bet.

George continued hitting Dominic's hand until it began to ache. Dominic's chest swelled with pride. Already the timid cabin boy was showing more determination.

A cabin door opened, and this time it was the young chaplain. George paused to glance at the orange-haired clergyman, who nodded in greeting.

"Will you be attending services today, sir?" the chaplain asked, adjusting his spectacles.

Ah, right. Sunday. Dominic scooped up his discarded clothes. "Of course, Mr. Doswell. I just need to fetch my prayer book." And dress himself properly.

Captain Woodall always wore his dress coat for services, and Dominic tried to remember to do the same. He still hadn't managed to form a friendship with the captain, something he'd never failed to do on his previous assignments. The captain had set firm boundaries with the crew, even with his officers. As far as Dominic could tell, no one had been able to penetrate those walls.

Except George, of course. Dominic wondered at that. They were barely relations.

George followed him to the door of his cabin. Dominic threw his things onto his cot and knelt by his trunk.

"Will we practice again tomorrow?" the boy asked.

"If you want to." Dominic glanced sideways at him. "Do you want to?"

The boy nodded, face still red from the exertion of their lesson.

"I will see you after forenoon watch." George was enjoying it, then. That pleased Dominic. The lad was as quiet as ever, but now he regularly looked Dominic in the eye, and he had even told a joke.

Dominic opened the lid of his trunk. A flash of gray shot out and latched onto his shirt. He yelped and jumped back, but it didn't fall.

A rat.

It clawed up the front of his shirt, racing toward his face. Dominic stumbled, an unintelligible scream spilling from his lips. George ran in and swatted the creature down. Its rough fur stuck out at odd angles. Those beady eyes set Dominic's insides wriggling. The rat scrambled back toward the trunk, but the boy kicked it out of the cabin. It sailed into the wardroom, squeaking and writhing. When it landed under the table, the pest rolled to its feet and scurried away.

Dominic panted, wiping the front of his shirt to rid himself of the feeling of claws racing up his torso. Where had the little devil come from? He must have left the trunk open a crack that morning. Of all the stupid mistakes to make.

He gripped George's shoulder. What a dolt, scared over a rat! Ships were rampant with them. "Thank you, George. I apologize for getting frightened like a little girl." He shook his head ruefully.

George didn't laugh as he expected. The boy fixed him with a flat look. Dominic couldn't read the thoughts behind those bright eyes.

He pulled on his waistcoat, hands still shaking from the surprise visitor, then reached for his coat. A curse slipped from his lips at the sight of a hole the creature had eaten through between the line of buttons and the sleeve.

"What is it?" George asked.

Dominic showed him the gnawed hole. "I'll be a shabby lieutenant until we get back to England." Not that they wore their dress uniforms very often. But every Sunday the hole would be there for all to see.

"I can mend that." George pulled the coat closer to survey the damage.

"You can?" Most men on board could do basic repairing, but their work was meant only to hold things together until a better solution could be found.

"I mend the captain's coat often enough. You can only see the mending if you know it's there." There was no pride in his voice.

Dominic looked at the hole. Did he trust the boy to fix something so expensive? George had trusted him enough to come back for more lessons. What sort of friend would Dominic be if he didn't offer trust in return? "Very well, I will bring it to the captain's cabin after services."

George nodded. "I'd best go see if the captain needs anything." He saluted and left.

Dominic scowled one more time at the glaring hole. No doubt the boy thought him ridiculous now. He chuckled. One thing he could count on — George would not tell a soul about his unmanly display. He'd have to console himself in that.

Bells tolled the end of the watch as Georgana scrambled up the ladder to the upper deck, a telescope tucked under her arm. She wondered if she would miss the constant ringing if she ever found a place on land to belong to.

She moved out of the way of the hatch to let the men go below. Her gaze flicked across the deck. Lieutenant Peyton stood at the larboard rail near the bow. His eyes were closed, a peaceful smile on his face — the picture of a man who knew where he belonged. Perhaps she could capture that scene if she were better at drawing. If only Grandmother had allowed her to draw more than dull landscapes.

But Grandmother wasn't here now, and the idea of drawing figures tickled Georgana's mind.

Lieutenant Peyton spotted her and raised his hand in greeting. The memory of Sunday morning and the terror on the lieutenant's face forced its way into her head. She kept her face passive, masking the giggle bubbling inside. What a world of trouble she would be in if she allowed such a feminine sound to escape.

The lieutenant walked toward her but didn't stop when he reached her. He stuck out a hand and tousled her cap as he passed on his way to the quarterdeck.

The quarterdeck! Georgana remembered

the telescope in her hands. Her father had sent her to the cabin to fetch it. She'd let herself get distracted by Lieutenant Peyton again. Georgana wheeled around and followed the lieutenant.

It wasn't as though she'd never seen a handsome man on the *Deborah*. Lieutenant Hargood had been severely handsome. Lieutenant Moyle was nice to look at. Even Mr. Jordan, the sailing master, though nearly as old as her father, still had pleasing features. But something about Lieutenant Peyton's hazel eyes, which twinkled as though holding in a laugh, and his firm jaw, offset by an easy smile, made Georgana hardly able to look away.

Tense voices carried across the quarterdeck as she climbed the steps up to the back of the ship. Most of the crew wasn't allowed on the quarterdeck, which was reserved for officers, but she was. One more thing for the other boys to hold against her.

Her father and Lieutenant Jarvis stood at the far end of the deck. She couldn't see her father's face, but his shoulders hunched forward like a cat ready to pounce. Jarvis's square face pulled into a snarl as he spoke.

"I am not the only one who feels we should have gone after the schooner we saw this morning," the second lieutenant said.

"Ask Peyton what he thinks."

Lieutenant Peyton had positioned himself a little to the right of her father. "I love a good chase but defer to Captain Woodall's judgement."

"Are we to sit here and wait until corsairs start firing on one of the merchantmen before we do our duty to protect them?" Jarvis's face flamed. "Must we wait until the fox is in the henhouse?"

Papa's hands balled into fists at his sides. "I will not expend our resources and men running after neutral ships. The schooner did not make contact, and we will let it be." He spoke through a clenched jaw.

Georgana crept forward, head down. She didn't want to draw their anger to her by calling undue attention.

Jarvis threw up his hands. "But —"

"There is more to being an officer in His Majesty's navy than lusting after combat, Mr. Jarvis. Every battle comes at a cost. As captain, it is my duty to determine whether a fight is worth the loss of life and ammunition. When you are captain, heaven forbid, you can take those chances with your men."

Georgana flinched. Jarvis would not take that slight well. Indeed, she could practically see steam rolling up from his face.

"I have chosen not to risk lives today," her

father continued. "You would do well not to question my judgment, Lieutenant." He turned toward Lieutenant Peyton, cutting off further conversation.

Jarvis did not move for a moment, eyes boring into the back of Papa's head. His shoulders heaved. Then he snapped a brisk salute and stormed from the quarterdeck. Georgana scuttled out of the way to avoid getting trampled.

Lieutenant Peyton quietly gave his report and retreated.

"I will be finished with your coat tonight," Georgana said as he passed. "Shall I bring it to the wardroom?"

"I'll fetch it. Thank you, George." His smile looked forced.

She understood the feeling. Papa and Jarvis had never agreed on how the ship was to be run, but the last week or so Jarvis had become bolder. Now a full-blown argument had erupted on the deck, within earshot of many of the crew. If this continued to escalate . . .

She did not want to imagine the results.

Papa was in the cabin when Lieutenant Peyton came to retrieve his coat that night. Georgana did not know why her stomach twisted when her father expressed his surprise at the visit.

Georgana put her head down. She quickly finished off a last stitch on the coat and wove the tail of thread into the other stitches. The location of the hole made the repair more obvious than the mending she had done on her father's coat. She hoped it would meet the lieutenant's expectations.

"George has been so kind as to mend my coat for me," Lieutenant Peyton said.

Georgana felt Papa's gaze. She had very little interaction with the men on the ship beyond relaying messages.

"Ah. I thought it was mine." He feigned interest in the notes before him on the table, but Georgana saw him watching them.

"I've finished, sir." She held out the coat to Lieutenant Peyton, but his eyes were on an open book sitting on the table. Her heart leaped into her throat. Her sketchbook.

The lieutenant picked it up and flipped through the pages. "Did you draw these, George?"

She wanted to pull his coat over her head. After finishing the mending, she had planned to make her first attempt at drawing a person. Thank heavens she hadn't already begun.

"These are very good." He held the book

toward the lantern light, examining each image.

"They're just waves," Georgana said. She hoped the confession would dissuade him from continuing his perusal.

It didn't. He gave each page more attention than the silly sketches deserved. "I can never grow tired of looking at waves. You have talent, George."

Hardly. She bit her tongue, hoping to avoid blushing under his praise. "Your coat, sir."

The lieutenant finally set down her book. "Thank you." He inspected the mending. "If I did not already know you came from a naval family, I would ask your father's profession, Mr. Taylor. Where did you learn how to do this?"

What did she say to that? Grandmother had made her learn mending.

Her father cleared his throat, turning the lieutenant's attention back to him. "Has Jarvis's temper cooled?"

Georgana relaxed. As much as she would have preferred to talk to the lieutenant alone, she was grateful her father had stayed in tonight.

"I believe so, sir."

"Very good."

Lieutenant Peyton held up his coat.

"Thank you, George. Good evening, Captain."

Her father followed him to the door and shut it behind the lieutenant. When the sound of Peyton's footsteps faded, he whirled.

"Does he know?"

Georgana's eyes widened. "No, Captain."

Her father let out a breath. His hand rose to his forehead. "Peyton has shown a marked interest in you of late. Does he suspect?"

Georgana swallowed. "I don't think so." Papa remained unaware of the defense lessons with the lieutenant, and she didn't think he would appreciate knowing. Keeping things from her father came easily. More easily than it should. She had kept Grandmother's mistreatment hidden most of her life.

"You must be careful in your interactions with the men on this ship. We cannot be too cautious." He returned to the table and sat heavily. He picked up his pen again, dipped into the inkwell, and continued the notes from before Lieutenant Peyton's visit. "I cannot understand why he would take an interest in you."

"Perhaps . . ."

He looked up and waited.

"Perhaps he saw a lonely cabin boy who needed a friend." Her voice came out small and shaky.

Papa stared at her, mouth open as if to speak. But no words came. Eventually he closed it and turned back to his work.

Georgana slipped her needle into its place in her trunk, then plucked up her book and pencils. She took them to the chair by the windows and set a lantern on a sill. Papa would have to be her first unsuspecting subject.

They didn't speak again that night. She drew until her father lay on his cot and let down the curtains. When his exhales deepened, she stopped her work on his likeness and turned to a fresh sheet.

Georgana drew lines for the bulwark, then outlined a head and shoulders. Arms resting against the rail. Hair flying back. Eyes closed. Ends of his lips lifted. She held the book back to examine her work. The picture did not look like the lieutenant.

Grandmother cried out in her head. *Mistake! Mistake!*

Her fingers slowly, quietly tore the page from her book. She eased the window open enough to stick her hand through and released the page into the night air. It drifted this way and that until coming to rest on the surface of the water. The paper tarried a moment, then faded into the deep.

CHAPTER 7

Georgana stared at the ceiling of the captain's cabin for a moment before realizing the hour. Bright light reflected off the white paint, making her squint. From the deck above, the bell rang three times. Half past nine.

She jolted up and tripped out of her blankets to the floor. Her father was not in the room. She hadn't even heard him get up.

Georgana rubbed her eyes with the heels of her hands. How could she have slept so long? The last two weeks she'd stayed up late every night drawing, but she never overslept. With bells every half hour, how could anyone?

She ducked behind the changing screen to pull on breeches and tuck her loose shirt in. Quickly she ran a hand over the bindings around her chest, her most important article of clothing. Not that she had much to hide in that regard, but she couldn't be too careful. Then stockings, shoes, and a neckcloth. As she fumbled with the buttons on the waistcoat, she wished for a moment she could wear fewer layers, as the other boys did. That would make dressing much faster on days like this. Last came her coat. Only the first-class boys, those awaiting a promotion to midshipman, wore so many articles of clothing. But they didn't have something to hide.

This was what she got for letting her pride get the best of her, as Grandmother always said. Georgana had started to grasp the basics of drawing people. Well, of drawing two specific people. She pulled her cap on and raced for the door. If she had been more humble about the drawings, she would not have stayed up so late.

Georgana headed for the galley, not stopping to wonder if her father had already eaten his breakfast. The ship bustled with seamen performing their morning tasks — cleaning guns from yesterday's drills, scrubbing the floors. In her haste, she smacked into one of the boys mingling on the gun deck.

Her throat tightened as Fitz's smirking face met her. "Sleep well, Prince George?" The boy put his hands on his hips. "Captain is above if you need to make your excuses."

Heat rose to her cheeks. She had managed to avoid him and his lot for several weeks, but she hadn't been thinking of them when she barreled out of the cabin.

"If you will excuse me," she muttered, taking a step toward the galley.

She anticipated Fitz's shove before his hand hit her shoulder and threw her weight into it to keep herself upright. She pivoted, facing her attacker. Out of habit from her lessons with Lieutenant Peyton, her hands clenched at her sides, ready.

"You think you're better than us, don't you, Georgie?" Before she could step back, Fitz lashed out and grabbed the front of her shirt with his soot-covered hand. She tried to pull away, but the action only tugged her collar out from under her loosely fastened necktie.

He leaned in, his face inches from hers. His breath reeked of grog. Georgana gagged. "You're no better than us, you little orphaned rat."

The button on her collar strained. Georgana yanked at his fingers to loosen his grip. "I never said I was." Her legs shook. The waistcoat covered most everything, but if the button popped free and the shirt fell open, the top of her bindings would be visible. Three years of secrets, gone in a moment.

Sound English cannon, the lieutenant's voice whispered in her mind. Georgana took a breath. Then she drove her fist into Fitz's face.

The blow glanced off his cheekbone instead of connecting with his nose as she had intended, but it accomplished her aim. He released her shirt and stumbled back, cursing. She stared at the hunched over Fitz. The boys stared at her.

What had she done?

The lads' leader raised his head. The skin under his right eye was pink and puffing up. There was murder in his eyes.

He didn't speak. Georgana widened her stance, heart racing. Peyton said if she defended herself, the boys would leave her alone. She prayed he was right.

With a cry, Fitz lunged.

Sails covered the deck for cleaning. Dominic walked among them, encouraging dawdling workers and chatting with the boatswain. Behind him, Captain Woodall paced the quarterdeck alone.

Jarvis and the captain had continued their quarrels since the schooner sighting. Dominic couldn't say if Jarvis simply needed to release pent-up frustrations for not getting promoted or if he was still stewing over the schooner they had let go.

Dominic hadn't seen George this morning. Odd. He usually attended the captain in the mornings, except on the days he washed clothes. He hoped the boy hadn't taken ill.

George had seemed fine the day before when they practiced in the wardroom. He was getting quite good, and Dominic couldn't help but feel a bit of fatherly pride — or what he imagined such pride would feel like, since he had never observed it from his own father. George had flipped Dominic flat onto his back yesterday. A real, if not painful, sign of progress.

He made his way toward the quarterdeck to give the captain a report. More encouraging than George's fighting skills, the lad had softened his reserved manner. A smile here. A joke there, so quiet and dry one might miss it.

Dominic passed the main hatchway as one of the men came through. Shouts echoed up from the gun deck. He stopped the man and pointed below. "What is all that?"

The sailor chuckled as he saluted. "Just a couple of the boys having a row, sir."

Walter Fitz, no doubt. That boy would

plague him this entire voyage. "Who is involved?" The fight needed to be stopped immediately.

"Fitz and Taylor, sir. And Taylor's holding his own. Lad won't give up."

Blast! Dominic spun around and practically threw himself down the hatchway. Boys' voices whooped and groaned all about him as his eyes struggled to adjust to the dimness of the lower deck.

It wasn't supposed to come to this.

"First the captain's pet, now the lieutenant's," Fitz growled. "How'd you manage that, pretty boy?" Blood dribbled down his chin from a cut on his lip.

Georgana hadn't landed a better punch than the first one, but she'd managed to stay out of the way of his swings. That cut had come from pushing at his face when he had tried to wrestle her to the ground. She hadn't let him, and she even tried to run for the captain's cabin, but he kept her in the fight by sweeping her feet out from under her.

"I don't want to fight anymore, Fitz," she said through clenched teeth. "Just let me go."

He and the other boys blocked her escape. A few of the men came to watch, but no

93

one stepped in to help.

"Don't want to fight?" Fitz breathed heavily, hands on his knees. He straightened and swept a hand to the side. "Well, we wouldn't want to keep a yellow-livered landsman in a fight, would we?" He moved aside as if to let her pass.

Georgana watched him, looking for a sign of deceit. He wouldn't let her just walk away. She edged toward the cabin, but the line of boys tightened, preventing her from passing through.

"Should have guessed a girl like you wouldn't stay to finish the fight."

Georgana spun, stomach leaping into her throat. "What did you say?"

Fitz grinned wickedly. "Where did the captain pick you up, Georgie? At a girl's school? Are you nothing more than a lass in breeches?" Fitz brushed off his hands.

Georgana stood frozen to the deck. He didn't know. He *couldn't* know.

Fitz crossed his arms. "Handsome cabin boy, indeed. More like ugly cabin girl."

Something within her snapped. "Stop!" She threw herself at him, knocking him to the ground.

"Girl!" he shouted. "You're a —"

Georgana clapped her hand over his mouth. He shook his head, and she had to scramble to keep his mouth covered. Every time he wiggled away, he shouted, "Girl!" How long until his suggestion stuck in the crew's minds, until they started guessing the truth?

Fitz tore at her coat, her cap, her hair, trying to get her off him. He tried to roll over, but she threw her weight to the other side. Louder, deeper voices called, but she didn't make them out.

She couldn't hold on much longer. Her arms shook, and her legs felt wooden and clumsy. Fitz, despite his bruises, wasn't tiring as fast.

Time for another sound English cannon. To end this. To protect her secret. Georgana pushed herself up, fist cocked to deliver the blow.

Arms clamped around her middle and dragged her away. She pushed and slapped, trying to break free. If they held her and let Fitz get the last hit . . .

But the iron arms holding her were covered in wool. Dark blue wool with brass buttons. Georgana relaxed just as Lieutenant Peyton hissed, "Settle down, George." She let him pull her back.

He released her several paces from Fitz, who wearily got to his feet. The lieutenant stood between them, glancing from one to the other with brows pulled low. He looked furious, but she spotted a little twitch at the corner of his lips.

Fitz's finger jutted at Georgana. "He threw the first blow."

"George did?"

"He wouldn't let me go," she mumbled. Her gaze sank to the floor. What a half-wit she was. She always made the wrong decision, and this time it would ruin everything. Her father would have to punish them both or risk making the crew suspicious.

Lieutenant Peyton didn't say anything for a minute. Movement and conversation from the upper deck sounded loud and clear in the silence. "I do not want to see either of you within ten feet of each other. I do not want you to speak. I do not want you to look at each other. Is that understood?"

Georgana's head moved up and down submissively.

"Walter?"

"Yes, sir," came the grumble.

"Very good. Mr. Fitz, go to the surgeon for that eye. Mr. Taylor, come with me."

He took Georgana's arm and marched her back to the captain's empty cabin. Once inside, he closed the door. "What happened?" He placed his hands on her shoulders, but she couldn't look at him.

"I already explained, sir." Her voice faltered. "I told you this wasn't a good idea." Her heart still pounded, but whether from the fight or from having Lieutenant Peyton's arms around her, she could not tell.

His hands fell to his sides. What would he tell her father? She wanted to crumple to the deck at the thought of Papa.

A moment later he slipped her cap, which she hadn't realized she'd lost, over her hair. The slight brush of his fingers against the short locks sent a peculiar tingle along her scalp. The sensation stilled the commotion inside her. When was the last time someone had gently touched her hair? Surely it had been Mama.

She lifted her head. His grin that had threatened earlier made a brief appearance. He tousled her cap and mouthed, *Good work.* "I'll have Étienne come up to look at those knuckles when he's done with Walter," he said. And then he left.

Georgana's shoulders sagged in relief. She was still in the lieutenant's good favor. She held up her hands. Despite her attempts to soften her skin with tallow, they had cracked and bled in the fight. She wondered if any of the blood was from Walter's lip. The thought made her flesh prickle. Disgusting.

Dominic didn't relish the task of reporting George's fight to the captain. Best to get it done with quickly. He leaped up the steps to the quarterdeck and nearly ran the captain over.

"What is it, Lieutenant?" Captain Woodall asked.

Dominic straightened his shoulders and touched his fingers to his bicorn. "There has been an incident, sir. With George and Walter."

The captain blanched. "What is it? What has happened?" Dominic was surprised by just how agitated the captain was. Of course, George was his relation and he was tasked in the boy's safety. But this was the navy, after all.

"I am not certain how it started, but I venture to guess that Walter provoked George, and George stood up for himself." Dominic bit the inside of his cheek to keep his expression in check. George had finally taken a stand. "After George's facer, he won't be able to open his eye for a week."

"George is hurt?" Captain Woodall hurried for the stairs.

Dominic held up a hand. "No, I apologize,

Captain. Walter is the one with the swollen eye. George landed the facer."

The captain stopped in his tracks. His head slowly came around. "George did?"

Dominic drew in a breath. "Yes, sir, and before you take disciplinary action, I wish you to know I consider myself partly to blame." His words rushed out like water from a cracked barrel. "I taught George to fight, so he could defend himself from the other boys' heckling. I didn't think it would go this far, but George did only what I told him to do."

Captain Woodall tilted his head. His hands clasped behind his back. "You taught him? When?"

"In the wardroom, sir, whenever our schedules allowed."

The captain paced toward the end of the deck. He stroked his chin. Dominic waited at attention for a response.

"He has been harassed by the other boys?" The man's voice lowered. "I didn't know."

"Forgive me, but there are many boys on this ship. You cannot protect them all." Which was why Dominic had tried to protect this one friendless lad.

"Gave him a shiner, you say?" An odd glimmer appeared in Captain Woodall's eyes.

Was he pleased? Dominic hoped so, for George's sake.

"Yes, sir. Quite thoroughly." He cleared his throat. "If I may be so bold, I would recommend not taking disciplinary action against either young man. I don't think it will happen again." Surely Walter had learned his lesson. George certainly had.

The captain waved a hand. "Oh, no. Of course not. After all, they were just being . . ." That strange expression returned. "Boys."

Georgana sat with hands clasped in her lap. The captain's meal was spread out on the table. Her father had stayed above decks nearly all day, and though she'd taken her turn helping clean the sails, he'd never come over to speak with her. He acted as though nothing had happened.

She looked down at her cracked knuckles, now smeared with lard. This time the surgeon had given the fat to her. The pungent scent of pig wafted up from her hands, mixing foully with the aroma of dinner. She preferred the less-fetid smell of candle tallow.

The door opened, and she jumped to her feet with a salute for the sake of the men who might see inside. Her father strode in, sweeping his bicorn from his head.

When the door closed, she waited for him to speak. He didn't.

Her father sat and helped himself to the sea biscuits and pork stew before them. Not once did he look at her. She remained standing, watching him dish up the food. Their looming discussion hung heavy in the silence.

He tapped the weevils out of his biscuit, then set it to soak at the bottom of his stew. The little larvae wriggled across the table, seeking their vanished food and shelter. Georgana used to shudder at the sight. Now she rarely glanced at them, except at this moment, to avoid her father's eyes.

A carafe of lemonade and a pitcher of grog sat between the dishes. Her father ignored the former and filled his glass with the watered-down rum. Cook thought the captain enjoyed lemonade, but it was a lie. The lemonade was for Georgana.

A lump formed in Georgana's throat. Everything was a lie. Her entire life these three years. Her interactions with the crew. Her friendship with Lieutenant Peyton. Lies, lies, and more lies.

The captain took a drink, then looked up. "Sit, George. Eat."

Georgana sank into the chair and slipped

a biscuit from the plate. Her stomach cinched tight, but she took a bite.

Her father leaned across the table. "Why did you not tell me the boys were harassing you?"

"I didn't want you to worry." The same reason Mama had told her not to tell him about how Grandmother acted.

His jaw clenched. Would he shout like Grandmother? He hadn't shouted at her in anger before, but she deserved to be scolded after what she'd done today. "You did not think I would find out?" he asked, voice still low.

"Boys have teased me ever since I boarded the *Deborah.*" Her wet eyes burned.

He covered his face with a hand. His chin dropped to his chest. "Why did you not come to me?"

"I didn't want you to be upset. If you favor me too much, the crew gets suspicious." And the boys' teasing would get worse.

Georgana stared at her food. If she ever left this ship, she wouldn't eat pork again. Or these biscuits. That day might be very soon if anyone thought too much about Fitz's jeers. She'd reacted too strongly to his calling her a girl.

"I've ruined you, George." The words

102

came out hoarse, pained.

Georgana usually refuted such statements. She didn't like to consider the possibility they were true. After all, he had tried hard to do what was best. But tonight she couldn't deny them. She didn't have the strength.

CHAPTER 8

Dominic didn't expect to find George huddled behind a cannon on the gun deck following afternoon watch. His knees were pulled up to his chest, and his Monmouth cap hung over his eyes. No one on the deck paid him any mind. Most probably couldn't see him.

Captain Woodall had kept the boy in the captain's quarters most of the day following the fight — Dominic assumed to help ease tensions. Word of the fight passed quickly and faded, as it always did. No doubt the only one who remembered now was Fitz, who could still hardly see out of one eye.

Dominic stopped in front of George. The sound of shoes on wood was hard to mask, but the boy didn't acknowledge Dominic's presence. He sat still as stone against the wall, leaning onto the cannon. If Dominic didn't know better, he would have guessed he was even younger than fourteen at that moment. He looked so small.

"George?" Dominic nudged George's shoe. No response.

Had the captain been more upset than he'd let on? Had he changed his mind and inflicted punishment? "Are you all right?"

The boy's hand rose to his cap, then slithered back around his knees. He looked unhurt.

Perhaps the shame of the incident had put George in this sorry state.

Dominic sighed and walked to the galley. He knew too well the loneliness of trying to find one's place at sea. As he entered, the hobbling cook nodded a greeting while stirring up a batch of grog for the impending meal.

"Might I have a couple mugs of that, Mr. Harold?"

The cook sent his mate for mugs and filled them with the warm liquid. Dominic thanked him and carefully made his way back to George with the sloshing cups. He sat awkwardly, trying not to spill all over himself.

"There you are, George." He tapped the tin mug against the boy's arm.

George took the mug, lifting his head enough to cradle the drink in his lap. He stared unseeing at it.

Dominic needed to make a report, write in the logbook, and prepare for the next day's gun exercise. But the dejected boy would plague his thoughts unless he tried to help. Dominic drank from his mug. He could spare a few minutes.

Charlie, the boatswain's son, walked by, a finger wrapped where a rat had bitten him the other night. A shiver ran up Dominic's spine. Wretched vermin. Charlie didn't look their way but continued on to the hatch. The eighteen-pounders secluded them. Enough, he hoped, to get George to speak.

"Would you like to practice today?" George always came to life when they practiced.

The boy shook his head. "Captain doesn't want me to practice anymore."

Ah. Well, they couldn't go against the captain's orders. Dominic disagreed with the decision, but he would respect it. "Have you been drawing?"

George flinched. "A bit."

"I always wished I had learned to draw. I'd probably rival you with how many pictures of waves I'd make." Most boys he'd looked after responded well to playful ribbing, but the goading didn't draw a smile from George. He tried again. "In the absence of talent, I will have to commission you for a piece to brighten my cabin."

The boy looked at him out of the corner of his eye. "It's pencil. There is no color."

"Well, to liven my cabin, then." Dominic leaned his head back against the wood. The sweet music of waves washing across the hull filled his ears. "I do love the sea."

"It's all around us. You can walk up and see it whenever you wish," George said, his voice pinched.

"I'd like a picture all the same." This wasn't working. The boy still stared into his cup, as though searching for something beyond his reach. "Where are you from, George?"

"London."

"I've never been to London. Not the city itself." He hoped speaking of home would draw the boy out.

"Lucky, you are."

Dominic laughed. "I assume you don't miss it, then."

"Not at all."

"And you don't like the sea." He winced as he said it. The observation had fallen from his lips before he could think better of it.

"I . . . do not know how I feel about the sea anymore."

Dominic sipped his drink and waited. He

sensed more beneath the surface. The boy did not speak again for some time.

"I wanted nothing more than to go to sea when I was young. I loved my father's stories, and I wished to be with him. But I fear . . ." The boy swallowed. "I fear I was not born for the sea as my father was."

Many boys in the navy, after their eyes were opened to the harshness of sea life, found it not for them. As a midshipman, Dominic had snickered over the boys who left the service. *Weaklings,* he and his comrades called them. As he grew older, he regretted those sentiments. Now, seeing the toll the navy had taken on George, his resolve deepened. This life seemed to be killing George from the inside. He would find another place for him when they got back to Portsmouth.

"Did your mother fight to keep you home, as mine did?" Dominic grinned. Many seamen could relate. Mothers somehow knew once they let their boys scramble up the gangplank, their sons were gone. Even if the boys came back unharmed, the navy changed them in irreversible ways. It hardened them or strengthened their unquenchable thirst for adventure. It didn't make them men. It made them sailors.

"My mother died just before I went to sea."

Dominic didn't know why the quiver in George's voice struck his heart. His own father had died not long before Dominic went to sea. But he never cried — at least not for the loss. Little had changed after his father's death. His mother was still uncared for, but with his father gone, Dominic could do something about it. Or start to. A twelve-year-old just beginning life at sea earned very little money. But he'd tried to make a life for them.

"What year did your mother die?" Dominic asked.

"Eighteen hundred and seven."

"Was that not also the year the *Caroline* sank?" Dominic set down his mug, turning toward the boy, who sat paralyzed in place. George's mother and father had been taken from him in the same year. Dominic felt sick.

Living this life away from the support of family was hard enough. But knowing someone was at home to welcome him back sustained Dominic when it felt as though no one cared one whit whether he lived or died.

Dominic put a hand over George's knee, covering the mismatched buttons on the side. "I'm so sorry, George." The lad's knee tensed, as though he wanted to pull away.

"Why does it concern you?" The pleading words burst from George's mouth.

It did not take long for Dominic to find the answer, though he had to dig deep. Deeper than he liked.

"It took me several years in the navy to find my place. Despite my love for the sea, this life is not for the faint of heart, and I worried I was not cut from the right cloth. I had plenty of men to tell me how to be a seaman, but not many to show me how to be a good man." He met the boy's intense gaze and offered a smile. "Not that I put myself forward as the best example. But a boy in the navy can never have too many friends."

George set his still full cup down between them and stood. "Thank you, sir." He trudged back to the captain's cabin, leaving Dominic alone with the guns and drinks.

Dominic drew a hand through his hair. It was longer than he liked it. What to do for George? If only he knew how to reach the lad — to show him he had a place, even if it wasn't at sea.

Georgana sat by a window at the start of the morning watch. Darkness still swathed

110

the skies, but the stars had begun to wink and fade. In these twilight hours, suspended between the magic of night and truth of day, she felt the most at ease. The whole earth held its breath, waiting for the hope of sunrise.

When she'd boarded this frigate, she'd practically still been a child. Hidden from Society on Grandmother's orders, then pulled away from the only world she knew while on the brink of womanhood. She had been unready to marry and eager to go to sea, but she was grown now. The excitement of being on the ocean wore off quickly under the weight of keeping her secret. If she'd stayed at home, she would probably be married. Possibly with a family.

She traced the panes of the window with her finger. She couldn't fool herself into believing she deserved respect from her shipmates. Fitz's heckling revealed what he thought about boys who couldn't adapt, and most sailors held the same view.

Her mind wandered back to her conversation with Lieutenant Peyton the day before. What would he think if he knew who she truly was? Would he dismiss her as the child she pretended to be?

Georgana rose and retrieved her sketchbook. She returned to her chair, flipping through the pages. In the faint light before dawn, she could barely make out her latest attempt at depicting the lieutenant at the bulwark.

Her father was right. She should be in London, moving forward with her life. Not suspended in adolescence in the middle of the sea. Would Grandmother allow suitors? No doubt she would skip the frivolous courting and shove Georgana headfirst into the hands of the first rich bachelor she met. Would Papa be brave enough to stop such a match? She couldn't say.

Georgana slid her fingers lightly across the page. What would it be like to be courted by a man like Lieutenant Peyton? Surely a wondrous experience, with the kindness in those eyes. It did not take great imagining to see them filled with love. They must resemble what they looked like when he laughed, so full of ease and warmth. She'd speak solely in jokes and riddles for the rest of the voyage just to see that joy on his face. And he talked about his mother in such gentle tones. If he adored a wife half as much as he adored his mother, she couldn't see herself wanting anything more.

Her fingers halted their progress. Was he already married? No, he had said he wasn't. But his heart could be taken already. He could be engaged . . . or soon to be engaged.

She shook the strange disappointment from her mind. Someone *like* the lieutenant was all she wanted, not the lieutenant himself. And the only way to get that was to leave this ship.

Her father's cot hung still, with the curtains pulled tight. She would have to tell him the time had come to quit this lie. He already sensed her unhappiness. They both knew in their hearts she couldn't hide from life much longer. But she would not bring it up now. She would wait until their return journey, when they were close to England. That would give them just enough time to plan her quiet escape.

Papa would return to a normal sea life, free from the burden of secrecy. And she would go back to Grandmother and her sharp tongue. As a young, single woman, there was no other option.

Georgana took a breath. Until then she would enjoy her last voyage — as she had enjoyed her first few weeks at sea — with her father. And with her friend, Lieutenant Peyton.

She seized the page with Lieutenant Peyton's likeness and tore it from the book. Then she crumpled it into a ball, opened the window, and tossed it out. The future

and any connected thoughts, good or bad,
would wait.

CHAPTER 9

A stiff wind nearly blew Georgana's cap from her head as she emerged from the hatchway. Lieutenant Jarvis would be pleased with the ship's pace today. His division could only hope that meant less shouting. Though she did not often participate in maneuvering the ship, she much preferred doing it under Lieutenant Peyton's energetic but kind command.

Clouds of sails strained above her, drinking in the incessant wind. Excitement pulsed through the crew, though no one said anything. Along the sides of the upper deck, men coiled lines to prevent them from tangling. They squinted against the late afternoon sun. With winds such as these, they would reach Antigua within the week.

Lieutenant Peyton stood on the starboard side, talking to the boatswain. He always seemed so alive in his beloved sea air. His smiles shone brighter, and his voice carried more intensity. After the dullness of her father's melancholy voice, she found the lieutenant's animation captivating.

She caught his gaze, and Peyton put a quick end to his conversation with the boatswain. He crossed the deck in a few long strides and greeted her with his customary mussing of her cap, interrupting her salute.

"I find myself in want of exercise, George." He nodded up to the web of ropes above them that steadied the mainmast. "Race me up the shroud."

Georgana followed the ropes with her eyes from their base up to the platform just above the lowest sail. "I've never been aloft."

The lieutenant's brows furrowed. "Three years at sea, and you've never been aloft?"

Her father hadn't allowed it. She glanced toward the forecastle, where Papa was holding up various instruments and speaking with the sailing master. He'd sent her below for paper and a pencil to make notes. She hadn't found his pencil and had to grab her last drawing pencil as a replacement.

"It's simple," Peyton said. "Left hand, right hand, left foot, right foot. You'll be up in no time."

Papa looked intent in his discussion. A climb couldn't take long, could it? She'd seen men race up the shroud in moments.

"It won't be much of a race," she said, pushing the pencil and scrap of paper deep into her pocket. Peyton chuckled.

She scrambled after him onto the bulwark where the shroud attached to the side of the ship. Several yards below them, waves beat against the painted sides of the *Deborah*. It was a long way to fall, with no certainty she could be rescued from the water. Georgana tightened her grip on the outermost line of the shroud.

"Now, swing yourself around and hold here and here," the lieutenant instructed. He pointed to the lines for her to use. Her stomach keeled. "Don't look down. On my word."

She threw him a scowl. "That hardly seems fair, sir."

His eyes glinted mischievously. "Go!"

Georgana swallowed, trying to calm her fluttering heart. Left hand, right hand, he'd said. She moved up the ropes and away from the deck below. The wind's snapping made the shroud quiver.

Keep going.

She paused only once, to find the lieutenant's position. He scrambled up the lines like a spider on its web, faster than many veteran sailors. Already he'd risen nearly to

117

the platform. She refocused on her own climb. Left foot, right foot.

At the top, her forearms burned and her legs wobbled. Now to get around the lines and onto the platform. She planted her elbow on the ledge and prepared to push herself up, but Lieutenant Peyton caught her under the arms and hauled her up beside him. She used the mainmast to help her stand, hoping the redness of exertion on her face covered her blush at his touch.

The lieutenant held one of the lines to steady himself. His chest rose and fell in deep breaths as he gazed out on the endless expanse of waves. Below, her father's attention was still toward the bow. Despite her fatigue, she itched to get back down.

"What do you think, George?" the lieutenant asked.

She lifted a shoulder. "It's the sea from a different angle." That earned her a laugh.

"Shall we go higher?"

Georgana shook her head, her eyes rising to the next set of lines. This height suited her just fine.

A young man staggered down from the platform above them. The ropes swung wildly back and forth as he moved. His head lolled forward, hands barely gripping the ratlines. He was going to fall.

"Lieutenant!" she cried, pointing.

Peyton turned and caught the youth as he slipped to the platform. It was Charlie Byam. His face was wet with perspiration, and his eyes were unfocused.

Peyton's jaw tightened. "We have to get him down."

"Ship," the young man mumbled. "There."

"Come, Charlie, let's get you to Dr. Étienne." Lieutenant Peyton guided him to the shroud and mounted it. "George, help him down. I'll go first should he fall. You come around beside him."

"Ship," the boatswain's son whispered again. Georgana glanced behind at the merchant ships to the north. Ship?

"George, hurry!"

She grasped the outside line and reached around the shroud with her foot. Her gut leaped at the thought of leaving the safety of the platform. *One, two, three.* She clawed at the ropes as she swung over. The lines vibrated beneath her.

"Ship," Charlie muttered again as Georgana helped him onto the shroud.

"Watch him," the lieutenant said.

A group of sailors noticed their plight and waited at the bottom to catch the sick young man and pull all of them in. Feet firmly on the deck, Georgana darted between the men and avoided crashing into the boatswain coming to fetch his son. She ran for the starboard side and caught herself against the rail.

She counted the merchant ships. Eleven, twelve . . . thirteen. "Ship!" she shouted. "There's a ship!"

Her father spun on the forecastle. He called for his telescope, but she wasn't there to get it for him. Jarvis hurtled up the steps to the forecastle, extending his telescope to the captain. Seamen joined her on the starboard side. Their muttering rippled the air.

Light popping cut through the noise. Everyone on deck fell silent, heads swiveling to the captain.

Her father shoved the telescope back to the second lieutenant. "Corsair!" A French privateer. "How did we not see this until she was right on us?" His snarl reverberated across the deck.

The boatswain's whistle screeched. Feet pounded the deck. Men yelled below. Across the water, tiny puffs of smoke appeared around the farthest merchantman.

A hand grabbed her arm and whipped her around. "Get to the powder room, George." Her father's wide eyes spurred her toward

120

the hatchway.

Two men carrying the boatswain's son descended before her. His eyes were closed, arms limp. Men poured onto the gun deck, while some continued to the upper deck.

"Clew up the mainsail!" came the shout from above.

Boys scurried about with bags of sawdust, coating the floor to soak up blood and prevent slipping in the heat of battle. Georgana coughed through the dust and hurtled down to the mess, then to the darkness of the orlop deck.

The yeoman and his mates already had a few sacks of gunpowder filled and lined up, ready for the powder monkeys to collect and carry to the cannons. She grabbed a bag and helped fill. The scent of charcoal filled her nose.

The ship tilted to one side as it changed course, and the powder crew braced themselves. She set down the sack, her hands shaking. Her eyes drifted toward the decks above, where her father and Lieutenant Peyton commanded the crew.

Their first battle of the voyage.

Cannon fire continued between the merchantman and the privateer as men tacked the *Deborah,* turning her to the north. From his position on the quarterdeck, Dominic could see the merchant crews. They madly hauled, turning their ships, with their meager collection of guns, away from the fight.

"Slack off the headsail sheets!" The crack of sails flapping in the wind drowned out the distant cannon. The ship rocked as it turned and crested white-capped waves.

Beside him, Captain Woodall adjusted his hat, then turned to observe the crew.

Midshipmen rushed about setting their gun crews in place. The boys carrying powder dodged to keep from getting trampled. Dominic looked for George on the chaotic deck.

"He's in the powder room," the captain grumbled.

"George is?" How had Captain Woodall known he was looking for George? No part of the ship was safe during battle, but barring a fire and explosion on the orlop, the powder room was one of the safer areas. Safe from gunfire and debris, at least.

The men finished tacking, and the *Deborah* stormed toward the attacking privateer. Dominic raised his telescope. *St. Germain,* the letters read. The wide blue, white, and red stripes of her flag flew straight out behind her, allowing no mistake as to her loyalties.

"I'd say twenty-eight guns, Captain," Dominic said. "Two carronades on the forecastle." The merchant ship blocked their full view of the enemy, but her size and shape pointed toward a lighter craft.

"We'll run her off, check the merchant-man for repairs, and get back on our course."

Jarvis wouldn't like that, and Dominic couldn't help thinking that ridding the seas of another corsair was worth the risk of a fight, but perhaps the captain was right. Their order was to see to the merchant-men's safety.

An age passed, as it always did when wait-ing for a ship to pull in range. The merchant ship was having difficulty maneuvering away from the fight. With its sails in shreds and one of the yards drooping from the fore-mast, it barely cleared the scene in time for the *Deborah* to force her way in.

Dominic checked his pistol and sword. His body thrummed as fourteen years of training took control, tightening his limbs and sharpening his senses. Every creak of the *Deborah,* every shout of a seaman pounded through his core.

Puffs of smoke erupted along the side of the *St. Germain* before the ships pulled even. Shots whistled overhead. The crew of the *Deborah* ducked, still tending to their guns. Boys carrying boxes of white powder cartridges poured up from the hatchway and ran for their gun crews. Powder was rammed in, then the shot and wadding.

"Run out!"

Dominic flinched as splinters rained down from a glancing blow to the mizzenmast. He'd been skewered by small shards of wood in nearly every battle, but so far he hadn't met any of the deadly ones that pierced a man through.

Men heaved at ropes — some attached to cannons, some to sails. Almost as one, cannons locked into firing position along the deck.

"Guns in position, sir," Dominic said.

Captain Woodall stared unblinking at the privateer before them, not a hundred yards away and getting closer. The small figures on the enemy ship swarmed about their guns as they loaded the next shot. "Fire when ready."

Dominic nodded. He jumped down from the quarterdeck, repeating the command to the midshipmen on the main deck and down the hatch to Jarvis on the gun deck.

A volley from the privateer preluded the *Deborah*'s deafening broadside. White smoke billowed around him as he propelled himself back to the quarterdeck. As much as he loved this life, he did not love the haze of war. Shouts and screams, both distant and near, pierced the sulfuric mist. Lead cracked against wood. His pulse roared in his ears.

All of it drowned out the whisper of the sea.

Sweat dripped down Georgana's face from beneath her hair, which stuck out at odd angles. Her cap had come off a while ago, but even in the heat of battle she didn't dare remove her jacket. Powder monkeys waited for ammunition to run up to their crews. As they waited, a few stood still as statues in a manner that even Grandmother would have approved. But most hopped back and forth or paced, anxious to be on the move.

Concussions rocked the ship. Those in the belly of the vessel knew little of how the battle fared, and Georgana pushed back the paralyzing fear that one could be the *Deborah*'s death blow.

Fitz ran up, towing two cartridge boxes. The whites of his bloodshot eyes shone prominently in the lantern light. Purple skin still marked one of his cheekbones where she'd struck him the previous week.

"Can't take two, Fitz," one of the mates growled.

Any ammunition near the guns could catch on wayward sparks. Powder monkeys took up only a few rounds at a time to reduce the risk of explosion.

"Locke went down." The boy's voice broke. "He's with the surgeon. The other crews need powder."

The mate took the canisters and shoved the tied-off sacks in. "Two will slow you down."

Four guns were sitting unused while they waited for powder, with more than four dozen men sitting idly, tensions high.

"I'll take one," Georgana blurted. Fitz's eyes narrowed, but no one else in the powder room reacted. She was only an extra set of hands forced on the powder crew by the captain.

"Be off then," the yeoman said, rolling out another barrel of powder.

Fitz stayed silent as she looped the box's strap over her shoulder. He took off toward the ladder, and she scrambled to keep up. Eighteen pounds of powder thudded against her back as she ran. They dodged other boys hurrying in the opposite direction.

"Take it to the *Hargood* and *Richards*," Fitz called over his shoulder as they cleared the messdeck.

She knew the first cannon. Once called *Queen Anne,* Jarvis had demanded a change of name to honor the fallen lieutenant. It sat on the gun deck, not the upper deck. Good. She'd be out of sight of her father.

Skidding on sawdust, she located the guns and deposited her ammunition. The gun crew didn't notice Locke's absence. As long as they had powder, they kept firing. Swab, ram, run out, fire — the endless round of battle.

Comrades pulled bloodied men down the hatches, and Georgana followed them. The walls of the captain's quarters had been taken down and her trunk and its condemning contents stowed below. The thought of a seaman accessing her things should have unnerved her, but the numbness drove out her fear.

She slid down the ladder after Fitz to collect more powder.

"Bring her around!"

Dominic ran to the larboard side. He couldn't hear the commands from the privateer, but he watched the French captain and coxswain for hints of their next moves. Bodies littered the decks of the enemy ship, holes speckled her sails, and she seemed to ride low in the water.

The *St. Germain* drifted away from the *Deborah,* heading south. But they couldn't be sure if the privateer was retreating or turning to get a better position.

The merchantmen behind the *Deborah* had drawn as close together as they dared, continuing slowly toward the Caribbean, out of the way of the battle.

"Hold fire!" the captain called.

A solitary shot from the *St. Germain* flew harmlessly by, burying itself in the waves. Then the French crew adjusted their sails and pulled away.

"Do we follow, sir?" Mr. Fitz asked.

The captain chewed the corner of his lip. Had he heard the question? Dominic opened his mouth to repeat, but the captain cut him off. "Put us between her and the convoy. Let us see what she does."

Men rushed from the guns to the lines to turn the ship about. Sweat and blood stained their shirts. Dominic could see their already fatigued muscles shake as they strained against the ropes and fierce wind.

Heavy footsteps bounded up to the quarterdeck, and Jarvis's crimson face materialized. "We aren't claiming her?"

Dominic closed his eyes. He'd hoped for a little rest from the battle with the *St.*

Germain before this battle of stubborn wills.

"We have done what was required, and now we return to our duty — the convoy," the captain said.

Jarvis's simmering glare made Dominic reach for his sword. Plenty of men struggled to regain normalcy after the heat of a skirmish, and he didn't expect anything less from a man like Jarvis. Over the second lieutenant's shoulder, the *St. Germain* diminished on her straight path toward the darkening horizon.

"We have the men, we have the guns — we have the stamina to take that ship. Why are we sitting here?"

Captain Woodall's eyes flashed. "You are not captain of the *Deborah*. And if this talk continues, I will consider demotion. Is that clear, Mr. Jarvis?"

"Yes, sir," the second lieutenant replied coolly.

"Bring me a casualty report."

Jarvis muttered under his breath as he left the quarterdeck. Captain Woodall's shoulders drooped. "Put Moyle on the forecastle. Watch that ship for any change of course."

"Yes, Captain." Dominic sent the third lieutenant to his post and put the gun crews to work cleaning the cannons. The deck was strewn with debris — pieces of masts and yardarms, rail and hull. The boatswain and carpenter rushed about with petty officers assessing the damage.

He stood in the middle of the deck and breathed in. The air wasn't the clear sea breeze he so loved, but still it eased the fire of combat coursing through him.

Jarvis returned, and Dominic moved closer to hear his report. "Four dead, thirteen wounded."

Captain Woodall nodded. "Bring me Mr. Byam to discuss repairs."

On his way to follow orders, Jarvis stopped by Dominic. "Your little friend made a passable powder monkey," he said grudgingly.

Dominic's brows pulled together. "George?" He was supposed to be in the powder room.

"He filled in for one of the boys who went down."

Dominic didn't know why the thought of George in the battle made his stomach twist. "Where is he?"

"I haven't seen him for some time. Check below," Jarvis said with a shrug.

That could mean many things. Dominic's mouth went dry. "How many boys went down?"

"A couple wounded, one dead. Étienne didn't tell me names." Jarvis's face soured as the French surgeon's name crossed his lips, and he stalked off.

Dominic swept the deck with his eyes, noting all men at their work. He then lumbered down the ladder. Hazy air shrouded the gun deck. Heart beating as fast as it had in battle, Dominic searched through the weary faces for the bright-eyed boy. If anything had happened . . .

He'd taken boys under his wing before but none quite like George. The other boys had the stature and temperament to get them far in the navy and needed only a little encouragement. George needed more than that.

"Do you need something, sir?"

Dominic whirled. Cool relief seeped through his limbs. There was George, standing with his coat on, cap off, hair in disarray.

And blood soaking his waistcoat.

"Are you hurt?" Dominic grasped his arms, observing the garish stain.

The boy's eyes looked him up and down in the same manner. He shook his head. "I helped some of the wounded below."

"You were assigned to the powder room. Why were you up here?"

George held his gaze. "Locke went down. They needed help."

As much as Dominic wanted to scold him for not letting the other boys fill in, he sighed and nodded. George had done his duty. "How is Locke?"

"Gone," George whispered. He squinted, as though struggling to keep back his emotions.

Dominic wondered at it. Wasn't Timothy Locke one of the boys who had mercilessly teased George?

"I need to find Fitz." The lad pulled away and made for the ladder.

What was he thinking? "George, this isn't a good time to renew quarrels."

George scowled. "This has nothing to do with that." And then he went below.

CHAPTER 10

Men moved about the messdeck, patching a hole from cannon fire and restoring stowed items to their proper places. Georgana found Fitz in a corner, head in his hands. Brown, dried blood streaked his fingers, arms, and clothes.

She sat on the bench beside him, much like Lieutenant Peyton had sat next to her the day after the fight.

She didn't speak. It was strange to observe a face she only saw sneering now pinched with grief. "Go away, Taylor."

Georgana blinked. All the boys in his group called each other by their surnames. He'd never used hers before.

"I'm sorry," she said softly, voice wobbling between her false masculine and true feminine tone. For all this boy had done to her, for all he'd said, she could not help but feel sorrow for his burden. She remembered floundering through the heartache of Mama's death in her early days in the navy.

Georgana rested her arms on her drawn-in knees. Her back ached where the powder canister bumped it as she ran, and she still had the acrid scent of burned powder in her nose. But worst of all, emblazoned in her mind were the images of writhing sailors, blood pooling from wounds they might never recover from.

The scene would have made her wretch three years ago. Now it just chilled her to the bone, even in the muggy center of the ship. She hadn't seen Locke's injuries, but Fitz must have.

"Thank you."

She nearly missed Fitz's words in the noise. He sounded younger than his fifteen years. Like a scared child in the night.

Georgana wanted to put her arms around him and tell him all would be right. Like her mother had done for her when Grandmother screamed. Like Papa had done when they carried Mama away in a box or when he'd found her bruised and bloodied from Grandmother's beating. Her eyes smarted. She knew Fitz wouldn't be all right — not for some time.

She reached out a hand and settled it hesitantly on his shoulder. He didn't pull away. They sat there, unmoving and silent, until the watch bells beat out their usual toll.

The morning after the battle, everyone arose and put on their best coats. Dominic stood on the quarterdeck, observing the trickle of crew members filtering up from below. Five still forms, wrapped in canvas, lay on the deck. One more had died from his wounds in the night. Fallen faces and bowed heads circled them.

This was a regular part of life in the navy. The worst part of it.

Captain Woodall came up the ladder, with George close behind. The captain positioned himself near the side of the ship and nodded to Mr. Doswell.

The young chaplain adjusted his spectacles and began his somber recitation. One of the forms was loaded onto the plank, draped in the country's Red Ensign. The bell tolled, the name was read, and the canvas-wrapped body slipped into the arms of the sea. They repeated the ceremony for the other causalities, and Dominic's heart sank a little deeper each time.

The last form was smaller than the rest. His eyes darted from George to Walter Fitz. He'd found them the night before, sitting together on the messdeck like long friends.

"Timothy Locke. Ship's boy, third class."

George's head dropped low on his chest, with no sign of anger or satisfaction about the death of someone who had treated him so poorly. Dominic had expected stoicism, not the pained distress he witnessed.

The men slowly dispersed after the brief memorial. Dominic didn't have watch again until noon. After the battle the previous day, he wanted nothing more than to go to his cot and sleep. But he stayed on the quarterdeck, wandering to the back of the ship.

"Mr. Fitz," Captain Woodall said to the coxswain, "let's catch up to the merchantmen."

The convoy was still in sight, but repairing and cleaning the ship had lasted through the remaining light the day before, wearying the crew and keeping them far behind. Without the help of his ill son, the boatswain had struggled to quickly set the rigging straight.

George made his way up the steps to the quarterdeck and joined Dominic at the rail. Dominic had somehow known he would come and offered as good a smile as he could muster.

"Good morning." The boy's cap had returned to his head, and he pulled his coat tightly around him. The crisp day didn't warrant more than a thin jacket. And if he felt the same inward cold as Dominic, the coat would not help.

"How are you this morning?" Dominic asked. Like the rest of the crew's, George's eyes had dark circles beneath them.

"Well enough." He leaned against the side of the ship. "How do you love this life when it can have such an end?" The boy said it softly, almost inaudibly. "How do you love this?" He waved a hand toward the main deck where they'd stood for the burials.

Dominic braced his arms against the rail. The water had a gray hue to it, or perhaps the somberness of his heart just made it seem so. "Can I not love the sea without loving its destruction?"

George sighed, his shoulders falling. "The destruction overshadows any good there is for me."

Dominic nodded. One couldn't sail without seeing many deaths. He closed his eyes. The wind played in his hair, threatening to tip his hat off his head. He could almost feel the salty water running through his fingers, though it lay out of his reach now. The life that pulsed through its depths resonated through him.

"I don't love this, George. Death is an inescapable part of navy life. I endure the battles, as any man does." He examined the cuts on his hands. "Each time I sail into action, I see a face through a window on a quiet little street in Portsmouth."

The boy looked at him for the first time in their conversation. Dominic couldn't read the guarded expression, but he could see he'd caught the boy's interest.

"If I'm not here doing my very best to stop our enemies, what sort of life might she have?" If he could do nothing else for his mother, at least he could do this. The thought sparked a little fire in his belly that scared away some of the cold. "If we lose this war, we lose England. Look how war has ravaged Spain, France, the rest of Europe. That could be England if I'm not here."

"Now there's a man who will do his duty," George said.

A chuckle escaped from Dominic's throat, earning him a harsh glare from George. "You sound like the captain."

"My father was in the battle at Trafalgar." George let go of the deck and folded his slender arms across his chest. Sometimes the boy seemed much older than the fourteen years he claimed. A mature soul trapped in a boy's body.

"As a lieutenant?" Dominic asked. If

George's father had died a master and commander, he would have been an old lieutenant at Trafalgar.

"No, as a . . . Yes, a lieutenant."

Dominic couldn't blame him for not remembering. George would have been only nine years old at the time of the battle.

"England expects that every man will do his duty," Dominic said, reciting the message Admiral Nelson had sent to the fleet that fateful day.

George pushed back from the rail. "And this is how they are rewarded. A watery grave."

Dominic watched him trudge off to attend the captain. He wanted to attribute the boy's despondency to his being unfit for sea, but he couldn't just now. He had seen that George could be as good a sailor as any man. If only Dominic could show the lad the wonder of living on the waves.

Though he didn't think he could muster the enthusiasm just now.

Georgana leaned over the desk, forehead in her hand. The captain's log sat before her, the last two days missing from the account. She needed to write about the battle, record the fallen. But all she could think about was how close she'd come to giving herself away to Lieutenant Peyton for the second time in as many weeks.

Her fictional father hadn't been at Trafalgar — her real father had. And she'd almost said he had been a captain even though their Mr. Taylor had never reached that rank. Sitting on the gun deck, she'd also let slip the year of her mother's death.

Her stomach churned at her missteps. Something about talking to the lieutenant made her forget. Was it his easy smile? His kind eyes? The way he looked at her as if she said important things, even though she was a third-class boy who could hardly climb the shroud? If he knew her true identity, he might not think her words so important.

The little happiness that sprouted in her chest withered. No, he most definitely would not treat her the same way if he knew she was the captain's talentless daughter.

Georgana dipped her pen and began updating the log. She didn't have to look at Papa's penmanship anymore to copy it.

11 September 1810

Merchantman attacked by French corvette *St. Germain* of twenty-eight guns. Engaged just after five o'clock p.m.

Some damage sustained, but repairable. Five dead, twelve wounded. Privateer retreated to the southeast and has not been seen since.

Georgana dropped the pen and moaned. She'd forgotten to mention the weather. Her father had not told her the wind's exact direction yesterday, and she hadn't reminded him. Another failure.

Mistake! Grandmother screamed.

Stiff wind from the east, clear skies, Georgana wrote in small print above the entry, pushing her grandmother from her mind. That would have to do for now. But before she began today's entry, she would need to consult him. Georgana stood, then wiped the quill and capped the ink, in case the ship decided to pitch in her absence.

And it was afternoon watch, which meant . . . Georgana sat down hard. No, she would not accomplish her duties based on which officer kept watch. She would wait until her father returned and leave space at the top of the entry for the blasted wind.

Shoulders hunched, she readied the pen again, making a valiant effort to not think of what the wind was doing to a certain lieutenant's brown hair.

CHAPTER 11

Stiff winds turned into powerful gusts two days later. The ship rocked to starboard, nearly knocking Georgana off her feet as she pulled herself onto the upper deck. Lieutenant Peyton hadn't come down after his watch, so her father had sent her to find him.

Waves threatened but hadn't spilled over the deck yet, or else her father never would have let her above. She shielded her eyes, sweeping the quarterdeck and forecastle. Where was he?

Ominous clouds gathered in the southeast, moving ever swifter toward the *Deborah*. A figure moved at the bowsprit, cast in shadow by the setting sun. He had no bicorn, but the longer Georgana watched, the more convinced she was she'd found the lieutenant. One hand on her cap so as not to lose it, she staggered up to the forecastle, fighting the wind that wished to blow her off the deck.

"Lieutenant, you're needed in the ward-room."

He stood with one foot on the bowsprit, as if he intended to walk out onto the spar extending over the rolling sea. "Isn't it wonderful, George?"

No sense falling for this one, she could almost hear her father say. He'd get himself killed in no time. She wanted to grab the lieutenant's arm to ensure he didn't step out. Whatever siren song the ocean sang, he was the only one who heard it.

"Can you truly say you enjoy these winds, sir?" The gusts pulled at her jacket, and she hurried to button it over her waistcoat.

He grinned through a spray of snowy foam. His eyes gleamed in the peach light streaming across the *Deborah.* "They haven't sunk us yet."

Belowdecks, a few men had already suc-cumbed to illness caused by the rocking ship. The crew members on watch walked carefully. Rain would start soon, as would the deck-pounding waves, and they needed to decide a course of action now, before the storm was upon them.

Lieutenant Peyton took her arm and pulled her in, resting his arm casually across her shoulders. She felt the beating storm move from without to within as she stood against his side.

"What do you think is out there, beyond that horizon?"

Had he been at the grog before his watch? She cast her eyes on the sliver of sun that was still visible. A few clouds ringed the spot of fire, sweeping purple against the gold.

"More water?"

Peyton lightly jostled her. "No, try again."

"Antigua?"

He sighed.

"Your senses? What is it?" She had to admit, staring into the sunset amid the raging wind sent a little thrill up her spine. The longer she stood with his arm around her, the more intense the thrill became.

"A world of possibilities, George. Adventures you have never dreamed of. People you can't imagine. Lands and discoveries and secrets waiting to be unlocked."

The corners of Georgana's mouth begged to pull upward at the boyish joy in his voice. He wasn't the experienced lieutenant just now but the lovesick lad jumping headfirst into the navy. A thought tickled her mind, a secret she wouldn't have to sail into the horizon to unlock.

"If you ever pick a woman," Peyton said, "choose the sea."

The surge of strange emotion deflated, just as the surge of waves increased. Water pelted them in the face, making Georgana sputter and the lieutenant laugh. She seized the arm over her shoulder and lifted it above her head. Untended, her cap flew off. The lieutenant snatched it before it dove over the side. He pulled it neatly down over her cropped hair, then ruffled it.

"If you wish to not be drowned by your dear lass, I suggest you get down to the wardroom," she growled, grabbing the brim of the cap to both steady it and salute.

He gave one last glance to the bursting waves. Then he turned and bounded across the forecastle, leaving her at the prow with the jeering and triumphant sea.

Dominic hurried down the ladder after midnight, shoes slipping over the rungs. The ship had caught the edge of the gale, but it wouldn't be long before it cleared the winds. He could feel it.

Soggy, weary forms stumbled down to the messdeck in the limited light. Jarvis handed him the sole lantern when the men had cleared the gun deck, then mounted the ladder to take his turn above. Water splashed through the hatch then cut off abruptly as they battened it down.

In an hour and a half, Dominic would be back up there at the mercy of the storm. The watches had been shortened to give everyone an equal turn in the gale. "An equal turn to be swept overboard," Jarvis had complained earlier. Dominic chuckled as he made his way to the captain's quarters to give a report.

Captain Woodall had gone below just before the end of the watch for a moment's rest. The captain stood near his hanging cot, wiping seawater from his face. His great coat still dripped as much as Dominic's did, forming a pool of water on the deck floor.

Across the room, George huddled under a pile of blankets in his hammock, many more blankets than the average seaman owned. Perhaps the captain had given up his blankets, knowing he wouldn't be using them. The lantern reflected off the boy's eyes, showing that despite the late hour he was still awake. The little sketchbook sat atop the blankets.

"Drawing tonight?" Dominic asked as he waited for the captain's attention. George's head moved from side to side. "I lost my last pencil in the battle."

"I'm sorry to hear it." They would have to remedy that in Antigua. Drawing seemed the only solace the boy found in sea life.

Captain Woodall finally turned. Even in the faint light, deep lines circled his eyes and mouth.

"Winds have died back down to seven, sir," Dominic said.

"Very good. If they hold, we'll try to run downwind shortly. Get out of the way of the storm." That didn't mean deep sleep any time soon, but there was an end in sight. The captain clapped Dominic on the shoulder. "Get some rest, Lieutenant. We have a way to go yet."

Dominic nodded a farewell to George, then began his careful climb down to his cabin. The messdeck reeked of too many bodies and sickness caused by the motion. The stench would easily carry through the wooden bars of the officers' cabins. He wondered if George would mind if he moved his cot up to the main cabin. Dominic snorted. For some reason he imagined George minding that very much, even with their friendship. Peculiar boy liked his privacy.

Dominic extinguished the lantern then let his great coat drop to the deck and collapsed into his cot. Another storm survived. He could not complain about that.

Dominic hated recording in his logbook. If

he'd accepted the promotion to captain, he could have hired a clerk to do it. But for now he would have to keep his own logbook. He threw open the lid of his sea chest, then braced himself against the wall as the ship swayed. The winds still held strong, but they'd beat last night's storm. With any luck, the force of the storm would propel them right to Antigua. English Harbour was no paradise, but after eight weeks on the water, everyone on board was ready for land.

Except him, of course.

And George, strangely. When he spoke to the lad about it the other day, he had not seemed concerned one way or the other. To be sure, George was not an excitable person, and he had taken on a more somber air since the battle, but Dominic knew few people who cared less about reaching land.

Dominic pulled the logbook from a corner of the haphazard trunk, where he'd stuffed it after making his last entry. He couldn't remember when that was. Then he dug around for the box with his pen and ink.

Perhaps George's solemnity came from not having his pencils and not being able to draw each night. Dominic popped up at the thought, smacking the back of his head against the lid. Idiot. He rubbed the sore spot and glared at the offending trunk.

Did he have a pencil to give George? He might somewhere. His mother always shoved random items into his trunk when she thought he wasn't looking. Usually sweets but sometimes more practical things.

Dominic pulled out the dress coat George had mended, then breeches, shirts, and stockings. If a pencil was in here, it would be at the very bottom, no doubt. Navigation equipment, a nibbled sea biscuit — no wonder the rat had been in there — and books Dominic hadn't read in ages.

He pulled a few of the thin volumes out — issues of *The Naval Chronicle* from 1807 and 1808. Good heavens, he had forgotten about these pamphlets. They had been at sea nearly as long as George. He thumbed through the collections of articles, amateur poetry, and letters. Nothing of great importance. He'd have to remember to leave these with his mother when he returned to England.

As he moved to toss them onto his pile of belongings, his arm froze. He had seen lists of lost ships in the *Chronicle* before, and each issue contained a section of death notices. Was George's father mentioned in one of these pamphlets? Something like that might interest the boy.

Dominic sat with legs crossed on the deck and examined the volumes more closely. Nothing in the January through June issue from 1807. He opened the edition for the second half of 1807 to a list of shipwrecks. *Pert, Maria, Subtle, Leveret, Prince of Wales, Boreas.* Odd. No mention of the *Caroline.* And when he found the death notifications, there was no one by the name of Taylor, master and commander or otherwise.

He ran a hand through his brine-washed hair as he closed the 1808 edition. No Taylors. No *Caroline.* He stared at the little books in his lap. What did that mean? When he'd spoken to other officers about it, they talked about the sloop as though they knew it. Surely a boat so well known among this crew would get a notice in the *Chronicle.*

Unless the sloop was only known to this crew . . . and no one else. Dominic fought the urge to go back through the collection again but finally gave in. He could feel a blister starting to form where he used his thumb to flip through the pages. This time he would do a thorough job of it, search every page.

The bell rang from the forecastle far above. Seven chimes. He had thirty minutes until the start of his next watch.

He reached the last page of the 1808 issue. Nothing. Dominic sat back and rubbed the nape of his neck. There had to be an explanation. An oversight perhaps by the *Chronicle* staff.

Or . . . there was no HMS *Caroline*.

But that made no sense. Why would George lie about such a thing? And if the captain was a distant relative, surely he would know if his cousin was in the navy and if his boat had gone down. If the *Caroline* was a myth, the captain would be in on the deception — a deception that could lead to a court-martial under the wrong circumstances.

"What are you doing, Peyton?" Jarvis's thick face appeared through the bars of Dominic's cabin door.

Dominic glanced around. Personal items lay scattered about the floor and cot. "I . . . lost something." A boat, to be exact.

"You'll need the boy's help to get that mess cleaned up." Jarvis pushed off the door, rattling the flimsy structure.

"Jarvis, a moment. Did you know the sloop *Caroline*?"

The second lieutenant shrugged. "I've heard of it, of course. Taylor's father commanded it."

Dominic pursed his lips. "But you never saw it?" Something told him he'd receive the same answer from each crew member.

"No, I've never sailed on a sloop." The man straightened his waistcoat. "Never paid much attention to them."

Some men reached the rank of captain without commanding one of the smaller boats, but Dominic doubted Jarvis would ever have the recommendations to take that esteemed path. Or if he would ever find a captain willing to nominate him for advancement.

The second lieutenant wandered off, leaving Dominic to stew over the meaning of his discovery. Suppose George's father wasn't actually in the navy — maybe the boy fabricated the connection to help his advancement. Plenty of boys joined crews with false credentials to make them seamen. But George's relation to the captain should have sufficed. And neither Captain Woodall — nor indeed George — seemed intent on his advancement.

Dominic got to his knees and tossed the books into the trunk. He didn't have a pencil for George, but he did have a multitude of questions.

When he had shoved everything back into the chest, his eyes fell on the logbook. Drat. He forgotten all about that.

Eight tolls of the bell. Time for his watch.

Dominic pushed his bicorn under his arm. He felt out of breath, as though he'd run from the orlop up to the quarterdeck. George and Captain Woodall had something they weren't sharing with the rest of the crew. And Dominic knew it would eat at him until he got to the truth.

CHAPTER 12

Seawater made poor wash water. What Georgana wouldn't give for a little lavender to freshen up the clothes. She dipped her father's shirt into the bucket and scrubbed it with harsh soap that stung her hands. Someday they wouldn't all smell like seaweed. At least she wouldn't.

Her hands stilled in the water. Papa would always smell like the ocean. She imagined Lieutenant Peyton would as well. And they wanted it that way.

She shook the thought from her mind. The lieutenant was not a man she could afford to think of. She could not fall for a naval officer or anyone attached to the sea in any way. She had spent eighteen years waiting on the tides and the whims of the Admiralty. She would not live the rest of her life that way.

After rinsing the shirt in another bucket, she hung it on a line strung from one side of the captain's cabin to the other. Then she turned to her last article, the waistcoat she'd worn the day of the battle. They had spent the day after the battle fixing and cleaning, including clothes and sails, but she still hadn't managed to completely remove the rust-colored stain on the side.

The cabin door opened and shut rapidly. Papa's set jaw made her stomach sink. Something must have happened. She guessed it was something with Jarvis, since that man enjoyed irritating her father in ways Papa couldn't combat.

"Mr. Marion said you weren't in the powder room during drills this morning."

Color drained from her face. Georgana focused on the stain, scraping the soap vigorously across it.

"Why weren't you there? Were you drilling with the powder monkeys, George?"

"They were missing one," she mumbled. Locke.

"The other boys can divide the extra duties. *You* were assigned to the powder room."

The lump that rose in her throat halted her words. She nodded, keeping her eyes on the bucket. Among the powder monkeys she was needed — at least more so than in the powder room.

"Do you know why I assigned you to the magazine?" His tense voice tightened all her muscles so much, she struggled with her task. "Look at me. I sent you there for a reason."

She didn't look. She couldn't. When her father's temper flared, she didn't see his face. She saw Grandmother's. Papa had never struck or belittled her, but his pinched brows and flared nostrils beat down her conviction as though his mother was standing in the cabin. This side of her father hadn't appeared before Georgana came to sea.

"Why won't you look at me?"

A tear wriggled out of the corner of her eye. She nearly brushed it away with her hand but at the last moment used the sleeve of her shirt. This soap in her eye would only bring more tears.

Papa's shoes clipped over the black-and-white floor. He sat beside her as she scrubbed at the stain that would never fully come out.

"I assigned you to the powder room for your safety," he said. He had lowered his voice, but it still held the same intensity. "By helping the powder boys, you are in grave danger of Timothy Locke's fate."

"I am in grave danger anywhere I am on

this ship," she whispered. If the ship caught fire, as ships often did during battle, the powder room was the worst location to be. "If you wanted me to be safe, you should not have brought me into the navy." Georgana clamped her teeth shut, horrified at the feelings she'd let escape. She had agreed to this. He hadn't forced her.

Her father rose without a word and retreated from the cabin, leaving her to her wash. Another tear pulled free, dripping into the soapy salt water in her bucket.

No, she could not choose to be a sailor's wife. Not even if by some miracle an exhilarating first lieutenant begged for her hand. It was lucky for her, then, that such a dream would never happen. She might find herself sorely tempted to accept the sea and all the ways it changed a person for the worse. Look what it had done to Papa. To Mama. To her. To all the men sunk in hammocks beneath the waves.

Only one person seemed unaffected by the ocean's wrecking grasp. Someone who laughed into the wind and smiled through the mists. Georgana groaned, burying her face into her shoulder. She was not falling for Lieutenant Peyton. She wasn't!

She couldn't.

But the energetic pattering of her heart

whenever she saw him suggested otherwise.

"Ship! Ship!"

The cry reverberated through the *Deborah* in the midst of their afternoon artillery drills.

Dominic adjusted his telescope in the intruder's direction. It wasn't large enough to be the *St. Germain,* thank the stars. It was another schooner, with perhaps ten guns.

Captain Woodall materialized on the quarterdeck and extended his hand for the telescope. Dominic gave it him. "She hasn't identified herself, sir." The vessel looked too close to the edge of the convoy for comfort.

Jarvis launched himself into their company. "It's the schooner we passed before. I'm sure of it. Back for blood this time."

"It's moving in the wrong direction to be the same boat," Dominic said, but Jarvis ignored him.

"Turn her about, Mr. Fitz," Captain Woodall called to the coxswain. "Every man to his station."

The boatswain's whistle pierced Dominic to his core. The possibility of another battle so soon after the first did not excite him. He pivoted and strode toward the main deck to get the midshipmen sorted.

George stood impassively by the hatch, watching the party of officers. He hadn't recovered yet from the last battle. Dominic's heart hurt for the lad. He squeezed his shoulder as he passed. "Get to the powder room, George. Captain wants you there this time."

The boy didn't respond but turned and hurried down the ladder. He wondered if George would listen or join the powder monkeys instead. Dominic knew what he would do in the same situation. But he'd chosen this life. Had George? Perhaps the captain hadn't given him a choice.

He rejoined the officers as wearing orders swept over the upper deck, and the crew prepared to turn the ship. Together the officers moved to the forecastle, dodging lines and seamen straining at their task.

Captain Woodall handed the telescope to Dominic. "Tell me the moment she posts her colors."

The captain didn't seem the sort to cruelly force an orphaned relative into the service. Then why fabricate a story for the lad?

Dominic put the instrument back up to his eye and adjusted the focus. It was strange the boat hadn't declared, and it didn't seem to be retreating either. A vessel that small could easily outrun a fully armed frigate and could do damage to a merchant-man carrying few cannons.

The *Deborah* came close enough to see the tiny dots of crew members without the assistance of the telescope before the flag rose. White and red stripes, with stars on a blue field in the corner. Dominic swore under his breath.

An American schooner.

Jarvis ran for the captain before Dominic could turn. His shrill voice carried across the forecastle. "American! We must ready the boarding party."

Captain Woodall held up his hands for quiet as Dominic arrived. "Patience, Mr. Jarvis."

"Sir, we must strike quickly, before they can form a plan," Jarvis said.

Dominic glanced behind at the convoy. "You don't think they've been forming a plan as much as we have in the last thirty minutes since we spotted them?"

"We thought they were French, Peyton," Jarvis spat. "This is a different situation."

"Gentlemen." The captain's graying brows pulled low over his eyes, cutting off whatever Jarvis had meant to say next. "What are your thoughts, Lieutenant Peyton?"

A neutral ship in neutral waters. "I think we need to tread carefully. Check their cargo and be done with them."

Jarvis's face reddened. "That is all? I'm sure there are British sailors on that ship. Why do we not bring them here to replace the men we've lost? Then your little George won't have to work with the powder monkeys."

Dominic gritted his teeth. He didn't know why Captain Woodall allowed this sort of insubordination, trite as it was. The captain had threatened disciplinary action before, but Jarvis continued to speak his mind without reserve and suffered no consequences.

"What sort of show of strength would that be," Jarvis said, "letting an American merchant go free? They'll infest the waters if they know they can get away with it."

"If they're sailing for France, they won't get past the blockade," Captain Woodall said. "More than likely they sail for England to obtain license."

Jarvis snorted. "American ships slip past the blockade often enough. How are we to be sure they are planning to legally trade in Europe?"

"We could follow them back to England," Dominic muttered. "There is no way to know their true design, but if we engage an honest crew and something goes amiss, we could have another war on our hands." He glanced at the captain. Another war was the last thing their country needed. "Remember the *Leopard,* sir."

Dominic didn't doubt Captain Woodall had read the reports. Americans screamed for English blood after the British fourth-rate *Leopard* fired a broadside at the USS *Chesapeake,* then boarded her and seized four Royal Navy deserters.

Orders by the British government prevented free trade with France for any ally or neutral country, which did nothing to ease tensions. Dominic hoped letting an American ship go without harassment would help relations between their countries, or at least do no harm.

The captain nodded. "Gather a boarding party, Peyton. Check their stores and let them be on their way."

"Yes, sir." Dominic touched the brim of his hat. Jarvis seethed beside him. This afternoon's proceedings would do nothing to establish a friendship between him and the second lieutenant, but then if eight weeks on the water hadn't done it, nothing would.

All too soon, Dominic stood on board the *Intelligence,* pistol loaded and sword at his side. Moyle and several men flanked him, keeping the way back to the *Deborah* clear in case of an ambush.

Dominic shook hands with the ginger-haired captain, whose gaze kept drifting to the British sailors and the *Deborah*'s guns. "The name is Captain Jacobs, sir."

"Where do you sail from, Mr. Jacobs?" Dominic asked. He counted the crew. Twenty, if all were on deck. Large for a boat of this size.

"Port Royal, South Carolina."

The crew looked healthy, though most had a darker complexion than he would expect from an American crew, not counting the three Africans. They all watched the captain with little expression on their faces.

"And what is your destination?" Out of the corner of his eye, Dominic could see Jarvis on the deck of the *Deborah,* staring daggers at him.

The schooner captain lifted his hat and scratched his head. He glanced at his dark-haired first mate, whose well-made coat outshone the captain's simple ensemble. "England, of course. Then on to the rest of Europe." They were sailing to France, then, but doing so legally. Just as he'd guessed.

"You've sailed farther south than I would expect of a ship bound for England."

The captain chuckled nervously. "Yes. Trying to avoid the storm." A reasonable answer.

"And your cargo?"

"Tobacco and rice."

"Might I see it, Mr. Jacobs?"

The captain motioned with one clublike hand toward the hatchway. Dominic left Moyle and all but two of the men above and followed the captain and first mate down. He worked to keep his breathing even and his manner relaxed. Anything could happen below. If the *Intelligence* wasn't what the crew professed, it would come to light in the darkness of the hold.

Dominic didn't see any additional sailors or anything out of order as they descended. They reached the bottom of the ship, piled high with bags and barrels. The captain barked an order to his accompanying crewman, who rushed to open one of the bags. White grains tumbled out and sprinkled the floor.

Well, they certainly had rice on board. Dominic went through and punched bags down the row. All rice. He kept one hand on his waist, close enough to reach for the pistol concealed under his coat.

"Does he want to see the tobacco?" the first mate quietly asked Captain Jacobs. His voice carried just enough for Dominic to hear the accent. London, for certain, though the man put an odd twist on that last word. If Jarvis had come, he would have dragged the man back to the frigate.

They moved on to the other stores, and the tension in Dominic's shoulders eased. The fearful Mr. Jacobs was no privateer captain. Just a merchant using whatever crew he could muster. Everything pointed to the *Intelligence* being what it claimed. There would be no battle today.

Georgana let out a held breath at the sight of Lieutenant Peyton coming up through the hatch on the American boat. He shook hands with the burly captain and then climbed over the rail and up the rope ladder to the deck of the *Deborah.*

She scuttled out from her hiding place behind one of the gun crews. The lieutenant spoke to her father for a few minutes, away from the other lieutenants. Then her father gave the command to let the *Intelligence* loose and send her on her way.

Georgana rubbed her forehead. Like steam from a hot platter, fear escaped her pounding heart and dissolved into the cool breeze. When her father turned his back, she jumped up and hurried to the ladder after Lieutenant Peyton. She caught him on the gun deck. "Everything all right, sir?"

He removed his bicorn. Many officers could walk the lower decks without removing their hats if they wished, but the top of Lieutenant Peyton's hat would be crushed if he tried.

The grin that lit his face melted away the rest of her uncertainty — uncertainty about the American vessel as well as her feelings. She *was* falling for Lieutenant Peyton. For his infectious zeal that ruled his every action. For the hazel eyes that twinkled in merriment when he was amused. For the perceptive heart that saw her loneliness and fear and couldn't stand by and just watch.

Her lips pulled free of the chains she'd set on them, returning his smile with a light that radiated from within. When was the last time she smiled like this?

Lieutenant Peyton put a hand on her head and ruffled her cap. "All's well. You're a good lad, George." He continued down to the messdeck.

Georgana shrank into the captain's cabin. A good lad — that was what she would always be to him. For a moment she'd forgotten the ship and her disguise. How utterly foolish to imagine he would ever think of her in the way she thought of him. When they returned to England, she would quietly slink back into Society under Grandmother's thumb and become a memory in his logbook.

The warmth of her smile faded from her lips, but she could not completely banish the heat from her heart.

CHAPTER 13

Dominic held the razor blade back from his face as the ship swayed. When it righted itself, he swept the blade down the line of his jaw and wiped it clean. He sat on the floor across from his little mirror, which was perched on top of his sea chest, and he continually had to catch it before it plunged to the deck. His shirt lay on the cot, and he put a towel across his lap to protect his breeches. With ships making such unsteady seats, Dominic had learned early to protect his clothes while attending to his face.

They'd be in Antigua any day now. The last time he had seen English Harbour, it was fading into the distance and Dominic had been more than ready to leave. But that ship had stayed in port for several weeks, tending to repairs and finding supplies. The *Deborah,* on the other hand, had orders to sail back to England as soon as they could manage, with letters from the commanding officers at the military compound to authorities in England.

At least he could find George some drawing pencils. Maybe that would bring another smile to the boy's face.

Dominic slid the razor across the cloth again to remove the suds. He used only the smallest amount of shaving soap today since it was running low. Just like everything else on the ship, other than biscuits and rum.

Light footsteps announced the boy's arrival. "Lieutenant?"

Dominic glanced up. He didn't know if it were a trick of the light, but George looked pale today. His wide eyes didn't help the appearance. "Good morning. Are you feeling well?"

The boy nodded and swallowed. "Yes, sir." It came out as a squeak.

No one could convince Dominic this boy willingly agreed to join the navy. Something must have forced him into it.

Dominic pointed the razor in George's direction. "Be grateful you don't have to deal with this yet. A rocking ship is a dangerous place to shave."

"But why are you on the floor?"

Dominic nodded toward the wardroom table where Mr. Jordan, the sailing master, had spread several maps and charts. "It would appear my grooming takes second place to getting the ship into port safely."

George's eyes flew about the room, but he avoided making eye contact. He chewed the corner of his lip, making Dominic pause. He'd seen someone else do just that recently. Jarvis? No. With the force that man put into everything, he'd chew a hole through his lip on the first attempt. Not Moyle. Perhaps one of the petty officers, or even one of the men from his division. Try as he might, he could not bring the other person to mind.

"What brings you to the wardroom this morning, George?"

The boy blinked. "Oh, yes. The captain wishes the lieutenants, Mr. Jordan, and the marine lieutenants to dine with him this evening."

A celebration of their safe arrival and last night at sea, no doubt. Dominic nodded, then swiped the razor under his chin. "I cannot complain about that."

Instead of running back to the captain, George stayed at the doorway. They had talked little the last few days. Dominic had missed their conversations and George's dry wit.

"Have you ever been to Antigua?" he asked.

"I've been in the harbor before, but not on land." The boy leaned half out of the door, watching the sailing master.

Dominic's eyebrow rose. "Never?"

"The captain doesn't let me on land." George didn't say it in anger or sadness, but as a simple statement of fact.

Dominic lowered his razor. "Why not?" Safety was a valid concern in port — naval law didn't extend to the land — but surely with a trustworthy guardian George could escape trouble.

The boy shrugged his shoulders. "I don't mind."

The sound of Dominic's razor scraping against stubborn whiskers, mingled with Mr. Jordan's mutterings, filled the silence between them. If what George said was true, he must not have set foot on land in three years. Even with his love of the sea, Dominic occasionally found himself restless to be back on land.

George inched out of the room. Now he looked flushed. Was he taking ill like the boatswain's son? Charlie had hardly left his hammock since the day of the battle with the *St. Germain* and didn't seem any better than when they'd eased him down the shroud. But George didn't look lethargic, despite his coloring.

"Tell the captain I am grateful for his invitation," Dominic said.

George grabbed the brim of his cap. "Yes, sir." Then he practically ran from the wardroom.

Mr. Jordan met Dominic's eyes from the table. "Frightened little thing, isn't he?" the sailing master said.

Dominic had thought George was getting past his nervousness, but it seemed old ways did not change easily. The sight of George chewing on his lip still tapped at Dominic's mind.

He finished his work, then wiped his face dry and folded up the razor. As he examined himself in the mirror, he thought of his mother's pouting face and could almost imagine her lamenting the fact there were no young ladies about. Dominic might even agree with her after this job well done.

After stowing the mirror and shaving kit, Dominic pulled on his shirt. He hadn't spent time in a young lady's company for a long time. His mother so wished for another daughter-in-law. Perhaps he could make some effort when they returned. For her sake.

Georgana removed reference books and writing supplies from the captain's table in

172

preparation for the dinner. The furniture could do with a polish. She didn't usually bother when they were at sea. But what would Lieutenant Peyton think of the dull table?

She straightened, hands falling to her sides. Lieutenant Peyton wouldn't notice one way or the other, just as he hadn't noticed the new softness in her hands. They were at sea, for heaven's sake.

She tried valiantly to banish the thought of him sitting in his cabin without his shirt, but the efforts were in vain. Her hands flew to her face. Heat seeped from her cheeks into her hands. He wasn't the first man on this ship she'd seen in such a state of undress. But it was the first time she had gawked, tracing the straight line of his back and lean muscles of his shoulders with her eyes when he turned away.

Grandmother would be appalled if she ever found out. That thought pulled a strange bubbling sensation from her throat, a girlish laugh she'd nearly forgotten how to use.

"What are you doing, George?"

Georgana jumped and whirled around to face her father at the door. "I-I was readying the table for dinner."

"What did you find funny about that?"

His eyebrow rose.

"Nothing. Nothing at all." She rushed to shove her trunk and bundled hammock behind the desk, out of sight of the visitors.

Papa stayed by the closed door, watching her. "It's been a long time since I've heard you laugh." She hadn't heard that softness in his voice for so long.

"I did not laugh . . . I coughed." She withered under his scrutinizing gaze. Pretending busyness, she rummaged through her trunk and played with the clasp that held it closed until she heard his shoes travel across the floor toward his own belongings.

Georgana wiped her sweating hands on her breeches. Papa was already getting suspicious. If he found out how much she cared for the lieutenant, he might cut off all interaction, and then, with how much time she'd spent at the lieutenant's side, the officers and crew would likely know something was amiss.

Only a few more months until she wouldn't have to worry about their questioning looks. Only a few more months left to enjoy her sweet friendship with the lieutenant.

It wasn't much of a celebration feast by their countrymen's standards. Salt beef, pickled vegetables, and rolls, with a pudding to finish. But Dominic didn't mind. He had never been one for elaborate food, so long as it tasted delicious.

Only six ate with the captain tonight. Most captains dined regularly with all the officers and midshipmen in the wardroom, but Captain Woodall kept his guests few and his dinners brief.

George stood near the opposite wall, his gaze wandering around the room instead of staying on the floor. The change pleased Dominic, as did the absence of any illness. The boy looked right as rain, though his thin brows lowered as he listened to Jarvis's drink-induced rambling. Dominic hadn't found good reason to bring up the mystery of George's past, but the more he observed the captain and George together, the more he spotted quick glances and unspoken dialogue that indicated secrecy.

"Will you receive word from home while we are in port?" Dominic asked. His own mother would have written at least once.

Captain Woodall swallowed a bite of roll. "I don't expect it." He seemed so calm. What man in the navy wasn't eager to see if he had received word of his loved ones? Correspondence would have left England soon after the *Deborah,* but any news was welcome news, even if it was old.

"Does your daughter write often?"

The captain lifted his glass to his mouth. "She does not write to me at all."

Beyond the captain, George fidgeted, pulling at his sleeves, and then he overlapped the sides of his coat. Did the boy know her well? Dominic's mother said she should have been out in Society by now, making her a few years older than the lad. George straightened, hands falling still as though forced.

Dominic fingered the stem of his glass. George knew something about the captain's daughter. Dominic saw discomfort hidden behind the lad's impassive stare.

"No doubt we'd have fresher provisions for dinner if we'd caught one of those vessels," Jarvis grumbled.

The other officers exchanged glances around the table. Captain Woodall ignored the jab and speared his last bite of food.

Dominic followed suit, finishing off his heavily spiced beef. He agreed that ignoring Jarvis would douse his ire more quickly than acknowledging it. At least for tonight. But if the captain continued to ignore his behavior, Jarvis would keep getting harder to manage.

"We can only hope we'll be reassigned a patrol in the Caribbean. Perhaps then we'll take prizes."

The captain cleared his throat, lifting hardened eyes to the second lieutenant. George also glared at Jarvis.

"We have our orders to return to England."

Confrontation at the table forgotten, Dominic looked from the captain to the boy. At first glance, one wouldn't see any similarities between them. The captain's light hair and weathered face appeared nothing like the dark-haired, pale-skinned boy.

"And we'll report to the Admiralty that we took nothing?" Jarvis asked.

Even in build, Captain Woodall and George did not resemble each other. The captain had a thick frame, the boy a slender form. But there was something similar between the two.

"We are doing our duty to king and country, not pursuing our own interests. Not another word, Mr. Jarvis."

The steward stepped forward with the pudding and divided it between the officers. Captain Woodall pulled in the corner of his bottom lip and gnawed it angrily as he watched the proceedings.

A prickle ran up Dominic's spine.

George had done the exact thing that morning in the wardroom. Dominic's eyes flew back and forth between the man and the boy, with their lowered brows and steely expressions. Dominic mindlessly took a bite of pudding and nearly choked when the idea hit him between the eyes. Yes, there was a resemblance. Too much of a resemblance to be distantly related.

Captain Woodall was George's father.

He sputtered and coughed until Moyle offered him his drink. The liquid cleared his throat, but it didn't clear his reeling head.

"Careful, Peyton," Mr. Jordan said. The older man's eyes twinkled. "Good as it is, the pudding isn't worth dying for."

Dominic laughed through another cough. Blasted pudding making him look the fool.

They were all fools. Captain Woodall had kept this secret for three years? Dominic couldn't fathom why. Plenty of captains brought their sons aboard. It was nothing to be embarrassed about.

Dominic didn't taste the pudding as he shoveled the rest into his mouth. But George was a third-class boy. What captain would put his own son in that position? Perhaps Captain Woodall thought the boy was not committed enough to advance in the navy. Since George didn't want to be in the navy, Dominic would agree with that.

"Thank you for joining me this evening,"

the captain said, pushing his chair back from the table. The officers rose and saluted before they left. Dominic lingered. He opened his mouth to spill his discovery, to ask the myriad of questions swirling in his head, then snapped it shut. George's serious face stopped him.

"Has there been any improvement in young Mr. Byam?" Dominic asked instead.

The captain would not take kindly to someone discovering his secret. No doubt he and George thought themselves safe after so long. Dominic couldn't risk losing the respect of the captain and the friendship of the boy by touting his own intelligence.

"I'm afraid not," the captain said, his previously stern expression falling. His eyes flicked to George. "He only worsens."

"We will continue to hope for a recovery." But cheery words did not appear to raise the man's spirits. Perhaps Captain Woodall imagined himself in the boatswain's shoes, watching helplessly as his son withered away. "Good night, Captain. George."

The boy saluted. Dominic studied his face once more, then the captain's, just to be sure he hadn't lost his wits. Yes, the resemblance was there in the set of their lips, the shape of their brows — hidden unless one knew to look.

Dominic skipped port with his fellow officers and went straight to his cabin and
closed the door behind him. No wonder he
hadn't found any Taylors or the *Caroline* in
the *Naval Chronicle*.

They weren't real.

He sat on his cot and let it swing side to
side. Light from the wardroom filtered
through the bars into his cabin.

The captain's treatment of George made
sense now. He worried for the boy as any
parent would for a struggling child. He'd
brought George to sea to try to form him
into the son he'd always dreamed of. Just as
Dominic's father had done with his heir,
raising John to be a copy of himself. Their
father had succeeded, but the captain
clearly hadn't achieved the same results.

Dominic kicked off his shoes and removed
his coat, which he draped over the stool.
The morning watch would come sooner
than he liked. He pulled off his waistcoat
and added it to the pile, then untied his
cravat.

George was the captain's son. How could
that be true, when everyone knew the
captain only had one child, a daughter?

Dominic rolled onto his back, not bother-
ing with his blanket. Roaring laughter came
from the wardroom. He tucked his hands

behind his head and stared up at the dark ceiling. A son no one had ever heard of and a secret they had never told. What did it all mean? He'd known gentlemen and officers to keep a multitude of secrets but usually not that sort. Only in the case of . . .

Dominic sat up.

Illegitimacy.

Yes, it was the only reasonable explanation. Why else would the captain be concerned about hiding the boy's parentage? Dominic couldn't fathom inventing a ship and an officer if not to cover a mistake. That would justify leaving George a third-class ship's boy as well, especially if the mother was of lower standing.

His head pounded with the new thought. Poor George. No wonder he had trouble finding his place on the ship. He didn't fit anywhere.

But with this new knowledge, Dominic determined to change that. George would have a place, and Dominic would help him find it.

CHAPTER 14

The murky waters of Antigua's English Harbour lapped against the *Deborah* as she slid into the bay. Georgana leaned against the rail for a better look at the shore. Shops and workhouses lined the streets, and stacks of timber studded the ground. Sitting high on the hill above, a walled military complex watched over the busy town.

Georgana loosened her cravat. Sweat already dripped down from under her cap, despite the midmorning breeze. She wished she could remove her coat. Several of the sailors had already taken off their shirts. Thank heavens Lieutenant Peyton wasn't among them. The officers wore dress uniforms today. She bit her cheek to stop the blush from spreading across her face.

Her father joined her on the forecastle and grasped the rail with both hands. His face glistened from the heat.

"I do not need to remind you to take caution while we are in port," he said quietly.

Georgana shook her head. "We won't be leaving the ship, will we?"

The captain pursed his lips. "The marine first lieutenant mentioned an old acquaintance stationed at the military compound in Antigua. I might be required to accept his invitation to dine."

The hair on the back of her neck raised, even in the sticky air. "What will I do?"

He sighed. "I haven't come to a conclusion. If you come with me, you will be sent to the servants' quarters. If you stay . . ." Ever since her father had learned of the boys' harassment, he was wary of being too far away from her. "Well, let us hope no invitation is extended."

Georgana nodded. He moved away to give instruction to the sailing master, and she turned back to watching the shore. One more docking after Antigua, and then she would leave this world forever. Return to the world she should be inhabiting, where she hoped she could soon find a home. Then she wouldn't have to worry about being left without the captain's protection.

Sailors swarmed up the hatch to see the harbor and guide the ship in. She shrank away from her spot and trudged back to the cabin. That world felt so far away. Her shoulders hunched at the thought of trying to become a young lady after being a ship's boy for so long. Could she meld back into the girl she used to be? Or would she struggle, just as she had on the *Deborah*? She wouldn't have a Lieutenant Peyton to show her how to defend herself against the gossiping tongues and probing gaze of Society.

Her eyes drifted upward and found the first lieutenant at the platform on the yard of the mainmast. She didn't want to be at sea forever, but for the first time, that life didn't seem so bleak.

"Two, please."

The shopkeeper nodded and took two thin pencils from a box. Dominic did not know if these were the sort of pencils George preferred for drawing, but they were the best he could find in the town.

The white-capped woman placed the pencils on top of a little blank book and wrapped brown paper around the lot before tying the parcel with string. She handed it to him and took his coin. Dominic nodded a farewell. He left the tiny shop and headed for the docks. Dirt from the streets stuck to his boots, and the humidity made his shirt stick to his skin.

Hammering and shouts from the dockyard filled the air. He planned to escape the filth of this town one afternoon and travel north to one of the quieter parts of the island. He'd bring George with him. The boy would enjoy that. If Dominic could convince the captain to grant permission, of course.

Raucous singing spilled from the alehouse he passed. A man stumbled out carrying a dark brown bottle. He tilted left and right, swiveling his head as though trying to determine a direction to go. No hat covered his head, but the blue coat and brass buttons marked him a navy officer.

Dominic groaned and closed his eyes. It was Jarvis.

"Shall I help you back to the *Deborah*?" Dominic asked, taking the second lieutenant's arm.

Jarvis shrugged him off. "I'm not going back to that filthy ship and its hen-hearted captain." His words slurred together. "If we're not to patrol, I might as well enjoy myself."

"You have watch in a few hours."

Jarvis guffawed. "You'll have to drag me back to the ship."

Dominic kneaded his forehead. Acting like this would land Jarvis in major trouble. As much as he believed the second lieutenant deserved discipline, he didn't want to be the one to tell Captain Woodall of Jarvis's misbehavior. He wasn't hurting anyone right now.

"Come back to the ship. I'll take your watch."

Jarvis grumbled something unintelligible but followed Dominic through the crowds of workers and seamen back to the *Deborah*. Dominic was exhausted from coaxing Jarvis by the time he deposited the second lieutenant in the wardroom. Dominic grabbed his hat from his cabin, secured the package in his sea chest, and returned to the main deck. After today, he didn't think he'd wait to find some peace. He'd go to Captain Woodall tonight and ask for leave for the next day.

They still had more than a week left in Antigua. Their departure couldn't come soon enough.

The next morning dawned bright and hotter than before, but a pleasant breeze blew in off the Atlantic, and that satisfied Dominic. A mail ship had come in earlier, and the upper deck teemed with sailors eager to receive their letters. Captain Woodall had put the purser, Mr. Greaves, in charge of dividing up the mail, and the poor man looked lost in the jumble. The small man caught Dominic's eye and waved him over.

Crewmen saluted as Dominic passed, but they gave him hardly any room to approach the purser.

"If you please, Lieutenant, would you take this correspondence to the captain?" Mr. Greaves shoved a handful of letters into Dominic's hand. "And there is one for you, as well."

Dominic took the letter with a grin. He had recognized his mother's swirling hand even before the purser placed it on the stack.

"Thank you, Greaves."

He looked through the letters as he walked away. Most of the captain's were from military acquaintances. The one on top had a familiar name — Mrs. Woodall. Everyone knew Captain Woodall to be a widower. This letter must be from his mother.

George's head popped through the hatch before Dominic could descend. "Ah, good morning, George. Will you take these to your . . ." Dominic mentally kicked himself. He'd almost said *father*. "To the captain?"

The boy nodded and took the bundle. At the sight of the first address, his face blanched.

Dominic wondered at his reaction. Did the boy, despite his illegitimacy, know the captain's mother? Often gentlemen would hide knowledge of such children from their families. George retraced his steps, slower than when he'd ascended. How could one letter put such terror on the boy's face?

Dominic knew how to remedy that. He followed George down, but instead of stopping at the captain's cabin, the boy continued down to the messdeck. Captain Woodall must have gone down to the wardroom to meet with Mr. Jordan.

After speaking with the marine on duty, Dominic crept into the captain's cabin and set the package of pencils and book on the boy's sea chest. The corner of his lips turned up. He wished he could see George's face when he found it. The lad didn't react much, but Dominic hoped the gift would bring George a little joy on the long journey ahead of them.

Dominic slipped a note under the string that simply read, "Best of luck in your drawing adventures. Lt. Peyton." Then he slid out of the room and back to the upper deck to read his own letter.

He broke the flower-stamped seal, heart swelling at the familiar writing on the page. Though he didn't often miss England, opening a letter from home always sparked a little flare of longing.

26 July 1810
Allam House, Portsmouth

My dearest Dominic,

Of course it would rain the week after you left. It tends to do that when it knows I most need the sun to brighten my spirits. But I took the gray days and threw them back at the skies. I finished a sweet little gown for Mrs. Talbot's new baby, with white roses embroidered on the hem. I think it shall do nicely for the christening, and babies make a much better subject for reflection than cloudy skies and an empty house.

On the subject of an empty house, I do hope you write as soon as you are able with news of Georgana Woodall. She has greatly been on my mind of late and —

Dominic blinked. He reread the previous sentence.

Georgana Woodall.

He gripped the paper, wrinkling its edges. Bumps ran up and down his arms. Could the captain really have two children with practically the same name? Captain Wood-all's Christian name was not even George, after all.

The rest of his letter forgotten, Dominic raced for the hatch. The marines on duty at the captain's cabin were just changing watch. He stopped the marine who had just been relieved from his post.

"Have you seen Mr. Taylor?"

"Yes, sir. He just went back into the captain's quarters."

Dominic didn't wait for the man's salute. Both doors to the captain's cabin were ajar. He moved to the door opposite where the other marine stood watch, the opening that gave him the best view of George's sea chest.

The boy stood unmoving before his trunk. After a moment he tentatively picked up the package and read the note. A soft smile touched his lips as he gently untied the string. The paper fell away, and George snatched the pencils before they rolled off the book. The smile grew, heightened by a growing pink across his cheeks.

Dominic stood frozen to the deck.

With small hands, the boy held the pencils up to the light from the cabin's windows. Then he pressed them and the book to his chest. He made no sound, but Dominic could almost hear the laugh of delight his mother made when he brought her roses clipped from their small garden.

Dominic staggered back. How had he not seen it? He put a hand to his brow and tried to catch his breath.

"Is everything all right, sir?" the marine asked from across the deck.

"Yes. Quite all right." Dominic distanced himself from the captain's cabin, not caring where he traveled. No wonder the other boys teased George. No wonder the captain gave George less work and kept George away from the crew as much as possible.

No wonder George had gone white as a sail that day he caught Dominic shirtless, shaving on the floor.

He let his hand slide down the side of his face. George was no illegitimate son sent to sea with a fabricated story to conceal his paternity.

George was a young lady.

He couldn't comprehend why she was here.

CHAPTER 15

Dominic wandered down the ladder, intent on closing himself in his cabin to straighten out his cluttered mind. He'd been treating her like a child, though she must be closer to an adult if she was supposed to be out in Society by now.

He opened the partition between the mess and the wardroom. Captain Woodall stood over the table, pointing to a spot on a map. Moyle, the sailing master, and the first lieutenant of the marines stood around. All except the captain looked up when Dominic entered.

"Lieutenant Tytherton, I want you to double the watch at the gangplank. There was a woman on the messdeck yesterday, and I will not have women aboard my ship."

Dominic nearly choked. No women on the *Deborah,* even though the captain was hiding a woman under their noses. Did Captain Woodall think by enforcing the rule, no one

192

would ever suspect he himself was defying it?

"Lieutenant Peyton, are you ill?" Captain Woodall asked, eyebrows knit.

Dominic shook his head. He was only in shock. Had the bell that signaled the end of his watch already rung? All duties had slipped his mind after his discovery.

"Could I have permission to take leave this afternoon, sir?" Dare he ask if he could bring the boy — or girl, rather — along? Surely that would be entirely improper now.

As improper as teaching her to fight alone in the wardroom? Every previous encounter sped through his mind. He'd been far from proper, though in the case of lessons, he had been protecting the lady by teaching her to protect herself.

An impish thought wriggled into his mind, a thought for which his mother would have cuffed him. If the captain and his daughter wished to keep their secret, Dominic would let them. They had come this far without detection, and it seemed a pity to ruin the secret now. He would pretend he was none the wiser.

"Might I bring George with me?" he asked. "He told me he hasn't left this ship in three years."

The captain opened his mouth to reply,

but Mr. Jordan cut in. "Come, Captain, let the boy have a little fun. Three years is a long time to be cooped up on a frigate, and Peyton is a trustworthy guide."

Dominic bit his tongue to keep from cringing at the label of "trustworthy." Did a trustworthy gentleman pretend not to know he was in the presence of a lady?

"The boy has served you faithfully, sir," Lieutenant Tytherton added. "Surely a short leave is overdue."

"I will have him home before nightfall," Dominic said.

"Oh, just let the boy go," came Jarvis's grumble from his cabin. Never had Dominic been so grateful for Jarvis's disrespect.

The captain's lips pressed together. Dominic squirmed under the piercing stare. Could the captain see through his act?

"Very well," Captain Woodall said with clenched teeth. "I expect you to take every precaution."

Dominic saluted. "Yes, sir." He hurried into his cabin and closed the door to gather his things.

"And if he isn't cautious, we can rest easy knowing ship's boys are easily replaced," Jarvis said, keeping to his room. "Especially those of the third class."

Dominic bolted from the wardroom, boots

on, knife shoved into his pocket, and pistol concealed beneath his coat. He raced up the ladder before the captain could reconsider his permission. He also did not want to witness the repercussions of Jarvis's comment.

This was madness. If his mother ever found out what he was about to do, she would be livid. Especially since he wouldn't be getting her a daughter-in-law from it.

He raised his hand to knock, but the door flew open. George walked right into him, smacking her head against his chest.

"Lieutenant!" The boy — girl — shuffled back and saluted. "I'm sorry. I didn't see you there."

Dominic straightened his waistcoat with jittery hands. When was the last time he had spoken with a young lady in private? He didn't know if he'd ever done so. In truth he had spoken to her only minutes ago when giving her the letters, but in his mind, she had been a boy then.

"The captain has granted permission for you to come ashore with me for the day."

Her eyes, wide and green as a Caribbean bay, flew to his face. "He has?"

"The officers all agreed you deserve a day away from the ship." Well, her father might not have agreed. Dominic had the pressure of the other officers to thank for the acqui-escence. "Come. We have a ways to go." And he had a massive line of questions to ask without drawing her suspicion.

The market near the harbor was boisterous, but after her time on the *Deborah,* Georgana didn't mind. Sellers of all races shouted their wares to passersby. Seamen and lands-men milled the streets, some intoxicated. Cleanly dressed men strolled down the middle of the dirty lane with servants trail-ing, crates in arm.

Lieutenant Peyton spoke to someone about securing the officers' food stores a few paces away from where she stood. Her eyes moved to a young girl's booth not far away. Trifles and trinkets lay over her dis-play, things Georgana would have loved before going to sea. She hadn't seen most of those kinds of items since coming aboard.

With a glance toward the lieutenant, still in deep conversation, she inched toward the booth to examine the wares. The items were not fine enough to be sold in most London shops. At least Georgana thought not. Grandmother hadn't let her go to many shops.

Brushes, mirrors, simple necklaces, a few hair accessories, a jar of rouge — all ridiculous things to have on a voyage. And yet Georgana wanted dearly to try on all of them. She fingered a little lace bandeau. It would look absurd in her cropped hair. All of it would look silly on her just now.

"You're too young to have a girl at home."

Georgana snatched her hand back from the lace as Lieutenant Peyton rested his arm on her shoulder.

"Do you have a sister?"

She shook her head.

"Cousin?"

"No. There is no one in my family except me and my grandmother." She turned, causing his arm to drop from its perch. "Are we finished here?"

The lieutenant's lips twitched. "Ready to be back on board?"

No, of course not. She stumbled as she moved away from the booth. Her body missed the swaying of the ship, but still it felt wonderful to plant her feet on solid ground. She couldn't fathom why her father had agreed to this outing.

"If you are done looking at trinkets, shall we be on our way?" Peyton asked. He continued up the street, heading for the edge of the market. Georgana moved into place behind, like the domestics she'd seen, but the lieutenant slowed and moved aside for her to walk next to him.

They hiked along a road shaded by trees on either side. When a wagon rumbled past, filled with crates, Peyton hailed the driver and asked if they could ride in back. The dark-skinned man agreed, and Peyton handed him a coin. They climbed up, legs dangling off as the wagon rolled forward.

"Are we going far?" Georgana asked.

The lieutenant laughed. "Only far enough to get away from the filth of the harbor." He twisted, putting his back against the side of the wagon and facing her. One leg still hung over the side. For a moment he studied her. She kept her gaze on the road retreating behind them, fighting not to blush. "What would you do if you had one day completely to yourself, with no worries about duties to the captain?"

She cocked her head, blocking her view of his face with her brimmed hat. What would she do? "Draw, perhaps. I'm not good for much else." Grandmother had made sure she never forgot it.

"I refuse to believe that. The captain says you have a steady hand."

Georgana shrugged. "Then I would draw and write letters to all the acquaintances I don't have."

The lieutenant set his elbow on his knee.

He didn't look at her now but watched the passing trees. "I find it hard to believe you lived in London and don't have acquaintances."

"And yet I do not." Grandmother had sometimes hosted dinners, but Georgana was never allowed to attend. Mama was only grudgingly invited. When Grandmother made connections with Society, she usually did so away from Lushill House.

"Now that you can hold your own in fisticuffs, you might find more acquaintances." His eyes danced with amusement.

Georgana raised her fists before her, as though ready to fight him. "Sound English cannon."

He grinned, lighting his face under the shadow of his simple straw hat. She let her hands fall to her lap, willing her heart to slow. His contented pose, his easy manner — she wished she could live like that.

"Did you live with your grandmother before joining the *Deborah*?" he asked. She nodded. "Tell me about your grandmother."

She pulled her knees into her chest and wrapped her arms around them. "We did not . . . That is, she . . ." Grandmother's sharp features filled Georgana's head. *Mistake. Mistake.* "She was not very kind."

"Is she the one who told you that you

weren't good for much?"

Her ears burned. What an ungrateful girl, criticizing her grandmother to someone else. Papa never did that, even though he knew what she was like. He hadn't known about the belittling, the shrieking, and the controlling until Georgana told him through streams of tears after the beating. He'd thought Grandmother's abuse had stopped after his own childhood.

A hot tear fell from her lashes. She cleared her full eyes with a swift wipe of her shirt-sleeve. For a moment she'd forgotten her act. She was a boy, not a blubbering girl. What would the lieutenant think?

His hand squeezed her arm, the strong fingers soft and gentle. They were tanned from long watches in the sun and rough from all the work he had to do on board. The touch pulled at her heart in a way that was both exhilarating and painful.

She didn't meet his eyes. Imagining the kindness in them was enough to hitch her breath. Before this voyage, she didn't know there were people in this world like Lieutenant Peyton. She thought Society was made of only powerful rulers who frightened their followers and tread on everyone else. But perhaps there were more varieties of people than she'd thought.

"Look at me, George."

With effort, she lifted her eyes. Looking into his face set her insides churning in lovely, terrifying ways. Papa had told her to be careful, and she had recklessly fallen heels over head down the very path he told her not to go.

"You are good for much more than drawing and recording. Whatever that woman said to you," he waved his hand, "forget it. Starting today. Starting now. It does you no service."

"I'll try." Though ridding that voice from the shadows of her mind did not seem simple.

The lieutenant released her arm, but the memory of his touch still pressed her sleeve. Peyton looked behind him, then asked the driver to stop. Playfulness twinkled across his face. "We've arrived."

Heavens above. That face would be her undoing.

Dominic hopped from the wagon and thanked the driver. George scrambled off as the wheels began to roll. Dominic stood awkwardly by and watched. His mother would be horrified if she saw him not assisting a lady down from a high perch, but that same lady would be horrified if he showed her any sort of chivalry. And he couldn't very well haul her down as he'd hauled her up the shroud. Respectable gentlemen didn't hold onto ladies in that manner.

"Why did we stop here?" she asked.

Dominic nodded behind him. "You'll see."

They left the dirt road and plunged into a line of trees. Earth turned to sand beneath their shoes, and then the trees opened to a crystal bay. Blue-green waters nestled against the shore, cloaked in white sand. No ships clogged this section of sea, and sailors didn't crowd the land. Here was the ocean as he dreamed it — pure and magical.

George's breath caught, a look of wonder on her face. She stopped in her tracks. All the reserve in her usually stoic features washed away. "I didn't know the sea could look this way." Her eyes matched the water before them.

"You've only been in ports, I'd wager." He removed his satchel and lowered himself to the soft sand near the tree line. Then he buried his fingers into its fine grains. The shaded sand cooled his warm skin. "I found this place the last time I landed in Antigua, after getting weary of the noise of the harbor."

She sank down beside him and pulled up

a handful of sand to examine. "Thank you for sharing it with me." The attempt at a gruff voice had fled with her surprise. He'd heard the switch plenty of times, but always attributed it to a boy's changing voice and the desire to appear older. That wasn't the case at all.

A frigatebird sailed overhead toward the sea. The sun caught its black wings, giving them a violet sheen. The bird flew lazily about the bay and eventually turned north and disappeared.

Dominic pulled off his jacket and tossed it to the sand. He'd prevent embarrassment for them both by leaving his waistcoat on. He leaned back on his elbows, savoring the sea breeze as it dried the sweat on his face.

"What of your childhood?" she asked.

Dominic opened his eyes. "My childhood?"

She shrugged. "We've been talking so often of me and my life."

That's because he found her life fascinating, especially after this morning's realization. He'd always sensed George was holding back something, though Dominic never had imagined the secret to be something like this.

"I spent my childhood near Winchester, then moved to Portsmouth with my mother after my father died. Then I went to sea." He held up his hands. "That is the whole of it."

She watched him with narrowed eyes but didn't ask anything more. Dominic pushed himself up and reached for his satchel. He pulled out a green, strawberry-shaped fruit as large as his fist which he'd bought from one of the stalls at the market.

"What is that?"

He retrieved his knife and cut the scaly skinned fruit into quarters, then offered her a slice. "It's a cherimoya. I take it you've never tried one."

George stared at the slice in her hand. Its white, pearlike flesh dripped juice over her fingers. "How do you eat it?"

Dominic took a bite and smiled through the bright sweetness that burst in his mouth.

Then he spit two seeds the size of almonds into the sand before he finished chewing. "Don't swallow the seeds," he said with a wink.

George considered the fruit for several more moments, then picked as many of the seeds out as she could with her fingers. Juice squeezed all over her hands before she finally took a bite. She moaned her delight as liquid trickled down her face. He reached for his pocket to get her a handkerchief, but she wiped her face with her sleeve before he could find it.

Boy. Right.

After they finished their sticky treat, Dominic peeled off his shoes and stockings. Sand stuck to his fingers, sticky with cherimoya juice.

"What are you doing?"

"Enjoying the sea in the second-best way to do it." He pushed himself to his feet. "You may join me if you like."

He jogged toward the gentle waves, rolling up his sleeves as he went. His feet squished into wet sand, and then the water came up to meet them. "Good day, friend." He kept his voice low enough so she couldn't hear.

He walked into the water a few steps and bent over. His fingers found the rippling surface. Water licked away the sand and juice. George stayed under the tree. Dominic couldn't see her face in the shadow, but just as well, since he might have laughed at what he imagined was a very stern expression.

Dominic swept off his hat, then cupped water in his hand and threw it over his hair. The mild water ran down the sides of his face and neck. He would never do this in the frigid waters of England's beaches. A few more scoops, and his hair and shirt were thoroughly drenched.

A soft splash brought his head around. George stood without her shoes and stockings at the place where the waves and shore met. She dragged a foot through the wet sand and waited as the water pulled away the trench she'd created.

"If I didn't know better, I'd think you had never been to the seaside before," Dominic said, coming back to stand beside her. Surely a captain's daughter had been to the ocean on many occasions.

She drew a second deep line in the sand, creating a small wall for the waves to find. "I haven't. Not like this."

Dominic made his own wall in the sand that met hers. It took several waves to wash his clear. She tried another one, this time extending hers farther to the side. He followed suit, hobbling along on one foot as he dragged his line several paces before the water ruined it. Soon they grinned and laughed as they raced the water to build little walls as long as they could.

How strange to see that smile on her face. He rarely saw it on the ship.

George stopped their game and stared out to the open sea beyond their little bay. "It feels like a dream, doesn't it? Soon it will be gone, and we'll be back to life as usual."

"That's the wonderful thing about memories," Dominic said. The water broke down the last piece of wall at his feet and smoothed the sand, as though it had never been disturbed. "We can relive it again and again, as many times as we wish to."

"Should we return?"

The afternoon sun still sat high in the sky, but if they didn't find a cart for transport, they would have a long walk back. "Yes, but there is something I must do first." His mother's loving face came to his mind. "I need to find a rock."

George's eyebrow rose. "A rock?"

"Or a shell or a bit of sea glass. Something." He crouched to sift through the sand.

"For what?"

Dominic pulled out a bit of shell, broken in half. He tossed it away. "As a present for someone dear to me."

She didn't respond, but when he glanced up, she was scouring the beach, lips pursed. Her feet left small prints in the wet sand. Dominic shook his head. How he'd ever thought those feet belonged to a boy, he wasn't certain.

"What is this?" She held up what looked like a translucent green stone. He held out his hand, and she set it in his palm, her fingers grazing his skin.

"That is sea glass," he said, turning it over. It was a lovely shade, far prettier than most of the murkier pieces he'd seen around ports. "It's made from bottles thrown into the water. Over time they get worn down and become like this."

"Beautiful," she breathed. "Whomever you are giving it to will love it."

He didn't mention that his mother already had several pieces of sea glass on her shelves. He enjoyed the awe on George's face. "You may keep it if you like."

"I have no need for something as fine as that."

She went for her shoes, and Dominic followed her. He'd have to show her how to get the sand off her feet, or she'd get blisters on the walk.

George stopped before she got to their things and cocked her head. "You said that was the second-best way to enjoy the sea. What is the best?"

Dominic pocketed the sea glass and caught up his shoes. "Standing on the bowsprit of a frigate in the open ocean."

George frowned. "In the middle of a gale?"

His lips twitched at her exasperation. "I wouldn't have it any other way."

CHAPTER 16

The sun was drifting down to the hills when they arrived in town. Georgana panted from the pace and gave a valiant effort to keep the corners of her lips from rising. She would always remember this afternoon, walking along a beach with a friend. Except she wasn't sure *friend* was the right word. She did not know if one could be so attracted to a friend.

As dark began to set in, the lieutenant increased his stride. They hurried past the empty market and closed shops. "The captain will have my head. I lost track of the sun," Lieutenant Peyton muttered, checking his pistol, which he had loaded before they left the beach. One couldn't trust the safety of port towns after dusk.

Twice they'd gone to fetch their shoes but had somehow wound up back at the shoreline with their feet in the waves. Georgana hadn't minded. She'd noticed the shadows getting longer while on the beach but didn't remind him. In less than two weeks they would be back at sea, sailing for England. Two more months with the lieutenant. Two more months as George Taylor.

Someone yelled from the shadows outside a public house, and Lieutenant Peyton nudged her toward the other side of the road.

"Best to stay away from that."

The shouting ceased, replaced by a cry. Georgana paused and stared into the blackness behind the alehouse. The arm of one large form swung down again and again, striking a person on the ground.

"Come away, George." The lieutenant took her elbow, but she stayed rooted to the dirt.

"He needs help."

Peyton followed her gaze and pressed his lips together. "I'll be in a worse mess after the captain . . . Stay behind me." Then he bounded across the road.

Georgana scurried after him, watching as he felt for the pistol under his coat. Her pulse raced.

"Leave him alone," Peyton growled as he moved behind the attacker. He seized the man's arm with both hands and jerked him away. The man stumbled to the side, then whipped around, snarling.

"Stay out of this, Peyton." The familiar snarl sent a chill down Georgana's arms.

The person on the ground tried to get away with a staggering crawl. He seemed thin, but Georgana couldn't make out his features in the dark.

"What is the meaning of this, Jarvis?"

"The boy was trying to rob me."

"I wasn't robbing him," came a strained call from the ground.

She knew that voice, too. "Fitz?"

"He asked me —"

"Silence, boy," Jarvis said. He jumped for his victim again, but Peyton hurled himself between them and stopped Jarvis with a hand to the chest.

Georgana's stomach lurched. They'd all seen Jarvis intoxicated. Even without co-ordination, the man could cause hefty damage. Though Peyton had the advantage in height, Jarvis was thicker.

"This is not your concern." Jarvis tried to bat Peyton's hand away, but the first lieutenant grabbed his wrist.

"It is my concern. This boy is in my division." Peyton leaned out of the way of Jarvis's fist and shoved the second lieutenant backward. Jarvis tripped and bumped into the neighboring building. "George, help

Walter back to the ship. I'll bring Jarvis."

Georgana slipped along the wall to where Fitz huddled on hands and knees. He cradled his head, breath shaking.

Jarvis snorted. "You train that whelp to beat the boy but won't stand for anyone else beating him? How noble."

"Come on, Fitz," Georgana whispered. She took his arms and tried to pull him up. He swayed, his weight nearly knocking them both to the ground. Fitz groaned at the movement.

"That was an even fight," Peyton said. "You are his superior."

"Can you walk?" Georgana put Fitz's arm over her shoulder and braced her legs against the burden.

"Yes." An odd whistling touched his faint voice.

They wobbled toward the street. The boy blocked her view of Peyton and Jarvis. Her throat tightened.

Focus. She needed to focus on Fitz.

They limped along, painfully slow. As they stepped into the waning light, she could see his mouth and chin covered in a dark stain, dripping onto his shirt. His head lolled from side to side, and his eyes kept closing.

Grunts and shuffling sounded behind them, and Georgana trained her ears on her footsteps to shut out the noise. An image of Peyton lying broken and lifeless on the ground filled her head. She blinked rapidly, trying to wipe the thought from her mind before it could cause tears.

Jarvis's chuckle, cold and deep, rang through the alley. "You have no right to force me anywhere, Peyton. I'm a lieutenant, same as you."

Georgana and Fitz turned onto the road, and she chanced a look back. Peyton ducked out of the way of Jarvis's blow but not far enough. The second lieutenant's fist hit Peyton's jaw. He careened back.

She halted and steadied Fitz. Her head screamed to keep going, but her eyes stayed locked on the struggle. Jarvis landed on the ground, but she couldn't tell if he'd tripped or Peyton had knocked him over. She prayed it was the latter.

Fitz sagged against her, and they nearly went down again. She had to get him to Étienne. But Peyton . . .

If Jarvis broke away, he'd come straight for them. Georgana reluctantly plodded on. The dock was still far, and if there wasn't a boat they'd have to wait. *Please let there be a boat.*

A faint click stopped her midstep. Everything went still. She turned them around, but a building blocked the alley from view. Her heart stuck in her throat.

"You can't do this." Jarvis's voice. It had to be.

"But I have the gun."

Georgana let out a breath. Peyton was all right.

"Now," he said, "we are going back to the *Deborah*. And we will go quietly. I have a feeling Captain Woodall wishes to see us all."

Lieutenant Peyton's words were meant to strike fear in Jarvis, but Georgana felt blood drain from her face.

They had to answer to her father.

Dominic steeled himself for the captain's reaction when he saw him, not just with the man's very late daughter, but also with a raging, drunk lieutenant and a half-conscious, bloodied boy. The marine standing watch knocked quickly as they approached the captain's cabin. In moments, the door swung open.

Captain Woodall's lips compressed, and he stared from one face to another, eyes lingering on George. "Inside. Now." He turned to the marine. "Fetch Étienne immediately."

Dominic had put away his pistol on the

214

boat ride back to the *Deborah*. Jarvis had calmed down enough to submit to Dominic holding his arm, but he still glared at everyone in the room. George set Fitz in a chair. Her narrow shoulders drooped.

"Explain," the captain growled.

Dominic opened his mouth, but to his surprise George spoke first. "Fitz said Lieutenant Jarvis was to pay him thruppence for coming to get him at the alehouse when it was time for his watch. But when Fitz came, Jarvis got angry and beat him."

"How were you involved?"

"The lieutenant and I saw the beating as we passed by the alehouse," she said. "Lieutenant Peyton stopped it."

"All lies," Jarvis mumbled.

Captain Woodall clasped his hands behind his back, chewing on the corner of his lip. His brows pulled down so low they nearly covered his eyes as he paced on the other side of the table. "We are men and officers of His Majesty's navy. This is not acceptable." He turned, eyes boring into Jarvis. The second lieutenant didn't flinch. "Jarvis, as a gentleman and an officer, this behavior is beneath you."

"I acted within the realm of my authority."

Captain Woodall pounded his fist into the

table, rattling a carafe perched on top. "You most certainly did not, and you can count on a court-martial when we return to England for abuse of rank."

Dominic bit his tongue to keep from showing his satisfaction. Served the scoundrel right.

The surgeon knocked on the open door. When his dark eyes fell on Walter's purple, splotchy face, he hurried to the boy's side.

"George, would you get the father of the boy?" Étienne asked.

"Send the marine," Captain Woodall snapped. "George isn't leaving this cabin again tonight."

George shrank into the corner, eyes on the floor. Dominic's hand clenched tighter around Jarvis's arm. Seeing her submissive posture made his heart ache.

"Jarvis, I will stand no more. I am demoting you to third lieutenant."

"What?" Jarvis's sleeve wrenched out of Dominic's hand as he threw his arms in the air. "You can't do that."

"I am the captain of this ship." Captain Woodall's cool tone cut through the protests. "You would do well to learn it."

Jarvis squared his shoulders as much as he could in his inebriated state.

"You will also be confined to the *Deborah*

216

until we sail," the captain continued. "If you are caught using corporal punishment on any member of my crew, justified or not, I will find one of the midshipmen to take your place in the wardroom, and you can return to life in the cockpit. Is that understood?"

Hatred burned in Jarvis's eyes. The cockpit, the orlop deck chamber where midshipmen and mates set their hammocks, was dark and dank. Dominic winced. No officer wished to return to those living quarters.

Jarvis didn't respond to the captain but burst from the room. His unsteady stomping echoed through the gun deck and down the ladder.

Dominic let out a breath. Living with Jarvis would not be pleasant for the foreseeable future. His eyes flicked to George. He'd have to keep watch on her in case Jarvis decided to retaliate.

"How is the boy?" the captain asked.

Étienne sighed as he dabbed a cloth across Walter's mouth. "He is missing a tooth and very dazed. I hope he will recover quickly, but he should not work for some time."

Captain Woodall nodded. "Peyton, you are dismissed." The stern set of his face showed he had reserved plenty of anger for his first lieutenant.

Dominic bowed his head. "I am very

sorry, sir."

"You should be. I will not allow an excursion like that again."

"Yes, sir."

Dominic trudged wearily from the room. He rubbed his jaw where Jarvis had landed a hit. He hoped he'd be able to sleep through the aching.

Moyle came down from the top deck. "Have you seen Jarvis?"

Dominic motioned below. "He's in his cabin. He won't be able to take watch tonight."

The third — now second — lieutenant pursed his lips. "Then shall I send for Mr. Jordan?"

"No, I'll go." The sailing master had taken Dominic's watches earlier that day.

Moyle clapped him on the shoulder, awakening new soreness Dominic hadn't discovered yet. The younger man's cheery smile did nothing to brighten Dominic's mood. "Thank you. I could use a little rest."

Dominic didn't bother mentioning Moyle's de facto promotion. He let the young man descend to the messdeck. The captain could tell him in the morning. Or Jarvis could. Dominic almost cracked a smile.

He took one last look at the doors to the

captain's cabin. Would Georgana stay in that corner all night? He hoped not.

The next watch had started, and he needed to get back to his duties. Dominic hoisted his taxed body up the ladder. The captain would keep her away from him now, wouldn't he? The thought made Dominic sigh. He'd enjoyed this day with Georgana, more than he anticipated.

Georgana. He mouthed the name. He liked the way it spun from his lips. He mouthed it again as he found his way to the forecastle to continue his already tiring night.

Dr. Étienne and Mr. Fitz eased the boy to his feet. Georgana wanted to help, but they didn't need her.

"Come directly to me if anything is needed for the boy," her father said as he walked them to the door.

Just before Papa closed it, Mr. Fitz turned back, his face grimly set. "Thank you, George."

She nodded. It had been luck they'd happened on the beating.

"Did you tell him?" her father whispered after the door shut. He moved toward the window to be out of earshot of the marine on guard.

Georgana stayed in her corner. "Fitz? Tell him what?" She didn't know what she had to tell the boy.

He threw a hand up to cover his eyes. "Did you tell Peyton?"

You stupid girl. You knew what I meant. Answer my question and no more of these games. Georgana squeezed her eyes shut against Grandmother's voice in her head. Papa was not Grandmother.

Whatever that woman said to you, forget it. Starting today. Starting now. The memory of Lieutenant Peyton's warm voice stilled her quaking heart. This was her father. She could speak to him. Reason with him. Explain.

"I have not told him, and I have no plan to do so."

Papa rubbed his forehead and lowered himself into a chair by the windows. He motioned for her to sit, but she stayed where she was. She knew what he would say next, and maintaining her stiff posture was easier from the corner.

"I don't think you should spend so much time with Lieutenant Peyton." Her father sighed and leaned forward, resting his elbows on his knees. His hands twisted together in front of him. "It is quite clear to me that . . . That is to say, I can see . . .

220

your feelings for him. And I worry that I am not the only one to see it."

Heat flooded her skin. If Papa saw it, how many others had? "If you were so worried, why did you agree to let me go today? You could have said no," Georgana whispered. Terrible as it was to cross her father, she wasn't sorry for what the lieutenant had done.

Papa straightened his coat. "I was wrong to agree to it. You do deserve some time off this ship before we leave, but you will only leave with me. I have to think of your safety, George. We also need to think of your reputation. Spending so much time with Peyton is not wise."

Georgana's head snapped up. The whirl of confusing emotions inside didn't let her pause to collect her thoughts. "My reputation was gone the moment I stepped onto this ship in these." She motioned to her rumpled waistcoat and loose cravat. "Do you think Society would ever accept a girl who lived on ship as a boy?" Tears threatened to choke her, and she pulled in her lips to keep them from quivering.

"If we maintain the secret, no one in Society will know." He slipped a letter from his pocket. "Your grandmother, for once, has made an argument with which I cannot disagree." He gave a short, mirthless laugh. "The longer you stay away from Society, the more difficult it will be to make a good match. She suggests that you return immediately so that she may work with you on practicing proper behavior."

Georgana's stomach sank. She'd wanted the same thing, to reenter Society and move forward with life. But when she imagined possible suitors, possible husbands, she saw only one face. One pair of hazel eyes. One confident smile.

"I agree." She didn't hear her own words.

"I will establish rules. We will hire a companion — anything we can think of to keep her from abusing you the way she did before." His eyes closed. "All the things I should have done instead of dragging you to sea." Papa rose and went to his trunk. "With any luck, you'll find a husband quickly and be rid of her."

After her father had gone to bed, Georgana took his seat by the window and pulled out the book and pencils Lieutenant Peyton had given her that morning. She turned to the first page but didn't draw waves. Nor did she draw the lieutenant leaning across the rail of the ship.

Her fingers smoothed over the crisp paper. She let her eyelids flutter closed, imagining the pristine bay so far from the bleakness of the harbor. Light shone on its white shore and traipsed across the waves. She could smell the fresh scent of the sea and sweet cherimoya juice that lingered on their fingers.

She sketched the curve of the bay, then added Lieutenant Peyton's lean form at the edge where the water met land. He gazed out to the open sea.

Georgana stopped before she filled in many details. Her father was right. It was foolish and hopeless to set her sights on the lieutenant. If the crew figured out who she was, they would both be in trouble. And if their friendship did go places Georgana could only dream of — courtship, or even marriage — she didn't think she'd be content with the same lonely life her mother had endured. Besides, he probably already had someone back at home — someone special enough to find little tokens for.

She quietly ripped the page from the book. She folded the paper, and just as she'd done so many nights before, she let it fall from the window. Though, this time, she didn't watch it drop to the water.

The sooner she got back to England and away from these silly fancies, the better.

CHAPTER 17

Georgana's father pulled at the coat of his dress uniform. He never seemed at ease in his captain's coat these days. "I wish this could be helped." They stood just inside a manor that was not grand by London standards but felt like a palace after her time at sea. His old friend had sent an invitation, days before they were to depart.

"I will be fine." She took his hat and walking stick and handed them to the footman. Again she was not needed. The footman could have taken these himself. But Papa insisted she join him, so she pretended to be useful.

"The stairs to the servants' quarters are down this hall on the left," the footman said. "You can get a bite to eat there."

She thanked him and followed his directions, but instead of continuing to the kitchen, she slipped out the first door she found and into a garden. It appeared empty, the only place in the compound not crowded with marines and sailors. Warm air pushed against her jacket as she wound through tropical trees and shrubbery. Many had brightly colored blooms with sweet scents that wove through the garden. A few diligent bees bobbed from flower to flower in the dimming light.

Georgana reached the southwestern edge of the garden and a low wall looking out over the harbor. Sweat dripped down her brow, and she wiped it away with a sleeve. She wouldn't mind a cool English summer again, and the safety of the rose garden at Lushill House. How very strange to miss that place.

The sun crouched at the peaks of the western hills, bathing the world in its evening glow. Birds called from the trees and insects hummed, but nothing else moved in the garden — her own little oasis until she had to return to the *Deborah.*

Georgana pulled off her jacket and set it beside her on the wall. The waistcoat and bindings disguised her figure well enough without the coat, but something about the extra layer gave her reassurance that her secret would stay safe. She wondered if the stays underneath a dress would feel awkward after so long of trying to hide who she was. They couldn't be as stifling as the bind-ings.

"Ah, there you are."

She snatched the jacket and spun. Her heart didn't slow when she recognized the intruder. "What are you doing here?"

"I finished my watch and had nothing else pressing, so I came to find you," Lieutenant Peyton said. He had a satchel slung across his chest and a melting grin on his face. "They told me you hadn't come down to the servants' quarters."

He'd searched for her. Hope peeked its head out from under the gloomy clouds that had filled her mind in the week since their outing. "I wasn't hungry. And I wanted a little time alone."

"Oh." His face fell ever so slightly. "Shall I leave you to it, then?"

"No, please stay." She cringed. No wonder her father was worried about someone noticing her feelings. Her tone was practically begging.

"Only if you wish." He rested his arms against the wall and settled his chin into his palm.

He stared at the sunlit hills. "Magnificent, isn't it?"

"Be careful. You sound like a land lover."

He laughed softly. "And if we don't get

you out of the navy soon, we'll never get the sailor out of you."

Her eyes narrowed. He knew she struggled as a sailor, but she hadn't told him she was planning to leave the navy. She realized she was still holding the coat up to her body, as though shielding herself. Face burning, she dropped it back down.

"You can't tell me you love navy life. Have you considered other occupations? Other positions?"

What positions could a lady have? She could be a governess, perhaps, but she knew little of children. A lady's companion? But that wasn't what Lieutenant Peyton was thinking, certainly. He was thinking of things suited to a boy of fourteen or fifteen who had no physical abilities — perhaps clerk or shopkeeper positions.

"I haven't, really."

"Why did you come to sea, George?" The lieutenant's fingers muffled his voice. He tapped thoughtfully on his upper lip. "Besides your father being a captain. Commander, rather. Why did you agree to it?"

There was only one reason. The true reason. And she couldn't think of a good enough lie to replace it. "To get away from my grandmother."

Peyton's jaw tightened. He didn't look at

her. His fingers tensed against his chin. "You won't go back to her, will you?"

"I . . ." She picked at a blade of grass sticking out between the cracks in the wall. How had it grown there, with hardly any soil?

"No, you mustn't." He pulled off his hat, the simple straw one from their time at the bay, and ran a hand through his hair. "I know of someone who would be open to a . . ." His gaze flicked to her, then away. "I believe I might be able to find you a position."

She sighed. Nothing he found would be suitable for a young lady.

"Please," he said. "I wish to help."

Dear Peyton. How could she say no, with the concern shining in his face? "Very well."

He reached into his satchel and pulled out two small flasks. "We'll drink on it." He offered her one, but she held up a hand.

"I don't like grog." It was true, but more importantly she couldn't risk losing her wits and saying something she didn't mean to. She did that enough with Peyton already.

His lips twitched. "I know you don't. I had Cook prepare this especially for you."

She took the flask and pulled out the stopper. "How did you know?"

"The captain doesn't drink all the lemonade sent to his cabin, does he?" A mischievous twinkle sparked in his eyes. "He never takes any at dinner, and yet a good amount is always brought to his quarters throughout the day."

Her face grew hot, and she tipped the liquid toward her mouth to try to cool the rush. A bright tartness trickled across her lips. But it wasn't lemon. "Limes?"

Peyton nodded and drank from his flask. "I found some in the market this morning. I thought you'd like a reprieve from your lemon water."

Georgana took a drink. It wasn't cold — few things on this island were — but the drink tasted wonderful in the heat of the evening.

"A refreshing change, is it not?" the lieutenant asked.

She answered by taking another sip.

He faced the sunset, which by now painted their skin a rosy hue. "Here's to tall ships and small ships. Here's to all the ships at sea. But the best ships are friendships" — he gave her a wink — "and may they always be." The lieutenant raised his flask in her direction.

A smile she could not keep back spread across her face. She tapped her drink against his, then put it to her mouth. Friendships.

She liked the thought of him considering her a friend. If only they could be more . . .

Why did she keep dreaming? Of course they couldn't be more than friends. He would be horrified if he found out who she truly was. And a man like Peyton surely had someone waiting back home.

Georgana tried to swallow back the words before they came out, to no avail. "To whom do you toast, when the officers toast their sweethearts and wives on Saturdays?"

"The sea, of course." He answered without hesitation. "She's the only lady I ever need." He winced. "That's not to say . . ."

Georgana cocked her head. "There isn't anyone waiting for you back home?"

He glanced at her out of the corner of his eye. "There is a lovely woman waiting for me back home, patient as Job."

Ah. She was right. If only being right didn't sink her spirits into the stone beneath their feet. Georgana pushed off the wall. She set the flask on the brick between them and plucked up her coat. "I should get back in case the captain needs anything." Even the rich sunset couldn't brighten her morale any longer. She hugged the jacket and made for the servants' quarters.

"You can't leave yet," he said. "You haven't answered my question."

She stopped. "You didn't ask a question."

"You didn't give me the chance. Come back and let me ask."

If her father found them out here, alone together once more, he'd demote Peyton faster than he'd demoted Jarvis. It would strengthen his fear that Peyton could figure out their secret. But all the lieutenant wanted was a little more conversation, and she couldn't resist. She walked back to the wall.

"It's only fair," he said. Unlike the way his smile pulled her in, which was completely unfair. He crossed his arms over the wall. "What do you throw out the window every night?"

"What do you mean?" Georgana's teeth pulled in the corner of her lip. How had he seen those?

"The papers. I've seen you throw paper into the water several times."

"They are mistakes. Drawing mistakes." She gritted her teeth. *Mistake.* How she hated that word.

"Why do you not keep them?"

Because she didn't want someone to happen upon Lieutenant Peyton's likeness in her belongings. "I don't need them anymore."

"You should consider keeping them. Often

we learn the most from our mistakes." He raised his arms, motioning to the garden. "That's why I came to speak to you here, instead of on the *Deborah*. After our last escapade, the captain's kept you under lock and key."

Hardly. But it soothed her dejected heart to hear he went through so much effort to speak with her. "He will have a harder time of it once we're confined to the ship for six or more weeks."

Peyton clapped her on the shoulder, more gently than he usually did. Georgana settled back against the wall and watched him down the last of his lime water. She would miss this place when they left.

A happy paradise in the middle of her lonely life.

Dominic wished they didn't have to put Mr. Byam to work so soon after losing his son. Charlie had succumbed to his strange illness days after landing in Antigua. His father now stood in the middle of the deck instructing the reparation of rigging, but he had a faraway look in his eyes. Poor man. He hoped Mr. Byam would be granted leave for mourning when they returned to England.

Men lined the upper decks, some washing

down the floor and others working on sails. A few hung from ladders over the sides, patching up forgotten holes in the hull or painting. The humid air pulsed around them with anticipation of the coming voyage. They were going home.

"Back to work," he said to a few boys sitting idle. They snapped to attention, then took up winding rope. They whispered behind him as he continued on his way. He thought he heard Walter's and Jarvis's names.

Jarvis hadn't made an appearance that morning. He had done all he could to alert the entire crew to his displeasure at the demotion without drawing more punishment. They might have pitied him if they weren't enraged over what he'd done to the Fitz boy. Walter still suffered from headaches and dizziness after more than a week. If Georgana hadn't made them stop . . .

Dominic shook his head. He didn't want to think about what could have happened. As much as Walter had aggravated him the first few weeks of their voyage, Dominic would have strung Jarvis from the yardarm himself for what he'd done.

Dominic descended from the forecastle in time to see Georgana pop through the hatch. She still wore her stone face, but she walked with a new spring in her step. Her mask nearly cracked when she spotted him walking in her direction.

"Good morning, George." Instinctively, he reached out to tousle her cap. He froze with his hand on her head. While continuing to treat her like a boy in front of everyone was essential, ruffling her cap now seemed like overstepping his bounds. He let his hand drop awkwardly to his side.

"Yes, good morning." She raised a brow but did not comment on his odd greeting. "I have a message for the boatswain."

He nodded and motioned her on. His head swiveled back to watch her bound up to the forecastle. She moved so nimbly. Had her grandmother allowed her to dance? He assumed she hadn't come out in Society before her father whisked her away, but he could see her picking up dancing quickly. He wouldn't mind dancing with someone like her.

Sails. Rigging. Paint. Dominic forced his head back around and skirted a wet patch that had just been scrubbed. If his mother agreed to take Georgana in, he might have a chance to stand up with her at a dance while they waited for orders in Portsmouth. He knew his mother would be delighted. Captain Woodall, on the other hand . . .

On his way up to the quarterdeck, Dominic passed Walter's father. Deep creases ringed his eyes. Dominic stopped him with a hand on his shoulder. "Are you well, Mr. Fitz? How is your boy?"

The man's mouth hardened. "Not well. If I weren't on this ship, I'd teach that no-account lieutenant to —"

Dominic sighed and held up his hand. "He is still your superior, Mr. Fitz," he said quietly. "I cannot allow you to speak like that. Even if I agree with you."

The coxswain nodded. "I didn't thank you properly for stopping Lieutenant Jarvis."

"Thank George. I never would have seen the beating if not for . . . him."

"Be careful, Lieutenant," Mr. Fitz said. "Men have heard Jarvis raging about you and the boy when you aren't around."

Dominic didn't doubt that he had made an enemy of the now-third lieutenant. He only hoped Jarvis could keep his mind clear enough to not do anything stupid until they got back to England. Captain Woodall would secure a transfer for Jarvis the moment the *Deborah* docked in Portsmouth, no question.

"Thank you, Fitz."

A party of men climbed over the rail before Dominic made it to the quarterdeck.

The carpenter's crew — a rather young, but jovial lot. One of them spotted him and hurried over.

"I found something while we were working, sir." He gave a salute, then reached into his pocket. "Stuck in a splinter on the side. What do you make of it?"

The square of folded paper had a torn edge on one side, as though pulled from a book. Dominic recognized it instantly. He'd seen a hand poke through the captain's window and throw similar pages into the sea several times during his night watches.

"Thank you." Dominic took the folded sheet. "I'll make sure this gets back to the rightful owner."

With a shrug, the young man rejoined his crew. Dominic hopped up to the quarterdeck and headed for the corner of the aft rail. With his back to the working men, he opened the paper. Fine pencil marks outlined the curve of the little bay he and Georgana had visited. An unfinished figure stood on the shore. Him?

His lips tugged upward. This is what she'd thrown out the window? Though he was no art expert, he didn't see anything wrong with this sketch, beyond its not being finished.

"Repairs are ready for inspection, sir."

Dominic stuffed the paper into the pocket of his jacket and turned. One of the carpenter's mates stood at attention behind him. "Yes, lead the way." He followed the boy down to the main deck.

He wondered what other subjects Georgana had drawn before throwing her sketches to the sea. Perhaps others had been of him?

He strode across the deck, lost in his thoughts. He couldn't say why the idea of someone thinking of him brought this peculiar lightness. And he couldn't say he disliked the feeling at all.

CHAPTER 18

"Captain?" Dominic hurried into the main cabin but found it empty. Captain Woodall must have already gone above with Georgana.

Most everyone had filtered up from the lower decks. Even the hardened sailors rarely missed a chance to see land one last time before putting out to sea. And with this faint breeze, they'd need everyone's strength to man the sails.

Dominic turned to retrace his steps but paused when his eyes fell on an unfolded sheet of paper on the table. It wasn't his concern, whatever it was, but his curiosity got the best of him. What if it was another of Georgana's drawings? He'd only take a peek.

He stepped to the table and smoothed the paper. Not a drawing — a letter. Before he could turn away, the name *Georgana* caught his eye. He quickly scanned the previous paragraphs.

Now is the time to put away foolish games. Georgana is already eighteen and has few merits. If we do not act while she is young, she may never find a match. Send to York and have her transported back to Lushill. I have already tried to send for her, but the name of the school is incorrect, as you knew when you gave it to me.

The grandmother. He set his jaw. No, the girl would most certainly not be going back to Lushill. Not that he held any say in the matter. But if he could present her another option, she would at least have the choice for once.

The girl will do whatever you say, Alfred. Stop this ridiculous hiding and put her where she can be of use to the family. Your own love match might have benefited you for a moment, but see where it has brought you. Don't let the girl make the same mistake.

He swept up the letter, prepared to rip it up and send it the way of Georgana's cast-off drawings. It took all his reasoning to lower it back to the table. He let go with stiff fingers and took a step away.

Dominic drew in a breath. He was late. He needed to get above to give the signal to haul up the anchor. And he couldn't let anyone catch him in here, reading Captain Woodall's private correspondence. He made for the door and ran for the ladder, shoes clicking on the recently cleaned deck. When he cleared the hatch, he snapped his bicorn onto his head and proceeded to the gathering of similar hats with feathery trim rustling in the breeze.

Dominic saluted. Captain Woodall didn't wait for his apology, but shouted, "Up anchor!"

Dominic relayed the message. Orders echoed across the deck, and men grunted as they hit the upper capstan's bars to bring in the anchor. Dominic found his place and waited for the report. When the anchor was raised far enough, he sent men aloft to ready the sails.

A small figure stood at the very back of the quarterdeck as the ship began to move. Tiers of sails filled. Men hurried between the lines and along the yards high above. But she paid the chaos no mind. The island drifted away while she watched, unnoticed by all except a lieutenant whose focus should have been fixed on the sea.

Georgana sighed and lowered herself down the ladder to the orlop deck. She headed to the powder room for the evening gun drills, as the captain had assigned her. Joining the powder monkeys again would be willful disobedience.

The belly of the ship didn't smell as foul as it did toward the end of a voyage. Two days on the ocean hadn't given the filthy bilge water enough time to collect. She hurried into the magazine, but neither the yeoman nor his mates acknowledged her presence.

"Jarvis is a fool," the yeoman grunted. "He'll get expelled from the navy if he isn't careful."

One of the young men laughed. "If Captain Woodall doesn't throw him overboard first. I've seen him with the lieutenant. Water and oil, those two."

Georgana poured black powder into its fabric cartridge.

"It's the captain's own fault, not putting the lieutenant in his place," the other mate said. "The last ship I was on, the captain would've flogged him, officer or no."

She tied off the cartridge and reached for

another. Her father's tactics were more lax than other captains' in some ways. He never resorted to clobbering his men when they were out of line. Discipline suffered only marginally because of it.

"Captain Woodall doesn't have the courage to stand up to his own officers," the yeoman growled.

The young men's eyes darted to Georgana, who kept her head down and continued filling bags as though she hadn't heard them. A chill slithered up her arms.

"You can't talk that way," one of the young men hissed.

"George won't squawk, will you?" She didn't meet the yeoman's gaze but shook her head. "There's a good lad."

The sound of footsteps made the mates jump into action. One of the gun crew captains appeared at the door. "George, we need you with the powder monkeys. With Fitz, Noyse, and Pearce down, we don't have enough boys."

"But the captain —"

The man snorted. "You think the captain cares one whit who fuels his guns?"

Yes. She knew well the captain *did* care if she fueled his guns.

"Go, lad," the yeoman said with a wave of his hand. "Don't think you're better than the rest of the lot."

Georgana tied off a bag and slid it into the canister offered by the gun captain. She added another, then followed him out.

"What's wrong with Noyse and Pearce?" She could barely see the man in the darkness of the lowest deck.

"Both had fevers this morning. They're in the sick bay."

She hurried to keep up with his long stride. Sickness on the ship meant trouble for all on board. Sometimes it affected only one, like Charlie Byam's illness. But in such a small living space, illnesses often spread rapidly through the crew.

Another thing for Papa to worry over.

"You'll take Fitz's place with the *Spitting Devil, Bess,* and *Victory,*" the gun captain said as they climbed the ladder.

Perfect. Jarvis's new post.

The gun crews snatched up the cartridges the moment she got to the gun deck, and she immediately turned and ran back for the powder room. With three crews counting on her, she would be running more than usual.

On her next trip up to the gun deck, she met with Jarvis's red face. "What kept you?"

Georgana glanced at the other powder monkeys, who'd gone down and come up at the same speed she had. She ducked her head and scurried to the crews, placing the powder far enough away it wouldn't get trampled. Best to ignore Jarvis and do what she needed to. And pray her father didn't catch her on the gun deck.

Minutes later she burst through the hatch with a full canister for her third round. A rough hand grabbed her collar and hauled her up.

"Do you think this a promenade in Hyde Park, Taylor?"

Jarvis sent her careening into one of the gun crews, and she narrowly avoided the gun's kick as white smoke exploded from its muzzle. Her ears rang from the boom that rattled her bones. A sailor caught her and pushed her out of the way of the men surging forward to clean the cannon.

She distributed her load and went for more. Her lip trembled, and she angrily caught it in her teeth to stop the movement. They weren't in battle. The crews didn't need powder as fast for training, especially since the captain frequently stopped them for correction. Too much powder on the deck and an errant spark could blow the ship into the sky.

Her ears throbbed, pushing sound back as though she had a blanket covering them.

Boys passed her going the opposite direction. They had to be close to finished. Her father tried not to waste shot on excessive practice.

The yeoman filled her canister, and she turned to make her trek back to the top again. Her stomach churned. Jarvis would be waiting at the hatchway to scream at her again. She shouldn't find it surprising he would try to retaliate against the captain and first lieutenant by pestering her.

At the top of the ladder, something swung at Georgana's face. She threw up her arm and deflected the blow, but the force of it sent her rolling to the floor.

Jarvis stood over her, face hard. "You dare to stand against me?" He raised his fist again, and she rolled out of the way. She sprang to her feet and spun to face him, ready for the next blow.

"Lieutenant!"

The gun master, Mr. Adams, had Jarvis by the arm. His balding head emphasized heavy brows that glared as he restrained the lieutenant, a man much above his rank. "This behavior is not called for, and it is distracting my gun crews."

Jarvis ripped his arm free. "I am acting within my authority."

"If you aren't careful, it won't be your

authority anymore." The gun master backed off, but footsteps on the ladder cut short Jarvis's advance.

Georgana didn't need to see much of the long legs to know who had descended to the gun deck. And while she was happy to see the face at the top of that well-formed frame, she bolted for the ladder on the other side of the ship. She hadn't been in company with Peyton often since they left Antigua, but she didn't doubt her father had made his commands clear to the first lieutenant. She was not to be on the gun deck.

Her arm pulsed where Jarvis's first blow had landed, but the ache didn't run deep enough to signal that anything was damaged. And her shirt would cover the inevitable bruise. Bringing attention to Jarvis's unwarranted punishment would only aggravate the strained situation.

She did not want to be responsible for that.

Georgana stood at the edge of the sick bay, a steaming cup of ginger tea in her hands. Lanterns illuminated three occupied hammocks. Most of the men now sat at dinner on the messdeck below, leaving this level quiet and undisturbed.

A figure moved between the two hammocks on the starboard side of the deck. Étienne didn't look up when she entered. The occupant of the third hammock was sitting upright, head in his hands. She moved to his side and cleared her throat.

"Captain sent this for you." Or at least the captain wouldn't be angry if he found out she'd brought it. She held the tin cup out to him. "Careful, it's hot."

Fitz moved his hands just enough to stare at the cup, but he didn't take it.

"It will help your head."

"Why are you doing this, pretty boy?"

She didn't know herself. Perhaps because she remembered the shattered boy sitting alone in the messdeck after his friend had been killed. Or because the scene of him struggling under Jarvis's abuse still haunted her thoughts.

She held the cup closer to him. Fitz was just a boy trying to find his place on this ship, as she was. And like her incessant memories of Grandmother, memories of Fitz's bullying did not serve her.

"I want to let go of the past," she whispered.

Fitz watched her, his eyes half covered by his hands, then hesitantly took the cup. "Did you poison it?"

"Only ginger and honey."

He took a slow drink, eyes narrowing in reaction to the spiciness of the ginger. One hand moved to his forehead as he sipped.

"Captain's sending food over shortly. He has fresh mango on the table tonight. Have you tried mango?"

The boy gave her a quiet yes.

"I think you'll enjoy the food. Rest well, Fitz."

He gave her a nearly inaudible "thank you" as she turned to leave. Perhaps she and Fitz would never be friends, but she hoped they were on the way to not being enemies. Having Jarvis as an enemy on board was difficult enough.

"Mr. Taylor, come here, if you please." The gravelly voice of the French surgeon stopped her before she left the sick bay. She moved to the other end of the ship, where Étienne's shadowy face held a grim scowl. He looked from one sick boy to the other. Even in the dim light, their faces shone with sweat.

"I believe they have the same fever young Mr. Byam contracted."

Georgana's hand flew to her mouth. It hadn't been an isolated incident, after all.

"I wish to quarantine them. Walter should be moved as soon as possible. Will you tell this to the captain?"

"Yes, sir."

"Thank you. And find the boy's father to help him back to the messdeck."

Georgana ran for the captain's quarters but crashed into a pair of blue-clad arms and a cream-colored waistcoat halfway across the deck.

"Where are you going in such a hurry?" Lieutenant Peyton asked.

Georgana touched the brim of her cap in a salute. She didn't meet his eyes, for fear he'd somehow see the flush of her cheeks, even in the darkness of the deck. "I have a message for the captain."

"I just finished speaking with him, and he is not in a pleasant mood." He still held her arms, gently but firmly. "He thought I'd told you to go against his orders and practice with the powder monkeys."

Her head snapped up. Her father hadn't said a word about it to her all evening. She thought he hadn't noticed her disobedience. "A gun captain fetched me up. Noyse and Pearse are down with the same fever Byam had, and the monkeys needed help."

Peyton's lips pressed together, and his eyes strayed to the sick bay behind her. "That is unwelcome news. What happened with Jarvis?" Peyton asked.

Georgana sighed and pulled out of his

249

hands, though her arms instantly missed the feel of them. Maybe someday she would let him stay like that, holding on to her.

No, dreams like this were dangerous. She shook her head, responding to her thoughts as well as to Peyton. "What happened with Jarvis was only to be expected."

"Did he hurt you?"

"No." At least no more than her grandmother had on multiple occasions. Her arm didn't smart anymore. "I've been cuffed plenty of times by officers. This isn't new."

"You must be careful, George. I don't want you getting hurt."

Georgana turned her back to him. His kind words were just as perilous as her thoughts. Seeing his face so soft and full of concern made her heart melt like sealing wax over her father's letters. And Peyton had already stamped his mark into the tender mess.

"I'll be fine," she said through a lump in her throat. "Did you tell the captain about Jarvis?"

"No, I wanted to speak with you first."

Those words gave her some relief. "Don't say anything."

Peyton let out a fierce breath. "This isn't a quarrel between ship's boys. Jarvis is twice your size and looking for revenge after losing his rank. He would have no qualms doing to you what he did to Walter Fitz."

Georgana knew he was right. She'd seen the fury in the third lieutenant's eyes after she blocked his fist. While she didn't know how far her father would go to teach Jarvis his place, if she were involved, he would throw Jarvis into the sea.

The words of the powder crew sprang to her mind. Water and oil, they'd said. She did not want to be the spark that ignited tensions. She would keep her head down and do her work. "I need to speak to the captain."

She didn't want him to leave her, but when she looked over her shoulder before entering the cabin, he had disappeared.

CHAPTER 19

Dominic lay in his cot, listening to Jarvis grumble to Lieutenant Rimmer, the marine second lieutenant, in the wardroom. Around them the ship was coming to life, though the sun had yet to rise. After taking the middle watch through the early morning hours, Dominic should have been sleeping.

Instead, he lit his lantern and pulled Georgana's drawing from his coat pocket. His mind drifted back to the sheltered bay and their afternoon alone. She'd seemed so free that day as they built walls against the tide and scoured the bright sand for a token to give his mother. He'd watched her search, following her small footprints across the beach before the jealous waters scampered over them. One corner of his mouth tugged upward. The sea did not like a rival.

Not that Georgana was a rival. He laughed silently at the thought. They were only friends, of course. If she ever suspected he knew her secret, she'd probably retreat behind her walls — walls that wouldn't come down with the simple touch of a wave.

Dominic traced the curve of the bay with his finger. He didn't want to lose this friendship. Didn't want to lose her trust. Their relationship was unlike any he'd formed before, though admittedly he didn't have very many female acquaintances since he had gone to sea at age twelve. He hadn't met many people with Georgana's dry wit and warm heart in those fourteen years.

"Spying for the captain, George?"

Dominic bolted upright at Jarvis's voice. He folded the paper and shoved it back in his pocket. How had she materialized, just when he was thinking of her?

"No, I'm here with a message for Lieutenant Peyton."

"Yes, you always are."

Dominic rammed his feet into his shoes as he rebuttoned his waistcoat. Jarvis had better hold his tongue. He ran a hand through his disheveled hair, then threw open his cabin door.

Georgana stood just outside the wardroom's entrance. The inward pull on the side of her lip belied her otherwise stoic face.

Dominic didn't acknowledge Jarvis's

glare. He nearly invited her into his room to avoid the third lieutenant, but the words halted on his tongue. Bringing her in felt wrong now that he knew who she was. If she ever found out he was aware of the truth, she could be angry with him for knowingly compromising her reputation.

Best to find a quiet space outside the wardroom. He closed his cabin door and joined her. With his head he motioned toward a secluded spot behind the ladder. She followed him over.

"There's no secret," she said.

He blinked. Of course there was a secret. This secret had completely changed their friendship, from that of a boy and mentor to . . . Well, he wasn't sure what it was now. A friendship truer than any he'd had before, and yet one where both parties kept significant truths from each other.

"The captain just wanted me to tell you there are three more."

Three more what? Three more women dressed as boys? Dominic's mind spun, and he put a hand to his head.

"This time it's men, too, not just boys." Georgana stared at a spot on the floor, face grave. "And the rash has started. Exactly as with Byam. Étienne still can't say what it is, but he thinks many more will fall ill before the end."

The gears in Dominic's head ground to a stop. He shut his mouth, teeth clicking together. Not women dressed as men. Ill crew members. What an imbecile. And he'd almost given himself away. Clearly he needed rest.

"Are you all right, sir?" Her strained voice kicked his brain into action.

"Yes, of course. Seven ill with fever. Unfortunate business." He wanted to hit himself for his stammering. "Tell the captain I appreciate the news and to keep me informed of any developments."

She saluted and hesitantly mounted the ladder. He hurried for his room and threw himself into his cot. Fool! Dominic pulled his pillow over his head.

Sleep. He needed sleep. And to stop those whirling thoughts in his head that centered on Georgana Woodall.

Georgana didn't usually mind the dark or being alone. She sat near the windows, sketchbook in her lap, gazing at the full moon's reflection on the calm sea. Tunes from a fiddle and Irish flute skipped through the open window, punctuated by men's laughter.

Her father had gone above to observe the

merriment. He had never invited her to join in on the nights of music and dancing. Most nights she did not have much desire for it.

But in a month or two, she wouldn't be able to refuse to join in the dance. After so many years of refusing to let Georgana learn to dance, Grandmother no doubt would implement a rigorous training schedule. Then she would watch Georgana's every move at balls and assemblies in order to belittle her for mistakes afterward. That routine would end only when Georgana secured a match.

"George."

The whispered name sent a tingle up her spine. She knew the voice before she looked up to see Peyton's head poking through the door.

"You are missing the amusement."

"I don't mind." But she did. Tonight she regretted being alone in the dark.

"I won't stand for it. You may draw tomorrow night. Come join your shipmates."

She glanced down at the book in her lap. Her father hadn't exactly forbidden her to come up. The music called to her, and before she knew it, she'd hidden her sketchbook in her hammock and was rushing out of the cabin after the beaming lieutenant.

■ ■ ■ ■

Stars glittered above, but no one on the *Deborah*'s deck paid them any mind. Lanterns were strewn around the company gathered at the mainmast. Men swung about to the fiddle and flute's duet, while their companions clapped with the music. It was a scene Dominic had viewed many times in his career.

He and Georgana kept to the outer edge of the gathering, on the opposite side from where the captain watched. He didn't know if Captain Woodall had seen them yet, but he suspected the protective father would have come over if he had.

Georgana watched the proceedings with a faint smile on her face. To most she would have appeared only mildly amused, but Dominic knew better. This rare smile meant that for once she felt comfortable above deck.

Despite the October chill, Dominic slid a finger between his neck and collar to loosen it. So many bodies on the deck made him warm.

"Are you enjoying yourself?" He could already see it in her face, but he wanted to hear it.

"Very much, sir." The sound hid in the roar of men's voices. "They all dance so well."

"Do you dance, Mr. Taylor?" He hadn't meant to emphasize the alias. If he didn't take more care, he'd reveal his secret and hers, and then the Woodalls truly would hate him. Lucky for him, she didn't seem to catch his tone in the noise.

"Not since I was small." Her hands beat together with the tune, and when it finished, she applauded with the others.

Someone called for a hornpipe, and other sailors eagerly seconded the motion. An idea tickled Dominic's mind. He glanced around and spotted an empty place behind the mast, sheltered from view of the officers but within hearing of the music.

He extended a hand to her. "Come, dance the hornpipe with me." He stared at his hand. What was he doing? He turned the gentlemanly gesture into a wave for her to follow him. Heat crept across his face. *Focus, Dominic.*

"But I don't know it."

"Follow what I do. I'll show you."

She followed him behind the mast as the fiddler began the introduction. Dominic folded his arms in front of him, one atop the other. Georgana followed suit. Her eyes flitted toward the rest of the group, as though worried the other men could see them.

"I'm not certain this is a good idea," she said.

He stepped in front of her, catching her gaze. "No one is watching."

"You are watching."

"But I am a friend. That hardly counts." He winked as the dance started. "First, we march in a circle, like this, then step back, step back. Good!"

She watched his feet on their first turn, shuffling through the steps with uncertainty. He bowed to one side, then snapped to attention. That step she did very well. She practiced coming to attention many times throughout the day.

"I feel ridiculous," she said.

"To dance is to be a little ridiculous, is it not?"

As they bowed back and forth with the song, the terror on her face melted away. Each turn, she stepped with a little more animation. Her face glowed. Before long they were both panting as they pushed through the steps, which mimicked hauling, winding, and rowing. Her movements didn't show fatigue. Indeed, she looked as full of life as he'd ever seen her. He had been right

— she made a lovely dancer.

At the end of the tune, the rhythm picked up speed. Georgana cried out as it forced her feet to move faster and faster. Dominic's heavy breathing and racing pulse silenced his chuckle at her distress. She kept up with the wild frenzy, stepping back in place until the fiddle struck the final chord with a glorious shout.

Georgana stumbled to the mainmast and collapsed against it. He stopped beside her, hands on his knees and gasping for breath.

A laugh — a warm flash that split the night — spilled out as she slid down the mast to sit on the deck. No one glanced their way, and the feminine tone was lost in the shouts of the next round of dancers. Little droplets glinted from corners of her eyes.

He sank quietly to the floor beside her, not wanting to disrupt the scene. She drew in gulps of fresh sea air as her peal of laughter wafted away like autumn leaves on the wind. It was no wonder she never laughed on board. She'd mastered the facade of a shy cabin boy, but he didn't think she could ever mask her laugh.

She wiped the moisture from her eyes and watched the bright moon above them. He ignored the moon and the way it tripped across the waves. Tonight he forgot the ocean. He watched her.

His heart pounded between his ribs, and he nearly let it push him forward to kiss that contented smile. How would it feel to have Georgana Woodall's soft lips caressing his own? To be wanted by someone like her would be a wondrous thing.

Dominic straightened, giving his head a sharp shake. What was he thinking? As though he could ever conceal a kiss with three hundred other men milling about or while this close to her father. Besides, he couldn't see her welcoming a kiss that could compromise her disguise.

"What is it? Are you sure you're well, Lieutenant?" She leaned toward him, face upturned.

He needed to get out before his reckless nature took over and he did something they'd all regret. "Yes, quite well." He leaped to his feet and offered her a hand up. She grasped it, rather than delicately setting her hand into his, as a lady would. This was how it was supposed to be. He pulled her up with enough force to lift her off the ground. She tripped into him before righting herself. He could almost see the pink in her cheeks in the lantern light.

"Are you certain? You seemed out of sorts

this morning, and now —"

He held up his hands. "I am well. I only need to collect my things before the next watch. Shall I take you to your . . . the captain? Or back to the main cabin?"

Her face fell, and he looked away quickly before it could convince him to stay. "I'll find the captain. Thank you."

Dominic ran for the hatchway but stopped to see she'd safely arrived at her father's side. Jarvis had stayed up on the forecastle with Lieutenant Rimmer, so Dominic needn't worry about a confrontation between him and Georgana.

The captain's brows went up at the sight of her. He said very little, and they both turned back to watch the dance. The gleam in her eyes had faded.

Dominic trudged down to the wardroom, trying to no avail to dampen the unfamiliar swirl of heat within.

CHAPTER 20

Water poured over the deck, and the scratch of rough bristles filled the air as dozens of crouching men and boys scrubbed. Georgana scrubbed too, at the black-and-white tiled floor of the captain's quarters. They'd taken down the walls and stowed her and her father's things below for the weekly cleaning.

The briny scent of seawater rose up from the deck. Though not her favorite smell, it made her stomach skip. If he were here, Peyton would drink in the concentrated aroma of his beloved ocean. Then that grin, the one that stopped time and worry, would light his face. She'd seen it more often since they left Antigua.

The first lieutenant and her father had gone above to oversee a course correction, since the winds had taken an odd turn. That left Jarvis stalking the gun deck with his usual dour expression.

Georgana kept to the corner of the deck in hopes he wouldn't notice her. On the opposite end of the deck, hammocks were strung across the width of the ship. All hammocks were usually removed when they swabbed the decks, but too many were sick today. Fifteen ill since Wednesday — three just that morning.

The crew gave the sick bay a wide berth, hoping to not be among the next sailors stricken. There had been no deaths since Charlie Byam's, but it seemed only a matter of time. The lightness within Georgana plummeted at the thought.

A shoe nudged her ribs hard enough to hurt. "Get to work."

Georgana rubbed her brush faster over the slick floor. Her fingers itched to reach back and feel the bindings to make sure they hadn't loosened at his kick, but she didn't want to provoke Jarvis further.

"Slow work will get you nowhere in the navy, lad," he said. "If this were my ship, I would have flogged you for laziness by now."

If this were her ship, she would have flogged him for insubordination by now.

"A pampered boy like you has no place on a ship."

Georgana kept her gaze on the tiles. Black tile, then white tile. Up and down, back and

264

forth. If she didn't react, he'd go away eventually. Grandmother always did.

His fist grabbed the back of her coat and her shirt and waistcoat with it. The bindings pulled tight as he dragged her to her feet. She dropped the brush and tried to pull away.

"Are you listening to me, Taylor?" His face jutted toward hers, inches from touching. The sickly sweet rum on his breath made her gag. "Tell me, do you swim?"

She didn't answer. He couldn't take her above without her father seeing, but still her pulse thundered in her ears. For all her years on board, she'd never actually been in the sea.

A nasty smirk split Jarvis's face. He snatched the handle of one of the windows and threw it open. The panes rattled as they hit the next window.

"I'd wager I could cram you through there."

Georgana struggled against his grip. The men on the gun deck behind them kept their heads down, as though oblivious to her plight. She pried at Jarvis's hand with numb fingers. "Why are you doing this?"

He slammed her into the wall, her head flying through the window. All the air fled from her lungs, and she fought to draw in breath as he pressed against her. The breeze ripped the tan cap from her head. It tumbled through air and into the waves below.

"You have no ambitions in the navy," he growled into her ear. "You couldn't care where you serve, so long as you have a plush cushion at the captain's feet and the bones from his table. But some of us have fought for every inch we've gained, and I won't lose it all to a sniveling little pickthank."

Georgana clawed at the windowsill, knowing it wouldn't do much to keep her inside. "Please, sir." She hardly recognized her own wheezing voice. The wind swept past her wet hands, making them tremble with cold. The shaking reverberated to her core.

"The next time you interfere with my disciplinary actions, I won't hesitate." Jarvis threw her to the floor and slammed the window closed.

Georgana crawled on hands and knees back to her brush. Her chest heaved, but she couldn't get enough air to soothe the panic.

"Sir!" a cry came. "It's Wallace!"

A man lay unmoving on his side by one of the guns. Jarvis walked calmly away from her, not looking back.

Georgana bit back tears. She had prayed Jarvis would let this go, but clearly he hadn't forgotten his grudge. She worried it was only a matter of time before he sought revenge again.

Men clambered up to the gun deck for services. Everyone huddled toward the captain's quarters, as far from the overflowing sick bay as possible. Twenty-seven were stricken now. Dominic shook his head. At this rate, half the crew would be down within a week.

Georgana sat in a corner across the room from the officers' gathering. Most officers had chairs brought up for services, but for several weeks Dominic had forgone the practice to sit with her. However, today she'd come out of the captain's cabin later than usual and taken a place far from him. He couldn't make sense of it.

The previous day, she'd hidden away after the crew had finished cleaning the gun deck. Dominic had attributed it to her father's orders, but now he wondered. She didn't meet his eyes. She pulled out a prayer book, set her sketchbook on top of it, and began to draw.

Had he done something to upset her? Or worse, had she seen through his ruse? She was a perceptive woman. Perhaps she had seen his ridiculous longing to kiss her

Friday evening.

Dunce. How had he let himself come to that?

Her hand reached up to pull on the back of her short hair. She wore no cap today. Odd. She always wore her cap and jacket. And she never brought her drawing things to services.

The chaplain stood to begin, and Dominic stood with him. He stole behind the officers' chairs and dropped down next to Georgana. She didn't look up.

"And ye shall serve the Lord your God," the chaplain read, "and he shall bless thy bread, and thy water; and I will take sickness away from the midst of thee."

Dominic nudged her rigid shoulder, but she continued to draw. A wave took shape on the page before her.

"What is the matter?" he whispered.

She lifted the pencil to put a finger to her lips, then returned the pencil to the page.

"I will send my fear before thee," recited the chaplain.

Dominic glanced around. Everyone sat in front of them, faces toward the chaplain. He wrapped his fingers around the pencil, brushing the skin of her hand. She instantly drew hers away, leaving the pencil in his grasp.

268

"I will make all thine enemies turn their backs unto thee."

He twisted his arm to write across the top of the page, out of the way of her work. *Why will you not tell me?*

Her lips pressed together. She took the proffered pencil and wrote, *It is of no consequence. It will pass.*

She went back to her sketch, but he slid the pencil out of her fingers again. *I can help.*

No.

Georgana didn't give him the pencil. She traced the crest of the wave, adding a line of foam. He rubbed his brow. He'd never seen her stew like this. At least not since he found her on the gun deck after her fight with Fitz.

Dominic stopped her drawing again. *Where is your cap?*

I lost it.

He scanned the deck for Jarvis, but the third lieutenant hadn't graced them with his presence. Dominic's stomach twisted into a knot. *Who took it?*

No one. It fell in the sea.

He let her resume her work. Jarvis had something to do with it. Dominic could feel it in his gut. Why she wouldn't tell him, he couldn't say. She still did not trust him completely. How could she, with her secret?

One thing he did know — he had grown tired of secrets. When she returned to England, he would try to form a real friendship with Georgana. One without all these lies.

A light tapping on his arm lugged him out of his thoughts. Georgana pointed with the pencil to a new line of writing on her paper. The letters now crowded around her sketch. *Are you listening to the sermon?*

Clearly.

You should be.

Despite himself, he had to swallow a laugh. How he wished he could understand what went on in that head of hers.

She didn't wait for a response before writing. *It is a good sermon and very relevant. You should set the example for your men.*

Dominic held up his hands. At her satisfied nod, he lifted his attention to the chaplain.

Though he tried to focus on the encouraging message and pleas for divine protection for the disease-riddled crew, his mind kept straying to the young lady beside him and the strange predicament in which he found himself. How much longer could he pretend to be oblivious while at the same time becoming completely preoccupied with Georgana Woodall?

CHAPTER 21

Étienne stood at the table in the captain's cabin. Dark circles stained the skin below his eyes, and his mess of curls hung wildly. Georgana hid in the corner with her mending. Her shoulders hunched a little lower with each sentence Étienne spoke.

"There are now thirty-six, and I have suspicions we will reach fifty before tomorrow has concluded."

Fifty. Georgana's stomach lurched. More than a quarter of the crew.

"I have reason to hope that Mr. Pearce . . . But I should not make these speculations. His condition has stabilized. However, Mr. Noyse is not doing well."

Her father sat with hands clasped on the table. "You believe Pearce will make a recovery?"

The Frenchman lifted his shoulders. "I only hope that young Mr. Byam was simply an unlucky case."

"And you still cannot say what it is? What caused it?"

Georgana bound together the seams of her jacket with needle and thread. The coat had been pulled too many times of late. She moved slowly since she had to work from the outside instead of the inside. Any poorly formed stitches, as she was prone to make, would show.

No, she would not think like that. No one but her Grandmother would think her stitching poor. If she did make a mistake, not a soul on this ship would notice.

"What causes any disease?" The surgeon sighed. "Bad air? Bad food? An incompatibility with the elements? I am doing all that I can, but there is only so much I can do."

Papa steepled his fingers in front of him. She didn't like to see the lines of worry around his mouth. Those lines echoed in the faces of every man on board. Their friends, companions, and kin were fading in the sick bay. And no one, not even the surgeon, knew how to restore them or prevent the disease's spread.

"Thank you for your work, Étienne."

The surgeon didn't give his usual wry smile as he quit the room. He only saluted and slipped out. When the door closed, Papa slumped in his chair.

"What am I to do, George?"

"What is there to be done?" She lowered her work. "We can only trust the surgeon."

"Perhaps Jarvis is right. What if the Frenchman is trying to sabotage the crew?" He didn't look convinced, but she heard seeds of doubt in his tone. Georgana did not know of Étienne's loyalties, but she had seen him in the sick bay as he cared for his patients. She did not believe him capable of poisoning the men, even if he was from an enemy country.

Georgana picked up her needle and stabbed it into the material. "Jarvis is never right."

"We at least have the same opinion on that."

She threw him a sharp look. What did he mean, suggesting there were things on which they did not agree?

Before she could ask, the door opened, and all thoughts of the previous conversation fled.

Lieutenant Peyton walked in, eyes flitting to her and quickly away. He stopped and stood at attention with a salute. As his hand fell to his side, a sliver of paper fluttered from his fingers and drifted to the deck. The table blocked her father's view of it.

"You called for me, sir?" the lieutenant asked.

Papa leaned forward. Georgana stared at the scrap and swallowed. Surely he wouldn't notice something so small.

"Has the ship behind us been sighted today?"

"No, sir."

The paper lay beyond her reach, though it had floated a little way behind Peyton. She sneaked her foot out, but her toes couldn't touch it.

"Good, and I would like it to stay that way," her father said. "We don't have the manpower for a confrontation. Set our course east-northeast."

Georgana twirled the thimble around her finger. Papa got to his feet, and her stomach gave an unwarranted leap. She flicked the thimble away, and it clinked across the deck. The little pewter bauble rolled, then stopped at the seam of two tiles.

Murmuring an apology, she dropped to her hands and knees to retrieve the thimble. Her shirtsleeve grazed the lieutenant's leg as she swept up the scrap of paper. Her breath caught from being so near to him. If she did not put a stop to this, she would give herself away. She scurried back to her seat on her sea chest.

Her father finished his instructions to Peyton, and she didn't miss his pointed look in her direction, though she pretended to. She kept the paper crushed to her palm with two fingers. The rest of her fingers awkwardly continued the repair of her coat.

"I'll be above directly," Papa said. She didn't watch Lieutenant Peyton leave for fear his grin would set her blushing.

"What was that?" her father asked when they were alone.

She blinked her eyes wide, trying to appear innocent. "What was —"

He motioned to the floor. "What was your little act?"

Her mouth went dry. She held up the thimble. "Just my thimble, sir."

"I see." His brow stayed raised.

"Do you have anything that needs mending?" Did her voice squeak?

He shook his head then left. Georgana took a deep breath, her hands falling still. Was she keeping secrets from everyone? Until recently, Papa had been the only person on earth she wasn't keeping things from. But now she had something else to hide.

She feared her affection for Lieutenant Peyton would anger him. But she would eventually leave the *Deborah,* and this infatuation would fade. No sense in troubling Papa about it now.

She opened her hand. The little scrap of paper had two hastily scrawled words — "first watch."

She scowled. Did Peyton have first watch tonight? She calculated the hours. Yes, he did. What did he mean by informing her he had first watch?

Then the answer clicked into place, making her heart skip. He wanted her to meet him.

Before she could stop the silly gesture, she pressed the paper to her lips. She dropped to her knees, opened her trunk, and tucked it carefully into a corner. What did it matter that he thought she was a boy in need of his protection and advice? She would treasure every moment she had with him. And when she set foot on English soil, she would keep these sweet days burning bright in her memory for as long as she lived.

Five chimes of the bell. Half past ten o'clock. Dominic tapped his fingers on the rail beside the bowsprit. He'd watched her pick up the note. Had she not understood it? Or the note had been too forward. Fool. What had he been thinking?

That he wanted to talk to her again —

that's what he'd been thinking. He wanted to know why she had been so withdrawn yesterday. He traced the constellations with his eyes up to Polaris, then over to Canes Venatici, the hunting dogs. The bowsprit pointed toward the southern hound's paws, whose stars hovered protectively over the ship's destination — his mother and home.

Dominic rested his chin on his fist. This voyage had been the strangest he'd taken. Few battles, discord among the officers, a young lady in disguise. But bizarrely, he did not want the journey to end. And this time his reluctance to reach land had nothing to do with the pull of the sea.

Timid steps across the forecastle deck brought his head around. A slender shadow stood in the lantern light from the foremast, and for a moment he imagined standing outside a ballroom waiting for a young lady to sneak away from her chaperone to meet him at the balcony.

He banished the fanciful image. He preferred the reality. "I didn't think you would come."

She joined him at the rail. "The captain stayed awake musing later than usual."

"He does have a lot to think on."

Georgana kept a safe distance between them, something she hadn't done while retrieving the note that afternoon. He had not expected her to come so close. His fingers had nearly touched her dark hair as she crouched to pick it up. They wanted to touch her hair again now, to smooth it out of her eyes so she could better see the tranquil night.

"You want to ask me again what happened Saturday," she said.

He chuckled. She wasn't easily fooled, which was why he needed to take caution.

"I won't tell you, so you might as well not ask."

Dominic huffed, half out of frustration and half out of admiration. For as shy as she was, Georgana had a stubborn streak. It was no wonder she'd survived so long at sea.

"Either Jarvis hurt you or he threatened you. Or both," he said. "I wish to know which it was."

She crossed her arms over her buttoned coat. "And what would you do, if I admitted to it?"

"I'd keelhaul his sorry —"

"And that is why I will not tell you." She glowered at the water below. "You shouldn't worry over a ship's boy who cannot even do that rank justice."

"That is your grandmother speaking."

Dominic turned his head to glance behind him. All seemed right on the deck. The movement cleared the steam rising inside him. Jarvis *had* done something. "You should keep yourself out of situations where Jarvis could catch you alone."

"Yes, the captain reminds me of that every day." She straightened and tucked her hands into her pockets. The autumn air must have felt too cold on her bare hands, but he didn't feel it. Too many sentiments, both pleasant and unpleasant, twisted within. "You cannot change what happened. We might as well forget it, as you told me to do with my grandmother."

Dominic pursed his lips. "But suppose I *could* change it. Would you allow me to?"

She walked away from him, pulling a hand from her pocket and trailing it along the rail. "The only way you could fix it would be to undo the past. It's useless to think that way."

He followed behind her and halted at the bowsprit. "I find it an interesting exercise." In an instant he planted a shoe on the base of the spar and pulled himself up. He grasped one of the overhead lines to steady himself. The bowsprit's wood was dry under his feet, minimizing his risk of slipping into the black water below. "If you could change anything about your past, Georg . . . . what would it be?" He had nearly misspoken and said *Georgana.*

It did not take her long to answer. "I would change my father's absence."

Dominic walked forward. He paused as the ship's bow rose higher than usual. The wooden shaft heaved, the power swelling up his legs and through his whole body, as though he were part of the vessel. The ship settled down again, and the rush lifted his soul. He walked out farther, drawn by the ocean's melody.

How would it feel to be in command of such a ship as this? To ride the waves at the speed of the wind on his own orders, with no care for what danger tomorrow would bring? There was no place in that dream for an anchor pulling him back to harbor. His mother was anchor enough.

"You would not have had him go to sea so often?" he asked.

"I would not have had him go at all."

Dominic's head swung around. "Why not?"

She watched him with a guarded expression. "Because my mother never smiled when he was gone. And my grandmother was at her worst."

A valid reason. "Perhaps he could not help

it. If he loved the sea, how could he not return to it?"

"Is it good to love the sea more than wife and child?" She glanced from Dominic's precarious position to the water many feet below. "It does not seem right to give more to something that cannot return love than to the people who can and do."

He could not tell if she spoke of her father now or hinted at his own position. Dominic retraced his steps and hopped lightly from the bowsprit to the deck. Her words filled him with a swarming confusion he hadn't experienced since determining whether or not to accept his promotion to post-captain.

One thing was clear. When Georgana Woodall returned to England, she would not seek out a husband among the ranks of naval officers. The idea brought a scowl.

"And what would you change about the past, Lieutenant?"

A facetious remark flew to his tongue, but he bit it back. The look of pride on his mother's face jumped forward, along with his guilt at having kept his promotion offer and refusal from her.

If he had accepted, he would never have met Georgana.

For the first time in months, his mind settled on that matter. No, he would not have changed his choice to remain a lieutenant.

The next thought to surface made him recoil. There was something he wished could be changed about his past, but it was something he had never said aloud. Not even to his mother, though she had lived the trial more horribly than he had.

Polaris hung suspended in Georgana's eyes, the star's attendants glittering around, as she waited for him to speak. She seemed to have no trouble waiting. She had waited for her father's return — she waited on her father now. Someday she might wait for Society to set her up as a wife, and then she would wait on her husband. How did she have such patience?

Dominic wouldn't make her wait any longer, and he wouldn't have another lie between them. "I would change something about my parents as well. I would change the way my father swept my mother into a corner and left her there, embarrassed by her low birth, and how he taught my older brother to do the same."

The words tore from his mouth, leaving a trail of unveiled hurt in their wake. Georgana only nodded, as though she knew there were no words that could ease the ache.

"He hardly spared me a glance either, but after his passing I only had to convince my brother to allow me to join the navy. My mother, on the other hand, had no way to escape the position he had put her in. He left her nothing."

A light touch on his arm made him freeze, except for his galloping pulse. "I think she did have an escape," Georgana said. Too soon she snatched her hand back, as though realizing what she'd done. She hid her hands behind her back. "I should return. The captain won't be happy if he wakes and sees I'm gone."

Dominic nodded. He should patrol the deck, check their location, and assess their speed.

When he had dropped the note, he didn't think she would distract him from his duty. But she had the potential to distract him from more than just his responsibilities on the *Deborah.* If he allowed anything beyond friendship to develop, it would be a disservice to his mother. He couldn't possibly have room in his heart or the little Portsmouth house for more than one woman.

Could he?

He muttered a farewell and watched the young lady drift down the step to the main deck, then down the hatchway. If only she could walk out of his head — and his heart — as easily.

Dominic adjusted his bicorn and tried to breathe in the wind off the sea. The aroma didn't invigorate him as it usually did. He stormed the length of the ship from bow to stern, the clomp of his shoes awaking sailors who had dozed in the quiet of the watch.

He leaned over the side to watch the wake as the ship moved dreamily on. With a metallic creak, a window from the captain's cabin beneath him opened. A hand crept through, clutching a page that glowed faintly in the light of the stars. He could just make out a ripped edge. The hand hesitated, then slowly drew back in with the paper still intact.

The sides of Dominic's lips lifted. And a little part of his soul whistled an old tune he hadn't sung in many years.

She hadn't thrown the drawing away.

CHAPTER 22

Georgana balanced a teacup in her hand as she climbed the ladder to the upper deck. The ship heaved to the side, and she paused to steady the dish. A little tea sloshed into the saucer. If her father got his hands messy, it would be his own fault for taking his morning tea on the quarterdeck.

"Careful, Taylor."

The unexpected voice brought Georgana's head up. "Fitz? Has Étienne given you leave to work?"

Fitz scratched his light hair with a shrug. "He says I'm well enough. My head isn't hurting as it used to." His teeth still whistled as he spoke. He kept his mouth half closed, trying to hide the missing tooth. When they arrived in Portsmouth, he could get a false one made, but he would never be the same.

"It must be a relief to be out of the sick bay," she said.

He glanced down toward the sick bay

beneath them. Even if he still wasn't well, she had the feeling Étienne would have approved him for work. With more than a quarter of the men unable to work, the ship needed as many hands as possible. If they should run into an enemy ship . . . Georgana didn't want to think about the results.

"It's good to see you up and about," she said.

He gave her a sharp look, then shrugged. "We both have duties to attend to."

Georgana remembered the cooling teacup in her hand. Fortunate for her, Papa was used to tepid tea. Fitz shuffled off before she could say anything more. She wondered if he still hated her or if they had moved to becoming neutral acquaintances.

She hurried up to the quarterdeck, where her father stood with a telescope to his eye. Moyle stood nearby, hands clasped behind him.

"I would have sworn it was a frigate yesterday," Papa muttered. "Now it looks to be a schooner."

Georgana could barely make out a speck on the horizon. Her insides wriggled at the sight of the other ship. Crossing paths with another ship rarely made for a pleasant day aboard a frigate of His Majesty's navy.

"She doesn't seem to be moving very

fast," Moyle said. "If we continue to lose her, she must not be in pursuit."

Papa snapped the telescope closed and exchanged it for his cup of tea. "We can only hope."

Georgana twisted her hands around the instrument, praying Moyle was right. While Jarvis would curse and shout about not getting any prizes this voyage, she didn't find prizes worth the loss of life.

"George, bring me Peyton," her father said, sipping at the now cold tea. "Moyle, you're dismissed. Get some rest before your watch."

"Yes, sir. Thank you."

She followed the second lieutenant down from the quarterdeck and then climbed up to the forecastle. Peyton stood at the bow, just like he'd done a few nights ago when they'd talked. She had hoped he would repeat the invitation for a midnight chat, but in the days since, he had hardly spoken to her.

She couldn't blame him. He had shared something so personal about himself with a mere ship's boy. Friends or not, she wondered if he regretted his decision to let her see a corner of his life he usually left covered.

The lieutenant stood with the triangular

sextant held to his eye. They sailed against the wind this morning, and the contrary breeze blew the tails of his blue coat out behind him. The brass buttons glimmered as they caught the sun. His brown hair rippled beneath his hat, and a hint of a smile graced his lips.

He fit naturally at the prow, as though he'd been written into the building plans and placed just so. A ship didn't need a figurehead if it could have a captain such as this. Why he hadn't received a promotion by now, she couldn't say, but a ship could not hope for a better commander than a Captain Peyton.

Peyton said something to the midshipman at his side, and the young man wrote quickly. Georgana waited a few paces away until he dismissed the midshipman to look up the numbers on charts to determine their location. She saluted as the young gentleman passed and again when Peyton turned to her.

"Ah, George. How are you?"

"The captain wishes to speak to you, sir."

He chuckled. "That did not answer my question."

"I am well, thank you." She pulled her lips into a frown, fearing they would do the opposite.

"I'm glad to hear it." He paused, and she waited with breath caught in her lungs for him to say more. But he walked away. Her posture slackened. She didn't know what else she had wanted him to say — how silly to have wanted more.

She fell in step behind him, and when they arrived on the quarterdeck, Étienne was speaking animatedly to her father. "They have all come from the same messes, five or six of them. Whole groups taken ill."

"You think it is food, then?" Peyton asked, putting a hand on the Frenchman's shoulder.

Not many members of the crew or wardroom treated the surgeon with such familiarity. The lieutenant had fought as many Frenchmen as any other man on board, and still he accepted this outsider with open arms.

"*Bien sûr,* the food."

Papa stroked his chin. "What does that mean for the crew?"

"We must inspect the food. Throw out the barrels already opened," Étienne said. "If we remove the bad food, we might see an end to the illness."

"The cook is not going to be happy about that." Her father nodded. "George, find Moyle again. I'll have him oversee the removal of the food. How many new sick crewmen today?"

"I have not seen one yet, sir," the surgeon responded.

Light touched Peyton's face at the news, and Georgana stared. She wanted to burn the image into her memory. With her meager skills, could she draw the hope that glowed behind that smile?

Papa blew out a long, slow breath. "Well, that is better news than we've had in some time. Thank you, Mr. Étienne. George?"

She snapped to attention, then hurried for the hatch to find Moyle. The sick still had far to go before they recovered, but perhaps the end was in sight.

Boisterous laughter hit her as she landed on the messdeck. Sailors were playing cards while waiting for their next watch. She almost ignored them, when her gaze fell on a well-tailored blue jacket in their midst.

Jarvis?

She crept closer. What was he doing here? Lieutenants didn't mingle with the rest of the crew on the messdeck. The men at his table all held mugs, attention fixed on the officer.

"You heard the surgeon's mate," Jarvis said. "Bad food."

"I don't see what the captain has to do

with it," one of the crewmen said.

Jarvis shifted on the bench, and Georgana leaned closer, crouching behind the nearest table. If he caught her listening . . .

"The captain's responsible for everything on this ship. If someone does their job poorly, and he doesn't reprimand them, is the fault not equally his?"

Georgana was hidden several tables down from Jarvis, on the other side of the aisle, but his words carried through the room.

"If the boatswain's son died of the same illness, the food must have been bad then as well. He's tried to poison the crew multiple times."

Her hands clenched into fists. Lies. She kept her head ducked behind the table, out of sight.

"Poison?"

"Why would the captain poison his own crew, sir?"

"He did not prevent the order of bad food," Jarvis said, retracing his steps.

The first man spoke up again. "If he didn't know it was bad, how can it be his fault?"

"Carelessness," Jarvis growled. "You've seen how he barricades himself in his quarters with that boy, not communicating, even with his officers. He allows the ward-room officers to do his responsibilities and doesn't inspect the warrant and petty officers' work. He's employed that Frenchman, who we all know couldn't care if we live or die."

"Étienne was pressed into service. I wouldn't doubt Captain's been fooled by the Frenchie," a new voice said. He sounded like the yeoman of the powder room. "What I've been wondering is how none of the officers have taken sick. If Mr. Jarvis is right, seems the captain's been skimping on the quality of the crew's food."

"I don't doubt it," Jarvis said. The pitch of his voice rose. "The officers have been dining like kings and not on our own funds."

Georgana wanted to scream. If the captain were only concerned about himself, why would he give such attention to the officers?

Footsteps on the ladder sent Georgana scrambling toward the wardroom. By the time she came back with Moyle, Jarvis had vanished from the messdeck. Thinking of his words made her insides contort.

When they reached the gun deck, Étienne's loblolly boy sprinted out of the sick bay, his face white as a sail.

"What is it, William?" Moyle asked, pausing with hands on the rungs of the ladder.

"Where is Monsieur?" The French came out awkwardly in the boy's cockney accent.

"He's above," Georgana said.

The boy barreled toward the ladder before she'd finished speaking, shouting, "It's Noyse!"

Another boy gone. Dominic pinched the bridge of his nose and closed his eyes, leaning into the bulwark. The steady creaking of the ship's hull rumbled through him, calming the anxious tension that had taken root within his heart. He didn't want to know how many would succumb to disease before they reached their destination. If he dwelled on speculations, he'd drive himself to distraction.

Not that he wasn't already preoccupied.

Dominic picked at a splinter on the rail. He usually enjoyed first watch. He liked the calmness of the black water and the moon reflecting on the crests of the waves. He liked the quiet of the ship and the murmur of men's voices as they sang songs or told stories in little circles across the upper deck.

And until Monday evening, he used the serenity of night to think. Now he thought only of Georgana Woodall standing beside him at the bow. Perhaps she infiltrated his mind because he worried about finding her a safe place to stay. He wasn't truly worried that his mother would refuse to help. She had put him up to this, after all. But what if Georgana refused his help? Or if her father believed he had some ulterior motive?

Dominic startled when his memory of Monday night materialized before him. Georgana walked quickly toward the prow, and for a moment he let himself enjoy it. He couldn't see her face in the shadows, but he imagined that elusive smile on her full lips.

"Are you well, sir?" She had asked him that question a thousand times since the onset of the disease.

"Of course. Are you?"

"I need to speak with you." Her voice trembled. Dominic straightened and reached a hand for her, but let it drop before he made contact.

"Is it Jarvis?"

"Yes, he . . ." She took a breath. "I overheard him talking in the mess with some of his division."

He blinked. What had possessed Jarvis to do that? He hadn't spent much time in the wardroom of late. He occasionally spent time with the marine second lieutenant, but he didn't seem the type to prefer common seamen's company to those of his station.

"He said awful things," she said.

"About you?" She'd survived awful things

being said about her before. And though it made his blood boil, he couldn't understand why it would upset her so much now.

"No, about the captain."

Dominic's shoulders relaxed. Jarvis hadn't threatened her. "Yes, I've heard that as well."

"But he blamed the captain for the illnesses."

"George, captains get blamed for many things outside of their control. It happens on ships. Do not let it worry you."

Georgana took a step back. "You think I shouldn't worry?"

She had sailed long enough — she should know that sometimes the small confines of a ship bred discontent. As the highest-ranking officer, the captain was often made a scapegoat when tensions heightened, but only in rare cases did it come to anything more than a meeting to discuss the issue. Good captains knew a crew with high morale performed better, and while he wasn't certain he would call Captain Woodall a *great* captain, the man certainly qualified as a good captain.

"All will be well. New illnesses have slowed, and Étienne will do all he can to care for the sick ones. Pearce and several others are on the mend already."

She retreated farther. "Sorry to bother

you, sir. Good night, sir."

A part of him wanted to beg her to stay, to spend a few more minutes talking in the dark. But before he could say or do anything, she had stolen down from the forecastle and was gone.

A hammock, its edges sewn shut around a still form, lay on the deck. Not even the wind moved it as it waited for the words of the chaplain. No more would the hammock hang in an orderly row, side by side with dozens exactly like it. Just another piece of canvas. Just another burial shroud.

Georgana didn't weep for the deaths anymore. They came too frequently. But she remembered every hammock that slid into the deep — every splash, every ripple as the ocean swallowed them. She recorded the deaths in her father's logbook, carving their names into her memory.

This burial could be only the beginning. She knew that. If Charlie Byam's illness was any indication, more deaths would come.

Étienne stood by himself, eyes on the closed hammock. No emotion marred his features, but his messy curls and disheveled clothes belied his state. He worked tirelessly to help the sufferers, and all he received in return was rumors and gossip.

296

Georgana ground her teeth and moved her gaze back to the deck at her feet. Lieutenant Peyton had greeted her when she came up that morning. She'd pretended not to hear, all while trying to convince herself not to blame him. He had curtly dismissed her worries over Jarvis's rumors about the captain, but she couldn't condemn the lieutenant for that. He didn't know the captain was her father.

The chaplain began his dour sermon, but his words drifted past her ears. The conversation with Peyton last night awakened her to the reality of her situation. She had let herself become too hopeful. For a few glorious weeks she'd nearly forgotten her disguise when in the lieutenant's presence. She had almost let herself believe there was something more between them.

Last night reminded her he did not understand, even if he seemed to. And continuing to hope for something that was impossible only risked her future. What would happen if she let her secret slip? No doubt he would be angry. She didn't think him petty enough to inform the crew, but Peyton's sense of honor would not allow him to treat her the same way he did before. He would treat her like a lady, and that would be enough to alert the other men.

At the end of the chaplain's words, Georgana said "Amen" with the rest of the gathering. John Noyse, ship's boy, third class. Then two men stepped up to lift him onto the board, covered in the Red Ensign. The board tilted, and the boy fell into the depths.

Georgana always looked for the other ship's boys at a burial for one of their own. Though she had little camaraderie with them, she knew they had a bond with each other. Not so hardened yet by sea life, true sorrow graced the young faces. Pearce, who had mostly recovered from the illness, slumped against the mainmast, face crumpling.

Before she could make her way to the boy, Fitz appeared and put a hand on his shoulder, as Georgana had done for him the day of Locke's death. A little flicker of pride swelled in her chest at Fitz's gesture. At the beginning of the voyage, she had not thought him capable of such compassion.

"We will not hold gun drills as usual today," her father announced gravely. "Wash your hammocks. Wash your clothes. We will resume drills Monday morning."

Lieutenant Jarvis rushed forward as the men dispersed. Georgana shrank back toward the quarterdeck to avoid him. "That is unwise, Captain. The men need practice."

Her father shook his head, brows lowered dangerously. "There are too many men unable to drill, and it is difficult to move seventy men from the sick bay just for gun practice."

"If we are attacked at reduced numbers, they need to be prepared," Jarvis said through clenched teeth. "What of the ship that's been following us?"

Georgana glanced to the west. She couldn't see anything on the horizon, but talk of a follower infiltrated every conversation on the *Deborah.*

"If she were a privateer, she'd be moving faster and would have engaged us by now." Her father drew himself up, nearly as tall as Peyton and much taller than Jarvis. "The men are tired. They need to rest and prepare for what lies ahead. We have many weeks to go."

Jarvis sneered. "Your giving them rest will not increase your favor with them, if that is your aim. An incompetent captain inspires disorder, and unstructured hours will only fan the flames." He turned on his heel and stormed off without a salute.

"Sir, that —" Peyton began from his side.

Papa held up a hand for silence. "He wants a battle. I will not give it to him on his terms."

Georgana avoided the lieutenant's face as she studied her father. He appeared so confident in handling Jarvis's insubordination, but he hadn't heard him spreading lies. Papa headed for the quarterdeck, and she followed behind him.

"George," Lieutenant Peyton said softly as she passed.

Once again she pretended not to hear, though it prompted an ache in her soul. Her father was right. Getting too close to the lieutenant had not been wise, and now she must suffer the consequences.

There were plenty of other boys on this ship he could take under his wing. He needn't miss her friendship, though she didn't think she could fill the void his warm smile would leave.

300

CHAPTER 23

Dominic rolled up the sleeves of his shirt and swung himself onto the foremast shroud. Hat and coat stowed safely in his cabin, he launched himself up the rows of ratlines with ease. A playful breeze rocked the lines as he climbed.

Too soon he reached the foretop platform. Up the next ladder to the higher platform he went. He didn't know what possessed him to climb that morning after his watch. When he reached the highest point on the mast, he did not stop to behold the breathtaking expanse of ocean. With a nod to the watchman, he turned around and climbed back down to the deck, then crossed the forecastle to the opposite shroud and started up again.

Heat ignited in the muscles of his arms and legs, slowly growing into a weary burn. At the top, he ignored the wary look of the watchman and immediately descended. His breath quickened. The rough lines bit into his hands. He could feel the stares of crew members as he jumped to the deck and trekked across to the other shroud.

He hoped the exercise would rid him of the looming realization he refused to acknowledge. The disappointment in her face yesterday morning would not leave his mind. She had very clearly been avoiding him since their encounter on the forecastle Thursday night. What he'd said had not pleased her.

Dominic's arms shook on his way down, slowing his breakneck pace. The pull in his shoulders and sides slowed him more. He sucked in the briny air, but it did nothing to rejuvenate him. When had his beloved sea stopped mending all that was wrong in his life?

Are you well, sir? She'd asked him that so many times.

"I certainly am not," he grumbled aloud.

At the foretop he stopped and collapsed onto the platform. His limbs cried out at their mistreatment. He hadn't climbed the shroud so many times in a row since his midshipman days.

Dominic wound his hand through one of the lines for stability, then closed his eyes. The *Deborah* swayed beneath him, the movement enhanced by his position on the mast. He wished the oscillating would alleviate the turbulence within him, like a mother hushing a child in a cradle.

How had he let it come to this — thinking of Georgana at all hours, getting distracted when he should be focusing on running the ship? She had been avoiding him for a day and a half now, and it was driving him mad. If she did not want to be with him, he would not force her. And yet he missed their interactions, more than he liked to admit. He wanted to tease out that elusive smile again.

The wind tore at his shirt, billowing it around him. His sweat dried at the wind's cold touch. It was easy to forget the seasons at sea. In England the leaves would be changing color now. His mother wouldn't see them well from the house in Portsmouth, not like she had at his father's estate. Back then, Dominic hadn't brought her shells, stones, and sea glass. Acorns and vibrant leaves had been the tokens of his adventures at the estate, and she had kept them in her private parlor, tucked out of sight from the rest of the world.

How could he make room for another woman in his heart, no matter how deserving? His primary duty was to his mother.

She had spent so many years forgotten by his father — Dominic couldn't forget her. She needed him more than she needed a daughter.

Georgana didn't need him. She had her father, and Dominic couldn't argue Captain Woodall's devotion. He'd gone to great lengths to protect his daughter, even backing down from battle to keep her safe.

Dominic opened his eyes and watched the spray rising around the bow of the ship. Surely everyone would be better to disembark as they'd boarded — unattached. The thought of not seeing Georgana again shot pain through his heart. She had ruined the sea for him. Could he ever sail without memories of her haunting every part of the ship? He would never stand at the bow without remembering her soft touch on his arm as he poured out his soul.

He clapped a hand to his forehead, then let it spill down the side of his face. His gut wound in an eager twist as he finally let the looming knowledge crash over him.

He was in love.

But the sea — she had always been his one love. He didn't need another woman.

Yet for all her beauties, the sea did not satisfy him like a few minutes with Georgana did. He ran a hand through his hair, stopping to tug at the ends, as he enjoyed watching Georgana do. He dropped his hand to his lap.

So he loved Georgana. What was he to do about that? Nothing. He couldn't change their interactions now that his heart had made up its mind. That would have to wait until they got to shore in more than a month. He didn't know if he could keep this strange sensation captive for so long.

The breath expelled from his lungs. He hadn't a clue how to love a lady. By the time of Dominic's birth, his father had fallen out of love with the sweetheart of his youth, blinded by his new fortune and her low birth.

Dominic leaned his head back against the mast. Creaking rumbled up through the wood's grains and into his skull. His brother, nearly as distant as his father, had married after Dominic went to sea. And he did not consider the common escapades of seamen and officers as valid examples of how to love a woman.

With a groan, he made for the shroud to drag his tired body back to his cabin. His limbs were loath to move again. Hand over hand he lowered himself down to the deck.

He loved Georgana Woodall. His lips crept upward. Somehow it felt wonderful to finally think it. He couldn't say what would happen, but for now he enjoyed the uncertain glow that flickered inside.

At the entrance to the wardroom, Georgana straightened and cleared her mind. She had to guard herself against the two lieutenants sitting at the table before her. She didn't know which she feared more just now, the glare or the grin.

Both looked up when she entered. They sat on opposite ends of the table, Peyton studying charts and Jarvis studying his drink. Peyton's face softened.

Georgana swallowed. She touched her thumb and forefinger to where the brim of her cap should have been. "The captain sent me to inform you he will dine in the wardroom tomorrow evening for Trafalgar Night."

"To celebrate true heroes, unlike himself," Jarvis muttered under his breath.

Peyton's hands tensed on the table, but he didn't favor Jarvis with a response. "Does he wish to see the menu?"

"He trusts your judgment," she said. Peyton's brow lifted at her answer.

"I will write it out for him all the same." He pulled a paper from under his maps. The corner had been torn off, the rip the inverse shape of the scrap she hid in her sea chest. She didn't like to admit how many times she'd pulled the note out to gaze at it.

She squirmed as his hand moved across the page. Even though he wrote slowly, the letters looked rushed. They matched their writer's windswept hair and rumpled shirt. His cravat hung loose and untidy. His sleeves were rolled up to his elbows, and no jacket or waistcoat was in sight.

"You'll excuse my state — I just climbed the shroud," he said quietly. He'd caught her staring. Her face flamed.

Peyton set down his pen and pushed back his chair. He looked as though he wanted to say something but closed his mouth and held out the list.

Georgana grasped the paper, prepared to run from the room. But before she could take a step, the deck pitched, sending her stumbling to the side. Her shoe caught a fastening in the deck, and she went sprawling across the lieutenant's lap. His arm flashed out to catch her. For a moment their wide eyes locked as he held her, her head cradled in the crook of his arm. His skin was warm against the back of her neck.

He was holding her.

She yelped and rolled to the floor. Her head bashed against the table on her way down and sparks flashed through her vision. She moaned, curling into a ball and holding her bruised crown. Heat crept up to her ears.

"Clumsy oaf," Jarvis said.

"Are you all right, George?" Peyton reached to help her up.

She pulled herself to hands and knees, blinking against the pain. Her throat tightened. She wanted to stay curled under the table. Maybe sink into the deck. She crawled out, brushing against his knee and past his outstretched hand.

A steadying touch on her back sent shivers along her spine. Falling into his lap was not the way to distance herself. She scrambled away.

"Are you hurt?" Peyton's hand still hung in the air, extended toward her.

"He's fine," Jarvis said.

Georgana shook her head and held up the paper to block her face. "I'll take this to the captain." Then she ran, before any sudden movements threw her back into his arms.

CHAPTER 24

Even though Georgana had already eaten, the smell of the officers' Trafalgar dinner wafting through the wardroom made her mouth water. Steam from salty beef, fresh rolls, and boiled potatoes rose from the officers' plates. A great pudding graced the center of the table, its fruity gems glistening in the light of a dozen lanterns.

She stood beside the door to Peyton's cabin, in reach in case her father should need something. That put her in plain sight of the first lieutenant, sitting to the captain's right. She should have stood on the other side. Staring at the back of his brown hair was easier than trying to avoid staring into his hazel eyes.

The wardroom buzzed with conversation. There hadn't been so big a gathering of officers since setting sail from Portsmouth in July. Several of the midshipmen joined the feast. Only two officers were absent — Jarvis, who had taken the watch, and Étienne. She imagined it uncomfortable for the Frenchman to celebrate the defeat of his homeland. He had excused himself, insisting he was needed in the sick bay.

Peyton stayed curiously quiet most of the meal. He generally loved the mealtime banter. His face often lit up as he conversed with his fellow officers. Now he mostly stared down at his plate, cutting his meat with precision. Each time his eyes lifted, she tore her gaze away. If her father hadn't insisted she come to assure him of her safety, she would have stayed behind in the main cabin. Just watching Peyton made her heart beat too fast for comfort.

It wasn't as though she could truly escape him on this ship. That wouldn't come until England. Until then she needed to learn how to remain firm, despite her longing.

The pudding was cut, and the aroma of sweet spices filled the wardroom. Georgana drank them in. The hasty puddings Cook had made for her and the rest of the crew had not smelled as rich.

She shifted to ease the strain on her feet. This dinner had lasted longer than her father's dinners with the lieutenants, and her hammock called to her from the deck above. Soon, she assured herself, as the last few officers finished their helpings of pudding. Soon she would escape his attention and guide her thoughts to safer harbors.

Her father cleared his throat. "Tonight we commemorate the sacrifice of British sailors who did not shirk their duty." Peyton's head lowered. "Sailors and marines who stood between their country and the enemy, that their families might not taste the devastation now surging through Europe. We remember with gratitude their leader, *our* leader, who would not sit idly by when someone threatened those he loved."

A lump formed in Georgana's throat. Papa had sacrificed and worried so much over her protection, but he would never be recognized for it.

Peyton watched the captain with a peculiar look on his face, as though he saw something different from the others in the gathering.

Papa lifted his glass, the liquid inside notably clearer than the others. The officers followed suit. Peyton's glass looked as full as when he'd first sat down.

"To the immortal memory of Admiral Lord Nelson and those who gave all for their king, their country, and their families," the captain said.

"To Lord Nelson!"

The gathering drank deeply from their glasses, except Peyton who barely allowed his drink to wet his lips. As glasses returned to the table, he kept his in hand. His chest expanded, pulling his waistcoat tight across it.

"Kind friends and companions, come, join me in rhyme."

Georgana jumped as the melody drifted from the lieutenant's mouth. *"Come, lift up your voices in chorus with mine."* Clear and strong, the words slid over the lilting notes with practiced ease. *"Come, lift up your voices, no grief to refrain. For we may or might never all meet here again."*

His voice stilled the room, as though he'd caught all in a trance. She froze, back pressed against the door of his cabin. His voice was gentle, imploring. It made her heart ache with its bittersweet tones as he sang the chorus.

"Here's a health to the company, and one for my lass. Let us drink to good fortune, all out of one glass.

Come, lift up your voices, no grief to refrain, For we may or might never all meet here again."

She recognized the tune. It was an Irish one the crew sang on occasion. She liked it better the way Peyton sang it, with sincerity

312

rather than raucous laughter.

Peyton's gaze grew distant. *"Here's a health to the dear lass that I love so well. For style and for beauty, there's none can excel."*

What woman graced his memory? How she wished he could look at her with the admiration that shone in his features just now. She flinched at the pang that reverberated through her. This. This was why she needed to distance herself. Loving Lieutenant Peyton would only lead to disappointment.

"There's a smile on her countenance as she sits upon my knee." Peyton's lips twitched mischievously. *"And there's no one in this wide world as happy as me."*

The officers joined him in the chorus, their voices rumbling across the deck. The sound might have stirred her soul, had her soul not been smarting from the thoughts she allowed through her mind. She needed to leave. It was close enough to the end of the dinner that her father shouldn't worry about her being alone too long in the dark. She glanced once more at Peyton.

"Here's a health to the company." His eyes locked on hers. *"And one for my lass."* He nodded ever so slightly toward her, lifting his glass. Her heart leaped into her throat.

She didn't hear the rest of the chorus,

even as she watched his grinning lips form the words. Heat drained from her face. She tried to step back, rattling the door with her movement.

Run, her head screamed.

Her feet obliged. So caught up in the song, the officers paid no notice to her flight. She flung herself up the ladder faster than she had at any other time during her sojourn at sea. From his post, the marine narrowed his eyes as she bolted past him into the main cabin and slammed the door.

Faint moonlight from the windows fell on the table in the center of the shadowy room. She'd cleared it before they went to the wardroom, but now something sat in the pale light on its surface. Peyton's voice filtered through the boards below her feet.

"Our ship lies at harbor. She's ready to dock. I wish her safe landing, without any shock."

Georgana's shaking hands lifted the flask from the table. She pulled out the stopper. The sharp perfume of tangy limes wafted through the cabin. When had he brought this here?

"And if ever I should meet you by land or by sea, I will always remember your kindness to me."

She brought the flask to her lips and sipped the brilliance of secluded lagoons and Caribbean sunsets. Had he figured out her secret? Surely her mind played tricks. Had she imagined the smile, the pointed nod? No one else seemed to see it.

He couldn't have figured it out. In three years, no one had. She held the flask, cooled from the chill of the captain's quarters, to her brow. It brought minimal relief to her burning face.

If he disclosed any of his suspicions to others in the crew . . . Georgana flinched. Her knees started to buckle as she staggered to her hammock. If word got out, she would be ruined. Her father could face a court-martial.

Peyton wouldn't do that, would he?

She sat and swung her legs into the hammock with the flask still nestled in her hands. The hammock swished back and forth.

"For we may or might never all meet here again."

In the wardroom, the last muted notes of the song fizzled out. She took another sip of the lime water. Her lovesick heart had pushed her to see things she longed to see. Yes, that had to be the answer. As brilliant as Peyton was about the sea, she didn't think he knew very much about women.

Except perhaps the mysterious woman he

had alluded to before — the one he probably sang about tonight. Georgana flumped back. The tenderness in his voice as he sang the lines about the dear lass sent her heart in a downward spiral.

She pushed herself up on one elbow, making the hammock swing. When he had sung those last words before she rushed out, he did not have a moonstruck look. Those eyes glittered with amusement. And stared directly at her.

Blast that lieutenant.

She dropped back to her pillow and curled up on one side, the flask of lime clutched in her arms. There was only one way to be certain how much he knew and calm her racing mind. Tomorrow, she had to confront him, but she would have to do so without giving her identity away, if he didn't already know.

Georgana closed her drooping eyes, tartness still clinging to her tongue. She didn't know how she would ask. She only hoped tomorrow would bring a plainer view of the situation. As she dozed, her subconscious hummed Peyton's song, swirling it about her head until it filled her dreams.

For we may or might never all meet here again.

■ ■ ■ ■

Pounding in his temples woke Dominic. The blackness of his cabin told him he'd awoken far too early for his forenoon watch. He would have turned over and tried to sleep again, but images of last night's Trafalgar commemoration bounded into his mind.

He'd heard of men being fools in love, but he hadn't expected to throw all care to the wind a mere day after realizing love was the cause of his jumbled emotions. She'd seen his acknowledgment, and she'd run.

The pounding continued but not from his head. Dominic sat up. Drums.

The screech of the boatswain's whistle pierced the frantic beat. Shouts of "Ship!" rolled through the messdeck, dampened by the bulwark between the wardroom and the rest of the deck.

Dominic jolted from his cot and fumbled for his sea chest in the dark. He could hear men breaking down the collapsible barriers already. He shoved two unfinished letters lower in the chest as he pulled out his coat and other effects. Though he had hoped to finish the messages before the next battle, he would have to pray he had the time to finish them later.

He strapped the holster for his pistol across his chest, then covered it with his coat. His fingers brushed the patch Georgana had mended. Nearly over his heart.

Where was she? He buckled on his cutlass, removed a folded page from his other coat, and slammed the lid of his trunk. A waft of lime swirled up from the little garland he had purchased for his mother. He shook his head, dismissing memories of the tropical sunset and slid the square of paper into his coat pocket. Bicorn tucked under his arm, he ran from the room.

He nearly knocked over a wide-eyed Georgana on the gun deck. His hands caught her elbows to keep her upright. What was she doing here? She should already have gone below. His grip tightened around her.

"You're going to the powder room?" he asked.

"Peyton!" someone shouted down the hatch from the upper deck.

"I need to speak with you after," she said, fingers digging into the sleeves of his coat.

"Yes." He pulled himself away before he could kiss her furrowed brow. Not now. He needed his wits.

Dominic pulled on his hat upon reaching the main level and strode for the quarterdeck on Moyle's heels. The captain barked orders. Midshipmen scattered over the deck toward their assignments.

"Whom do we face, sir?" Dominic asked. "Is it the American merchant again?" He blinked. The barest hint of morning light from behind him caught the sheets of not one but two vessels bearing down on them. The stiff wind filled their sails. Around the deck of the *Deborah,* men shouted and pulled at lines.

"Have them wet the sails," Captain Woodall said, raising the telescope. "I want to outrun them as long as we can. Get some light before we do battle."

Dominic relayed the orders, then returned to the captain's side. "How did they catch us in the dark?"

The captain shrugged. "Last night we probably had enough lanterns on deck to alert any ship within thirty miles."

The risk of celebrating at sea.

"They'll come along either side," Captain Woodall said. "Prepare the crew for an all-out attack."

"Yes, sir." Surrounded. Dominic fought to keep his hand from tugging at his stock. He couldn't let the crew see anything but confidence. The *Deborah* outgunned the privateers, but in the chaos of firing guns from both port and starboard sides, anything could happen.

The captain grabbed his arm before he left. "Where is George?" The strain in his voice echoed Dominic's own fears.

"I sent him to the powder room."

They both knew the order wouldn't necessarily keep her there. But with both of them needed on the quarterdeck, it was the best they could do. How strange, to care so much for a person Captain Woodall also held dear. Dominic had never experienced the camaraderie of protecting someone else. He'd always been on his own.

"He'll be fine," Dominic said. He clapped the captain's arm. "We're in far more danger up here than he will be."

Captain Woodall nodded. "Carry on."

CHAPTER 25

Georgana didn't stay in the powder room long. With almost sixty men still down with the sickness, how could she? A few were trying to fight through their malady, but most were safely deposited in the cockpit. The help of every healthy person was needed.

Very little light touched the gun deck, only enough to see faceless shapes. Lanterns were forbidden. One overturned candle in the chaos of battle, and the whole ship could go up in flames.

"No more powder," came the order when Georgana deposited her load. Gun crews on both sides of the ship crouched in readiness. She'd never experienced a battle on both sides. Her dry mouth made it difficult to swallow.

She followed the other powder monkeys to their stations near the center of the gun deck. No one spoke. She met Fitz's eyes, barely visible in the twilight. For all his earlier bravado, she could feel his terror.

The ship pulsed with it.

Against her will, her mind fled to Lushill House — the soft greenery of the gardens, the serene architecture. If she wanted a better chance of seeing that place again, that place of so many bittersweet memories, she should have stayed in the powder room.

She chewed the corner of her bottom lip to distract herself from the quaking inside.

Jarvis uttered a long string of curses. Dominic almost joined him.

The glow of morning had increased enough to see the enormous flags flying from the approaching vessels. Blue, white, red.

The third lieutenant lowered the telescope and slammed it into Dominic's waiting hand. "It's the *St. Germain* and the *Intelligence.* I told you we should have taken the *Intelligence.* Now we get to suffer from *your* lack of intelligence."

"It can't be." Dominic raised the instrument to his eye. The *Intelligence* had been American. He sighted the frigate. It certainly appeared to be their previous foe.

Twenty-eight guns on the *St. Germain.* A thirty-eight-gun frigate like the *Deborah* should have the advantage, but add the ten

322

or twelve guns of its schooner companion . . .

He set his jaw. It would be a fair fight.

He scanned the deck of the smaller boat,
looking for a sign that Jarvis's assumption
was right. The crew looked to be an unas-
suming mixture of nationalities, like many
crews. He dropped the telescope to the man
at the wheel, and his fingers contracted
around the shaft. Thick red hair topped the
burly man's head. Dominic remembered the
stammering captain. Now the man shouted,
but he didn't seem to be in charge. The
dark-featured man, who had acted as a mate
when Dominic inspected their cargo, was
giving orders and striding the forecastle.

They'd been fooled.

"It is the *Intelligence*." His stomach tightened, as though it had been rammed into
the barrel of a cannon. He'd walked that
boat. He'd heard the odd accent of the real
captain pretending to be a first mate and
the uncertainty of the American acting as
though he was in charge. The red-haired
man was probably the only American that
ship had on board. And they'd duped him.
Rice and tobacco. No doubt they had only
enough to make a convincing storeroom.

Dominic spun on his heel and raced to
where Captain Woodall stood with the sail-

ing master, Mr. Jordan. The ship hadn't come up to speed as quickly as they had hoped.

"The *St. Germain* and the *Intelligence*," Dominic said.

The captain's eyes closed. They should have listened to Jarvis. The lieutenant would gloat when this was over.

"If every man does his duty, we will see this through," Captain Woodall said.

Dominic nodded. The flags that bore Nelson's last message to his men as they sailed toward the Battle of Trafalgar waved in his mind. *England expects that every man will do his duty.* How many men, like him, drew strength from that phrase?

A pop echoed across the water, and as one, the entire crew hit the deck. The cannonball whistled harmlessly off the larboard side. Dominic's mind shifted, more slowly than usual, into its practiced numbness.

"Turn her about," the captain shouted. "To your post, Jarvis. Ready a broadside and load the chase guns. We need to throw as much as we can at them before we're surrounded."

The third lieutenant ran for the hatch. Dominic almost followed him to check that Georgana wasn't with the powder monkeys. Instead he turned and relayed the wearing orders to the crew. She'd told him she'd go to the orlop deck, had she not? He couldn't remember.

Seamen drew in the sails above him. They couldn't run anymore. Now was the time to stand and fight.

Georgana gripped the ladder as the boy above her swung his feet. He'd already kicked her face twice, and they had only made it to the messdeck.

Someone had called for more ammunition, even though the ship hadn't fully turned yet. She moved more slowly than usual, not wanting to put up too much powder at once. Some of the boys moved at regular pace, mindlessly following the ill-advised orders. They were on their third round of powder as though in the midst of battle already.

A broadside shot from above rocked the ship back. She braced herself against the next ladder, then mounted and continued her journey. Now they could move at normal speed, though with all crews working short-handed, loading would take longer than usual.

Darkness still prevailed on the gun deck, but they were starting to see clearer. The gun crews' faces glowed blue in the light of the rising sun seeping through the ports around the cannons. Midshipmen snapped orders, and powder monkeys scuttled about to avoid getting trampled.

Georgana set down her cartridges. With two enemy ships, this battle could last hours. She jumped to her feet and ran for the hatch.

Her head didn't turn at the boom — not until it knocked her flat. She skittered across the deck, bowling into men and boys. Arms and legs, waistcoats and petticoat breeches, lay in a jumbled mess across the floor.

Smoke filled the room. Georgana's ears whined so loudly they nearly blocked the cry, "Fire! Fire on the gun deck!"

She pushed herself away from another stunned powder monkey and cringed at the burning in her palms. They bled through the dust and powder coating her skin. She stared, her brain not engaging. What . . . ?

Someone grasped her under the arms and hoisted her up. Fitz shook her shoulders. "Fire!" She saw his lips move more than heard him.

Fire.

Flames licked the deck, and men beat them with shirts and jackets, whatever they had. Guns abandoned, crew members ran for the elm-tree pump to fill buckets. Lifeless bodies lay scattered across the floor.

Fitz dragged her to the messdeck to get out of the way of the men fighting the fire. Crewmen laden with bleeding comrades eased down the ladders toward the surgeon on the orlop deck.

Too much powder. They'd had too much powder. Fitz shook her again. "Are you hurt, George?"

Despite her stinging hands, she moved her head slowly left and right.

"Good. Come on," he said as though the explosion hadn't happened and men weren't lying dead on the floor above them.

They headed for the magazine and more powder.

CHAPTER 26

Dawn brought clearer views and smoke rising from the hatchway. The crank of the elm-tree pump beat time with the steps of men towing buckets down to the gun deck. Cannon fire punctuated the steady rhythm, its thunder reverberating up through Dominic's shoes.

The *Deborah* rocked back and forth each time a ball hit her hull. The *Intelligence* had ridden up on the larboard side. She didn't have many guns but enough to drive the carpenter's crew across the ship patching holes. The *St. Germain* had neared, placing the *Deborah* in range of the French ship's twelve-pounders, though she'd already used the swivel gun at her bow to inflict damage to the *Deborah*'s mizzenmast.

Dominic ran across the deck, shouting orders to the midshipmen for how to set their guns. He couldn't stop moving. Stopping would give him time to think about the fire on the gun deck. Though she was supposed to be two decks below it, the blaze started near the bow of the ship, just above Georgana's position in the powder room.

They'll put it out, he told himself repeatedly, trying not to let the fears consume him.

The *St. Germain*'s masts nodded toward them as the ship sailed closer. The large French flag snapped defiantly.

"Give them a broadside the moment she's in line," Captain Woodall said, voice tight. His gaze kept darting to the hatchway's smoke.

"Yes, sir."

A ruddy head lifted through the hatch before Dominic could give the command. Captain Woodall jumped toward the edge of the quarterdeck, eyes piercing.

The crack of another round of enemy fire echoed across the water.

"Back to your post, Jarvis!" the captain screamed, jabbing a finger at the lieutenant in the hatchway.

Grapeshot whizzed past Dominic's face, its hot lead beating the air against his skin. His eyes clenched, and he waited for the pain of a piece hitting its mark. But that was not the shock he should have been bracing for.

Dominic heard a scream that rattled his

soul, and his eyelids flew open to splinters and rope raining down on the quarterdeck over a writhing figure. Blood stained the sawdust and planks beneath a mangled hand.

"Captain!" Dominic dropped to his knees. The whites of the man's wide eyes shone in the growing light.

Jarvis ran up. "Stupid oaf, I came to tell him the fire is out."

Dominic ground his teeth. "Stow it, Jarvis," he said, jaw taut. Jarvis withered under his glare. "Take him below."

Jarvis was the last person he wished to entrust the captain to, but Dominic had to stay on the quarterdeck. Someone must be in command.

Dominic shouted for sailors from the surrounding gun crews, and they lifted the battered captain from the deck and eased him toward the hatch.

Dominic had watched this scene before. It had played over and over through his mind for months. A different captain, a different ship, but both then and now Dominic was left alone on the quarterdeck with three hundred men at his command. Only this time it wasn't just the captain who was wounded. It was Georgana's father.

Dominic caught the arm of a powder

330

monkey running past. "Find George Taylor in the magazine. Send him to the surgeon."

"Yes, sir!"

The boy ran off after the men carrying Captain Woodall. The captain's eyes were closed, and he pressed his arm into his stomach. Crimson stained his waistcoat and jacket.

Dominic's heart begged him to run for Georgana himself, but his feet stayed planted. Now was not the time. He was acting captain, not a lovesick lieutenant. With all his fortitude, he slammed an iron door shut against the impulse and let his battle instincts take over.

"Run out the guns!" he cried. "Fire!"

White smoke filled the air, heralding the start of his command.

Georgana met them on the ladder. For a moment she stared, not comprehending the scene before her. Jarvis hauling her father down to the orlop. She saw red. So much red.

"George!" Jarvis snapped. "Back to your duty." He guided the group holding Papa toward the ladder to the orlop.

Georgana's feet didn't move. Her stomach heaved. She couldn't . . .

"Lieutenant Peyton wants him to go with

the captain," one of the boys said, coming down on the heels of the group.

Jarvis's eyes flashed. He quit his position, making the men stumble under her father's weight. Georgana dashed in. She didn't ease the load of the sturdy crewmen much, but she helped keep her father steady.

The third lieutenant stood to the side, watching the struggle. Hot indignation, thicker than the smoke that filled the gun deck, billowed inside her. She urged to launch herself at the smirking officer.

"Come, sir," she said quietly to her father as they descended. "Étienne will help you." The deep lines across Papa's face wrenched at her heart. Though partially covered, she could see the mutilated flesh of his arm. Could this much blood have come just from his hand?

Scorched and broken men filled the surgeon's workroom. The curly haired Frenchman quickly tied off a bandage before running to the captain's side. "Here. Put him here."

They laid her father on a stained table amid a display of surgeon's tools. Georgana balked at the sight of their sharp edges.

"My arm," Papa wheezed. "My arm."

Étienne took one look and turned, motioning to his mate. "The arm, it has to come off." A mate jumped forward to grab straps to secure Papa to the table.

"It . . . what?" Georgana's tiny voice got lost in the groans of the wounded around them. They couldn't take his arm. How would he function as a captain? He wouldn't be able to write. Grandmother would shame him. What sort of life could he lead? "No, you can't!"

Étienne glowered. "If I do not take the arm, infection will eventually take his life. Plenty of men will line up behind him waiting for my care. Will you help, or must I send you out?"

"George," her father whispered. He panted under the straps the surgeon's mate tightened about him. Étienne made a cut in the sleeve of her father's coat and tore it off.

Georgana flinched at the callousness. Her eyes burned. She wasn't supposed to be here. She should be sitting at Lushill in the breakfast room listening to Grandmother's shrieking and the clinking of china. She should be a young lady, naive and sheltered from the horrors of the world.

But she wasn't a lady. She had seen war and helped fuel cannons that maimed and destroyed. She didn't fit into the genteel life anymore, and she didn't fit into this one either.

Her fingernails dug into her palms. Papa needed her. She pushed herself forward to the end of the table and knelt. "I'm here." She put a hand on his head. Her chin trembled. "I'm here."

She closed her eyes and ducked her head, steeling herself as the surgeon took Papa's strong arm that had lifted her to his shoulders in the few happy moments of her childhood, and sawed it away.

CHAPTER 27

Georgana carefully lowered her father onto the makeshift bed in the corner of the carpenter's workshop with the help of a blood-covered surgeon's mate. The young man retreated quickly, leaving her and Papa alone in the dark room. Here the deck didn't rock so violently with the ship's movement. Walls muted sounds of wounded and dying men. Bringing him to the workshop was the best she could do.

She moved the little lantern she'd found in the room to a secure place near him. Then she sat on the floor to watch. His shuddering breaths had strengthened a little since the trauma of surgery. She couldn't break her gaze away from the knob that ended just above where his elbow should have been.

"The ship," he said. His eyes stayed closed. "The fire."

She took his shaking hand, the only one

he had left. "The fire is gone. The deck was damaged, but the men worked fast enough that it didn't eat down to the messdeck."

"Thank the heavens."

"Would you like something for the pain?" she asked, thinking of their brandy stores. He gave one curt shake of his head.

"Please, sir." *Papa.* "You're hurting."

"I will not put you in danger."

Georgana rested her forehead against her knees. Of all the times to risk revealing their secret, now was it. What crew member would think twice about a wounded, delirious captain talking about his daughter?

Papa lay silent for several minutes, and she hoped he was dozing. Soon she'd need to go for a blanket. His skin was hot and slick now, but she didn't want him to catch cold in the chill of the orlop.

"Peyton is commanding?" her father asked.

"Yes." Walking the same deck where Papa had suffered his wound. She murmured a prayer, not knowing if it would ascend past the carnage of the upper decks. *Please, keep him from harm.*

Dominic whirled as Moyle met him on the quarterdeck. "Gather a boarding party for the *Intelligence.*"

The second lieutenant glanced at the floundering ship off the larboard rail. Its crew frantically hacked at the grappling hooks slowly pulling them toward the *Deborah.* "She hasn't struck her colors, sir." Indeed, the French flag still waved behind the *Intelligence.*

Dominic clapped him on the shoulder. "She will soon. Or you will do it for her."

"Yes, sir," Moyle said through a grin.

"Once we silence those guns, we'll double our efforts on the *St. Germain.*" The French frigate had drifted out of range to regroup but kept launching periodic shots. Geysers exploded up from the sea around them. "What say you to a pair of prizes for the return journey?"

The lieutenant's smile widened. "I don't think even Jarvis could frown at that." Moyle hurried away to gather his party, and Dominic turned to the mizzenmast. A cannonball had taken a bite from the side of the mast and wreaked havoc in the rigging. Mr. Byam stood aloft, untangling and fixing the lines. Too much pull in one direction or another could topple the already weakened spar. They could sail with two masts, but not well.

"Hold her steady, Mr. Fitz," Dominic said as he passed by the wheel. The coxswain nodded.

Dominic could practically taste the victory. The *Deborah* had sustained damage in the hour and a half since the first broadside, but much of it had been to her masts, yards, and rigging — all of it difficult to repair, but none of it a threat to the immediate safety of the ship. The *St. Germain,* however, had taken several hard hits at the waterline. Her pumping crews would be working frantically to clear the flooding.

Just as the sun burst up from the horizon, he ordered men to fire a volley at the *St. Germain* from the long-range cannons. The sailors cheered. The deck shook as the long guns let go their loads. At least one shot hit the *St. Germain.*

Yes, they would win the day. Dominic brushed a trickle of sweat from his cheek. When he glanced down, a smear of blood lined his hand. Blasted debris.

"She's coming back around!"

To his right, the enemy frigate pulled in, as though on course to collide with the *Deborah.* "Ready a broadside," he said, then turned to the opposite rail. The captain of the *Intelligence* raced aft and pulled down the French flag in surrender as Moyle and his party climbed aboard with pistols raised.

A midshipman ran up beside Dominic.

"The *St. Germain* is leaving, sir."

He swore. The French ship intended to turn tail, bold enough to start a row but not honorable enough to finish it. They couldn't cut the *Intelligence* off and give chase now, not with Moyle and his group aboard. The *St. Germain* lumbered just out of range of the *Deborah*'s eighteen-pounders, tacking south. She rode much lower in the water than she had almost two hours ago.

"Fire the long guns until she's out of their range."

On the main deck of the *Intelligence* below, the captain handed his sword over to Moyle. The decimated crew drew together behind him, their red-headed pretender nowhere in sight. Dominic couldn't believe he'd mistaken them for Americans. They were almost as obviously French as Georgana was female. The corner of his lip curled.

The popping of faraway cannon signaled that the *St. Germain* hadn't quite given up, or at least the privateer wanted to leave behind as much destruction as possible. It was to be a battle of the long guns until she finished tacking and moved away.

Dominic strode toward the starboard rail. They'd send their own parting gift. "Ready the —"

An ear-splitting crack cut off his words. Wood flew in all directions, and he threw up his hands to shield his face. The *St. Germain* wasn't finished. He tried to draw breath to shout his command again.

No air came. Only blinding pain, searing through his side.

Dominic hit the deck, splinters digging into his palms. His lungs beat uselessly as they fought to pull in the sweet ocean air. Roaring in his ears drowned out the crash that shook the deck beneath his hands and knees.

A little air seeped in. Not enough. He gasped, digging his fingers into the sawdust that coated the deck.

Distant shouting circled him. The stabbing agony in his side wouldn't let the words through the haze. The deck jumped beneath him. Feet pounded. A cold wind touched his face. He tried to draw it in, but it wriggled away.

He let his head drop to the rough planks beneath his quaking limbs.

One thought flashed through his clouded brain. Georgana. Where was Georgana?

CHAPTER 28

Shouts of victory reverberated through the orlop deck as Georgana scurried for the captain's storeroom to retrieve the brandy. It had taken almost an hour to convince her father to take something for the pain.

Deep inside, Georgana wavered. The sight of her father collapsed on the deck, shaking from the ache of the missing arm, still muddied her mind.

Yelling carried down the ladder, and several men heaved someone to the orlop as she passed. She darted down the corridor toward the storeroom, gaze trained on the ground.

More wounded. More dead. She'd seen enough already to haunt her the rest of her life.

Her legs wobbled as she moved. The lantern pulled down on her hand as though it held a cannonball instead of a candle. She sighed, attempting to quiet her skittish heart in the shadows of the orlop. All would end soon if the shouts of triumph could be believed. In no time they would have the captain's cabin restored, and she could begin properly caring for Papa.

She stopped outside the storeroom door and pulled the key from her pocket. The marine usually on guard was above with his comrades, defending the deck. She held the lantern up before she entered the storeroom, disrupting a rat nibbling something on the floor. Her footsteps sent the rat scampering away.

The memory of Peyton's wide eyes when the rat had jumped out of his sea chest relieved some of her anguish. She moved to the back of the room to the meager store of bottles nestled in straw-filled boxes. No doubt they owed this victory to the first lieutenant.

She longed to see him, to gain strength from that reassuring grin. But he wouldn't have time for her now or any time soon. If the enemy ships had surrendered, he would be receiving swords, inspecting the vessels, giving orders for detaining privateers, and organizing crews to man the prize ships.

Georgana resealed the box and made for the door with one of the bottles. There were many things one could count on while at sea — storms, repairs, battles, deaths, rats. She would not regret leaving these behind. But what of Peyton? Could she stay if it meant a little more time with him? The thought spun through her mind as she cautiously made her way back to her wounded father. She had already made the decision to return to normal life — how could she rethink it now?

An officer left the carpenter's shop as she approached. Georgana hurried forward, but the lantern revealed Moyle's rigid face instead of Peyton's. The young man opened his mouth as if to speak but closed it and moved past before she could salute. They had all seen and experienced so much today.

She entered and knelt beside her father, offering him the bottle. His eyes were open but distant, and his jaw was set.

"Here, take this," she said.

Papa didn't move. He didn't look at her. "Lord Nelson went back to the quarterdeck after losing his arm."

She sighed. It would do no one any good to compare themselves to a foolhardy, ambitious vice admiral like Nelson.

"I am not Lord Nelson."

Georgana pulled the stopper from the bottle for him. "I know of only one who was."

"I suppose we cannot all be heroes." His remaining hand closed lightly over hers on the cool glass. She had never seen him so devoid of energy. Even after Mama's death.

"You *are* a hero," she insisted. He had saved her from his mother's clutches, after all. From living a life alone. A life at sea had plenty of troubles, but he'd brought her into it out of love.

He looked up. In the dim light, torment swirled through his bloodshot eyes. "The greatest heroes are always taken the soonest."

Georgana swallowed as her father laid his head back and turned it away from her. She didn't press him to drink again. His words had sent a chill through her she could not shake.

A few hours passed before they could return to the captain's cabin. When Georgana had settled her father in his chair, he mumbled a request for a jacket. She located his undress coat and gingerly pulled its sleeve over the stub of his arm. She wondered if the limb would ever be of any use to Papa again.

"Are you certain you want to wear this?" she asked. "It seems you would be more comfortable without your coat."

He answered with a glare, so she continued helping him into it. She understood. Normalcy had been wrenched from him. Pain and the unknown had been left in its place. Now he grasped for anything that could return him to some semblance of the Captain Woodall of yesterday.

Georgana had searched for Peyton as she helped her father back to his cabin, but the lieutenant must have had many tasks to oversee. She would find him after her father was resting. The thought of confronting him about his pointed looks last night made her stomach fidget.

Papa leaned heavily against the table, an untouched mug before him. She wanted so badly for him to drink it, to take away a bit of the hurt. But he wouldn't. For her. His refusal made her want to reveal her secret to everyone on board, just so he could find some relief.

At a tap on the door, her father straightened. He pasted on a mask of stern strength that nearly broke her.

Lieutenant Moyle strode in and saluted. Strange that Peyton had sent him to make reports twice. A surgeon's mate followed behind him on spindly legs. Red-brown stains snaked up his previously white sleeves.

"We've secured the *Intelligence,* sir," Moyle said with a slight tremor in his voice. "The *St. Germain* is nearly out of sight."

"We can only pray she won't be back," her father grumbled.

"She rode low in the water and had several yardarms missing. She'll need repairs before she can challenge a bigger ship again."

Papa nodded. The skin around his eyes pulled tight in hidden pain. "What are the casualties?"

"Thirteen dead, including Mr. Byam. He was aloft when the mizzenmast came down." Her father ran a hand across his brow. With both Byams gone, the ship had no boatswain. When they refitted the mast, the carpenter or yeoman of the sails would have to sort out the rigging. That would delay their journey.

"And wounded?" Papa asked.

Moyle looked to the surgeon's mate. The young man stepped forward. "Thirty-two, sir, but several are just holding on to life."

"How is Peyton?"

Georgana's head snapped around. "Peyton?" Father avoided her stare.

"Not well, sir. He isn't lucid, and Mr. Étienne doesn't think he has long."

Peyton? Wounded? No, it couldn't be. They were wrong. She wanted to run to the surgeon's mate, make him explain, confess to misspeaking, but her feet stayed paralyzed. *It can't be. It can't be.* The spiraling words in her head numbed everything.

The surgeon's mate adjusted his spectacles and ducked his head. "Poor man keeps calling for Georgiana, whoever that is."

Georgana's heart froze. She clenched her teeth against a sob that threatened to tear free. She pulled at her neckcloth, trying to still her anguish. He wasn't calling for her. The surgeon's mate said Georgiana, not her less-common name of Georgana.

"Are you certain he wasn't calling for George?" her father asked in a low, distressed voice. She almost couldn't hear him in the fog that had encircled her.

The young man cleared his throat. "I distinctly heard Georgiana. Perhaps a sister or a sweetheart."

The lady Peyton thought of when he sang at dinner? The memory of his soft gaze was too much. Georgana's legs wobbled. She reached a hand out to her father's chair. Whomever he called for, he'd never see her again.

"We've moved him back to his cabin in hopes he'll be more comfortable there," Moyle said. "It won't be long."

At his words, she shot from the room,

Papa calling after her. Her pounding feet and racing heart muffled the shouts. She slammed into a blue officer's coat. Jarvis. She shoved past, not stopping to listen to his protests.

Peyton. She needed to get to Peyton.

Her feet hardly touched the rungs of the ladder on her way down to the messdeck. She slipped on the final rung and fell to the floor, her knees cracking against the wood. The still fresh wounds on her palms screamed as they pushed her back to her feet.

Peyton.

CHAPTER 29

Georgana jerked to a halt at the door, Étienne's stocky form blocking her view of the cabin. She willed her feet to carry her inside. Trepidation countered her longing to run to Peyton. What would she see when Étienne turned?

"Ah, George. There you are." Étienne's hoarse voice grated against the raw uncertainty she felt. The Frenchman hadn't moved enough to provide her a view of the lieutenant.

She could see only his lifeless hand, so pale it blended with the blanket covering the cot.

"I wondered when I would see you." The surgeon motioned her over. When she didn't move, he crossed the tiny cabin and took her hand. She let him pull her in, step after faltering step to stand at Peyton's side.

The lieutenant lay propped at an odd angle, his chest and arms uncovered. A bubbling splotch of blood ran from a deep gash the length of a finger and seeped into the pile of bandages sitting beneath his ribs. His ashen face clenched weakly.

And his breath. Each rattling, whistling gasp slashed at her heart.

"I think you should seat yourself," Étienne said gently. He removed a lantern from the stool by the bed.

Georgana dropped to her knees. Her hand wound through Peyton's. She found no warmth or strength in the icy touch.

"What happened?" she managed to choke out.

"A shard from the mizzen struck him," the surgeon said. "It pierced through his coat to his lung and hit his arm as well. I have removed all cloth and splinters, and I have stitched up the arm, but . . ." He sighed. The weight of his hand rested on her shoulder. "There is not so much a doctor can do in this situation. I have leaned him to the side, to keep the blood from getting into the hurt lung. I think, however," he squeezed her shoulder, "you should make your farewells. We have little time left with our lieutenant."

Georgana's body shook. She ground her teeth to keep in the torrent. But waves do not like walls, and just as the sea broke down their walls of sand in the bay, her sobs surged through her defenses. She lowered her head, her brow brushing Peyton's arm.

It couldn't be the end. She'd prepared for separation, but not this. She had consoled herself knowing he would be on his beloved ocean, taking in the fresh, briny air as though his life depended solely on the sea. Now he would never again glimpse the roaring tide or stars freckling the night waters.

"I must see to the other wounded," Étienne whispered. She hardly heard him. "I shall return when I can." His footsteps drifted away. Her sobs and Peyton's rasping were the only noises that sounded in the wardroom.

Georgana pulled herself up. She inched toward the head of his cot, which softly swayed with the rocking of the ship. Her hand came to rest over his heart. His faint pulse echoed Étienne's warning. So little time.

Her fingers traced up to his face, smoothing along the line of his jaw. For a moment his eyes fluttered, and she held her breath, but they did not open.

"Peyton?" she murmured. "Can you hear me?"

There was no movement, only the haggard rise and fall of his chest that seemed to wane with each repetition. "I wish I had known you under different circumstances. Perhaps we could have . . ." The lump in her throat did not let her continue the thought. "I only wish I could have seen your smile once more." She brushed the tip of a finger across the corner of his mouth.

She leaned her head against the side of his cot. Finally she had found someone to make life brighter, only to have that light snuffed out before her eyes.

Georgana didn't know how much time passed, how long she watched his paling face, before Étienne returned.

"How is he?"

"Fading." She should be worrying about her father, but she didn't have the strength to go above. Her will was broken. She would stay with Peyton until the last, even if it meant days.

The surgeon took Peyton's uninjured arm at the wrist and pulled out a watch. He nodded grimly. "Soon."

The word battered through her mind. The surgeon's simple response cut through her more than his mate's announcement had in the captain's quarters. She thought she'd understood, but now she withered under the glaring reality.

"Is there nothing else that can be done?"

352

Georgana shrieked. She didn't know where it came from — some hidden well deep inside that could no longer be contained now the ramparts had fallen.

She covered her mouth with a hand, horrified she'd let the outburst slip out.

The Frenchman held up his arms. "I have done all I can. If we block it up . . ." He pursed his lips, eyes darting down to the open gash where Peyton's life was flooding out onto the bandages. "Unless . . ."

Georgana spun around. "Unless?"

He held up a hand for quiet. "Monsieur Larrey spoke to me once about a patient of his during the campaign of the Nile."

"What is it? What did he do?" Her voice cried in desperation.

"*Un pansement.*" Étienne threw off his coat. "*Rapporte-moi un pansement!*"

She blinked. "What do you mean?"

"Ah, this stupid language." He slapped his forehead. "*Pansement, pansement* . . . plaster! Bring me a plaster. And wine. *Rapidement.*"

Georgana didn't need a translation of that. She hurtled out of the cabin, tripping over her shoes. The key to her father's stores beat against her leg through her pocket. He had plenty of untouched wine. She collided with the surgeon's mate on the ladder, knocking his spectacles askew.

"Take a plaster to the wardroom," she cried. "Hurry!"

She didn't wait to see his reaction. Étienne had offered her a glimmer of hope, and she wouldn't let go.

"I have been taught that such injuries to the cavity of the thorax are to be left open and clear," Étienne muttered as he worked. His mate held the lantern above the surgeon's hands, while Georgana watched from the corner, knees curled up to her chin. "But I recall that Monsieur Larrey mentioned an incident of this sort, where he sealed the wound. Bring the light a little closer, please."

He dipped his head, and Georgana leaned forward. She couldn't see what the surgeon did. His body blocked most of the light. Eerie shadows waved across the walls and ceiling.

"What happened, sir?" she asked quietly. *Please let there be hope.*

"The soldier survived."

Her nails dug into the fabric of her trousers, and she rested her forehead against her knees. What if Peyton didn't? All this hope would be for nothing. And yet she couldn't push its fluttering wings from her aching heart.

"I have not seen this done, but the lieutenant has nothing left to lose." Étienne straightened and picked up a cloth at his feet. He wiped smudged fingers on the already tainted scrap. "There. It will have to do. Now, help me lift him for the bandage."

Georgana scrambled to her feet. "I will do it." She skirted the stool where Étienne sat.

Peyton's countenance hadn't changed, but his breathing had. The whistling had stopped, and the breaths came in without so much strain. Or perhaps she only imagined the change.

She slid her arm under his neck and shoulders. Then she lifted Peyton's listless body enough for Étienne to wind a bandage around his torso. Her arm shook with the effort.

His head rested on her shoulder, the lines of pain faded. His skin was still so cold against her hands, and his lips had taken on a blue tint. But that wondrous, regular breath continued.

She had once been horrified to find herself with him in such a state of undress. Now she held him to her, never wanting to let go.

Étienne secured the wrap, then removed the mound of crimson bandages that sat beneath Peyton's wound. Georgana eased him back into the cot. She paused, still cradling his head.

"What now?" she asked.

"Pray that I remembered Monsieur Larrey's story correctly."

Georgana gently pulled her arm free and nestled Peyton's head back into the pillow. Étienne thanked his mate and sent him to check on the other patients. He put a hand on her back. "Do not get your hopes too high, George. This might not work, or he might get an infection. There are many things that could go wrong."

She nodded. She didn't think any intelligible words would make it through her constricted throat.

"For now," the Frenchman said, "we wait."

CHAPTER 30

On Étienne's orders, Georgana trudged up to the gun deck, legs hardly keeping her upright. He'd put William, the loblolly boy training to become surgeon's mate, in her place at Peyton's side until the next watch.

So many had been wounded. So many were still sick. Étienne worked tirelessly as though he wasn't serving his country's enemy. She had seen no hesitation when he treated Peyton or her father.

Her father.

Georgana ran for the captain's cabin. How selfish to have forgotten his plight. She threw open the door to find him hunched over the table, face in his lone hand. A carafe and cup sat at his elbow.

"Are you well?" She flew to his side. The drink was only lemon water. Where had the brandy gone? "I am so very sorry, I completely —"

"How is Peyton?" he asked, raising his head.

Georgana tried to speak, but words wouldn't come.

"You loved him, little one," her father said quietly.

Her chin trembled. Yes, she loved him. More than she realized. Watching him cling to life, while she stood helpless by his side, had sapped away what little strength she had left. She dropped to her knees, face crumpling as the weight of the morning plummeted onto her weary shoulders. Her father's uninjured arm wound around her, and she buried her face into his coat as sobs racked through her. He hadn't embraced her in so long. Not since Mama's death. Her tears fell onto his coat and rolled down the blue wool.

"He was a good man," Papa said. "A good lieutenant." A priceless friend.

At a knock on the door, Georgana pulled away and wiped at the wetness of her father's coat. Moyle entered, hat in hand. "All is in readiness, sir."

Her father nodded. "What of the repairs?"

"I have two of the carpenter's mates at work now, and the crew running the pump. The worst of it is under control, and the rest of the repairs can be made on the way."

"Congratulations, Commander." Papa moved as though to shake Moyle's hand, then flinched and pulled what was left of his right arm back in.

Commander? It seemed Moyle was to take the *Intelligence*. With her father wounded and Peyton at death's door, that left Jarvis running the *Deborah*. She held her stomach.

"We wish to leave after the burials." Moyle picked at a spot on his hat. "Will you come above, sir?"

Her father's head moved slowly back and forth. "Please lead it, Lieutenant."

"Yes, sir." Moyle's face remained impassive.

When he left, Papa rose and dragged himself toward his cot. Georgana hopped up to help. "Do you not think you should attend?" she asked. She could only imagine his suffering, yet the crew needed his presence.

He paused. His eyes closed for only a moment before he continued to his bed. Shoulders slumped, she helped him remove his shoes and lie back. Then she closed the curtains.

The chaplain's unsteady voice floated down through the hatchway. Despite her struggle to stand, she ducked from the room and made for the upper deck to watch the fourteen burials — thirteen from battle, one from fever.

Jarvis stood unmovable, an image of strength beside the less-composed chaplain. He had brushed the debris from his lieutenant's uniform. Just the right amount of grief and determination showed in his lowered brows to commend him to every man on deck.

He'd take advantage of this situation, this power. If her father did not find the will to keep going, he would have to deal with consequences beyond just Jarvis's insubordination. But Papa would rally. She knew it. He just needed time.

Each time they lowered a man into the sea, Peyton's pallid face shimmered before her full eyes. She pulled her coat tightly around her, wishing for the warmth of a friendly touch. The only men on this ship who cared whether she lived or died lay below, one in despair and the other in a battle for his life.

Back in the captain's cabin, she sat against the wall and leaned her head back. She hadn't the strength to hang her hammock. The floor would have to do.

"Has there been any change?" Georgana asked the loblolly boy at the door of Peyton's cabin. An hour or two of sleep hadn't done much to refresh her spirits.

"Not a great deal, but if he wakes, you're to get Monsieur immediately." He blinked as though just waking from sleep himself. She wanted to be angry with William for not keeping watch, but she couldn't blame him. What man on this ship didn't look asleep on his feet?

She nodded and changed places with the boy, then closed the door after him. Grandmother's screech at the impropriety of the situation filled her ears for barely a second before Georgana threw the recollection out. She had no room for the woman today. Not in here.

She sank down onto the stool beside Peyton's cot and reached for his hand. It still felt cool.

Perhaps he needed another blanket. She stood again and went to his sea chest. A bloodied shirt, waistcoat, and jacket sat on top with his holstered pistol. After checking the gun wasn't loaded, she gathered them in her arms, then laid them neatly on the floor. The jagged tears where the shard of wood had gouged him made her stomach turn. If scraps from one of these garments remained in the wound, infection would set in with certainty. She pulled her eyes away from the gaping rips and fished a key from the pocket of his coat.

Her fingers wound along the carved "DP" just below the lock before she fit the key and opened the lid.

She wasn't prepared for the scent of lime to overwhelm her. Her eyes, dry and itchy from weeping, smarted. Several slices of dried lime, strung together on a ribbon, sat atop his clothes. She reverently lifted the little garland and brought it to her nose. Brilliant sunsets and impossibly blue water swirled through her memory until she pulled the limes away.

Georgana tried not to disturb anything as she searched for a blanket. When she finally found one, she carefully removed it from between clothes and books. For all her efforts, the blanket pulled a few folded pieces of paper out with it. They fell open on the floor.

She hugged the blanket to her chest, willing some of her warmth to flow into it. If only she could do more. The weave had taken in the dizzying smell of the lime garland. She knelt and draped the covering over him, then tucked his chilled hands beneath it. Her chin settled onto the side of the cot near his head. Hesitantly she smoothed his hair back from his face. "Sleep well, my love." She couldn't hear her own voice over the creak of the ship.

How humiliating if he should wake at that moment to find George Taylor saying such things. She would give anything for that embarrassment.

Georgana returned to the trunk to set it to rights. She scooped up the papers. Letters, it seemed. Her eyes trailed down the page before she could think of the invasion of his privacy.

My dearest mother,

I pray this finds you in good health if not good spirits. Life is never certain in the navy, and perhaps it is this fact that makes life so much sweeter for one such as I, who cannot tear himself away from the sea. I know such notions have never been a comfort to you who must remain behind, constant and patient. Have I ever thanked you for the support you've given your Dominic these fourteen years? I think to every day.

Georgana's hand covered her mouth. She shouldn't read this — and yet she couldn't look away.

You sent me to sea in July with a mis-

363

sion, and I am pleased to report I have succeeded.

A mission? She held the page closer.

I have found Georgana Woodall.

She whirled around to stare at Peyton's sleeping form, her mouth going dry. He had been searching for her? Images from the Trafalgar dinner came back. The odd looks. He *did* know.

I can say for myself that she is well, though I worry what will become of her when she returns to England. I have not spoken to her or her father of this, but I wonder if you might open your doors to her. She is a quiet young lady of great courage, and I think

The words didn't continue. With quivering hands, she pulled the second page forward.

Only three words marked the top: *My darling Georgana.*

Not Georgiana. Not some distant, bewitching lover. Just Georgana — a foolish girl pretending to be a cabin boy.

She covered her face with her arms to

stifle her crying. He knew. Peyton knew, and he'd played along with her and her father's game. His eyes had twinkled in merriment as he sang of the dear lass. As he sang of her.

Dare she believe it? Her heart raced faster, and she was at once in despair and elation. If he died tonight, she might have discovered this without the opportunity to see his face.

She put everything back as it should be in his trunk and set the stained clothes on top. Tomorrow she would clean them with her father's uniform. The pistol would need cleaning as well. If only she could wash the effects of this terrible day from their owners' battered bodies.

Georgana collapsed to the deck at Peyton's side and listened to his soft breathing. As long as that sound continued, there was hope. Hope that he would once more smile and that she could return it knowing he saw her for who she really was. Her hand crept under the blanket to grasp his.

Sometime later, the door opened behind her. No doubt it was Étienne to send her back to her father. She didn't turn around. Grandmother's voice scolded her to do her duty, to return and care for her flesh and blood. She miserably argued that Papa would be there in the morning to care for.

Peyton might not.

The thunk of wood on wood brought her head up. A square plate piled with hot beef, vegetables, and ship's biscuits sat on the stool.

"You should eat." It wasn't Étienne. Fitz sat beside her and settled his own plate onto his lap. He did not look at her. He only watched his food.

She didn't know if she'd be able to swallow through the tightness in her throat that rose at Fitz's thoughtful act. She took the plate from the stool. It wasn't the fare she was used to at the captain's table, but it warmed her as nothing had since last night. That seemed an age ago.

They ate in silence. Georgana hardly tasted the food. Fitz took her plate when she'd finished as much as she could. Then he squeezed her shoulder, as she'd done to him after Locke's death.

"Don't let Jarvis catch you," she said as he turned to go.

He threw her a smirk, then stole out of the officers' quarters, leaving Georgana with a clearer mind and thankful heart.

Chapter 31

Georgana sighed as the wind played through the shorn ends of her hair. Its tender strokes sent tingles along her scalp. Was this what Peyton loved about the ocean breeze?

Something hard tapped her face as she rocked with the motion of the ship. Not hard enough to hurt — just hard enough to irritate her. What a way to ruin a liberating moment on deck.

Her back groaned, and she forced her eyes open as one hand fell from her knees and rapped against the deck. She wasn't standing on the forecastle at all. No sea, no sky. Just the gentle wind through the open cabin window.

Something yellow blocked her view of the dark room. Her eyelids fluttered closed. She hadn't set up her hammock again. That was it. Her stiff body protested another sleep on the floor of the captain's cabin, but she ignored it and leaned into whatever insisted on tapping the side of her head. She could afford a few more minutes' rest before tending to her father and Peyton.

Dominic Peyton. She whispered the name, enjoying the taste of it. Bright, strong. Like limes.

Dominic. It suited him.

The fingers of the wind caught a lock of hair and smoothed it behind her ear. A breezy caress wandered from the crown of her head to the nape of her neck, spreading the magic of its touch.

Her heart beat lighter than it had since before the battle.

The fatigue had nearly crushed her yesterday. She couldn't even remember slogging back to the captain's quarters after checking on Peyton during the first watch.

Her hand slid across the wood grains along the deck and froze. Those were not the smooth tiles of the captain's cabin. They were planks.

The wind continued threading itself through her short hair. Her hand flashed up to her head, catching the warm fingers, halting their progress. She hadn't returned to her father's cabin in the night. Canvas from a hanging cot gently bumped against her face as it swayed.

Her eyes flew open to a bandage, yellow

in the wardroom's light coming through the door. The cloth was wrapped around a bare arm, which reached over the edge of the cot.

Dominic.

Georgana twisted to her knees to see into the cot. She met half-open eyes reflecting the dim light and a weary grin. His hand cupped her cheek, and she held it there with her own.

"Georgana." The whispered word scratched through his throat, so different from the silky voice that had sung to her in a crowded wardroom. Yet she'd never heard a sound more beautiful.

With a sob, she pressed a kiss to his wrist. His pulse thrummed, weak but steady, against her lips. Warmth had returned to his skin, warmth that spread from her cheek to her heart despite the coolness of the lower deck.

"Oh, Dominic, I thought I'd lost you," she breathed. His thumb traced the tears down her face. The tingling sensation that wove through her hair now continued over her arms. She'd imagined so many times how it would feel to have him look at her in that gentle way. The dream had fallen utterly short of the reality.

The corner of his mouth lifted, and her

face flamed. She hadn't meant to let the name slip out. It had sat too long on the tip of her tongue.

"How long have you known?" She brushed at her tears.

He pulled her hand in and laid it over his heart. His chest lifted in a regular cadence beneath her palm. Only a blanket separated their touch. She gulped in the lime-scented air.

"Since the mail ship arrived in Antigua. My mother included your name in her letter, and . . ." He coughed against the roughness of his throat.

Georgana grabbed a tin of grog and helped raise his head to drink. "Rest. We can talk when you've regained strength." She nearly placed a kiss on his brow as he drank, but she held it back. Already she had displayed her affection in no uncertain terms. She glanced toward the wardroom. It remained empty.

Dominic sank back. Stubble dotted his face. His eyelids began to droop.

Uncertain if he'd fallen back asleep, Georgana kept her voice low. "I'm going to fetch Étienne."

His eyes flickered open, and he reached for her fingers. "No. Stay. Please."

She squeezed his fingers. "He wanted to

know the moment you woke. And I need to see to my father. I will return as soon as I can."

But he didn't let go. His eyes begged her to stay. She'd never seen him this pleading, this vulnerable.

She brushed her lips across the tips of his fingers, then lowered his hand back to the cot. "Rest." After one last look, smiling at his attempts to keep his eyes open, she sped from the cabin. Could the sailors she passed see the glow she held in? Surely it shone clear as day from her face.

Georgana hurtled down the ladder to the orlop deck to retrieve the surgeon.

Peyton was back. Peyton was alive. And Peyton wanted her.

Dominic lay still at the sound of footsteps at the door. They sounded too heavy to be Georgana's. Pretending to sleep wasn't difficult. He could hardly move his limbs. Just grabbing for her hand had taken all his energy. And his left side throbbed, though the pain wasn't as crushing as it had been on deck.

The battle. His brain muddled through the hazy memories. They'd won, but at what cost?

"I would suggest that you not concentrate

so hard at this moment, Lieutenant." The gravelly French accent gave away his visitor. "Your duty is to rest."

Dominic cracked one eye open. The surgeon wore a tired smile. He checked Dominic's pulse, then pulled aside the bandage wrapped around his torso. Dominic winced at his inspection. Though careful and brief, the movement sent stabs of pain shooting between his ribs.

"You, my friend, are a fortunate man." Étienne resettled the bandage.

Dominic's brow rose, but he didn't waste breath on asking what the Frenchman meant.

"Your friend Mr. Taylor." Étienne's eyes flicked to his. "We had all but given you up for dead, but his pleas to help you brought to mind a solution I had heard of but never practiced."

Georgana. He hadn't been able to see much of her face in the darkness when she awoke, but the elation in her quavering voice had been enough to thrill his heart.

"That boy has been at your side any moment he can. Whatever you did to inspire his loyalty, it saved your life."

Was it only loyalty? The stroke of her lips on his wrist suggested otherwise. Darling

Georgana. How he wanted her back at his side.

"How is the captain?" he whispered, closing his eyes again.

"As well as can be expected. Men mourn the loss of their independence with wounds such as his. It can take much time to accustom oneself to such a change." Étienne cleared his throat. "You, sir, will stay in bed until I deem you well. This wound is significant, and I still fear for your health. You are not one to sit quietly, but perhaps I can enlist the aid of your little friend, Mr. Taylor, to help convince you."

Yes, Dominic was ready to do anything Georgana asked of him just now. He didn't hear the remainder of the surgeon's instructions as he drifted into unconsciousness with her sea-green eyes running through his foggy mind.

Georgana burst into the captain's cabin, nearly upsetting the breakfast tray. Pale light came through the window. Her father was already sitting up in his cot, curtains pulled back.

"George, what is it? You looked flushed." Shadows covered Papa's face. "Is it Peyton?"

"He's awake." Dishes clanked together as she tried to walk steadily to the table. She set down the food and hurried to help her father from his cot.

He grunted at her assistance but did not pull away. His shirtsleeve hung limp at his side. Georgana retrieved his banyan and draped it around his shoulders. She ushered him to the table.

"How do you feel this morning?" she asked.

His head hung as he picked at the food on the tray. She didn't see the captain who'd commanded from the quarterdeck these last three years. She couldn't even see the tortured man who'd stolen his daughter away to hide her from her grandmother's cruelty.

She set her hand on his. "We will survive this," she whispered. "Together."

"Together?" He whisked his hand away to reach for his tea.

Georgana took a step back. What did he mean by the growl in his voice? He sounded like Jarvis. "Is something the matter, sir?"

"No. Go tend to your lieutenant."

The words stung. She did want to go down to Dominic. Her heart yearned to sit at his side and watch every relaxed breath that filled his lungs. But didn't Papa need her as well?

"Do you not need —"

374

Her father swore and pounded the table. "I lost my arm, not my head, boy." Georgana retreated, pulling her coat tightly across herself.

"Send Jarvis to me before you go down. I need his report."

"I can help," she choked out.

Papa stood, flinging back his chair. "You are not needed. Why I made the mistake of bringing you here, I shall never know."

Grandmother's slaps had never penetrated so deep. *Mistake.* That word again. Hot tears gathered across the surface of her eyes, blurring her vision. "I-I'm sorry, sir."

She scurried to her sea chest and pulled out her sewing kit as well as her sketchbook and pencils. He had never shouted at her before. Not out of anger. She shut the lid of her chest and squeezed her eyes closed, pushing the tears past her eyelashes and down her cheeks. Her head ached from all the crying she'd done in the last twenty-four hours.

Papa righted his chair and sat, dropping his head to his hand. She wanted to go to him, to comfort him. But how? He didn't want her here.

Georgana tiptoed through the door and closed it behind her. She kept her eyes on the floor as she made her way to the hatch.

She had neglected her father, hadn't she? In his hour of need, she'd been at the bedside of another. She had traded Papa for Dominic.

"Something wrong, Taylor?"

Georgana pulled her eyes from the floor. Fitz had just come up the ladder. She rubbed her eyes with the heel of her hand. "It's the captain. He needs help, but he doesn't want it from me."

"Shall I check on him for you?" Fitz asked. "I finish watch in an hour."

She nodded. "Yes. Thank you."

"Now I best get this to Lieutenant Jarvis." He lifted a sextant box.

"Will you tell him the captain wishes to see him immediately?" Georgana was glad to miss that meeting.

Fitz's nose wrinkled. "I still can't figure why Moyle was sent off."

She shrugged. If Papa continued to push her away, she might never know. The thought sunk her spirits so low that even the promise of seeing Dominic could not raise them.

Short, dark hair peeked over the side of Dominic's cot when he awoke. It brought a smile to his lips. Georgana sat just out of his reach, head bowed.

"Good morning," he mumbled.

"Afternoon, rather." She got to her knees beside his cot, setting her drawing book on the deck. "How do you feel?" Her haunted eyes sent a jolt of fear through him.

"Georgana, what is it?"

She shook her head, eyes closed. "It is nothing."

"That is what you have told me before, even when it was something." He tried to catch her hand, but he moved with an aggravating slowness. She slipped away before he could raise his sore arm.

"It is time you ate. The loblolly brought in some broth." Georgana slid an arm behind his shoulders, her cool fingers sending shivers across his skin. She tucked a folded blanket behind him and eased him back onto it. "There."

Steam rose from the tin mug she retrieved. She dipped in a spoon and blew gently. Little ripples fanned out across the broth. She touched the broth to her lip to test the heat, then held the spoon out to him. Her lips pressed together as she licked away the drops left behind. To kiss those lips . . .

"Broth again," he said, unable to look away. Surely it was only the effects of his wound that left him feeling this weak.

"Yes, broth. Hush." She held the spoon to

his mouth, and he obediently drank.

He chuckled uneasily. "I feel like a child."

"Don't." No humor traced her features. She offered him another sip. "You should feel cared for."

Dominic sucked in a deep breath at her words, then flinched at the flash of pain in his left side.

"Be careful," Georgana said. "It will take time to heal. You cannot move about as usual."

He couldn't even take a breath to still his thundering heart. He had suspected she cared for him, but hearing the words filled him with a brilliance that pushed some of the clouds from his mind. "How is your father?"

Her gaze dropped to the cot. "He doesn't want me in his cabin. He told me it was a mistake to bring me on board." She faltered on the word *mistake.*

Dominic bristled at the captain's words. He touched her arm, stopping her from dipping the spoon in again. "He is wounded and not in his right mind." He kept his voice soft. Captain Woodall should know his daughter well enough to realize such a comment would pierce her to the core.

"I know." The quiver in her voice tugged at his heart.

"I do not think it was a mistake you came here." He knew what he wanted to say, but the sorrow on her face scrambled the words in his head. "I am very grateful you came." Some of the tension around her eyes faded. "Don't let his despair wear on you, Georgana."

Her lips pressed together. "You mustn't call me that. Someone will hear."

"You prefer George?"

She stirred the broth in the cup. "I do not prefer it, but if I am to keep any semblance of a reputation after this journey, I must keep my identity a secret."

He nodded. Bother reputations. He liked to say her name.

She resumed feeding him, slowly and deliberately. When he'd finished, a glimmer of a smile stole across her face.

"What?" Dominic asked. "Are you to tell me I've been a good boy for finishing my soup?"

Georgana shook her head, unaffected by his teasing. "This time yesterday, I couldn't imagine sitting beside you and conversing like this. You seemed too far gone."

He wove his fingers through hers, ignoring the ache in his wounded arm. "Were there many casualties?" He hated to ask, hated to wash the smile from her eyes. But he was first lieutenant. It was his duty to know.

"Fifteen, as of this morning," she said, looking away. He had almost joined them. "Étienne thinks the rest should survive, barring infection. And two more have passed from the fever."

"Were any of the dead officers?"

"Lieutenant Tytherton and Mr. Byam."

Dominic sighed. He'd forgotten Byam had been aloft when the mast fell. Poor man. And his poor wife, who lost both son and husband on this voyage. He would seek her out when they landed in Portsmouth.

"They were both good men," he said, a lump forming in his throat.

"Yes, they were." She rubbed the side of his hand with her thumb. "Moyle took command of the *Intelligence*."

It should have been Dominic's command, had the shards of mast not hit him. But he found himself grateful to not have the position. It would have separated him from Georgana, and he never would have been able to convince the captain to let her accompany him.

That put Jarvis in control on the *Deborah*. Dominic sat up. The flesh around his ribs screamed at the idiocy of his action. Georgana cried out.

"What are you doing?" She threw her arms around him to steady him.

"Jarvis can't take charge," he wheezed.

She huffed. "It cannot be helped now. You are certainly in no state to command the ship."

Blast his wound. He had no trouble picturing Jarvis's smug face as he paced the quarterdeck alone.

"While you are up, we might as well replace the bandage," Georgana grumbled. Her fingers untied the knot on the side opposite his wound, then worked their way around his ribs to remove the cloth. To have her so near, practically embracing him as she stretched the new bandage around his back, threw his mind into the dizzying mists once again. Her short breaths tickled his shoulder, sending prickles across his skin.

"Are you cold?" she asked, the corners of her mouth pulling down. "Would you like a shirt?"

Dominic reddened. He didn't know why. She'd seen him without a shirt before, and it had discomforted her. He'd thought the situation humorous when he learned who she was. Now she was the one who didn't mind, and he blushed.

"Yes, thank you." His stomach turned, and his hands shook at the effort to keep himself

381

upright.

She returned quickly and slipped his shirt over his head. He felt helpless. She threaded his arms through the sleeves. He couldn't even lie down without her support.

Georgana didn't immediately remove her arm from beneath his neck after settling him back onto the cot. Her bright eyes searched his face. "You'll listen to Étienne, won't you?"

His own eyes felt heavy. "Yes, of course." He wouldn't mind falling asleep in her arms.

What was he thinking? He couldn't fall asleep in her arms unless a very serious promise were made. Could he make such a commitment to another woman when he could hardly give the first what she needed? His earlier doubts poked their way into his head.

"I don't believe you," she said. The words weren't accusatory, just a statement of fact. His lips curled.

"You might have to remind me." He didn't feel her slide her hand away, nor did he hear her walk out of the cabin, but the next time he woke the light was gone, and he hadn't the power to raise himself to find it.

Jarvis met Georgana at the entrance to the

wardroom, arms folded. "Your services are no longer needed here. Do your duty to the captain. The surgeon will tend to Lieutenant Peyton."

She clutched the bloodied clothes and bandages, which she'd wrapped in one of the blankets. "Lieutenant Peyton wishes me to help him, and the captain does not object." The captain didn't even want her in his quarters.

Jarvis took a step toward her and pulled himself up to his full height. Georgana huddled back.

"Lieutenant Peyton is not in command of this ship."

And Jarvis thought he was? She knew she shouldn't say it, but the simmering in her stomach flung out the words. "My understanding is that neither of you commands this ship."

Then she ran. Jarvis cursed at her but didn't follow. She stopped at the bottom of the ladder, her whole body going cold. Dominic was alone, asleep, unprotected in his cabin. Jarvis could take advantage of such a situation.

"Mr. Taylor, are you well?"

Georgana jumped at the French surgeon's greeting. "I . . . Yes, I . . ."

"What bothers you?" Étienne grasped her

shoulder, concern in his eyes.

"Dom— Peyton. Lieutenant Peyton. Jarvis is . . ."

The surgeon glanced at the wardroom and nodded. "I will send William to sit with him. Will that help?"

She nodded. The loblolly boy couldn't do anything if Jarvis had a mind to make trouble, but she prayed the lieutenant wouldn't try anything with others present.

"You are going to the captain?" Étienne asked.

She nodded. For all the good it would do. She had never seen such anger on Papa's face directed at her. She'd seen him angry at her grandmother, at the crew members, and even at God for taking her mother. But never at her.

"That is good. I worry for him. He needs the help of his friends, and of his family."

Georgana peered at him, but the Frenchman gave no hint of the meaning behind his words. His family? Of course, they had said George Taylor was a distant relation. Surely the surgeon referred to that.

"Take care of yourself, Mr. Taylor, not just the captain and the lieutenant." He must think she was getting sick. A midshipman had taken ill with fever despite nearly a week with no new cases. The surgeon suggested

384

this case might have been caused by infection from a nasty rat bite.

Étienne strode away, and Georgana watched until he entered the wardroom. She climbed the ladder, steeling herself for what she would find above.

CHAPTER 32

Georgana absently dipped her brush into the bucket. Water dribbled across the black and white tiles as she lifted the brush out. The floors weren't usually cleaned on Wednesdays, but slow repairs after last week's battle had interrupted the regular schedule.

So had the deaths. She pulled her brush along the tiles, wishing it could erase the memories of standing on the upper deck waiting to say goodbye. They should be grateful, all things considered. The fever had claimed only a few lives, and many men had recovered enough to resume work. But two crew members had passed since the battle, and the captain had not attended the ceremonies.

She glanced to her father, who sat at his desk on the opposite side of the cabin. He stared into an open book in front of him, but she knew he wasn't reading. He hadn't turned a page since she came in with the bucket to clean. Most cleaning days they took down the cabin's barriers and furniture, but given the captain's condition, the surgeon urged them to leave him undisturbed.

Georgana wished Étienne hadn't made the recommendation. Taking down the cabin would have forced Papa into the company of his men. The more days that passed, the more he withdrew. She tried to speak with him, but he rarely engaged. He hadn't left the cabin since the day of the battle, and the crew didn't like it.

At each burial for victims of the fever, the mutterings had grown louder. And ever since the midshipman had contracted the fever last week, everyone was on edge. The men needed their captain. With Dominic's slow recovery, they had no one to look to. Except Jarvis.

Georgana crawled forward to the next spot on the floor, dragging her bucket with her. Papa didn't look up at the noise.

Jarvis had taken advantage of the situation, for certain. The petty officers didn't even try to bring their questions and reports to her father anymore. She'd worried Jarvis's command would lead to beatings and stiffer punishment. But it hadn't. He had not come after her or Dominic, as she feared.

This time when she shoved the brush into the water, something tickled her wrist. She jerked her hand back and peered into the bucket. A little flash of red floated in the brine, which hadn't turned murky yet from cleaning. She cupped her hand and scooped it out.

A starfish. She grinned. It must have clung to the ship and come off when they pulled water in. She settled it back in the bucket and sought out a cup, which she filled with water and then put the creature inside.

A certain officer below, who had begun complaining about staying in bed, might enjoy seeing this.

When she'd finished scrubbing the floor, she asked the captain for permission to leave. He didn't respond, so she left. She tried valiantly to divide her time between the two men. The hours flew by too quickly.

Dominic looked up from a booklet when she entered his cabin — a good sign. Most times she found him dozing.

"I couldn't find news of the *Caroline* in the *Chronicle,*" he said, tossing the thin volume to the side. "That raised suspicions."

She and Papa had not counted on anyone trying to verify the story of a lowly ship's boy. "I've never taken you for a reader."

"I enjoy it sometimes." His eyelids lowered, as did her shoulders. She'd hoped they could talk. She'd had little more than silence in the captain's cabin. "Have you brought me something to drink?"

Georgana gazed at the starfish in the cup. "I don't suggest it, but if anyone enjoyed drinking seawater, it would be you."

Dominic chuckled. Not his usual lively chuckle, but a stronger one than she had heard since the confrontation with the *St. Germain.* He slowly sat up in his cot, and she knelt beside it, extending the cup to him. Lantern light danced in his eyes as he observed the creature. He swirled the water with his finger.

"A little bit of the sea," she said. "I know how you miss it."

He caught the starfish in his fingers and brought it closer to his face. "I am told if I am good, I might go above soon." He brushed the creature's bumpy surface with his thumb. It wiggled its arms. "What a sorry situation, trapped in a tin cup. I understand your plight, sir."

"You are talking to a starfish."

He gave her a sidelong glance. "Is there something wrong with that?"

"Has the surgeon administered laudanum today?"

He shook his head. "Come now, George . . ." His voice lowered to a whisper. ". . . Ana."

She pressed her mouth into a firm line, even though the edges so badly wanted to raise. What had she done the last three years without him on board? She had not smiled so often since living in Portsmouth as a very small girl.

"Shall I read to you?" Her mother had liked that whenever she fell ill.

Dominic gently set the starfish back in the cup of water. He leaned back in his cot. "I would rather you tell me about the sea. How does it look today?" The longing in his voice nearly made her jealous.

She shrugged. "Much the same as it does every day, I suppose. Wet, blue, with waves and wind."

His expression soured. "Thank you. Now please enter that in the log for the Admiralty."

"What am I to say?" She threw up her arms at his feigned exasperation. "I am not poetic about it as you."

"Perhaps Lieutenant Peyton would prefer to see it for himself." Étienne stood at the doorway, arms crossed. He watched them with a raised brow.

Dominic nearly leaped from the cot. "I will not say no to that." He swung his legs over the side.

"Slowly, slowly," Étienne said, raising his hands. "Have Mr. Taylor help you, sir. We do not want to sap your strength on your first outing." He winked at Georgana. "Do not keep him long."

"I won't, sir." She saluted, and the surgeon quit the cabin.

"Traitor," Dominic mumbled.

She retrieved his shoes and helped him into his jacket. He looked a mess, with more than a week's worth of stubble on his face and no waistcoat, but that didn't keep her insides from soaring like gulls through the sails.

"Ready?" she asked.

He paused before pushing up from the cot. She supported him on his right side. They had walked him around the cabin a few times, but the upper deck was a much farther journey. He made to step forward, but she held him back.

"Remember that I am George Taylor, not . . ." Her eyebrows lifted, and she hoped he understood.

He beamed. "You might have to remind me."

"Will that be your answer for everything now?" They walked slowly to the door. She cleared all emotion from her features. In the cabin they spoke softly enough not to draw attention from the other wardroom officers, but out in the open they would have to guard their chatter.

Before they stepped through the door, he bent forward so his lips brushed her ear. "If it means keeping you near to help me recall, then yes."

Dominic expanded his lungs as much as he dared to take in the ocean wind he'd missed so much. The fresh air dried the sweat on his face. He had never struggled so much to get from the messdeck to the quarterdeck, but the effort had been worth it.

Skipping waves reflected the afternoon sun, and he squinted against the brightness. He supported himself against the larboard rail. Georgana stood at his side, ready for him to collapse, judging by the pinched expression on her face.

"Are you enjoying yourself?" he asked, resting his elbows on the rail. The breeze whipped at his hair, now almost long enough to tie back. Longer than hers.

Her eyes softened. "Not so much as you, I'm certain."

He tore his gaze away. If she didn't want him to let her secret slip, he'd best not linger on her upturned face or full lips. He should have kissed her when he'd had the chance — that night they'd danced behind the mast. Each morning when he awoke to her standing above him with breakfast, he regretted his forbearance.

"What is it?" The wind caught her voice and filled his ears with it.

"It is nothing." Or everything. Could he keep up this act for three or four more weeks? "When we return to England, I have a proposition. Instead of you going back to your grandmother."

Her face reddened. "Yes, I . . . I read your letter to your mother. I didn't mean to. It fell out when I was finding a blanket, and —"

He caught her arm, and he would have pulled her into an embrace if dozens of men weren't walking the main deck. To hold her in his arms, to feel her curl her head against his chest, to kiss her without worrying about sailors and wagging tongues — what bliss that would be. He let go quickly, before he drew suspicion.

Someday they wouldn't need to hide.

"I love you," he breathed into the wind, his mouth barely moving.

She scanned the deck, eyes wide. "You cannot say that."

"But it's true all the same." He forced his attention to running a finger along the grooves in the rail's wood, just to keep from staring. "And if I am to keep it from the world, I will not keep it from you. I wish to never hide my thoughts, my feelings from you again." He couldn't help another glance.

Her eyes glistened in the late afternoon light. Until very recently, he would have thought no sight more thrilling than an open sea, her waves capped by bubbling foam, carrying him toward the horizon. Today he knew his happiness would not be complete without the lady beside him. No matter that she wore trousers and a coat overlapped in front. The smile she tried to bite down set his pulse racing. This. This was perfection — the waves, the wind, and his darling Georgana.

He didn't know if his head whirled from the exercise or the picture before him. He wished it would never end.

"Taylor."

They both turned. Walter Fitz stood just off the quarterdeck, staring over his shoulder at Jarvis and Rimmer, the marine second lieutenant, conversing on the forecastle.

Georgana hurried over to the boy. Her strange friendship with the former bully made no sense to Dominic.

"There's been more talk about the Frenchie," the boy said in hushed tones. "And the captain. Some think he's a spy."

"Which one?"

"Either. Both." Walter took another look behind him. "Jarvis has been in the mess again."

Georgana sighed. "Thank you, Fitz." She returned to Dominic, the lightness in her face gone.

"What is happening?"

"Unrest among the crew because of the captain's absence."

Something that was out of his power to fix. For now.

"Come, let's get you below," she said. "We've stayed too long already."

He wouldn't object to her putting her arm around him once more. It was as close as he would get to holding her until they landed.

Georgana shut the door to the captain's cabin and leaned against it, choking down the giggle that rose to her throat. Dominic's words on the quarterdeck melted all her resolve.

Someone loved her. And not just any someone — Dominic.

She covered her mouth with a hand. How long had it been since someone told her they loved her? Her father never said it, though he'd implied it on several occasions. To hear those words — spoken so tenderly by the lieutenant, who she thought would always remain a dream — left her breathless.

"Does he know?" Her father's growl upended the euphoria. He sat in his hanging cot. The curtains cast shadows across his face.

"He . . ." Georgana gulped. She didn't want any more secrets. "He does."

"He's a man of the sea. Do not forget that."

She waited for his reprimand, for him to rail about the impropriety of her actions. That was what Grandmother would have done.

Papa didn't. He lay down and turned his back to her.

Her hands fell limp at her sides. Must she choose one man over the other? Papa had thrown up walls around himself. How was she to give him the care he deserved?

She crept to his cot. Just as he hadn't mentioned his love for her in the last three years, she couldn't remember telling him either. In her younger life, he had chased away the storms with his return. For years he and Mama had been the only two people in the world who saw her as something other than a mistake. So many times he'd cradled her and told her she meant the world to him, and that helped carry her through the days when Grandmother screamed the loudest.

Georgana reached out her hand. Dominic was right. Sometimes things had to be said, no matter the risk. She touched her father's arm. "I love you, Papa."

He did not respond. She backed away and busied herself hanging her hammock. The day's work had drained her, as it had every day since the battle almost ten days ago. She couldn't complain. Everyone on board was working harder than usual to repair the broken mast and yards, restore the rigging, and mend the sails. Others, like her father and Dominic, worked to get well.

A sniff came from the other side of the cabin. Her father didn't move, and Georgana said nothing.

CHAPTER 33

Georgana didn't mind mending. She had done so much of it at Lushill and more since coming to the *Deborah.* And she certainly didn't mind mending for him.

Dominic's uniform coat lay across her lap. The jagged tear across the left side gaped open. For weeks she'd put off this work. Just looking at the holes in his clothing made her stomach turn. She rethreaded her needle with blue. Anyone who looked closely would see the repair, but it would do until he could commission a new coat. She stabbed the needle into the material and pulled the two sides of the rip together.

"Jarvis hasn't come with a report for three days." Though more than a week had passed since her attempt to reconcile with Papa, and two weeks since the battle, the sound of his voice surprised her. He still did not speak much, but he was slowly letting down some of the walls.

He sat at the table, a map before him and a teacup in his remaining hand. He'd allowed her to pin up the sleeve of his jacket, as she'd seen similarly wounded men do. He stared intently at the map.

"Shall I fetch him for you?" she asked.

He immediately shook his head. "Send one of the other boys. That man is not in his right mind."

She didn't mention that Jarvis had been shockingly less violent since shouldering most of the responsibilities of the captain and other officers. Many of the crew had even begun to speak highly of Jarvis, despite their earlier dislike after Fitz's beating. Fitz and his father avoided him at all costs, but the rest of the crew had forgiven and forgotten the incident under his newfound aptitude for leadership.

Her fingers smoothed over the coat blanketing her legs. Dominic had come far in his recovery, though he still came below looking haggard and faint after his watches. He didn't have the strength yet to step into the role Jarvis had taken. She hoped Dominic wouldn't have to, with how much better her father was doing in recent days.

"Don't fall for a navy man," Papa said.

Her head snapped up, and her hands fell still. "You are a navy man."

He set down his cup and ran his hand through his hair. It looked grayer than it had a few weeks ago, or perhaps his perpetual weariness made the fading more prominent. "And look what that did to your mother and to you. Would you drag yourself and your children through this?"

Georgana winced. She stared at the needle stuck into the fabric on her lap. If he had told her this two months ago, she would have readily agreed. Now she saw the love in Dominic's eyes and felt the warmth of his voice, and her convictions faltered.

"You have a tender heart and are prone to love, even when it is not earned." He fiddled with the buttons on his jacket. "After all you've endured at your grandmother's hand because of me, I do not wish to see you hurt anymore."

"Yes, sir."

She lowered her head and set to her work, images of her mother filling her mind. Given the choice, would she choose the same path as Mama? Her plans to return to London and seek out a husband had faded into the muddle of caring for Dominic. Each time a thought of the looming arrival came to her mind, she pushed it out with thoughts of Dominic's progress and their quiet flirtations.

One day soon, she would have to choose.

A life with Dominic meant being alone. Was that challenge worth the brief moments of paradise? She did not know.

"Your watch is in half an hour, sir."

Dominic smiled and opened his eyes. He had lain down for a few minutes after readying himself for the day and fallen asleep. What a sorry excuse for an officer. Waking to that voice, however, made it all worth it. For more than a week he'd made excursions around the ship, sometimes with Georgana and sometimes alone, and taken occasional watches. His strength was returning, but he still had bouts of fatigue and dizziness.

Georgana set the breakfast tray on the stool by his cot. She hadn't stopped bringing his breakfast, even though he'd recovered enough to do most things himself. He hoped she wouldn't stop until they got to Portsmouth. As a matter of fact, he hoped she would never stop greeting him in the mornings.

He glanced out the door. No one sat in the wardroom, so he grabbed her hand. "Now there's a face I'd love to come home to." He got slowly to his feet.

Her hand went rigid in his. "Come home to?"

Dominic took a breath, but it did nothing to slow his raging pulse. Only a week or two remained until they set foot on the dock in Portsmouth. If he stayed with the *Deborah,* it would be only a matter of weeks before the Admiralty called the crew into service again. He didn't know what would happen or where they would assign him. One thing he did know: he would not leave for his next voyage uncertain of his relationship with Georgana.

"Yes. Home." He tried to catch her gaze, but her eyes stayed fixed on the lapels of his coat. "I want that home to be wherever you are."

Footsteps traveled through the wardroom, and Georgana wrenched her hand away. Étienne passed, hardly giving them a glance.

"I will not be left at home," she whispered after Étienne left.

Dominic blinked. "But you do not want to waste your life away on board a ship. You hate the navy."

She nodded, and the hand he'd held came up to pull at the cropped ends of her hair. "I cannot marry a navy man." A question hung on her voice.

"I don't understand."

"Look at what it has done to my father." She retreated one step. Two. "Look what it's done to you. I can't continue this way. My mother . . ." Her voice caught.

Heavens above, he'd forgotten her mother. He swiped a hand across his brow. "You are not your mother. And my mother is not your grandmother. Your life would not be the same, I promise."

She clutched her coat around her. Her face carried the haunted look he'd tried to clear away so many times in the last few weeks. "How long would you be mine? Six weeks in a year?"

He rubbed his temples. This was not the conversation he'd imagined having. Dolt. "Possibly more than that. If I thought you would be happy, I would bring you with me on some occasions, but you have made it clear that is not your wish."

"You are married to the navy, Lieutenant Peyton." The dejection in her tone rattled inside him. His chest constricted. "That is a life I will not live. A life I cannot live."

Ears ringing with the beat of each word falling from her lips, Dominic sank back to his cot. He couldn't erase a lifetime of prejudice against the sea. Two weeks of considering, deciding, and gathering the courage to ask her to be a part of the simple life he lived, and he hadn't imagined her refusing him. She understood sea life. She understood him. She . . . cared for him. He had assumed she loved him enough to see past his occupation and its trials.

He sucked in a breath, the action as difficult as it had been in those hazy moments after he'd been struck with the shard from the mizzenmast. His heart wrenched as he opened his mouth to speak. "No. I suppose you could not."

"I'm sorry. I truly am," she said, cowering toward the door. "I'm sorry." She turned on her heel and fled.

The energy to stand fled with her. He needed to ready himself to take his watch. Instead he dropped his head to his hands. This was the reason he had never bothered with young ladies on land. The only woman he needed was the sea.

Dominic stayed hunched in his cot until numbness took over, cooling the heated chaos of his mind. It wasn't the same apathy he fell into when preparing for battle. This deadening fog clouded out everything from his mind and heart. He didn't touch his breakfast. He didn't even move until the bell for his watch rang eight melancholy times. Then he dragged himself off the cot and up the ladders to the life he'd loved before Georgana had staked a claim on every last part of it.

CHAPTER 34

Heated voices above made Georgana and her father look up from their dinner. When the noise began, she'd thought it just the rising winds. Now she couldn't mistake the shouts.

"A fight on deck, no doubt," Papa said. "The officers will take care of it."

Georgana took a sip of lemonade, but it didn't calm her. The taste of lemons made her wish for vibrant limes, which only turned her heart to other things she longed for and couldn't have.

Wouldn't have, she corrected. She chose this. For the first time, she had the power to decide something about her life, and it made her sick.

"George, will you go to Dr. Étienne for a poultice? He will know which one I mean."

Her brow furrowed. The voices above had not quieted. "A poultice? What for?"

"My arm."

He hadn't asked for one in some time. "Yes, of course." She got to her feet, leaving her meal unfinished. The tightness of her stomach hadn't allowed her to eat much. She took one of the lanterns with her to help her find the surgeon in the blackness of the orlop deck.

No marine stood at attention by the door when she exited. Several men climbed the ladder, their movements masking the sounds from above. She hurried to the ship's fore ladder, passing the long scorch mark on the deck where the fire had burned during battle.

Few sailors roamed the messdeck. Her father generally ate after the men did, but the crew liked to linger over cards and grog if they weren't on watch. Had they all gathered to watch the fight?

Georgana walked quickly through the narrow corridors of the orlop deck, between storerooms and holding chambers. The marine guarding the officers' storerooms had also left his post. Georgana paused at the door. The hairs on her arm stood on end. Something was amiss.

The marines had been more unruly than usual since the death of their first lieutenant. Lieutenant Rimmer did not enforce discipline as strictly as Lieutenant Tytherton had. Or at all.

She rushed on, hoping the surgeon could quickly prepare the poultice, so she might return to her father.

Étienne sat at his desk, making notes in a ledger. Georgana knocked on the doorframe and saluted when he turned around.

"The captain wants a poultice, sir. He said you would know which one."

Étienne's eyes flicked to the deck above them. "Ah, yes." He stood and stretched, then set about gathering supplies. Slowly.

"How are you this evening, Mr. Taylor?"

Georgana shifted her weight from one foot to the other. "Well enough." Better if he hurried.

He put various ingredients into a bowl and pounded them with a pestle. He added a few more things, sprinkling them in as though mixing a pudding rather than a poultice.

"Do you prefer Mr. Taylor or George? I have heard Lieutenant Peyton and the captain call you George more often." His dark eyes glinted. "Or perhaps you prefer Georgana?"

Her mouth went dry. How had he known? If the story was out to the crew, she was ruined when she returned. She inched backward, preparing to run. Though she had seen kindness in Étienne's ministrations, she suddenly worried about being on the orlop alone with the foreigner.

He watched her reaction, then chuckled. "Your secret is safe with me, *mademoiselle.*" The Frenchman wandered over to a chest and rummaged through, one hand still holding the bowl. "Though I am immensely curious as to how a lovely girl such as yourself ended up in this position."

"Who told you?"

He arched a thick, dark eyebrow. "I am a man of medicine. Do you think I cannot recognize a woman?"

Georgana flushed. Had the bindings not worked as well as she thought?

The surgeon held up a little bottle, unstopped it, and added a few drops to his bowl. "In truth, I had suspicions since the early days of our voyage. But it was when I saw you at Lieutenant Peyton's bedside that I knew for certain." His eyes focused somewhere far away. "Something about a woman's love — it is hard to disguise. Especially to one who has known such a love."

The air rushed out of Georgana's lungs.

"I could not help noticing the lieutenant looking poorly this morning," he said. "He insisted all was well. Just as you did a moment ago."

Georgana's eyes burned, and her mind raced to the image of Dominic's stricken face when she'd panicked about being left behind. She hadn't let the tears fall since their conversation yesterday morning. She'd avoided the wardroom and the upper deck when he was on watch, and when she had to go below, she used the ladder near the stern instead of the one near the officers' quarters. But everywhere she looked, she saw him.

"Trust can be very hard to give," Étienne said. He sought out yet another ingredient. She'd never seen such a complicated poultice. "I am guilty of it, to be certain. It is hard to trust my shipmates." He gave her a sidelong smile. "You may relate to that situation."

Georgana didn't return it. She only nodded. "They find it hard to trust you."

"Yes, yes. *Bien sûr.* It is difficult to see the face of an enemy. They think me a spy." Étienne snorted. "As though I could gain any useful information from this voyage."

He continued to talk, describing his home of Marseille and his seaman father. He had trained to be an army surgeon, but his heart was always with the sea.

Just like Dominic's. Like most men who left their wives to sail for adventure and glory. She wrapped her arms around herself. She needed to return to the main cabin, to find a corner to hide her tears that had begun to well up from the void inside.

"I must go." She ran for the door, but the surgeon caught her wrist. His pestle clattered to the floor, splattering his green-tinted concoction over the deck.

"The poultice is not ready."

She pulled against his grip. "I'll return for it." A chill ran up her spine at Étienne's creased brow and the intensity in his dark eyes.

"I do not suggest you go above just now."

She leaned away from him, but his hold did not loosen. "Let me go. Please. The captain —" She grunted as she tried to break his grasp.

"It is too dangerous, *mademoiselle*. He does not want you above."

Georgana stilled mid-pull. The surgeon's weary face watched her with sadness. "What is happening?" But she knew. Bile rose in her throat. She should have seen it coming. Jarvis's endearing himself to the crew, his taking command, his refusal to bring reports to her father. It meant only one thing.

Étienne nodded. *"Une mutinerie."* Mutiny.

Papa! She jerked her hand free and bolted from the room. Étienne cursed in French.

The sound of his bowl falling to the wood deck echoed through the orlop.

She lost herself in the black, trailing her hand along the walls. She had left her lantern in the surgeon's room. Several times she smacked into doors and tripped over rope or debris, but she kept moving in the direction of the ladder. She had to get above. She had already lost Mama. And Dominic. She couldn't lose Papa, too.

Dominic knelt by his sea chest and inserted the key into the lock. His hands slipped as he pushed the lid open. Standing on watch would get easier. He had to keep reminding himself of that.

The hole Georgana left did nothing to help his fatigue. It was nigh on two days since their conversation, and he couldn't rid her frightened eyes from his head. They were there each time he looked at the sea or tasted the wind. Wherever he went — the wardroom, the gun deck, the forecastle — he pictured her pained face. And yet, he had not actually seen her since their conversation. Somehow she had managed to hide herself. Perhaps it was for the best.

He loosened his thin black cravat and pulled it from his neck. If he wanted to regain his strength, he needed to rest.

411

Sitting atop his clothes was the square of paper the carpenter's mate had salvaged from the side of the ship, the image she'd drawn of him at the bay. Dominic didn't look at it long. He tucked it beside the unfinished letters and little package he should have given her before everything broke apart. The gift could easily go to his mother, but he didn't want to give it to his mother. He'd imagined Georgana wearing it too often.

Footsteps in the wardroom nudged him out of his ruminating.

"This way, Lieutenant."

Two red-coated marines blocked the doorway to his cabin. They carried muskets with bayonets fixed. A pair of irons hung from one marine's arm.

"What is this?" He thrust himself to his feet. Their grim expressions sent tension through his muscles.

"We're to take you to the captain's cabin." One of the marines lifted his musket, training it on Dominic. Well, they weren't heading to a meeting to discuss sailing conditions, he should think. Something had happened since Jarvis took watch.

"On whose orders?" He couldn't think why Captain Woodall would have him escorted to the gun deck under armed guard.

"Captain Jarvis's."

Dominic went cold. Jarvis! What would push him to such idiocy? He ground his teeth together. They'd trapped him in the tiny cabin with no way of escape. If he were healthy, he'd take his chances in a round of fisticuffs with these two. But they had muskets, and he could hardly stand unsupported after walking the deck so long on watch.

"Come, Lieutenant." One of the marines strode forward and seized his arm. The man's sharp movement pulled the tender flesh still healing around Dominic's ribs.

He followed the men out of the wardroom. Where was Georgana? He prayed not in the captain's quarters, but where else could she be? She'd shut herself inside that cabin since yesterday.

His chest tightened. If Jarvis discovered what she'd been hiding these three years . . .

Before he could think, Dominic rammed his fist into the jaw of the man holding him. The marine swore and stumbled to the ground. Dominic spun back around to face the companion.

A blur of wood slammed into his wounded side. He cried out as fire raged across his ribs. His breath caught in his throat, and he plunged to his knees.

"Lieutenant Rimmer said to put him in irons first, you fool," the second marine growled, pointing his musket in Dominic's face.

Hunched over, the edges of his vision blurred, and a moan escaped his lips. The marines ripped his hands away from his injured side. Cold metal clamped around his wrists.

Dominic couldn't straighten when they hauled him to his feet.

They had to wait on the stairs as crew members carried furniture and trunks below. Then the marines dragged Dominic above.

Georgana burst into the darkening captain's quarters and found them empty, not just of people but of furnishings.

"Captain?"

Nothing moved. The privy doors on either side of the room hung open, empty. They must have taken him above. Georgana pivoted, but voices on the gun deck stopped her from fleeing the cabin. A sight of red on the ladder made her stomach drop. Marines.

She ran for the starboard privy and pulled the door most of the way closed, then flattened herself against the wall. Chains clinked, and gruff voices rumbled. She dared a peek through the crack between the door and its frame. Marines shoved several men into the cabin. One of the red-coated traitors shackled her father's uninjured hand to his ankle, which was already chained to the other foot. The other men — the sailing master, the masters-at-arms, the chaplain, and the gun master — entered, shackled at the wrists and ankles. As they shuffled in, the gunner tripped and went down to his knees.

Dominic wasn't with them.

"Where is the boy?" a marine demanded.

"I sent him above," her father said.

The man muttered something, not sounding convinced. The marine questioned the other officers on her whereabouts and then walked out and closed the door. Lantern light cut off, leaving only the weakening evening light from the windows.

She began to ease the privy door forward, but the main doors flew open once again. She pulled back as another man dropped to the floor. Her heart lurched to her throat. He didn't try to get up. His manacled hands grabbed at his side.

"The captain wants three guards at all times," one of the marines said. "If someone should —" The click of the door closing cut off his words.

Georgana waited for another moment. Then on hands and knees she scrambled from the privy.

"George, what are you doing here?" her father hissed.

"I came looking for you." She reached Dominic. His face creased with pain, and he didn't look up when she touched his arm. "Are you all right? Please say you're all right."

Dominic slowly nodded, breathing hitched.

The men sat on the floor, except for Mr. Adams, the gun master. He shuffled around one of the secured cannons, chains clinking. He pushed on one of the gun ports, but it had been nailed shut and didn't budge.

"What are we to do?" Mr. Jordan asked. "They wouldn't set us afloat tonight, would they? There's a gale to the south."

"I think that's exactly what they intend to do," the gunner said. "I saw them readying the boat."

The chains of Mr. Jordan's shackles rattled as he rubbed his face. "They'd send us to our deaths?"

"I don't think Jarvis cares one way or the other," Adams said. "Not a wit about the man, and he's been at the last of his liquor stores tonight."

Georgana lowered her lips toward Dominic's ear. "Can I help?" she whispered. He shook his head.

Her father cleared his throat. "How far off is the *Intelligence*?"

"Far enough they won't be able to turn around in time to reach us before the storm, even if they see a call for help," the sailing master said. "We have only sixty to ninety minutes of light left."

Dominic's breathing deepened, but he didn't release his hold on his injured side. Georgana knelt helplessly beside him. She let her hand fall to the floor, where his hair splayed out across the planks. Gently, she stroked his hair, the action hidden from the others.

"You are certain the storm is heading north?" the captain asked. Georgana hadn't seen this commanding side of her father in many weeks. Hearing his confident tone gave her a small spark of hope.

"Yes, Captain."

"Our best option is to delay them as long as possible," Papa said. "If they keep us aboard for the duration of the storm and set us adrift after, we have a chance. We'll make for Ponta Delgada. Can you get us there, Mr. Jordan?"

The gun master cut in. "I think they'll cast us off as soon as they are able. What are we to do to dissuade them?"

A shiver wriggled down Georgana's back. The little boat wouldn't stand a chance in a storm, no matter how experienced its sailors. Jarvis might as well sew them up in hammocks and drop them in the sea.

The young chaplain, Mr. Doswell, huddled in the corner, eyes darting from one speaker to the next behind his spectacles. His already pale face took on a green hue.

"Our only hope is to signal the *Intelligence* and pray the storm holds off," the gunner said.

"Impossible," came Mr. Jordan's response. "She's too far ahead of us to see anything from the stern."

Georgana wanted to curl up beside Dominic and bury her head in his shoulder. They had no chance.

Once when she was small, she and her mother had received word of a mutiny in the navy. The crew of HMS *Hermione* had massacred the officers, including a few of the young midshipmen. Mama cried harder the next time Papa left. Georgana never dreamed at that time she'd find herself in the middle of a mutiny one day.

Perhaps her final day.

The deep, agonized furrows slowly cleared from Dominic's face. She slid her thumb down to brush against his neck. She focused on the caress, trying to still her quavering heart. If today had to be her last, at least she could spend the remaining hours with the two men she loved more than all the world.

"What about the boy? He isn't chained." Georgana shot the gun master a confused look. He nodded toward the windows. "I think you could fit through one of those."

Mr. Adams wanted her to climb out? She chewed the corner of her lip.

"Out of the question," Papa said. "The boy would fall to his death."

The gunner sat back against the wall. "If he doesn't try, he'll meet a watery death all the same."

"What am I to do?" she whispered.

"Surely there are still some loyal men on this ship," one of the masters-at-arms said. "Or some who are not loyal to Jarvis. We need only convince them to take a stand."

That didn't sound so simple since most of the men opposing them were marines with muskets. The guards outside their door spoke loudly, but she still worried they'd hear the plans.

"Who will side with us?" her father asked.

"The surgeon? The carpenter and his crew? The only reason they aren't here with us is because repairs and treatment are needed. I can think of few who owe me more loyalty than they do Jarvis."

"You're their captain," the master-at-arms said.

"I have not been the captain they needed." Papa lifted the stub of his arm. "This crew wanted leadership. Encouragement. Things I deprived them of. Jarvis gave them a source of strength through the aftermath of battle and disease."

Georgana winced at the truth in his words. "Mr. Fitz and Walter are loyal," she said quietly. "And some of the ship's boys." Still, not many. If Jarvis had whipped three hundred men into anger, what could a handful of people do against them?

"It's the best chance we have, even if a small one." The gunner raised his hands. "The longer we sit without acting, the less time we have."

"I will do it." Her voice trembled as she spoke.

Dominic's eyes opened and caught hold of hers. How she'd missed looking at him the last two days.

"I forbid it," her father said. "She is not risking her life for the rest of ours."

Georgana stared, and Papa blanched when he realized what he'd said. The room went still. Everyone's gaze turned on her.

"She?" someone whispered.

Her father sat paralyzed beneath the windows, breathing sharply. Three years at sea. Three years of watered-down spirits. Three years of hiding, scraping, lying. Three years — gone in a moment.

Georgana let the air in her lungs dissipate slowly. Though her pulse beat and her face burned, her shoulders loosened as the mantle of secrecy slipped away. They would tackle her reputation when they got to shore. For now, she was their last hope.

Only Dominic moved. He rolled his head to the side to face her father. "She can do this."

Georgana squeezed Dominic's arm, then moved to her father, fueled by the warmth of his confidence. The light in the room was waning further. She needed to leave quickly.

"Let me try, Papa." With the secret out, she had nothing to hide. She kissed her father's cheek, took one last glance at Peyton's reassuring face, and pulled open one of the windows.

Chapter 35

Cold wind ruffled Georgana's shirt as she clung to the embellishments on the stern. She'd left her coat, shoes, and stockings behind and kept the gunner's cap pulled low over her eyes. Once on deck, she'd have to move quickly.

Her toes barely fit on the decorative ledge below the larboard window. Had she not been standing on such a precarious perch, she might have blushed at the thought of all the men staring at her through the glass. She should have worn trousers instead of breeches, which left her lower legs exposed.

But then, she hadn't counted on a mutiny when she dressed that morning. Georgana forced her feet to inch along the ledge and her eyes to stay on the side of the ship. Water rose up just under her feet, and though the waves increased, they didn't touch her.

Breathe, Georgana, breathe.

She reached out for the booms, horizontal

boards that secured the shrouds to the side of the ship. Once she had a firm grip with her hands, she stretched her leg down to find footing. Her toes dug into a line that ran the length of the ship, but her hands held most of her weight. The gunner said to follow the booms around to the sick berth, where she would have fewer chances of getting caught.

The sun nearly touched the horizon. In the distance, she could see the tiny schooner commanded by Lieutenant Moyle. Even if she could find a signal to hang from the gun ports, they might not see it in the dimming light.

She moved her hand forward, then her foot, then brought the other hand and foot to meet them. Her arms already ached from the strain, and she hadn't yet cleared the captain's cabin gun ports.

Halfway across the ship, the boom ended. She had to extend herself to catch hold of a square gun port cut through the hull. This position made her fingers visible to anyone on the upper deck looking down. She pulled herself from gun port to gun port, murmuring a prayer under her breath for stealth. She was nearing the next boom but not fast enough.

The *Deborah* pitched toward the starboard

bow, and Georgana clawed at the edge of the gun port to keep her grip. A whimper escaped her throat as her stomach leaped. When the ship righted itself, she doggedly pushed on. Everyone chained in the main cabin was counting on her to set them free. *Keep going. Keep going.*

The next boom came into range. Her arms burned and shook. Only a little farther to get to the sick bay gun ports. She sighed and closed her eyes, gathering her strength to swing her weight down to the boom.

As she extended her arm toward the ledge, another deep wave sent the ship lolling to port. Water shot up around her, drenching her clothes. She yelped. Her grasp on the boom slipped, and with the momentum her feet skidded off their slender perch.

With one hand still clinging to the gun port, she tried in vain to get her other hand back up to the boom. Her wrist and fingers screamed as her weight jerked against them. She grabbed for an overhanging line, but it was too far away. The sharp breeze whistled over her, giving her gooseskin. Her teeth chattered, and her muscles refused to move.

She can do this. Dominic's sure voice echoed through her head. She'd broken his heart, but he still had faith in her.

Georgana caught her lip between her teeth

and set her sights on the boom. Her shoulder united in the screams of her other joints. She blocked them out, just as she had Grandmother.

With a grunt, she threw her hand toward the boom and caught hold. Balanced between the two holds, she paused to steady her breath, then grabbed for the boom with her other hand. Her feet glided across the sides of the ship, still dripping from its dive. She paused to find a grip for her toes.

Only a little farther.

She spied an open gun port a few feet beyond her reach. It was still in the main area of the gun deck, not quite in the sick bay but close enough. The salty aroma of dinner from the nearby galley wafted through the opening.

Hand by hand she went, fingers slipping as the pressure on them increased. Her energy was failing, and this was only her first of many tasks.

Georgana had never been so happy to see a cannon. She clutched the gun's maw with all the strength she had left and squeezed between it and the hull, pulling herself inside. The cannon's surface pulled at her wet clothes, but she didn't care. Deck finally under her, she collapsed in a shivering heap.

■ ■ ■ ■

Fitz lay in his hammock on the messdeck, a length of rope in his hands. He twisted it this way and that with a scowl on his face. Georgana stole over to him, keeping her face down.

"Fitz, I need your help."

The boy jumped. "What was that, sneaking about all —"

Georgana cuffed his arm. "Hush!"

Fitz glanced behind him. A few marines hung about the messdeck, but most had gone above with the crew. "I thought they locked you up with the captain."

"They didn't catch me." Her arms throbbed. "Is all the crew behind Jarvis?"

Fitz shook his head. "Maybe half. The other half doesn't necessarily support Captain Woodall, though. He couldn't convince them to help when Jarvis's lot presented their grievances."

Georgana wound her fingers through the ends of her hair.

"Where's the surgeon? Carpenter?"

"Below. Jarvis has a dozen marines on them. There's talk of setting Étienne afloat with the rest of the officers, but Rimmer worries the surgeon's mates aren't skilled

426

enough to take the full duties in battle."

"Battle?"

"We're going after the *St. Germain*. Jarvis hopes to use it as a peace offering when we get back."

Georgana wanted to pound her head against the hull. The doughty privateer had caused enough problems for the *Deborah*. What's more, the Admiralty would hardly accept the proffered olive branch after Jarvis practically ordered the deaths of several of its officers. She blew out a sigh. How could the crew get behind such a simpleton? Surely they knew this time of peace wouldn't last once Jarvis was rid of the other officers. Not to mention anyone found in league with him risked hanging back in England.

"There's a gale to the south," she said. Everyone knew that. They were about to stand by and watch as Jarvis set the officers out in a little boat to die in the storm. "We have to stop them."

"How do you suggest we do that? I don't think the crew will listen to a couple of third-class ship's boys." His words whistled through the gap in his teeth. Fitz motioned above with his head. "By the time Jarvis is done with his speech, we'll be turned around and heading west again."

"We have to try to convince the rest of the crew. Where are the boys? Together we might have a chance." Just the thought of speaking to the men bolted her feet to the deck. For three years she'd tried to escape their notice. Now she had to plead with them for her father's life.

"Most are above."

"Why aren't you?"

The boy reddened. "My father didn't want me up there if things got out of hand."

She understood that. Her father hadn't wanted her involved, either. "Gather the boys and meet me at the sick berth. Maybe they won't shoot if there are enough of us."

Fitz's eyes glinted. "They wouldn't shoot regardless."

"What do you mean?" Her brows lowered. The marines were undisciplined, and she didn't trust Lieutenant Rimmer could keep them from shooting whoever they fancied.

"They can't get into the powder room. Magazine's locked." He grinned wickedly. "I heard the marine lieutenant muttering about it in the wardroom. The key the captain gave them didn't fit the lock, and the carpenter won't take out the door. They plan to break it down themselves once everything is settled."

They didn't have ammunition. Georgana

sucked in a breath. Perhaps the boys had a chance.

"Hurry, Fitz. We don't have time."

She skirted through the hammocks, avoiding the marines who hadn't gone above. The wardroom stood unguarded, its interior dark. The officers were either on the upper deck or in chains in the captain's cabin. Georgana darted into Dominic's cabin, her bare feet silent on the wood floor. She didn't need to see to find her way around his room.

Trailing fingers along the aft wall, she found her way to his sea chest. The key still sat in the lock. Praise the heavens.

The scent of lime wafted up when she raised the lid. The letters and package tucked into the side of the trunk crackled. Her hands brushed over layers of wool and linen. The scratchy dried limes snagged her fingers, begging her to pull them to her nose and lose herself in memories of Antigua. She pushed the lime garland to the other side of the chest. The bittersweet thoughts would turn more painful than she could bear if she didn't succeed tonight.

Her hand hit a slender wood box where she'd stowed it weeks ago. She pulled it free of the mess of clothes and books. It slipped from her grip and clattered onto the deck.

She tensed, listening for footsteps.

Hearing nothing, she unhooked the clasp and opened it. The long-barreled pistol fit nicely under Dominic's coat, but she didn't have her own coat to try to conceal it. Weeks ago she'd cleaned the weapon while the lieutenant slept. The smooth handle and cold shaft slipped around in her quavering hands. Cleaning pistols didn't give her any shooting experience, not that she even had any shot to fire. Would Jarvis fall for his own ruse?

Georgana shoved the gun into the waistband of her breeches and tried to cover the handle with her waistcoat. It bulged horribly. Even in the fading light, anyone could notice it.

It would be as difficult to smuggle as the next item she had to bring above. She shut the trunk quietly and scurried toward Lieutenant Tytherton's old cabin. Her heart pounded hard enough to alert every man on deck to the thief in the wardroom.

Georgana knotted the sleeves of Lieutenant Tytherton's coat around the muzzle of the eighteen-pounder. She hated disrespecting the dead man's things, but there would be more dead men if she didn't.

"Run it out," she whispered. She grasped

the rope, and all the boys leaned back. For a moment, the cannon didn't move. The low grumble of the wheels in the tracks grated in her ears. Finally the brilliant red coat dropped out of the gun port and snapped to the side in the strengthening wind. The knot held for now, but she didn't know how long it would last. Or if the *Intelligence* would see the signal.

The sun sank lower on the horizon, cutting off precious light. Around them, occupants of the sick bay turned their heads to watch, but no one spoke.

"Secure the gun," Fitz said.

One of the older boys didn't crouch to help. "How can a few lads stand against the lieutenant? We don't even have powder."

Georgana's resolve wavered. "We're the captain's only hope." She said it as much to encourage them as to reassure herself. "The captain will reward you handsomely."

"Rewards aren't much use if Jarvis throws us over the side," another boy muttered.

She tried to piece together an answer, a reassurance, but Fitz spoke first.

"You'd let good men go to their deaths when there was a chance to save them? Whatever you think of the captain, the other officers don't deserve this fate for sticking to their duty."

Fitz's words stung. The boys only saw a withdrawn captain shirking his responsibilities. "Let's get Taylor to the quarterdeck. I take it you'll do the talking?" Fitz turned to her.

Georgana nodded, her throat closing off. Papa's face flashed before her eyes, then Dominic's. Would this pitiful effort do anything to delay the inevitable?

Fitz put a hand on her shoulder and motioned to the ladder. "We're their last chance."

Georgana rested her hand on the pistol sticking out of her belt. Then she ran for the hatchway, with the boys following behind.

CHAPTER 36

Jarvis traipsed the quarterdeck, looking every bit the captain the crew desired. The southern wind rippled through the feathers of his bicorn as he faced into the gale. Rimmer stood nearby in his red marine's uniform. The uncertainty in his eyes calmed Georgana's racing pulse.

She dodged between seamen, keeping the gunner's cap pulled low. The boys followed behind, trying to blend in with the crew. On the larboard side, men lowered a boat into the swirling waters.

"And now I entreat you, my comrades and brothers-in-arms. Let us go and take what is rightfully ours — the prize our captain denied us."

She wiped sweaty palms on her breeches and tried to paste on a confident mask. If Jarvis saw her deceit, she'd get worse than Grandmother's slap to the face.

No, she wouldn't think of Grandmother.

Not now.

Jarvis glanced at Rimmer and nodded. The marine lieutenant left the quarterdeck and headed for the hatch.

"All those," Jarvis continued, "who find fault with our plan, please step forward."

Two hands shoved Georgana forward. "Go," Fitz hissed.

She ran, slipping through the line of marines with their unloaded muskets. Bayonets glimmered on the tips. Even without powder, the marines had some defense. Footsteps pounded onto the quarterdeck, and within moments ship's boys surrounded Jarvis.

A chuckle wound through the gathered men.

"Ah, George, I knew you would turn up," Jarvis said with a sneer. He addressed the group. "Does anyone have a veritable reason we shouldn't go after the *St. Germain?*"

Georgana whipped out the pistol and aimed it at Jarvis. "I do." Her chest rattled with each shaky breath.

Jarvis eyed the gun. "Do you even know how to use that?"

"Shall we find out?" She prayed he couldn't hear the tremor in her voice.

The lieutenant flicked his hand toward the line of marines, who leveled their muskets at Georgana and the boys. Even with the knowledge that the marines lacked ammunition, a few of the boys stumbled back.

"If you try anything, you will be dead before you hit the ground," Jarvis growled.

"So will you." Her arms already ached from holding the pistol. "Do you think Lieutenant Peyton taught me to fight with only my fists?"

"What reason do you have against proceeding?" Jarvis eased back. He was frightened.

Georgana took a step forward. "The officers have done nothing wrong, besides tolerating you in the wardroom." She sounded like a squeaking mouse instead of a boy. "They don't deserve to be set adrift in a storm. In doing so, you sentence them to death."

"It is not unheard of to rid the ship of an unwanted captain." Jarvis watched something behind her.

"What will you do after securing the *St. Germain*? Do you think any port will allow an honest sale after what you've done? You have no sanction from the Crown for your privateering."

Jarvis's mouth pressed into a hard line. "We will return to Portsmouth with a prize for the Admiralty. And if we don't, there are

435

ports that allow for sales without a letter of marque."

"How much of the cut would you take, Jarvis?" Fitz called. "Would you leave any for your crew?" The murmurs of conversation from the men on deck began to rise.

The lieutenant held up a hand against the seamen's mutterings. "A contract will be drawn up. Every man shall get what is fair."

"Even if you can sell it, remember the *Hermione*!" Georgana cried. That halted the men's discussions. The mutiny ended in twenty-four hangings after the mutineers returned to England. "Do you think the navy would pause for a moment before stringing every last man of this crew from the nearest yardarm?"

"The crew of *Hermione* had good reason to rid themselves of Captain Pigot," Jarvis said.

Georgana's knuckles turned white around the handle of the gun. "You do not have so good a reason. Your pride and your greed will send this ship to the bottom of the ocean."

The lieutenant threw the onlookers a patronizing smile. "I think the men have more trust in my seamanship. Surely more than they have in our former captain's."

None of the sailors moved to help

Georgana and the boys, except for Mr. Fitz who inched toward the quarterdeck, eyes on his son. Several crewmen had mugs of grog in hand. Of course Jarvis would pass around extra rations before taking the ship. It was the only way to get the men to agree to this ludicrous plot.

"Think of your families," she said, her eyes flashing between Jarvis and the crowd. "Your mothers, your wives, your children. No good will come of this for them." Her words drew jaded looks from many, but a few whispered uneasily to their companions. She silently plead for their support.

A disturbance at the hatch stole everyone's attention. Marines spilled onto the deck, drawing her father, Dominic, and the others out after them. Georgana's legs wobbled. The guards herded the officers toward the larboard rail, where a sailor let down a ladder over the side.

"Let them go." She pulled the hammer back fully. The click of the cocking pistol echoed over the deck. A chorus of empty muskets cocked in response.

"Lieutenant," one of the marines said. "Shouldn't we try to sort this out?"

"Silence." Jarvis looked Georgana up and down, no doubt sizing up the distance between them. Unless she was a very poor shot, she'd hit him somewhere. He didn't know her gun wasn't loaded.

"Release the officers, Jarvis," Georgana said. The prisoners stood near the dangling ladder. Her father stared at the deck, but Dominic watched her. His clothing disheveled and face pale, he still flashed her the briefest of grins. The grin, in defiance of his circumstances, pierced through her heart. "Don't do this. You know it will be more trouble than it's worth."

Her father went over the side first, gripping the rail with his one good hand. Bayoneted muskets circled him. The ship bucked on a wave. Foam spilled across the deck.

Papa slipped. He grabbed in vain for the wet rail, but his flailing hand disappeared below. "Papa!" Her shriek rang through the yards. She lunged for the lower deck, but a hand around her wrist yanked her back.

You stupid, stupid girl. Why did you think you could succeed? Grandmother screeched.

Jarvis wrenched the gun from her hands and shoved the muzzle against her skull. "I knew there was something between you and the captain." He cackled. "Good Captain Woodall, with an illegitimate whelp. I should have known."

438

Georgana couldn't see for the tears. She lunged for the ladder but couldn't break Jarvis's grasp.

Papa. The last person she had in this world. One more thing the sea had taken from her.

"And good riddance to the good captain," Jarvis snarled. He whirled toward the rest of the crew. "Any man who wishes to side with the boy may come forward and have his brains blown out as well."

When the captain vanished, Dominic's guards happily let him throw himself over the side. He clutched the rungs of the ladder, hands still manacled, as the ship pitched and swayed. The boat below pulled free of one of its ropes and swung toward the stern.

A groan forced his gaze down.

Captain Woodall clung to the end of the rope with his good arm, his legs submerged in the rolling sea. The movement of the ship battered the captain against its hull. Dominic scurried down the ropes, the pain in his side slowing his pace.

"Hold on, sir."

"I can't," the captain gasped. The wind muffled his voice as it tore at their hair and wet clothes.

Dominic bumped against the ship's side,

cracking his fingers against the wood. "Yes, you can." His feet hit the end of the ladder, but the chains on his wrists stopped his hand short of reaching the captain. He needed to go lower.

Bitter cold water raced up his legs as he swung down even with Captain Woodall. The man's pinched face stared back. "You're endangering yourself, Lieutenant."

Dominic grasped him under his injured arm. Their wool coats were soaked, pulling them into the deep. "Georgana needs you."

"She has you now."

Dominic grunted, pushing the captain up with one hand and pulling down on the ladder with the other. The force did not get them very far. "Bring your feet up," he said through gritted teeth.

Captain Woodall pulled up his legs, but he couldn't get them high enough to get his foot on the rung. "I can't."

"Pull with your arm." Dominic tried again to hoist the thicker man. The manacles bit into his wrists. This time the captain's shoes slid across the ropes before crashing back into the sea.

"Harder. We're almost there." The ladder skidded across the hull as the *Deborah* hit another wave. "Hold!"

The captain's face relaxed, and his body

slackened. "It's no use." The sea roared over his calm voice.

Dominic dug his fingers into the man's coat. "You're not giving up now." Waves lobbed the ship hard to port and sucked them both downward. The captain's head sank almost beneath the surface, only his weary face showing.

Curse this water. Curse the mutineers and their stupidity. Curse this rocking ship.

"Let go, Peyton," the captain said as the ship leveled for a moment. "Take my place. I'm not needed here."

Dominic's limbs shook. His numb hand threatened to let go of the soaked wool coat. Ocean water seeped down his face, stinging his eyes. Georgana was above, facing Jarvis and a swarm of muskets to save them. Until his strength failed, he would not betray her by letting her father commend himself to the deep.

Dominic shouted and heaved once more. He didn't breathe, only yanked with everything he had.

The rope tightened as Captain Woodall's feet caught the rung. Dominic cried out in relief. The captain grabbed higher up the ladder with his hand, and the weight lifted. Dominic's muscles shuddered. He tightened his grip on the side rope with both hands.

His face clenched at the ache in his side.

They made it up only a few rungs when the captain looked down at him, gasping. "Why did you do that? You owed me nothing."

"You are my captain," Dominic said. Then he softly added, "And Georgana doesn't want me. She only has room in her heart for one navy man." He had meant to say it with a smile but couldn't muster one.

After a painstaking climb, they rolled over the rail and hit the deck on hands and knees.

In front of them, Jarvis held Georgana, a pistol leveled against her head.

"Stop this, Jarvis." Mr. Fitz stepped up to the quarterdeck. "We've lost enough on this voyage. Let the boy go."

"Get down, Fitz, or you'll be next." Jarvis pressed the pistol harder against Georgana's head, making her tears fall.

Papa.

"He doesn't have enough powder for that," Walter Fitz called. "Not one of them has any powder. Every musket's empty."

Jarvis stiffened against her. Angry voices rose among the crew. A few pushed past the marines and clambered onto the quarterdeck.

"What is this, Jarvis?"

"Some mutiny!"

"We were better with Woodall."

"Not a proper officer."

Some seamen scowled, but relief flashed on several men's faces. From the corner of her eye, she saw Jarvis staring at them, veins popping out on his temples.

"You won't escape this, you little mistake." He pressed her to him and twisted the pistol's muzzle against her scalp. Someone shouted her name.

Georgana ground her teeth, pulling at the man's arm as he tried to tighten it around her neck. He'd taken almost everything she had left. She wouldn't let him take anything else.

The ship pitched as it crested another wave. Georgana crouched as she yanked Jarvis's arm and thrust forward. The lieutenant tripped and tumbled over her, aided by the motion of the ship. The pistol dropped from his hand. His weight pressed into her back as he rolled, but she stayed upright. He hit the deck with a thud then lurched to his feet, uttering a string of curses.

Georgana tensed, ready. One step. Two steps. Her fist curled. *Sound English cannon.*

The pop against her knuckles reverberated up her arm. Pain flashed through her shoulder from the impact with his face. Jarvis careened backward, eyes wide.

Georgana stumbled and collapsed to the deck. Boys and a few men pounced on the lieutenant. On the main deck, sailors wrestled muskets from marines.

A cry from the forecastle brought everyone's head around. "It's the *Intelligence*!" The schooner had cut the distance despite the wind. Her bow pointed toward them. The impending presence of more loyal officers and crew made the last of the mutineers' confident stares falter.

Looking out at Moyle's boat, her eye caught two dripping forms lying against the larboard rail. Georgana had to squint to see their faces in the waning light.

Papa. Dominic.

A sob emerged through her pursed lips. She pushed herself up, her hand falling on top of the pistol Jarvis had dropped.

"I will not be beaten by a chicken-livered captain's mistake child!" Jarvis thrashed against the men who held him.

Georgana stood and turned to him. Her body quaked, the vibration shooting through all her limbs. She stooped to pick up the gun.

"I am not a mistake," she hissed.

She cocked the gun. Her grandmother's withering screeches and Jarvis's threats tumbled through her mind. She took a fierce breath and forced them out — for good, forever.

"And I am not the captain's illegitimate son." She raised the gun toward him.

"Taylor, no!"

The empty gun clicked when she pulled the trigger. She cocked it again and pulled. And again. Jarvis's face hardened with each tick of the hammer, murder in his eyes as the realization dawned. He'd been beaten by an empty pistol. Shaky laughs erupted from the men holding him.

"I'm his daughter."

As the deck fell silent, Georgana spun on her heel. She stepped down to the main deck and ran past her father and Dominic. Men aided them to their feet. She should go to them. Help them. But the welling inside didn't let her stop. Everyone's eyes followed her progress.

"I knew it," someone said. Probably Fitz.

Pistol still in hand, she climbed down the hatchway ladder. Men coming up from the messdeck didn't give her so much as a glance. Through the darkness of the gun deck, she easily found her way toward the stern.

She walked into the captain's cabin, then shut the door. The gun slipped from her fingers and clattered to the black-and-white tiles. Her damp footsteps slapped against the barren floor.

Georgana sank into the corner of the room where her sea chest normally sat, buried her face in her hands, and wept.

CHAPTER 37

Georgana stood at the windows of the captain's cabin. Portsmouth's harbor stretched before her, but she didn't see it. Her gaze fell no farther than the glass panes.

In the reflection across the squares of glass stood a young woman she hadn't seen for so long. This reflection couldn't be right. The white gown she wore hung loose and pulled tight in all the wrong places. Even with the stays beneath the dress holding her upright, her shoulders hunched.

And the dark, cropped hair . . . She cringed and wrapped her arms around her middle. When ladies wore their hair short, it wasn't supposed to look like the fur of that rat the lieutenant had found in his trunk.

Two tedious weeks had passed. After the attempted mutiny, everyone walked on eggshells, especially around her. No one spoke to her except her father and Lieutenant Peyton. And even he acted strange, but she could hardly blame him. He had hoped to secure her hand, but she wouldn't be left at port while he sought adventure at sea.

She closed her eyes. Someday the soreness inside would fade. She had nearly taken back her refusal just to banish the hurt in his voice. And to see that grin again.

Each time she tried to convince herself that perhaps she could live the life of a navy wife, without him for months on end, Mama's image forced itself into her mind. The thought left her paralyzed. She couldn't do it.

Georgana reached toward the window. Her fingers drifted down the cold panes. One good thing had come in the last two weeks. Grandmother's voice didn't shout at her anymore. Even as she stared at her unruly hair and yellowed, wrinkled gown, the woman's voice did not penetrate her defenses. The image didn't stop Georgana's own voice from finding fault, but perhaps that too would fade with time.

The planks of the deck outside the cabin creaked under approaching footsteps. She glanced to the reflection of the door in the window. Her tall, blue-coated visitor stopped in the doorway.

"Miss Woodall." Those two words pricked her heart. He'd never called her that, even after her revelation to the crew. It made him sound like an indifferent acquaintance rather than a friend.

But they were supposed to be indifferent acquaintances, she supposed. She was to go to London and find a husband as quickly as possible before word of her time at sea spread. That left little room for friendships with other young men.

She touched the ends of her hair. "It looks a mess, doesn't it, Lieutenant?"

He stood too far away for her to see his eyes in the glass, but she imagined they twinkled. "I wouldn't have it any other way." His boots echoed on the floor as he walked up behind her and pulled something from inside his coat. "But perhaps, if you find it lacking, this may help."

He rested a strip of lace across the crown of her head and tied it at the back. The magic tingling as his hands brushed against her hair made her breath snag. She fingered the delicate material around her head. It was the lace bandeau she'd admired at the market in Antigua, the day Lieutenant Peyton took her to the lagoon.

"You may need to retie the bow." He stepped back to observe his work. Or to be proper. "I am not the best at it."

"I don't think I could do better." She

hardly knew anything about propriety any-more. She finally turned to him.

The lieutenant bowed, his brown hair fall-ing across his face. She clasped her hands together to keep from brushing it back. He needed to have it cut, though she was glad she'd be gone when he did. She would always remember him standing at the rail with the wind running through his unruly hair.

"I've taken the liberty of inviting you and your father to dine with my mother and me this evening. He accepted, but I do not wish to hold you to it if dinner will make you uncomfortable."

"Oh, no. That would be wonderful. Thank you." She had never dined with him before, despite their many weeks together. Only on cherimoya and lime water. It would be a fit-ting last meeting.

He held out his arm to her. "Might I escort you to the carriage? Your father will join us in a moment."

"Yes, let me fetch my cloak. And bonnet. And gloves." She had to remember these things now. The flattened poke bonnet, more a summer hat than a winter one, settled nicely over the bandeau. She tied the cloak over her gown, squeezed her fingers into the too-tight gloves, then returned to his side. This would all have to do for dinner, since she'd brought only a single ensemble aboard, crammed in the bottom of one of her father's trunks and disguised as covering for books. She would fix the horrifying attire when she arrived in London.

Lieutenant Peyton took her hand and wrapped it tenderly around his arm. The act pulled her close against him. She fought the urge to lay her head on his shoulder. The time for that had passed. He led her out the door, and she leaned on his arm as they walked into the main area of the gun deck. No one had seen her in women's clothes yet. The thought made her face burn.

The lieutenant preceded her up the ladder, then held out a hand to help her through the hatch. Not many men remained since the ship was paid off. Peyton moved them quickly to the gangplank, where a lone figure waited.

Fitz.

The boy stuck out his hand as they made to pass. She hesitated before setting hers in his.

Fitz shook it, and none too gently. "Farewell, Taylor."

"Thank you, Fitz." Her eyes blurred, and she blinked the mist away as they proceeded down the gangway. Never would she have guessed she would miss that boy.

Slippers firmly on the dock, Georgana halted and looked back. The late afternoon lit the *Deborah*'s freshly washed decks. She saw the quarterdeck, where she had followed her father around so many times, and the bow, where she and Peyton had spoken late into the night. Her eyes stopped on the mainmast, where he'd taught her the hornpipe, and the mizzenmast, whose falling had nearly killed Peyton. A crew of carpenters were making more repairs to it now. Her gaze drew down to the many gun ports, marking the gun deck, where she'd carried powder in battle. And the main cabin, where she spent so many quiet hours.

Beneath that, obscured by the hull, was the messdeck and wardroom. She sighed. The wardroom. She'd spent so many horrid, but mostly wonderful, moments there.

"Will you miss her?" he asked.

She paused. "I think, after all, I shall miss her."

Dominic squeezed her hand, then helped her into the carriage. She closed her eyes and closed the book on George Taylor and his meager existence on HMS *Deborah*.

Dominic settled in beside Georgana. The

cool November day leaked into the carriage, but he didn't dare close the door. That would be highly improper, and she didn't need any more rumors spreading.

"When will you leave for London?" he asked to break the silence.

"As soon as my father can settle his affairs with the ship." Captain Woodall had requested leave to recover from his injury. Dominic, whose side was now almost fully healed, would oversee the *Deborah*'s business until his return.

He shifted, then pulled off his gloves. Restrictive things. Gloves were of little use on board — one of the many benefits of being at sea.

Typically he didn't want her father to hurry, but this afternoon he hoped to see the man soon, before Dominic did something he'd regret. Sitting this close to her, after so many days of near separation, sent his emotions both soaring and plummeting in turn.

"Are you excited to see London?" he asked.

Her hands folded in her lap. "Not very. There are so many things I must relearn."

Her timid voice pulled at his heartstrings. He laid a hand on her knee without thinking, as he'd done often before knowing who she was. "You will succeed, and I daresay you will find yourself a fine . . ." His thumb brushed against a button hidden under the soft layers of her cream-colored dress. He traced his fingers along a cuff sitting just under her knee.

"You're wearing breeches." A laugh billowed up, so freeing and delicious he didn't try to stop it. All this time she wanted to return to being a normal lady, and here she was, wearing breeches.

Georgana yelped and batted his hand away. "It felt . . . That is to say, I didn't think . . ." She caught the corner of her lip between her teeth and cast her eyes down to her lap.

Dominic couldn't keep it in any longer. He touched her pink cheek, loving the warmth of her blush against his skin. "Darling Georgana," he whispered.

"Dominic, I'm so sorry." She held his hand against her face and leaned into it. "For everything — for shutting you out, for not speaking to you."

He dipped his head forward, until their foreheads touched. Her soft breath beat against his. How he wanted this wonderful woman in his life.

"For not being strong enough."

He kissed the corner of her mouth she

incessantly mistreated, and when she didn't pull away, he skimmed his lips over the surface of hers. A sound escaped her lips — a laugh or a whimper, he couldn't tell. But when he pressed lightly against their smoothness, she returned the kiss with longing ardor.

One of her hands found the line of buttons on his coat. The other rested tenderly over the jagged repair she'd made in the wool, stitch after careful stitch to make it whole again. Could he ever be whole again, once she tore herself away?

The scent of the sea clung to her, reminding him this kiss would have to end. Too soon he would have to return to his first love. As his lips covered hers with the caresses he'd longed to give before and would always yearn for after this moment, he shoved the ocean's inviting waves from his thoughts. Surely if there were any chance for him to kiss her like this for the rest of his life, he would take it.

A clearing throat pushed them apart. Georgana let go of his coat and threw herself against the wall of the carriage. The pretty pink of her cheeks was replaced by crimson humiliation.

Captain Woodall pulled himself into the carriage and sat across from them, one thick eyebrow raised and his mouth pulled into a flat line. Dominic looked out the window, but he wanted to cover his face. The door had been open. Dullard.

Dominic knocked on the roof of the coach, and it pulled into the streets. His eyes passed over shops and houses, but he did not register what he saw. He kept waiting for the captain to rebuke their behavior, though he couldn't regret it. Kissing Georgana had been sweeter than he had first imagined that dark night behind the mast, when her carefree laugh had washed over his soul. He may never have the opportunity again.

"They've scheduled the court-martial for Lieutenant Jarvis," the captain finally said. "He's in luck, since there are enough captains in port this month. We shall remain for another week at least."

A week. Dominic chanced a look at Georgana but couldn't read her flat expression. "And if there is to be another court-martial, it could keep us here a month."

"Another court-martial?" she asked.

Dominic nodded. He had expected the possibility.

"Whenever there is a mutiny, the navy must get to the bottom of what went wrong." The captain tapped his leg with his hand.

Georgana clutched the bow at the neck of her cloak.

"It is nothing to worry yourself over, Miss Woodall," Dominic said. "Your father will not be blamed." He certainly hoped there would be another court-martial — if it kept her near him a little longer.

The coachman helped them down at the steps of his mother's townhouse. It looked much smaller today. He could only imagine how it compared to Lushill House.

They'd barely arrived at the door when it burst open. A white cap and lavender shawl jumped into his arms. "Oh, Dominic! My Dominic. You're here," his mother cried. She stepped back to examine him. "And in one piece, praise heaven." Tears pooled in her merry eyes.

Dominic smiled. He'd relay the story of his wound in private later. If Georgana heard him try to misrepresent it as a minor injury, he could only imagine the glare he would get.

His mother looked past him, and her mouth formed a little O. "Mercy, you've brought me a daughter."

A daughter! He wanted to clap a hand over his eyes. What would Georgana think?

"Oh, no, Mother," Dominic said hastily. "May I present Miss Woodall. And Captain Woodall."

The joy in the woman's eyes did not dim. She held out her arms to Georgana. "Miss Woodall! Oh, my dear child, I've been looking for you."

A tremor shook Georgana's chin as she embraced his mother. Dominic blinked rapidly, overcome by the sight of his whole world together on a small porch in the middle of Portsmouth. The sea breeze sighed down the lane, and all was almost right.

If only for a moment.

CHAPTER 38

"I cannot believe your stamina, Miss Wood-all," Dominic's mother said as she sat near the fire. "One woman in the midst of all those men for three years? I love my boys, but I could not tolerate them without some female company once in a while."

Dominic winced. They hadn't told her the complete details of Georgana's stay on the *Deborah* yet. He didn't want to embarrass Georgana in front of someone she'd only just met.

When his mother rose to see about the status of dinner, he excused himself as well and stopped her in the hall. "Mother, there is something you should know about Miss Woodall," he said in a low voice. "She has lived these three years under the disguise of a ship's boy."

"*She* was a member of the navy?" His mother glanced past him toward the draw-ing room. He flinched at her stare. "Why

459

have you not married her yet?"

He should have known the knowledge wouldn't shock her. Dominic ran a hand through his long hair. "She does not wish to be attached to the navy any longer. She told me in no uncertain terms. They will return to Town and find her a husband with a London house and a country estate, not a sailor on a ship."

Mother's eyes squeezed nearly shut. "I'm sorry, my son." She took both his hands. "Do not give up hope."

He didn't want to. He so fiercely did not want to. But Georgana's mind was made up. What could he do against a determined lady? "You did not give up hope on Father and his treatment of you, and nothing came of it." He hated bringing up his father and the sorrow that appeared on his mother's face.

She gripped his hands. "No, nothing did. But that hope sustained me for many years. It gave me strength to face the dark times. All is not lost, Dominic."

He smiled to reassure her, but inside he did not believe it. His love of the sea aside, the navy was his livelihood. Without it, he couldn't care for Georgana. With it, he couldn't have her.

"Perhaps you could start in the other

direction," Mother said, dropping his hands. "I've secured a fine port for you and the captain tonight."

The captain? The man's stern face from the coach ride burst into Dominic's thoughts. He did not want to spend time alone with the captain just now. "Oh, I'm certain he wouldn't mind forgoing port, since our company is so small."

"Nonsense." Mother waved a hand. "I insist you take the opportunity." She raised her shoulders to her ears and beamed. "I'll see to dinner."

And so, after a comfortably quiet dinner in which his mother had no qualms doing most of the talking, Dominic remained in the dining room for a post-dinner drink with the man he had at one time hoped would be his father-in-law. The captain wore the same look he had upon entering the carriage and finding his daughter in his first lieutenant's arms.

Dominic sat at the head of the table, twirling his glass in small circles around the tablecloth. He didn't have the appetite for the drink tonight, and the captain seemed to feel the same since his also sat untouched. The silence made Dominic squirm. How long did he have to wait before suggesting they join the ladies?

461

"I am recommending you for advancement to post-captain," Captain Woodall said after several tense minutes. "You have proved yourself an able officer, and you will make a fine commander."

Dominic's shoulders sank. Twice in the same year, he would have to refuse promotion. "I am very grateful for your confidence in me, sir, but I cannot accept it."

The captain's brow rose. "Why not?"

Dominic rubbed the back of his neck. "I refused my last chance at promotion for the sake of my mother. If a command cannot be soon secured, I worry she will suffer for the cut in funds. She lives much lower than her station as it is."

"You'll have the dowry — that should make up the difference until a suitable command comes forth."

The dowry? Dominic paled. The captain thought everything was settled between his daughter and Dominic. It certainly would have appeared that way to anyone who happened upon them that afternoon. "Sir, I have already discussed an arrangement with Georgana. Miss Woodall." He swallowed. "She is not in agreement."

Captain Woodall traced the foot of his glass with his thumb. "That surprises me. She adores you."

Did she? The words both excited and saddened Dominic. "She will not be left behind as her husband goes to sea." He couldn't fault her for that.

The captain nodded thoughtfully. "Then don't leave her behind."

"The Admiralty . . ." Dominic stared at the man beside him, who had faithfully followed the Admiralty's orders to keep women off the ship — with one exception.

"If you are the captain, you enforce the rules." Captain Woodall shrugged. "Or don't."

"I would not put a lady in that situation, to live in such crude and humble . . ." His voice trailed off at the captain's wry look.

"I think we both know Georgana is cut from tougher cloth than that."

A little spark in Dominic's chest glimmered. Of course he'd known officers whose wives journeyed with them. But many did not enjoy the close quarters and harsh life, and Georgana had said she wanted to leave the navy. She didn't want any part of it.

"Did you discuss such an arrangement when you asked for her hand?"

Dominic sighed. "No. She wouldn't hear any more after I suggested I would enjoy coming home to her smiles."

He and the captain both cringed at the

stupidity of his suggestion.

"Might I suggest a different approach?" her father asked. "Perhaps by giving her the choice, she will see things in a different light. Heaven knows she deserves to choose her own path."

"Then, you give your blessing?"

The captain rested his hand on the table and opened his fingers as though to thread them through the fingers on his other hand. Realizing his mistake, he closed his hand slowly and patted his fist against the table. "All that I want for Georgana is what I couldn't give her during her childhood. Love. And peace."

"She never doubted you loved her, sir."

Captain Woodall smiled sadly. "Yes. She wouldn't. But I couldn't protect her. I couldn't give her the love she needed, and her mother couldn't make up for the pain inflicted by her grandmother. We failed her in so many ways." He sniffed and adjusted his seat, turning his face from Dominic for a moment. "You are a passionate man, Peyton. You don't attach yourself to something without giving your whole heart to doing the job right. You are also very *com*passionate, and I think after all she's been through, my daughter needs some compassion in her life."

464

Dominic stood, sending the chair skidding across the floor behind him. The rushing in his ears made it hard for his mind to engage. He wanted this. Her father wanted this. And the warmth of Georgana's kiss made him hope she wanted it as well. The captain watched him with glistening eyes, then reached for his glass and took a sip.

"Will you send her to the study, please?" Dominic's voice wavered in excitement, like a ship's boy promoted to midshipman. Her father's chuckle rumbled behind him as he made for the door.

What would he say? He'd never been a man of words. Only a man of the sea. He prayed that could be enough.

Georgana found her way down the dim hall, lit only by a few candles. Their flames swayed, the light pulsing across the walls like waves across an open sea. She had to walk slowly to keep her balance. Her body missed the sway of the ocean. It wouldn't do to stagger like a drunken sailor now that she was a lady again.

She paused at the door to the study. Inside Dominic paced before the hearth and brushed his fingers through his hair. She stayed to watch for a moment, capturing the image in her mind. The fire reflected off the gold trim on his uniform jacket.

She pushed the door open wider. Dominic looked up and graced her with that grin that melted her insides. She'd missed it.

"You called for me, sir?" She lifted her hand to the lace bandeau in a salute.

Dominic stared at her a moment before shaking his head. He crossed the room and pulled her hand down. "None of that." He didn't let go of her hand.

She laughed and let him pull her into the shadowy study. Little things — shells, driftwood, stones — lay scattered across the shelves. Slips of paper stuck out from beneath them.

"I thought you said you collected these for someone." She walked down the line of shelves, reading the looping handwriting. *Jamaica, April 1804 to January 1805. Aboukir, January to November 1801. Malta, October 1807 to August 1808.*

"I did. For my mother." From the desk, Dominic withdrew a quill, trimmed it, and uncapped an ink bottle. A scrap of paper rested before him on the desk. He extended the quill to her. "Will you write for this voyage?"

How silly. She'd been jealous of a fictitious young lady when, really, the tokens were a gesture of thoughtfulness from a son

466

to a patient mother. "Your mother doesn't want to write it?"

"She won't mind."

Georgana took the pen and dipped it into the inkwell. *Antigua, July to November 1810.*

She lifted it and blew to dry the ink.

Dominic reached into his coat and pulled out the piece of green sea glass they'd found on the clear beach in Antigua. Had she ever experienced a more perfect day? Would she ever again? Despite the pristine sand and sparkling water, it was Dominic who had made it perfect.

"Where will you put it?" he asked.

She slid the glass, warm from being tucked so close to his heart, out of his hand and retraced her steps. She found the slick black stone from Malta labeled 1807 and placed the sea glass beside it. Dominic followed behind her to observe.

"Why there?" His voice tickled her ear.

She loved the feel of him so close. The taste of his kiss still lingered on her lips. Would it last when she was gone? He'd nearly been taken from her once. How could she allow it to happen again?

"Because I began my life at sea in 1807," she said. "And I ended it in 1810. The beginning and the end, right together." That beginning had been so black, like the stone from Malta. Firelight caught the piece of sea glass, making it glow. But she had finally found some light.

Dominic laid his hands on her arms. "Does this have to be the end?" She couldn't see his face, but the pleading in his voice stung her already raw emotions.

She slid her finger across the polished glass, made lovely by the endless beating of the waves. Did it have to end?

His arms encircled her waist from behind, and he pulled her in. So many times on their voyage, she had longed to feel those arms around her.

"Georgana, I cannot promise there will never come a time when we have to be apart," he whispered, resting his head against hers, "but any ship I captained would not feel whole without you on it."

Her tears choked another laugh. "You will have the sea. Is she not the only woman you need?" He had sounded so sure of it that night at the bow.

"The sea will never be the same without you beside me. It wasn't the sea who sat at my bedside day after day. It wasn't the sea who saved me. It wasn't the sea who made each day brighter than the last." His lips grazed her neck just behind her ear. "It was the girl with oceans in her eyes and love in her heart."

Though he held her tenderly, she found she couldn't breathe. "We would have to marry soon. You might only have a few weeks before you're sent to sea again." She wished so desperately to agree. But the thought of watching his ship sail away while she stayed ashore . . . She didn't know if she could do it.

The corners of his lips curled against her skin. "I will agree with your first thought but not your second. Your father has recommended me for promotion. I shall have months before I leave again. Before *we* leave again."

Georgana whirled to face him. "Truly?" Before they left again. He and she. Together.

He gave her brow the barest kiss. "Will you come with me, my darling Georgana? Share in whatever adventures the sea has for us?"

She rested her hand on his waistcoat over the wound that had almost removed him completely from her world. The life he offered would not be an easy one. Rough seas, cramped and dank quarters, the carnage of battle, inescapable sickness. Weevils. Could she endure all that and more to be with him?

A few months ago, she had known her answer. She had harbored no desire to set foot on a naval ship again. But she'd already overcome the worst the navy had to offer and discovered some of the best. And now the sea meant more than loneliness and suffering. It meant love.

Her arms wrapped around him. How could the darkened room feel so bright? "I never imagined I would find such happiness on a ship," she said.

"Sometimes we find what we need in the least expected places." He chuckled. "I never thought I'd fall in love with a cabin girl."

Georgana pushed herself up on her toes to kiss him, but he pulled back. "You haven't answered my question. I've already put myself in trouble with your father once today for kissing you without an agreement."

"Yes." She giggled as he crushed her to him and lifted her from the floor. And then he kissed her, settling her back on the ground as light as a gull landing on a yardarm. She took his face in her hands.

His fingers wound into the short ends of her hair, just as they did the morning he awoke and she learned to breathe again, and to hope again. The past still lurked in the shadows of her memory, but the light of his grin kept it at bay. And while she still had to push back worries of the future, she knew she could face them by his side.

He pulled away, breathless. She nestled her head against his chest, and he held her tight until their breathing slowed.

"Will we have to invite your grandmother to the wedding?"

"I know how to manage her." She closed her eyes and tightened her grip around his waist. That woman would never control Georgana again.

"Oh? How is that?"

She raised her fist, mischief bubbling in her joyful soul. "Sound English cannon."

He stared.

Then grinned.

Then laughed. And covered her knuckles with little kisses until her mouth got jealous, and she pulled him in once more.

EPILOGUE

Georgana Peyton stood on HMS *Marianne*'s quarterdeck, watching her husband climb aloft. The boatswain and his mate surveyed the little frigate's rigging on the deck below and cast curious glances at their new captain's wife. They'd not been aboard five minutes before Dominic thought to climb the shroud.

A few crewmen milled the deck, but most hands hadn't been hired yet. Dominic would set about securing a crew as soon as he made a thorough inspection of the ship — which included climbing to the top of the mainmast. The crew would have to get used to such a passionate captain.

One of the only familiar faces on the ship popped through the hatchway. He grabbed the brim of his cap in a salute and made his way in her direction. He stopped before

472

ascending to the quarterdeck.

"Good morning, Fitz," Georgana said. Now sixteen, the boy had begun to fill out his lanky form, and she was glad not to call him an enemy anymore.

"Taylor," he mumbled in greeting. "Ready to sail again?"

Georgana's stomach flipped. She didn't know how to answer that. Eight months on land had made her appreciate a warm fire and a cup of tea that wasn't constantly at risk of sloshing over the sides. She nodded above them. "If he is ready, then I shall be."

The boatswain made his way over to them, giving Fitz a reproachful stare. The boy didn't wither under the look. Perhaps if the boatswain knew their history, he wouldn't disapprove of the lad's familiarity with the captain's wife. But then again, it might shock him.

"Pardon me, ma'am. When will he come down, do you think?" the boatswain asked.

Georgana watched the blue-clad figure standing on the topmost platform, waving down at her. "He might never come down."

"The lady might have to fetch him," Fitz said, then turned and hurried away before the boatswain could react. The older man shook his head, muttering an apology about ill-mannered ship's boys. Georgana waved a hand to dismiss it. She'd seen much worse manners from Fitz. And a small part of her did want to climb the shroud to fetch her giddy husband.

He would make a very different captain than her father. Though she appreciated that Papa had done his best on the *Deborah,* she looked forward to seeing how this crew would react to a more lively captain. Papa, still on an extended leave to recover from his wound, had hinted at a desire to leave the navy in his last letter. The thought saddened her. His Majesty's navy had been her father's home for so much of his life, but she couldn't argue that he needed retirement.

When finally Dominic made it back to the quarterdeck, he was out of breath, disheveled, and beaming like a little boy given his first pony. He gathered her in his arms, and she thought he would have kissed her if not for her stern look.

"Shall we move to the captain's cabin so that you may let free all your sensibility out of the public view?" she asked. Workers, sailors, and officers walked the street just beyond the dock, in sight of the *Marianne*'s quarterdeck.

He chuckled. "Ah, Georgana." He squeezed her tighter. "I love a good August breeze from the top of the mainmast." His hand grabbed hers, and he pulled her toward the hatchway.

"Is there any breeze you don't love from the top of the mainmast?" But she couldn't help a smile at his exuberance. She'd seen his restlessness the last several months, though she knew he tried to hide it.

Dominic closed the door when they reached the cabin, which was much smaller than her father's on board the *Deborah,* but she didn't think Dominic noticed. He swept his arms out. "Look at this. Our own cabin."

Georgana nodded thoughtfully, releasing her bonnet from its pins and letting it fall to her side. "We won't have to squeeze ourselves into a wardroom cabin to be alone anymore."

"I cannot say I minded that." He grinned and grabbed her arms, pulling her close. "Think of it — the two of us, in command of our own ship. And whenever we are tired, we may retreat in here for time to ourselves. No worries of officers suspecting what we are up to, no crew members thinking us odd. Just us."

Georgana pulled the corner of her mouth between her teeth. Yes. Of course. Just the two of them. He rested his chin atop her head, and she sighed into his embrace, trying to banish a flicker of guilt. She wasn't really keeping a secret from him again. A few weeks more, after they set sail, she would tell him. She hoped his joy would outweigh everything else.

"This is to be the greatest adventure of our lives, my darling," he whispered, fingering a little curl that had wiggled out of its hairpin. Her hair wasn't very long yet — just long enough to increase the pleasure of his fingers running through her locks. His mother had helped her find an acceptable way to style it in its current state. Georgana would be sorry to leave her mother-in-law's cheeriness. The woman remained in good spirits, even with her son whisking his new bride off to sea and leaving her alone again.

"Indeed it will." She turned her face up to him. The duties of a ship's captain would call him away very soon. They had best take advantage of this quiet moment.

Dominic grinned. He kissed her forehead. Then her nose. And when he found her eager lips, she could not suppress a little laugh. She had found home — not on the safe shores of England, but on the deck of a lilting ship and in the heart of a navy man. Though the days ahead would bring with them both hardship and happiness, all she and Dominic needed to face this life was each other.

And perhaps someone to teach her what one does with a baby.

ACKNOWLEDGMENTS

I am so grateful to the many people who have helped me in my writing journey and in publishing Georgana's story. First, I am grateful to a Heavenly Father who gave me a passion and has helped me develop it throughout my life.

Thank you to the Shadow Mountain crew, especially Heidi Gordon, Alison Palmer, and Lisa Mangum for all their hard work in making this story the best it could be.

Thanks to my critique partners — Joanna Barker, Heidi Kimball, Megan Walker, and Sally Britton — who have encouraged me from the start of our friendship, and to Deborah Hathaway, whose love for this story has kept me going through the rough times. And thanks to Jennie Goutet for helping with my French.

Thank you to all who betaread this story for me — Deborah, Jo, Meg, Heidi, Jill Warner, Alayna Townsend, Collette Campbell, Melissa Crandall, Caroline Huball, and Susan Perry; and my sisters-in-law — Kathryn, Corie, Arielle, and Kalle — who have been some of my biggest fans.

Thank you to my family — especially Mom, Dad, Mama, and Papa — for your inspiration, teaching, and unwavering support.

Lastly, a huge thank you to my husband and three children, who let me write for long days and late nights to chase my lifelong goal. Thank you for sharing this dream.

ABOUT THE AUTHOR

Arlem Hawks began making up stories before she could write. Living all over the Western United States and traveling around the world gave her a love of cultures and people and the stories they have to tell. With her travels came an interest in history, especially the history of her English heritage. When she isn't writing, Arlem is baking her characters' favorite foods, sewing Regency dresses, learning how to play the tin whistle, and watercoloring. She lives in Arizona with her husband and three children.

The employees of Thorndike Press hope you have enjoyed this Large Print book. All our Thorndike, Wheeler, and Kennebec Large Print titles are designed for easy reading, and all our books are made to last. Other Thorndike Press Large Print books are available at your library, through selected bookstores, or directly from us.

For information about titles, please call:
(800) 223-1244

or visit our website at:
gale.com/thorndike

To share your comments, please write:
Publisher
Thorndike Press
10 Water St., Suite 310
Waterville, ME 04901